STERLING FIGHT

L.B. DUNBAR

WWW.LBDUNBAR.COM

Cover Design: Lori Johnson Designs

Photographer: Katie Cadwallader Photography

Cover Model: Cole

Editor: Nicole McCurdy/Emerald Edits

Editor: Gemma Brocato

❀ Created with Vellum

OTHER BOOKS BY L.B. DUNBAR

<u>Sterling Falls</u>

Sterling Heat

Sterling Brick

Sterling Streak

Sterling Clay

Sterling Fight

Sterling Touch

Sterling Stone

<u>Chicago Anchors</u>

Elevator Pitch

Catch the Kiss

Parentmoon

Holiday Hotties (Christmas novellas)

Scrooge-ish

Naughty-ish

Grouch-ish

Road Trips & Romance

Hauling Ashe

Merging Wright

Rhode Trip

Lakeside Cottage

Living at 40

The Heart Remembers

BOOKS IN OTHER AUTHOR WORLDS

Smartypants Romance (an imprint of Penny Reid)

Love in Due Time

Love in Deed

Love in a Pickle

The World of True North (an imprint of Sarina Bowen)

Cowboy

Studfinder

THE EARLY YEARS

Legendary Rock Stars Series

Paradise Stories

The Island Duet

Modern Descendants – writing as elda lore

PROLOGUE

Nineteen-years old

[Genie]

As I round the stacks in the university library, my gaze catches on a lone student sitting at a dark wood table amid the numerous empty ones. The hour is late, nearly closing time. The lights are low. The scent of leather bindings and old paper is more prominent in the emptiness, and I'm on my final stretch of reshelving books. Work-study for financial assistance isn't glamorous, especially when it cuts into your Saturday night plans.

From where I stand, I simply admire the man I know is a senior. His head is bowed. His wet-sand colored hair is shaggy and flopping forward against a prominent forehead. He dresses in dark colors giving off a broody vibe, like a poet from the 1960s. He's quiet, reserved, and often alone.

But he didn't have to be.

The first time I met Judd Sylver, I was in third grade. It was February 11, National Make a New Friend Day, and I wrote him a note on lined paper decorated with a unicorn.

Do you want to be my new friend? Check yes or no.

WITH EYES the same shade as the brilliant blue sparkles on the cover of my notebook, he looked up at me from underneath that disheveled hair and stared. An entire conversation went on behind those eyes, like he was actually considering being my friend, then he blinked once, narrowed his gaze, tugged one of my French braids, and said, "Why would I be friends with a girl?"

I might have only been a skinny eight-year-old, but my arms had enough strength to push him right off the low desk chair.

Judd was a reading buddy in the elementary school program that paired fifth graders with third graders. I don't know why third graders needed reading buddies. I'd known how to read since I was six. While at first, I'd been excited to have Judd as my buddy, hopeful of a new friend, I'd wished for someone else after that encounter.

Then, there was a brief period in middle school when I had a crush on Judd. He wasn't the most popular kid in Sterling Falls, our small mountain town in West Virginia. He was considered shy and aloof. Sometimes he looked a little dirty with matted hair, pants too short for his long, thin legs. He had the saddest blue eyes, and that was something which constantly drew my attention. A time or two, I caught him glancing over at me across the crowded lunchroom or in the library where I'd wait for my mom to pick me up after school. An eighth-grader rarely looked at a sixth-grader, but I'd feel those eyes on me and glance up, knowing exactly who was watching. My innocent heart would flutter in my chest, like the wings of a majestic bird taking flight. A slow pump on liftoff before the thumping wings gracefully flapped faster and faster. Sometimes, I'd ship Judd's name and mine together in a pretty floral notebook where I kept all my precious thoughts and important dates.

Such a silly girl back then.

Finally, Judd and I connected for a while in high school. Being two years ahead of me, seniors didn't often associate with sophomores, but we were in Math Club together. By then, Judd was no longer a scrawny mountain rat but a young man on the verge of adulthood. He'd bulked up but kept his head down. He was in the extra-curricular activity to beef up his college applications. He was so smart. He was also quiet but polite. Teachers adored him. He was your average good guy, and that was the best of compliments. I dare to say, we were friends. My secret crush on him was renewed.

And I made the bold move to ask him to *his* senior prom.

I have an obsession with national dates, the odder—*the quirkier*—the better, and I'd been a trendsetter when I hadn't even known it. National Promposal Day, which takes place on March 11, would not become a thing until years after I graduated from high school. Back then, I thought I was so clever, finding that old unicorn notebook from third grade in the bottom of a dresser drawer, and ripping out a blank piece of paper, then handwriting my promposal question in a similar fashion to how I asked Judd to be friends when I was a child.

Finally, in high school, Judd checked yes.

Excitement brewed with every minute I stood in my living room, twirling around in the dress that I'd picked because it matched the bright blue of Judd's eyes. He was special to me. Important even. He'd be my first kiss, and I couldn't wait.

Until those minutes added up to an hour, then two, and then the clock struck midnight.

Judd never showed. He never called either.

He missed his prom. He even skipped his high school graduation.

After finally winning his friendship, which I did consider a rare prize, the hurt I'd experienced from his absence was unbearable. I already had an aversion to being abandoned, as in, I didn't want it to ever happen again.

Judd had been that *again*.

Next thing I knew, he was here in Tennessee. Maybe I should have known he attended the same university I did, but I didn't. Then one day, I spied him working in the dining center. After that, I noticed him a time or two, or twenty. *Who was counting?* And each time I saw him, my opinion of him changed from anger to grief to confusion.

The quiet of the library, on late Saturday nights, was the place I found him most often.

He never noticed me.

Head down, book in hand, he wasn't the boy I'd pushed off a chair or the teenager who stood me up for prom. He was solid, refined, haunted-looking, like ghosts followed him, and he was determined to ignore their presence. That buzzing energy also suggested I keep my distance.

I'd learned my lesson with Judd long ago and swore he'd broken my fragile heart for the last time.

But as I watched him at the ripe age of nineteen on another National Make a New Friend Day, despite all that happened between us, I wished silently Judd Sylver and I were friends.

He looked like he could use one.

1

[Genie]

I cannot believe I've agreed to this date.

The last place I want to be is in this dimly-lit pub just outside of Knoxville, Tennessee. And the last person I want to be meeting is Ralson Meyers.

The forty-something, portly man is the son of a friend of a friend of my mother's and newly moved to the Knoxville area. By default, my mother thought I should know him despite the relationship distance—the son of a friend of a friend of hers—and *she'd* decided I should meet him. Like I was a personal welcome to Knoxville committee.

Honestly, I'd like to ship him back to Sterling Falls, our hometown in West Virginia.

However, being a cordial, dutiful daughter, I agreed to meet Ralson. I'd even allowed him to pick the location, which happened to be a decent looking place from the outside, featuring a green canopy over the large, mullion window and a deep-red, oak door. The Boxer had a cute logo with the patch-work face of the corresponding dog breed in black, white, and brown on the wall opposite the door of the small entryway. I might have passed this place a dozen times and never given it a thought.

Ralson had heard of it and wanted to check it out.

Once inside, Ralson thankfully recognizes me compared to the vague description of him I'd been given from my mother.

"He's got brown hair and a sweet face."

She meant that the limited hair he has is brown and his face is unremarkable. But I wasn't here for his looks. I was doing my mother a favor.

"Huh," he says after an awkward moment where he goes in for a hug and I hold out my hand to shake his, thus causing me to jab him just above the beltline. "You don't look anything like your Instagram photo."

My Instagram is a graphic image with a distorted face, wavy, short hair with blond and brown stripes, and a wide smile. Quirky_Girl_Calendars is my handle, and I don't know how he'd know that nor why I'd look like a caricature. Since my mother hardly gets my business name correct, I'm surprised Ralson found me on social media.

I smile tightly at him before he leads me to a table. The pub only has a few as the majority of the space is taken up by the physical bar lining one wall. A swing door is in the back corner and each time it opens, the sound from that space invades this area like the roar at a football game. Cheers and jeers filter into the rectangular area, continually distracting me.

"It's been difficult living without my mom."

"Oh, I'm so sorry. I didn't know your mother passed away." Mom hadn't warned me Ralson was in a sensitive position or that he'd lost his mother who was the friend of Mom's friend. Now I feel bad.

"Oh." He chuckles, the sound heavy and wet. "No, no. She's

still very much alive. I mean, it's been difficult living without her because I used to live *with* her."

I want to whole-heartedly believe he means temporarily. Like he went to college, earned a degree, and lived on his own before something tragic happened, say a job loss or even a temporary transfer.

But he continues. "It's the first time I've been on my own." He smiles, pleased with himself, and sitting taller. "How do you feel about laundry?"

"Uh . . . I do it regularly?"

"Wonderful." His muddy-brown eyes flare but the gleam is unnerving, just like this conversation.

One drink and I'm out of here. I pride myself on being single and willing to mingle, and *not* interested in marriage. Still, there are multiple reasons not to mingle, and just embrace singlehood. Like the improbability of finding the right-for-me man.

"I like to have mine done on Fridays."

O-*kay*. I nod.

"So, I'm happy to drop it off, if you want to just pop me your address."

What the . . .

He slides his phone across the table toward me and I stare down at the device. Is he serious?

"Um. I don't own a laundromat."

He chuckles, his shoulders jiggling. "My mother told me you were funny. Quirky." He tilts his head, like he's pleased with his own joke and I'm starting to wonder if this entire setup is one bad prank. Any minute someone is going to pop through that swing door and tell me I'm being punked.

That a forty-three-year-old man did not just proposition me to do his laundry because he's no longer living with his mother.

Sweet succulents, save me.

We haven't even ordered that drink I suddenly, desperately,

need—the one that starts the very short time clock on this evening—when a server approaches and tells us our table is ready. He tips his head toward the swinging door with a pleasant smile on his face.

With a confused expression, I glance at Ralson. We're already seated at a table. A very open, very public, very visible by the bartender and a bouncer at the door, table.

"Uh." I seem to be stuck on monosyllabic sounds because I'm truly at a loss for words.

Ralson stands, and without a glance back at me, *as his date*, he proceeds to follow the server. Thunderstruck, this would be the moment to swipe right and leave this situation. Just bolt for the door and never look back. Just what the ever-loving-eff-ity is going on here?

Typically, I'm quicker on my feet to leave a situation, so I'm surprised at myself when I'm suddenly standing as well and hesitantly following Ralson, thinking a separate dining room must be behind the swing door. A room that is overcrowded and has bad acoustics.

"I really only planned on one—"

I cut myself off as I slip through that dividing barrier, catching the door before it swings back to hit my stunned face. In front of me is a boxing ring. A four sided, roped off, raised roughly eighteen inches off the floor, boxing ring, and in the center are two men punching the daylights out of each other.

In silky, violet-purple shorts is one man facing off with another man in white shorts with a green stripe up the sides and around his waist. Each is a powerhouse of strength. Corded muscles. Bulging veins. Boxing gloves on their fists. They also wear a padded helmet which is the only sane thing about this situation.

Standing inside a backroom boxing ring has never been on my bingo card.

Ralson is several feet in front of me and readily takes a chair offered by the server. I close the distance between us but remain standing.

"Hey, I think I'm going to head out."

Ralson swivels his head almost as fast as the punch I see out of the corner of my eye. I'm trying not to look. The last thing I want to watch is too grown men pummeling one another, and I definitely do not want to hear the breaking of bones. Or worse, see the sight of blood.

Keeping my concentration on Ralson, I'd really like to throat punch him, despite my aversion to violence. Finally, he blinks up at me from his seated position.

"But we didn't have a drink yet."

"Yeah, and suddenly, I'm not thirsty." I'm downright dehydrated, desperately in need of a martini or six, but not with this guy. And not in this bar.

"I was going to order champagne."

I have no earthly idea why he'd think champagne was a bargaining tool or a platitude to sway my decision.

"I never drink the stuff." Bubbly and I have a history that's long and bitter, unlike this date which will be short and quickly forgotten.

"You've got to see this guy," Ralson continues, turning his attention toward the ring like I didn't even speak. Didn't reject his offer or suggest I'm leaving. Because I'm going home.

Or better yet, today is National Indie Bookstore Day, and I think I'll hit up my local favorite. A good book. A gin martini. A warm bathtub. Best date ever. *Party of one, please.*

"Ralson, I'm not—"

Ralson flinches. His eyes are trained on the ring. He grimaces like whatever he's witnessed hurts *him*. Inhaling deeply, I close my eyes, willing myself not to look. But like watching a horror film, I feel the pull to peek when I know I won't like what I see.

For half a second—no lie—not even fifteen milliseconds or

whatever it would be called; more like thirteen, my favorite number, I turn my head and then turn it back toward Ralson who is fixated on the fight.

But in that microcosm of time, I don't miss the boxer in purple looking at me. Or at least, facing my direction, eyes appearing to be aimed outside the ring over his opponent's shoulder.

Ralson winces.

I'm not falling for the temptation to look again, but a strange energy surrounds me.

Snap-crackle-pop.

Or maybe that's the punch-crunch-break of a bone.

I don't want to know.

"Jesus," Ralson hisses, rather loudly, though the sound blends in with the uproar around us. "He's so damn good."

Don't ask. Don't ask.

"Ralson, I'm—"

"Have you seen this guy?" His voice rings incredulous, as he finally turns back to me, pointing in the direction of the boxing match.

Of course, I haven't seen him. I don't want to look now. I don't want to ever look.

"Good luck in Knoxville, Ralson." I say, stepping to the side to walk away. *How about losing my number?* And thank goodness he doesn't have my address, although I'm momentarily nervous my mother will give it to him. Telling me I should help a friend of a friend and do the damn man's laundry for him.

Another thing that is never going to happen.

"I didn't know Judd Sylver was in Knoxville." Awe fills Ralson's voice.

My head whips back toward the ring so fast my neck cracks.

"What?" I drag out the word like the sharp crook of a right arm before—*bam!*—a hook to the jaw.

Staring at the ring, I see the man in purple shorts turn into a beast of aggression. His arms move like a pinwheel. Left. Right. Right. Left. His vision is tunneled on the man before him who slowly moves backward until his back hits the ropes.

The view is both disturbing and intoxicating, and there is no way that spiraling man in the ring is the thoughtful, quiet, poet-souled Judd Sylver.

A bell rings—*ting-ting-ting*—breaking me out of my reverie.

Then Purple-Shorts-Guy is stepping away from his opponent. The once-reserved man I knew is now a heavily breathing machine, layered in perspiration with a wickedly delicious energy coming off him and his eyes are trained in my direction. The referee dressed in black pants with a white shirt is lifting Judd's arm by his wrist and declaring him, "Winner".

Ralson is on his feet letting out an impressive whistle. One of those where he inserts his fingers into his mouth. The inflection is perfect, ear-piercing and shrill.

And that's my cue to leave.

I don't want to be here with Ralson and the last person I want to see is Judd Sylver.

I MARCH HASTILY to my car, parked purposely underneath a bright lamp in the middle of the lot, and click the button on my key fob to unlock my Camry. It's not a glamorous car but she's been dependable and I'm grateful for how easily she unlocks without the trouble of inserting a key into the handle.

"Genie?"

I close my eyes as I near the side of my car, wishing I could disappear in the dark night, but the lot's light illuminates me.

Clenching the door handle in my fist, I spin to face Ralson.

"Hey." He bends at the waist and clutches at his knees like he just ran a marathon instead of crossing fifty feet of pavement. With exaggerated breaths, he stands tall again, winces as he pinches his side, and then speaks. "We didn't have that drink."

Yeah, and we aren't going to have one either. "I'm sorry. I have a sudden headache."

Ralson slowly smiles. "I thought you weren't supposed to use that line until date number three."

Does this sad man ever get to three dates with a woman? Does he not understand complaining of a headache isn't a positive thing?

"Maybe we could reschedule," he continues.

"Ralson." I sigh. It's never easy to let someone down. Even if he is the son of a friend of a friend of my mother's. Despite the distant, nonconsequential acquaintance, I don't like hurting anyone. However, I'm good at knowing how these things work . .. and when they don't.

"Like I said inside, I wish you all the luck living in Knoxville. It's a great city."

"You could show me around." He steps closer to me and my hand squeezes tighter on the door handle.

And I also could not. There's a thing called the internet and map searches. Even GPS. "I'm . . . sorry." I don't know why I'm apologizing. I'm not sorry. "I have a big meeting coming up in a few weeks. One that could change my career and it's really my only focus right now." Not playing tour guide to my city.

"Quirky Girl Calendar, right?" He tips a brow and for half a second, the other half of the one from earlier, I think Ralson might have something positive to say. Something encouraging, like asking me about my company, or wanting to know more about my meeting. Maybe he is slightly redeemable.

"Your mom told me about your little hobby."

Nope. There goes the credit I wanted to give him.

"Ralson, it's been . . ."

Nope. I can't do that either. I can't even pretend this has been fun. Or real. Or whatever might soothe *his* ego.

Singling and mingling. It's been my choice, although it's also been daunting lately, and I don't have the strength to fake my enthusiasm for a date that was more like a meetup. It's almost worse than faking an orgasm. *Almost.*

"I've got to go," I blurt, turning away from Ralson who is suddenly leaning against the side of my car. His hip presses into the back passenger door.

My heart hammers. A split decision is needed. Do I risk opening the door, hoping I can get in fast enough to close it behind me? Do I worry he'll catch the door and push me further inside then follow me? Or do I hesitate, knowing he could easily step forward and block my entry once I have the door open?

These are all fears I don't want to have. Ralson doesn't feel threatening, even if he is a larger man. In general, I'm just tired of having to calculate how a *man* will respond in these situations.

The not-so-easy letdown situation.

"Genie, I just want to—"

"She said she had to go."

I spin at the sound of a masculine voice. One rich and deep, and a bit threatening on a different level. A protective pitch. A commanding trill.

And I stare into somber, sad eyes that ironically flame the brightest blue I've ever seen. A blue I recognize, because the shade matches a dress I once bought.

"Judd," I whisper-choke.

His hair is slicked back yet that familiar flop of his bangs falls forward against his forehead. His face is pink in the light of the overhead lamp. His shoulders are broad in a tight tee. Broader than I remember when he was eighteen, and my prom date. When he'd *finally* been my friend, or so I thought. When he stood me up for that singular right-of-passage back in high school. And that night hadn't even been *my* prom, but his.

He'd *said* yes but I heard the resounding no loud and clear at his absence.

Judd stares at me a long minute, as if trying to place me. I'm out of context, I assume. This isn't high school Math Club. Or even Sterling Falls. Judd is four hours from his home and only miles from mine. Our paths have not crossed in over twenty years. Almost twenty-two.

I'm torn between pointing out who I am and letting him continue to ponder the recognition when Ralson speaks.

"Damn good fight, man."

Judd grunts.

"I heard about you back in Charleston," Ralson continues, fanboying. Judd has apparently made a name for himself, enough to at least have one follower.

Judd still doesn't respond to Ralson's enthusiasm. Those sorrowful eyes are trained on me, and I shiver in the mountain air.

"Anyway . . ." Ralson clears his throat at Judd's unnerving silence. "Genie and I were just leaving."

I spin toward Ralson. "Not together." I don't know how much clearer I need to be. I'm not leaving with him. I'm not interested in seeing him again, and the last person I want to see as well is Judd Sylver.

While I appreciate this interruption, considering the timing a momentary savior situation, I don't have any desire to catch up with him.

The boy who stood me up. The one who stole my heart.

I can't really fault him. He was always a bit quiet. Shy and aloof. He didn't ask for my crush on him. He barely offered me his friendship.

And right now, I have nothing to offer him.

Still, Judd and I are locked in a moment. One where unfamiliar energy swirls around me, winding me up. He steps toward me. His gaze focused. His mouth open, as if he's about to speak.

The movement flips a switch inside me, and I quickly turn away from him, giving him my back as I'm not prepared to hear his voice after all this time.

"Good night, gentlemen," I mutter before swinging open the door of my Camry and slipping inside, keeping my eyes forward until I need to reverse out of the parking space. Only then do I see that Ralson is nowhere in sight, but Judd remains standing a few feet away, underneath the parking lot light as if he's some ominous creature.

Snap-crackle-pop.

I lean forward to check the sky. Not a cloud in sight. No spring storm brewing, and yet I sense one coming.

Especially after I reverse out of the parking space and glance in the rearview mirror one more time to find Judd has walked out from beneath the parking light, standing directly in my line of sight behind me.

And behind me is where he belongs. In my past.

2

[Judd]

From the moment I saw Genie Webster a week ago, I haven't been able to stop thinking about her.

Normally, I don't notice the crowd around the ring. My intention is to get lost in the motions of my body and out of my head. However, for a brief second, no more than a blink, I saw her in backroom of The Boxer. Like the flash of a firefly in the darkness of night. And that blip surprisingly blinded me.

Or rather, awakened me.

Even though my mind has been full of Genie, I wrangle my concentration into submission. The beautiful, blonde woman sitting across from me in Curmudgeon Bakery deserves my momentary attention. Especially with how this conversation is about to go.

Our small town is located on Milton Peak, and the woman across from me is a local celebrity, recognized as the pin up girl for Remington Autos annual calendar. Her daddy owns a set of successful car dealerships in the area, and she's his pride and joy. She's also been my girlfriend of sorts for two and a half years.

And we are breaking up.

As we sit at a small bistro table in the front corner of my brother's bakery shop in the business district of Sterling Falls, we have a clear view of the crossroads of Main and Corner. The few other tables near us remain empty. The long, wooden bench taking up one full wall hosts several tables in front of it. Another customer is tucked in the back. My brother Sebastian is behind the counter along with his newest baking assistant.

I already ordered a coffee for myself and the complicated iced caramel macchiato with one pump of caramel and an extra splash of milk that Heather likes.

This will be my last act of kindness.

Our relationship has been unsettled for a while. As in, Heather wants to settle down, and I've been uncertain she's the one for me. She's beautiful but bossy. Sexy while stubborn. And brutally honest while not always polite or considerate with her opinion.

I'd be the first to admit I'm not perfect. Heather would be the first to tell you she is.

"So, I've been thinking, maybe today, during the Buttercup Society Garden Party, we could..."

I internally groan, tuning Heather out at the thought of the local women's club and their garden affair. Even though Clay begged me to go in his absence, I had no plans to attend.

"It's good business," my older brother by eighteen months said.

As the Sylver Seed & Soil is our family business, and we are the leading place for garden supplies and landscaping needs, among many other goods and services, it *is* good practice to be present for these types of events. However, I'm not the face of Sylver Seed & Soil; I'm the books. Accounting and financial advising, actually, which includes Chief Financial Officer as my official title, although I feel strange about the label.

"I'm not attending the party."

"But, Judd, we need to—"

"Break up," I interject.

Heather rocks back in her chair and stares at me. Her icy blue eyes are frozen for a second. I've seen those eyes be seductive or stone cold, with rarely a shade in between.

She wants us to get married. And I don't. At least, not to her.

"I don't want to hurt you," I admit.

"But you will." Her voice grows louder as she sits taller. She's wearing a flannel shirt over a bandeau top, a term I only know because of her, but she has each shoulder pulled down to her elbows, and I just don't understand the appeal. Dangling her shirt in the crook of her elbows looks uncomfortable, but what do I know about women's fashion? I have one sister, and Heather has been my longest relationship.

I do know she's wrong for me. We're missing that *sizzle* I see between my brother Sebastian and his wife, Enya. Or the solid fountain of Knox and Halle. Or the unbreakable ease of Clay and Mavis. We definitely lack the electric energy of Ford and Cadence.

My family has never liked Heather. They never understood our relationship. And in the last few months, I've noticed what they've seen.

Heather and I don't fit.

"Don't tell me you don't feel it," I say, certain she must be aware of the disconnect between us. I'm quiet; she's loud. I'm reserved; she's not. I want communication and connection; she just wants to come, yet she's quite critical about how that happens.

"The attraction?" she states.

I choke. "The differences."

"What differences? Is this because I come from money?"

Another contrast. One not easy to ignore when it is continually put in my face. I was once poor. Very poor.

"Heather, I don't—" A cold sweat breaks across my forehead. I don't want to say I don't love her, but I want her to know that I don't love her. And shouldn't love be the basis of a marriage? Through all the hell my father put my siblings and me through, at his core, he loved our mother. You wouldn't have known it after her death, but he had. Once upon a time.

"What's love got to do with anything?" she states, like she read my mind. "You have money now," she adds, like that's the heart of the matter. "And we make a beautiful couple. Everyone says so. We're perfect."

"But we aren't." I swallow hard. As I've never really had a girlfriend, I've never had to break up with someone, and this is difficult.

Ford suggested I have this discussion someplace public. Sebastian offered the bakery.

"Judd, you're going to buy me a ring . . ."

I'm already shaking my head.

"And then, you'll get down on one knee in front of my family," she continues, lifting her plastic cup toward her mouth while giving me her ice-cold glare.

"I'm not," I argue keeping my voice low, and side-eyeing the bakery which thankfully remains mostly empty.

"And you're going to ask me to fucking marry you." Her command cracks like a whip before she sips her complicated drink and stares at me over the straw. Her cackled demand does nothing to change my mind.

"No," I say a little louder. "I'm not asking you to marry me."

Stillness fills the bakery. My voice carries. Sebastian pauses his movements behind the counter. The woman in the opposite corner, whom I can't see from my position, probably heard me as well.

"Don't be a coward, Judd."

The very last thing I want to be accused of is being a weakling. I never want to be considered a chicken, and it's taking a lot of strength to stay calm right now.

Heather's problem is Heather doesn't want to listen. She likes to hear herself talk. About herself. About her plans for us. About our future. What I should do, buy, say for her. Without really being engaged in us. Or rather me, as the other part of *we*.

"I. Am not. A coward." The cowardly thing to do would be to continue this farce of a relationship, but I can no longer pretend Heather and I are going anywhere but this dead end. "I'm sorry, Heather. We're over."

"We aren't over until I say we're over," she says loud enough for the entire Milton County to hear. Her chair screeches against the tile floor and she stands, caramel macchiato in hand, and tosses the icy drink in my face.

"Now we're over, Judd."

Stunned, I swipe my hand down my face and blink the sting of a sweet drink out of my eyes. The distinct sound of the bakery-door bell jangles as Heather storms out.

Then, I sense a presence beside me.

"Sorry about that," I mutter to my brother, my voice hushed and hoarse. Heather made a mess. *I'm* a fucking mess. My eyes burn. My shirt is soaked. Macchiato is dripping from my cheeks.

"Are you okay?" The voice asking is distinctly *not* Sebastian, not even masculine, but soft and sweet, decidedly concerned and definitely female.

And when I look up, it's like the macchiato is surging through my veins instead of soaking my clothes. The shock is something cool, rich, and incredibly sweet.

"Genie?"

                                    3
                                  ____

                               [Genie]

Witnessing this fallout between Judd and my long-standing nemesis was not my intention.

One minute, I'm minding my business, randomly scrolling on my phone in the back corner of Curmudgeon Bakery, listening to my queen belt out "You Belong with Me" while enjoying the sweet, sticky goodness of a cinnamon roll with a thick layer of frosting, and the next minute, I'm trapped by the unexpected sight of Judd Sylver and then the entrance of Heather Remington.

My mother's best friend's daughter and total perfection in my mother's eyes.

She's a dutiful daughter. *She's* appreciative of her mother. *She* is such a good girl.

Appearances are everything to Janet Hurley, my mother's fourth married name, which made it difficult for her to have a daughter who couldn't keep her mouth shut or follow rules.

"You just march to the beat of your own drum, darlin'," my daddy used to tell me when I was a child, and he was still alive.

Mother would interject, "Let's try to have a little less rhythm, Virginia."

And *she*, being Heather, wanted to get engaged to Judd Sylver, according to her, a few minutes ago.

Apparently, Judd disagreed.

My stomach feels a little nauseous that Heather Remington almost snared Judd. I'm also disconcertingly grateful Judd had a different plan. Deep down, my heart whispers Judd is mine. I liked him first.

The idea is ridiculous. Judd made it abundantly clear he was never available to me.

Still, I feel sorry for the guy covered in something light brown and saturating his white shirt beneath a flannel one.

I heard what Heather said. They made a beautiful couple. They'd even been dressed complementary to one another in flannel shirts, each a shade of blue, like Judd's eyes.

Since seeing Judd a week ago, he's continually crept into my thoughts. The look in his eyes as he stood near me in that Knoxville parking lot. The flare of his nostrils. The width of his shoulders. The electric energy between us.

Snap-crackle-pop!

Despite those melancholy eyes, there was an edge to Judd I'd never seen when he was a boy. And he isn't a boy anymore but all man. And I shouldn't be thinking about him at all.

He just broke up with someone.

In the recesses of my mind, I probably knew Judd and Heather were dating. My mother most likely told me the small-town gossip, but after the sixth retelling, I tune out her stories. Maybe I shut down on the details because I didn't want to believe Judd Sylver could end up with someone as cruel as Heather Remington.

My mother could never understand that being the daughter

of her best friend did not automatically make Heather *my* best friend. Friendship was not by osmosis; it was earned. It was fostered. It was a rare find. I have few friendships but the ones I have are tight.

Handing Judd a stack of paper napkins, I'm reminded I once asked him to be my friend on National Make a New Friend Day, and he shot me down.

"Guess you heard all that?" Judd mutters after thanking me for the wad of napkins I held out to him and swiping in a circular motion around his face. He flicks at ice cubes collected near the zipper of his jeans and shrugs out of the flannel which didn't catch as much of the drink as the front of what turns out to be a white wife-*pleaser* tank top.

Sucking in air, I hold my breath at the glorious sight of tattoos covering both his muscular arms. I hardly noticed them when I saw him at the boxing match, where I did my best not to look at him and his opponent in the ring. But up close and in his personal space, I cannot ignore the colorful designs decorating his lean muscles.

My eyes narrow at what looks like a unicorn beneath faded lines like old-school notebook paper on his bicep.

Strange how another memory related to Judd hits me hard. Didn't I have a notebook once that looked like that unicorn?

"People in Rogue River might have heard that finish," I tease about the next small town over.

Judd glances up at me, those eyes warm but sorrowful, while he dabs at the hopeless wreck of his white shirt.

"What are you doing here?" His voice isn't cruel but curious.

"I'm enjoying a cinnamon roll, as one does in a bakery."

Judd scowls while dismissing my attempt at humor. Those lost-boy eyes remain focused on me. "No, I mean here in Sterling Falls."

I've been asking myself the same thing since I left my place in Knoxville at six this morning. The last time I was here might have been at least five years ago, maybe more, and any visit is always short. One day max. Originally, I'd planned to arrive next weekend for a four-day visit, but my mother somehow talked me into attending her annual garden party.

"I'm here for the Buttercup Society Garden Party."

Judd groans, understanding who and what that means, before he eyes my outfit.

No, I'm not wearing the mandatory yellow dress required *yet*. That torture will happen later today. The current torture is this shift in Judd's eyes while looking at me. From forlorn to flaming. Like I'm a gooey bakery treat, and he has an insatiable sweet tooth. Then again, I might be projecting my own thoughts on him, and I do not want to be thinking of Judd in this way.

Because he still has that floppy whisp of hair falling against his forehead. His hair is still wet-sand, now freckled with gray here and there, and a matching beard on his round face. Plus, those eyes.

He's pure catnip.

"Want to take a seat?" Judd invites, pointing to the open chair Heather left behind.

Never a fan of her hand-me-downs, I respond, "I should probably decline. Caramel isn't my favorite flavor." I smile to lessen the blow of my joke.

Judd glances down at himself again.

"Sorry about all that with Heather." *Are condolences the correct response to a breakup?* I sound like a loon. Instead, I should question him about the fight he participated in last week, but I quickly decide against asking.

Judd Sylver hasn't been my business for a long time.

"Anyway, it was great seeing you again," I state, albeit a strange *second* re-acquaintance.

"How long are you in town?" he asks, reaching out toward me like he might capture my wrist before I walk away but then thinking twice about it and dropping his fist back to his upper thigh.

"Roughly ten days." And not a day longer if all the rest of the days are this exciting. I can't remember the last time I witnessed a breakup other than the continual stream of my own, most of which had been my doing.

Judd nods, noncommittally, and I assume he was only making conversation.

Now we're both just awkwardly staring at one another until he clears his throat and says, "Well, thanks for the napkins."

Of course, I have to take this moment one step further toward *more* awkward because my mouth lacks a filter sometimes. "Any time. I'm great at cleaning up messes."

Judd's brows pinch and even I question why I've said such a thing. I'm better at making a mess than fixing things.

The longer Judd looks at me, the more uncomfortable I grow. Perhaps he recalls my date from last weekend. I must have looked pathetic and desperate to be there with Ralson. Nearly forty and I'm still accepting random dates with the son of a friend of a friend of my mother.

Silly Ralson even tried to text me this week, asking if he could still drop of his laundry, even without a second date. *Bless his heart.* I didn't have time nor the inclination in my overly non-busy schedule to do his laundry or respond to such a text.

"If *you* ever need help getting out of a mess, let me know what I can do for you."

"Can you help me find a date by one this afternoon?" There is no earthly reason why that question pops out of my mouth, especially as Judd is the last person I'd want to know I'm in need of a date.

His brows hitch and even I'm surprised by the snark in my tone and the bluntness of my response. Admitting I'm still single as a Pringle, I've just slapped another layer of awkward on my awkwardness.

Even if a date would halt my mother from asking the inevitable question, when will you be getting married?—*answer: never*—Judd isn't a miracle worker and that's what it would take to make a date magically appear.

I laugh, dismissively, waving off my question. "I'm kidding. Of course."

Judd continues to watch me. His eyes seem to take me in, holding on mine before touching on my forehead, nose, and cheeks then dipping down to my lips. Like he's either cataloguing the changes of twenty years or memorizing my face in case another twenty years passes before he sees me again.

Either way, the look is intense and unnerving, a conflict between flattering and uncomfortable. I don't know if any man has ever looked at me like Judd is right now.

For a moment, I wonder if he remembers what happened between us.

Or rather, didn't happen.

How he stood me up when I was sixteen and how I still sound pitiful at thirty-nine. Then again, I don't need Judd's pity. I feel sorry for him. He just broke up with someone and why would I make a joke about a date?

The awkwardness grows thicker than a layer of frosting on the Curmudgeon Bakery's cupcakes, and the time to excuse myself and take what's left of my pride with me elsewhere has come.

"See you around, Judd," I mutter.

But hopefully not.

My fragile ego wouldn't be able to handle it.

4

____

[Judd]

"**W**ell, that was messy," Sebastian states, finally approaching me and I wonder for a moment if he means Heather or Genie.

As I watch Genie Webster exit the bakery, her question about finding her a date rattles through my brain. I'm well aware that years ago I stood her up.

My chest aches when I consider a young girl waiting on my arrival, dressed in a prom dress she excitedly told me the color of and then refused additional details, telling me I'd have to wait and see her in said dress to learn more.

I never learned more. I had my reasons. And while those reasons haunt me, one of my biggest regrets is hurting Genie.

Currently glancing down at myself, I'm further embarrassed by *my* appearance. I lift my arms to my sides and shake them once as if that will make any difference in the stench coming off me or the wetness that is seeping into my skin.

My younger brother stands beside me with a mop and a bucket. "I was trying to give you a minute, but I really gotta get this cleaned up."

Pushing back my chair, I see the drips of macchiato that haven't been absorbed by my shirt, jeans, or skin. Liquid had puddled between my legs on the seat of the chair. Melting ice drips down to the tile floor.

"Are you okay?" he asks, his typically rough voice softening.

"I will be." Maybe I should be more distraught over my breakup with Heather, but as I'm the one calling it quits, I'm not. I can already hear the tale Heather will spin to her friends and family. I'm the asshole. She broke up with me.

Let people believe what they want. I typically don't care about anyone's opinion other than my family's, and even with them, I try to keep my distance. It's a strange dichotomy as I work with a few of my siblings.

I prefer being alone. Sadly, I'm used to it, but I'm also tired of being lonely, which was one reason Heather appealed to me. But sometimes, even being in the presence of another, one can feel invisible. In my case, I often try to make myself disappear.

My two oldest brothers have tried very hard *not* to allow my non-existence to happen.

With gradual return to Sterling Falls of the remainder of my brothers, all younger than me, I've been slowly coming out of my shell. A snail's shell, which means it's been a languid unfurling.

"Who was that woman speaking to you?" Sebastian arches a brow before he begins mopping around my feet.

"Genie Webster."

Sebastian doesn't shift from his sweeping motions, his non-response evidence he doesn't remember her. Genie would have been roughly be between Knox and Ford back in school. Sebastian is younger than them.

Genie Webster. I didn't get a clear enough visual of her the other night, but in broad daylight, I caught some of the finer details. Her hair is cut to her chin with loose waves, streaked strawberry blond and hot chocolate brown. Her dark, expressive eyes are a richer color than her hair. Her smile is still the same. Bright and vibrant.

"Anyway, sorry again about the mess."

Sebastian shrugs. "It happens."

"Really? Women toss drinks in guys' faces every day around here?"

Sebastian snorts and lifts the mop to wring out the wetness. "People break up."

We stare at one another a second. Our family doesn't hold a strong belief in romantic love; as in, many of us don't think we'll experience it. Stone, our eldest brother, however, has been adamant we all deserve the powerful emotion, and love will happen in different forms for different people.

Sebastian fell deeply into the didn't-think-he-deserved-it camp until he met Enya. Surprisingly, I'd met her first in a professional manner. We're both accountants and shortly after working with our family business she decided to move to Sterling Falls. *Then*, she met my brother.

And I want to feel the kind of sparks I see between them. That fire in his eyes when he looks at his wife, and the smile on her face when she looks back at him.

Heather and I did not have that kind of flame.

The thought returns my mind to Genie.

Firefly.

She'd been this brief flash of light during my fight. A flicker that popped in the darkness, held, and then extinguished.

I didn't want that light to burn out.

"Want to go for a ride later?" Sebastian asks, still watching me.

For one of the first days of May, the beautiful day is perfect for a ride around the mountaintop passes near us. Since his return from jail, Sebastian and I share a similar love of motor-cycles and the quiet understanding that sometimes you need the rumble beneath your legs and the open road before you. We don't need to talk. We can just be silent.

Then again, the silence surrounding my loneliness and the chatter of Heather in my ear are two things I've been wanting to do away with. Today, I checked one item off my list.

"Rain check?" I suggest, my head a few steps in front of my heart.

Sebastian shrugs and I get busy helping him clean up the bakery before excusing myself.

Suddenly, I have new plans for the afternoon.

THE LAST PLACE I really want to be is Janet Hurley's home or the Buttercup Society Garden Party. I'm not the face of Sylver Seed & Soil; that's Clay's job. Actually, our business logo contains a newly sprouting plant coming out of a clay pot, a symbol of rebirth and growth after our father ran the business into the ground.

As much as I hate that I've given in to Clay's request, because he has other plans that deserve his attention, namely his new little family, I have a change of heart and ulterior motive for being present.

If only I can avoid Heather. Then again, I want everyone to know we are no longer together. And we never will be.

I'm familiar with the concept of wallflowers because I read all kinds of books, so I make myself a plant, stiff and still in a corner near a window, hoping my presence is noted but no conversation is required.

I can tell Clay I did my due diligence. The society is happy Sylver Seed & Soil is represented. And I can get the heck out of here once I see . . .

Genie.

She's dressed in a monstrosity of a yellow dress. Something poofy, with bows and scalloping, making the bottom look like the layers of a wedding cake. The top portion is fitted, which leaves very little to the imagination, hinting at every curve and dip, and the ampleness of her breasts, although they look a little constricted. To further prove my observation, Genie slips her thumb into the strapless dress right between her breasts and attempts to heave the top portion upward. Her elbow sticks out and she almost clocks the waiter cautiously walking among the crowd with a tray of champagne.

He turns to her as if she were trying to grab his attention, but her nose cutely scrunches as she quickly waves off his offering of the bubbly drink.

Glancing around the room, Genie's deep brown eyes catch on me. I smile timidly.

I might not want to be here, but it's my chance to see her again.

Her proposition earlier still haunts me. *Can you find me a date by one this afternoon?* It might look a bit suspicious to appear as her date within hours of a breakup, but I'm here to keep Genie company, if she'll let me.

I owe her. An explanation. An apology. Maybe even some groveling.

For some reason, I envision myself on my knees, hiking up that extra wide skirt and diving beneath the fabric to bury my face between Genie's thighs as a form of apology.

Quickly, I glance away from her. What the hell am I thinking? I can't do *that* with Genie. I just separated from someone else. Then again, it's been months since I've done anything remotely close to my imagination with a certain someone.

I don't even want to think her name, and I'm grateful I haven't seen her yet.

Slowly, Genie makes her way to me, every few steps

nodding at someone, but not stopping to engage in conversation. Pulling up beside me, she mirrors my position, standing close to the corner and staring out at the gathering.

"Whatcha drinkin'?" she eventually asks.

"Whiskey on the rocks, although I'm not really drinking it." I'm simply holding the glass to give my hand something to do. Plus, the alcohol is a reminder of someone else I don't want to think about, but a good reminder of where I need to be later.

When this day is over, I'll have extra energy tonight in the ring.

"May I, then?" Genie is already reaching out for the short crystal glass and removing the drink from my hand. As the two ice cubes within clink, she chugs down the whiskey in one steady stream. Lowering the glass, a quiet sigh of relief escapes her wet lips, and suddenly I'm thinking about them.

If she'll taste like the harsh alcohol. If she'll allow me to lick it free from her lips.

I scrub my hand down my face, willing my thoughts to dissipate.

When I was in middle school—*no, even before that*—I had a crush on Genie. As I aged, the crush turned from innocent schoolboy interest to a burning desire to be closer to her.

And I'd fucked up.

"Did you know today is National Naked Garden Day?" Genie says, startling me both with the tenderness of her voice and the random information.

"I—"

"Yet everyone here is clothed." She focuses on the room and grimaces while continuing to hold the empty glass, waving it outward to emphasize her observation. "But who would want to see Mrs. Chapman naked?"

I glance at the eighty-something, retired librarian and then quickly look away, not wanting *that* image in my head.

"Of course, I'm the only one in this custard-colored atrocity that even an empty donut wouldn't desire."

Genie glances down at herself while holding out the empty whiskey glass without looking in my direction. Our fingers brush as I take it from her, and a spark crackles over my skin where our hands touch. Genie's head quickly turns in my direction. *Did she feel it too?*

But just as quickly, she looks away again and cups beneath those restricted breasts, shimmying a little, appearing to adjust those luscious swells. I glance away to avoid a glimpse of something I shouldn't see.

She sighs, which sounds more frustrated than revealed by her adjustment.

"You look . . . pretty," I mutter to the room. She looks uncomfortable and the dress appears a bit dated, but again, what do I know about women's fashion.

"I look like Didi Conn in the role of Frenchie in *Grease*. And I feel like an overstuffed banana." Genie tugs at the sides of her skirt, while mumbling, "If this is a size ten, I'm a fucking princess."

I snort. *She's funny.* Humor and I are not playmates, though, so I don't have something witty to say in response. Then again, I don't need to speak because Genie continues.

"It's also Kentucky Derby Day, but is there a mint julep in sight?" She pauses without looking at me, waving outward toward the room. "No, there is not." Her voice raises just a touch, and a couple nearby looks our direction.

"It's also National *Star Wars* Day."

"You certainly know a lot about this day."

Genie huffs, continuing her streak. "The *Force* does not feel like it is with me today."

This reference I understand, and I laugh. One short puff of air.

Genie turns toward me looking startled, like she'd momentarily forgotten I'm standing next to her despite her chatter. "I know a lot about dates because it's my business."

"Like asking me to find you one?" Maybe I'm misunderstanding *her* situation. I definitely did not like the assignment. If she's looking for a date, I'm ruling out husband or boyfriend for her relationship status. She already knows my hours-old position. Single.

"No," she chides with a smile. "As in, I make calendars. Quirky Girl Calendars." She presses a hand to her chest like I should understand the reference.

"Anyway," she continues. "I didn't know you'd be here."

I arch a brow. "I'm not supposed to be. But I thought I'd be reinforcements for you." Maybe the Force will be with her after all.

"Why would I—"

"Virginia, there you are." Janet Hurley is a force. One I don't particularly like. I've had occasional interactions with Janet because of the woman I'm no longer going to name having a connection to this pillar in our community. She's one of the reasons I'm standing next to Genie.

Because Genie asking me to be her date becomes clearer as Janet takes in my proximity to her daughter.

"Judd." Janet nods stiffly. She doesn't care for me anymore than I care for her.

"Mother, I see you know my . . ." Genie pauses and glances up at me.

I arch a brow, almost daring her to call me her date. In my gut, I know it's premature to say such a thing. And it's definitely impetuous to say what pops out of my mouth next.

"I'm her fiancé."

5

[Genie]

His *fiancée*. Just what the *eff-ity* is happening here?

Before a moment to process that Judd went rogue passes, my mother crosses her arms, hitches her hip, and glares between Judd and me. Her processed-blonde coif doesn't move despite the rapid movement of her head.

"*Real*-ly?" My mother draws out the word then pauses for emphasis. "Where's the ring?"

Instantly, I fist my left hand, debating about wrapping my arm around Judd's back in order to hide my naked finger.

Here's the thing; I'm allergic to marriage and standing in front of me is the reason why. My mother is on her fourth husband.

And despite the strange burst of energy between Judd and I, that *snap-crackle-pop!* sensation I felt last week at his fight, I do not want to marry him. He's lucky we're even cordially speaking at the moment.

Plus, he just broke up with his girlfriend, less than four hours ago.

"Could you excuse us a second?" I grip Judd's suit coat sleeve just above his elbow.

The moment I saw him across the room, my lungs constricted. Judd in a flannel shirt earlier was one thing. Judd out of it with that tight-fitting tank and those colorful arms another. But Judd in a royal blue, custom-made suit that matches is eyes is almost lethal. The material is silky and smooth beneath my grip as I tug him toward a door a few steps from the corner we'd been standing in that leads us outside.

The yard is packed with people for the garden party, admiring my mother's pre-summer collection of greenery and the potential for future flowers.

Needing more privacy, I drag Judd around to the side of the house into a shaded area which hides us better from the garden viewers.

Glancing up at him, I snap. "What the hell do you think you're doing?"

"I—" Judd swipes his hand through his thick mass of hair and blinks down at me. "I'm sorry. I panicked."

"Well, panic elsewhere." Looking at his stricken face, I sigh and take a deep breath. "I'm sorry. *I'm* panicked. My mother is going to have a million more questions, especially if you can't magically produce a ring."

"Actually . . ." Judd digs under the collar of the white dress shirt he wears beneath his suit jacket and brings forward a silver chain with two rings dangling from it. Removing the linked chain from his head, he works at the clasp and removes the daintier of the two rings.

Between his pinched fingers he holds out a sliver of a gold

band with a small amethyst stone and two diamonds on either side of the gem. It's pretty and sweet. A bit antiquated and . . .

"Are you *fucking* serious?"

Judd and I both turn at the sharp loudness of Heather's voice. In a slinky yellow dress that hugs her curves and slithers down her body like a drizzle of soft serve ice cream, Heather Remington is a vision of brightness. Her boobs almost pop out the top of her strapless contraption and her blond hair even matches her dress.

"You have *got* to be joking." She glares at the ring Judd is holding before narrowing in on me.

"And you." She jabs her finger in my direction.

Judd shifts, partially blocking me from Heather's menacing glare. The move is protective and endearing but unnecessary. I've been dealing with Heather Remington my entire life.

Heather steps closer to Judd, getting right up in his face. He turns his head, giving her his cheek, like a noble man. He's preparing for her to strike him, and I swallow at the realization he'll take it.

Instead, Heather attempts to push Judd out of her way and aims at me with a raised palm.

Judd body blocks her, keeping his hands out and upright, the ring still pinched between his fingers. Her chest bumps his.

"Heather," he warns. "Attempt to touch her and you'll be sorry."

Heather instantly snaps her attention back to Judd, narrowing those icy eyes to shard-like slits. "Are you threatening me?"

"I'm stating a fact," he warns, his voice calm but from my view of the set of his shoulders and the stiffness of his back, Judd isn't letting Heather get anywhere near me.

Hoping to defuse the intensity of their staring-contest, I curl my hand around Judd's bicep.

Heather's head whips to her left. "Is that it?" She glares at the ring in Judd's pinched fingers as if it offends her.

My lack-of-filtering cannot be stopped. "I think it's precious."

"Precious?" Heather reiterates like Golem within his dark cave. Spittle might even release from her disgust. "It's pathetic."

"It was my mother's." Judd's voice grows bolder, louder, almost menacing. *Almost.*

Shock strikes me. Why on earth would Judd give me something so special to him?

Heather's gaze leaps back to Judd's face. "You're pathetic, Judd Sylver."

Spittle actually leaves her mouth but does not quite make it to Judd's chin, if that was her intention. Instinct tells me to step around Judd. Wedge myself between him and her, but then Heather turns on her spiky high heels that are not conducive for the uneven flagstone and she wobbles toward the back yard.

"Are you okay?" I ask, still standing behind Judd. He hangs his head a second before turning around.

"Yeah."

We silently stare at one another a second. The *snap-crackle* between us is missing the *pop*, but the fizzy energy slowly rebuilds.

He said I was his fiancée. He has a ring.

"You should have just told her it wasn't what it looked like."

Judd continues to watch me. "Maybe I want it to look like what it looked like."

"You want Heather to think you got engaged to someone else on the same day you broke up with her."

Judd lowers his head. "Well, when you put it that way, it doesn't sound so great."

"What way would you put it?"

Judd hesitantly lifts his head while holding up the ring

between us and dropping his gaze to it. "I was going to ask you to wear my mother's ring."

"I don't know, Judd." This isn't a symbol of his love or a sign of future commitment. This would only be as a means of getting out of something complicated. A complete misunderstanding. For a minute, I picture Heather running to my mother like the little tattletale she once was, and the look of disappointment on my mother's face that I've somehow hurt poor Heather's feelings.

God forgive me, but for once, a little *ding* toward Heather would feel good.

Most of all, though, I'm not certain I'd feel right wearing Judd's mother's ring.

"It's only for show. For now." Judd's voice sounds a little trembly, almost panicked again, like he's trying to convince me this isn't for something other than getting out of a messy situation. Not for something real. But then, Judd gently takes my left hand and lifts it between us. "Genie Webster, what do you think? Check yes or no."

Funny, that's how I'd communicated with Judd when we were kids. On lined paper with unicorns. My thoughts flash to the tattoo on his bicep. The one familiar and . . . *It can't be, can it?*

One thought bulldozes the next and I realize Judd isn't really asking me anything. He isn't proposing. He's simply offering me this ring. His mother's *special* ring.

And while I'd be saving face in front of my mother, I'm terrified of losing something that holds so much importance to Judd. Then again, I can always give the ring back to him later, right?

Because Judd is positioning the ring at the tip of my third finger and then I'm watching as it slides down to the notch, settling against the webbing at the base of my finger. I spread all my fingers wide, then pull them back together.

The band is delicate. The stone a pretty shade of purple. The diamonds only pinpricks, but sweet.

The ring feels strangely right on my finger. Too right. I should return it to him immediately. I should demand he take it back.

Instead, I curl my fingers, forming a fist. *Just one more minute.* I'll give it back after sixty seconds. Just let me marvel at how good this looks. How nice it feels.

Hesitantly, I glance up at Judd, who is also staring down at the ring.

"Now you officially look like my fiancée."

Am I? Why am I not contradicting him? Why can't I negate this strange rumbling in my gut and stop the thumping of my heart?

"Want to get out of here?" Judd asks.

It's the first sane thing that's been said in the past twenty minutes, and I do want to leave. I want to shed this dress and skip this party and disappear from my mother's house despite having just gotten here.

But I don't want to give the ring back yet, which feels all kinds of wrong.

"Yeah," I whisper.

Then my hand is clasped in Judd's larger one, and he's leading me the rest of the way around the side of the house.

6

———

[Judd]

I don't know what possessed me to say it. *I'm her fiancé.* The words came out of nowhere and yet everything about them felt . . . good. I felt better than I'd felt in a long time, and all from a few words linked together.

Now, Genie's hand is cupped in mine and I'm leading her down her mother's driveway.

The moment I saw Genie, I should have simply asked her if she wanted to run away. I was happy to be her escape. Now, I've made her my fiancée.

The practical side of my brain is already calculating how many days she'll be present in Sterling Falls and what that means once she leaves. For now, I have ten days with Genie and a lot to explain.

She shifts her hand, so her fingers entwine with mine, and I glance down at how our fingers link. The distraction pulls me from my thoughts. I lead Genie down the street to my Harley and she stumbles as I draw up beside the powerful machine.

"You opposed to motorcycles?" I ask, my voice lighter sounding than it's been in years.

Genie glances down at herself. "I just don't know how I'll ride that thing with this dress on."

I pause a beat, observing once more the fullness of the bottom half and the constriction of the top. "Want me to wait while you change?"

Genie is already shaking her head. "I am *not* going back in there." Not yet, her bright dark eyes say.

I nod once and hitch a leg over the seat, then hold out my hand to help Genie climb on behind me, telling her where to place her feet and to be careful with her legs. When she's seated, she tucks and wraps and positions her dress in such a way her bare legs are mostly exposed. She sits with too much distance between us, and I worry she'll fall off the back.

I also just want her close to me.

Every boyhood fantasy I had of Genie included her pressed up against me somehow and I'm not going to miss out on this opportunity to bring her closer.

With her knees bent, I curl my hand behind one of them and tug her forward, forcing her legs to spread wider and her inner thighs to hug my outer ones.

Better.

Genie grunts and her hands come to the sides of my suit coat, clutching at the fabric, but it's still not close enough. I take her right hand and tug it forward so her arm wraps around my stomach. Then I cover her left hand, pulling it forward and pausing a moment to admire my mother's ring on her finger. My thumb flicks over the tiny gemstone. Then, I curl my hand around hers and purposely position her left palm near my heart.

Much better.

With my hands on the throttle and the engine suddenly revving, Genie leans into my back. Her hesitant hold in the position I've placed her tightens. Her thighs clench. Her arms stiffen and her left hand momentarily fists in my shirt. Then, she's simply hugging me from behind, leaning her face against my back, and nothing has ever felt so right. Nothing.

She who shall not be named never rode on my bike. She liked the idea of motorcycle riders but the practicality of riding . . . she didn't want to get dirty. Her hair would tangle. She didn't trust me.

The last excuse was a difficult one to swallow and should have been my first clue that we were not right for each other.

As Genie squeezes my mid-section, returning my thoughts to her at my back and the road before me, I let go of everything else and just drive.

"Where should we go?" I eventually holler over the roar of the engine.

"I don't know. Your place?"

Any other time, Genie's answer might sound like a pickup line. *Your place or mine?*

Heather had used one on me. We met at a Chamber of Commerce get-together. Not the most romantic setting and certainly not where I expected to meet anyone. Clay asked me to attend on his behalf back when my over-worked brother was still over-working himself. Heather was there representing her dad's dealerships.

She asked me if I'd like to join her for a cup of coffee, then made a joke by tilting her head toward the carafe at the back of the meeting room. After I'd poured coffee into a Styrofoam cup, we stood next to one another when she propositioned me.

I could wet that dry spell of yours. It was the most forward anyone had ever been with me. I'd been flattered. Combined with my loneliness, it was a bad mixture.

I haven't answered Genie about where to go, but I have made a decision.

Spiraling down the winding road, I pull up to the iron gates of my property, where they automatically open at our approach. I pick up speed again and zip swiftly along the drive until I slow in front of my home.

The house is dark limestone, with wooden exterior beams and a steep black roof. Rustic mountain cabin meets French Alps, or something like that, the realtor told me when I purchased the place a few years ago. It's hardly a cabin with two wings off the main common area, including five bedrooms in addition to the primary suite.

Only my family has ever been here. Until now. Now Genie has been here too.

After I park in the garage, I help Genie off the Harley. She steps back on shaky legs, and I quickly reach out for her hip to steady her.

"You okay?" Through all that's happened, I haven't asked her how she's feeling.

Her mother's piercing gaze. The altercation with Heather. The ring on her finger.

I need to do better. *I will do better*.

"I'm good." Her warm smile accentuates her response.

Once inside, we pass by several rooms before entering the great room, which is a living room and open concept kitchen area. With a vaulted ceiling that includes thick beams and a large wrought iron wagon wheel chandelier, the space feels grand, which is one reason I love it. I also fell in love with the fieldstone fireplace that encompasses the entire wall opposite the kitchen. A huge kitchen island with four high-back stools on one side and another one at each of the ends divides the space. The dining room is offset to the right.

But all I can focus on is Genie, who takes in the two caramel-colored, soft leather couches and a pair of plaid swivel chairs that face into the room. Most nights, I take a seat in one and turn it to face the windows. A set of three glass panels offer a grand view of the small, private lake on the property. Those three panes have another set of windows above them culminating in a triangular one that matches the pitch of the ceiling. Natural light filters into the room, and from my position, Genie practically glows.

A firefly in broad daylight. An anomaly.

"It's breathtaking," she whispers, wrapping her arms around her middle.

"Yeah," I reply. "It is." *She* is. She's prettier than I remember, only because my memory fails me. Breathtaking, like she said.

"So, this is home?" She twists at the waist to glance back at me and I slowly remove my suit jacket.

"This is it." Maybe it's not sweet and cozy but it's mine. Seeing it as if through her eyes, it might look a bit masculine, foreboding, and dark, but I love this place. And I want her to love it as well. "Make yourself at home."

Suddenly, I'm nervous. "Want a drink?" I pause, considering our unusual circumstances—fiancés for ten days. "Maybe champagne to celebrate." We did just get engaged, right? At least, on some level.

Genie spins fully, still hugging herself. "Maybe another time." She pauses, lowering her gaze. "Do you know how to make a gin martini?"

I sigh. "Unfortunately, yes." She who shall not be named coached me into perfecting the drink.

Genie nods once in understanding. "How about wine?" she hesitates.

"Wine I can do," I offer with more of a smile. "Red or white?"

"Red, please."

I cross the room for the bar tucked behind the kitchen,

facing the dining area, and make quick work of opening a new bottle.

When I return to the great room, Genie has moved into the space between the back of one couch and the high back stools. She's still gazing around the room when I stop in front of her.

She accepts the glass of red wine I hand her and then I lift mine, speculating what we should toast to.

"To old friendships?"

7

———

[Genie]

Friendship is certainly one thing, but fiancée is quite another.

And my mind is still reeling with scenes from the garden party.

My mother's shrill question about a ring. Heather's haughty tone when she caught Judd and me in the side yard. Judd's quiet hesitation.

What do you think?

He meant the ring, right?

Still holding my wine, I stare at Judd. He's so . . . handsome. Classic looking. All American boy with billionaire vibes. *My God, look at this place.* But, a melancholy aura surrounds him. Take in the fact I know he's a fighter and those tattoos add to the edge I saw in him only a week ago. He's the full package, and a lot to unpack.

"What are we doing?" I whisper.

First, I can't say Judd and I are old friends. We were friendly. We were in Math Club together. And that's where I grew bold enough to ask him to *his* prom. The high school ritual is a rite of passage, and Judd didn't want to attend. I thought it was more likely he didn't have anyone to go with to the dance. And I didn't want him to miss out.

He'd been so aloof throughout most of high school. That dark soul in the back of a classroom with moody eyes and a permanent scowl. However, he wasn't a troublemaker. He skated underneath the radar. Of teachers. Of admin. Of other students.

But I noticed him. I sensed he was different. Special. Unique. Like a unicorn.

My gaze flits to his covered bicep and Judd sets his glass of wine on the island counter, without taking a sip. He takes my glass from me and sets it down as well, then pulls out one of the stools.

I'm still wearing this atrocious dress in putrid yellow. Judd doesn't even comment. He grips my waist and hikes me onto the raised seat, then pulls out a stool for himself. We face one another and my left arm rests on the island countertop.

"What do you want us to do?" Not a trace of anything salacious is in his question and yet everything in me lights up.

I could list a few things I want to do with Judd as he is now —a gorgeous man with a body that rocks.

I hadn't missed the tightness of his abs beneath his dress shirt when my arms were wrapped around him while riding his motorcycle. Or the firmness of his thighs pressed against mine as we rode. Even the thumping of his heart was a turn on when he placed my left hand over his chest before we took off.

But Judd and I have some unresolved issues between us. Twenty-two-year-old issues that might best be left alone.

"Maybe we should talk about Heather."

"Maybe we shouldn't." Judd mirrors my position, and he

swipes through his thick hair, brushing back the floppy strands against his forehead. "Honestly, we're over. We've been over for a while, we just needed to have that final conversation."

The official end. I understand that.

"I'd like to focus on new beginnings," he says next, his eyes lowering to the ring on my finger.

With some strange instinct, I flex my fingers, as if emphasizing the ring under his appraising gaze.

Once again, I admire the ring as well. The gold band. The lilac-colored gemstone. The ring is simple while lovely.

"If you weren't planning to marry Heather . . ." Because I distinctly heard that portion of his argument with Heather earlier today—how he would not be asking her to marry him. "Then why did you have this ring at the ready on you?" Had he been planning to ask Heather to marry him at some other time? Before today?

The top three dates for engagements are Christmas Eve, New Year's Eve, and Valentine's Day. Rather cliché, if you ask me. If I ever was to get engaged, which I don't suppose will happen, I'd like the proposal to happen on a random day. A date that becomes significant *because* I got engaged on that day.

Judd sighs and his hand covers mine. He toys with the ring. A strong forefinger and thumb pinching the gemstone. He gently rocks it side to side. His eyes never losing focus on it.

"Once upon a time, I'd *thought* about asking her. Last summer. Once. Then, my brother Ford and I had a discussion." Judd is pensive a moment, thoughtful as his brows crease. "I sounded shallow when I described her." He swallows. "And even shallower when I thought about the reason I might marry her."

"Which was?"

"She liked me." He pauses his movements with the ring and looks up at me. His tone is sharp as he spews the juvenile-sounding words. The look in his eyes strikes me, though, and I realize that sorrow in them might not be sadness, but a lonely boy turned into a lonely man.

"But I had an entire checklist of reasons why we weren't right for one another."

"And today just felt like the day to breakup."

Judd lowers his eyes again, staring down at the ring on my finger once more. He slides his fingers down the length of mine, pressing the tips of his to the tips of mine, forcing my hand upright. He twines our hands together and, with our wrists resting on the countertop, we hold onto one another.

Being single as long as I have, I've had time to evaluate handholding. In some cases, it can be the most intimate contact between a couple. In other cases, it can feel distant, uncomfortable, almost distracting. Like how long do I hold his hand before I can pull away.

Judd holding my hand lands firmly in the intimate column, and leads me to wonder once more; what are we doing?

More importantly, what is happening between us?

We aren't those kids in a grade school classroom. The one where I asked him to be my friend when he was *assigned* to be my reading buddy. We aren't angsty middle schoolers, staring across a crowded library wondering: is he looking at me or someone else? And we aren't those high schoolers on the cusp of adulthood, using Math Club to fulfill a college application (him) and earn extra credit in geometry (me).

We're different people now, and I don't know him.

I might have never known Judd.

I certainly didn't know why he'd stand me up for his prom.

Like I don't know why he'd blurt I was his fiancée in a state of panic.

"Today felt like the day for lots of things," Judd whispers, staring at our fingers that are clasped together.

We're linked.

"Endings and beginnings," I whisper, afraid to pop this

strange bubble that seems to be expanding around us. "So, this is your mother's ring?"

As if heading off a question I hadn't asked, Judd lifts his head, and says, "I never intended to give it to her."

Judd sits upright and runs his other hand down the buttons of his dress shirt. The movement reveals the chain he wears underneath the crisp material and the ring remaining on it.

"I've been wearing that ring"—he nods at our clasped hands—"since I was eighteen. I've been holding onto it."

I swallow hard. "Did you ever intend to give it to someone?" Maybe he'd planned to keep it as a keepsake.

And now I was wearing it.

"I'd always planned to give it to the woman I love. A woman I hope to spend the rest of my life with." Judd lifts his lids, his focus narrowing in on me. A strange shiver runs down my spine.

Along with a cold sweat.

"Well, I never plan to marry," I state bluntly, sticking a pin in the bubble around us and gently tugging my hand free from his.

Judd's expression shifts, first stricken, then tense.

I glance down at the ring myself. "This is too much. I shouldn't be wearing it." This ring is important to Judd. Special and unique, like I've described him. He should continue to hold onto it. Save it for that woman he'll love.

I grasp the top and bottom of the ring and give it a tug, struggling to remove it. After three attempts to pull it over my knuckle, I hold out my hand. "Maybe you should remove it." It might hurt like hell for him to tug at my finger, but if that is what it takes to get this *thing* back off me . . .

Then something else aches. An unfamiliar pain in my belly. A sharp jab to my sternum. It's nothing, I tell myself.

"And maybe . . . it's exactly where it should be."

"Judd," I whimper. He can't be serious.

"Look, I'm not proclaiming we're actually engaged, but you did proposition me for a date."

I stare at him, blinking although I'm not innocent. "Well, not you, directly. Just you *finding* me a date, in general."

"Consider me your date in general." He straightens and pats his chest. "For whatever you need for the next ten days."

"Judd, I can't ask you to do that."

"You didn't ask. I'm offering."

I sense there's something he isn't saying. Like he's offering because he owes me. Like he remembers standing me up when I was sixteen and thinks he can make it up to me at thirty-nine.

"Judd, you don't want to pretend anything with me. Not dating. Not an engagement. You would not want to marry me." I scoff.

"Why not?"

"Because I'd be shit at marriage. Look at the role model I had. My mother is on her fourth husband."

"You aren't your mother. And I had a shit father as well, but I still want—" Judd cuts himself off and pulls back his shoulders. He turns his head, his eyes avoiding me.

"You still want what, Judd?" *Marriage? Love?*

Judd exhales heavily. "I'm not opposed to dating you. Or even pretending to date you."

"You just came out of a relationship."

"Which was more of a falsehood than faking something with you will be." His voice rises just a touch but there's depth to his tone. Sincerity and honesty and something that frightens me.

Does Judd want to spend time with me?

"So, what you're saying is that you are open to a pretendship?"

"A pretend *engagement*," Judd clarifies. "We already told your mother I'm your fiancé."

Actually, he said he was mine, but semantics.

"For ten days," I counter, like we're negotiating terms.

"Ten days," he quickly agrees.

I don't want to think about how we'll break up or what excuse we'll use. The simple answer is he lives here, and I live in Knoxville, four hours away. But those details, how we'll end, feel like a discussion for another day.

"To new beginnings." I hold out my hand to shake his. "A pretendship."

"An *engagement*," Judd clarifies, lifting his hand and taking mine with it. "And old friendships."

For half a second, Judd's eyes flash, like lightning in a summer storm. No more sorrowful puppy dog gaze, but heat and hope flares in those blue eyes that perfectly match a clear afternoon sky.

When our hands connect, that *snap-crackle-pop* turns into *bing-bang-boom*.

And I don't know if it's that metaphorical drum my dad said I marched to or the thumping of my heart.

I'm afraid to admit how much I like the sound of option two.

8

———

[Judd]

As we hold hands a little longer than a typical handshake, my phone buzzes in the pocket of my suit jacket which dangles over the back of a couch. The tingling sound is a reminder I set, and I twist my wrist to check the time on my watch.

"Shit." I hate to do this, but I need to get going. "I'm so sorry, Genie. But I have to go. I have a fight tonight."

While fighting is my deepest kept secret, the cat is out of the bag so to speak, with Genie. She saw me last week.

"You're leaving for Knoxville now?"

Reluctantly, I release her hand and stand to retrieve my phone to shut off the reminder. I chuckle softly at Genie's skepticism. "No. Being in Knoxville was a one off."

I don't typically travel for fights, but The Boxer's management reached out and I figured, what the heck. Why not take my talent elsewhere? However, I'm not certain my family would agree that I have talent. Or understand the underlying desire to have the skills I have.

"I fight just outside of Charleston." The city is one of the largest in West Virginia and roughly thirty minutes from Sterling Falls. Mack's is much like The Boxer, with a pub as a front for the boxing ring in the back. Harvey Mack is a decent guy. He respects his boxers. Knows how to schmooze sponsors. Allows bets. Keeps the place clean.

And I'd never want to be on his bad side.

"Why do you fight?" Her tone is curiosity mingled with concern, and my answer is too complicated for the first night of our reunion.

"I just do." The answer is a bit curt and a lot nonexplanatory.

Genie watches me as I slip my phone into my back pocket and then loosen my cuff buttons to roll up my shirt sleeves. With each fold of the starched material, her expressive eyes widen and then glitter brighter. At one point, she licks her lips and chews at the corner.

Does my fake fiancée appreciate the ink? Will she appreciate it even more when she understands the meaning behind most of it?

"I'm not judging you," Genie finally states, pulling her eyes from my forearms, now exposed with my shirt sleeves rolled to my elbows. "I just want to understand."

I want to tell her. I am certain I could trust her with my secret, but another day.

"Want me to take you back to your mom's? Or get your car for you?" She's still wearing that godawful dress. Her car and phone and a change of clothes are at her mom's.

Genie lowers her head and sheepishly asks, "Would you mind if I hang here?" Maybe she isn't ready to face her mother again. She swings her feet which don't touch the footrest on the stool. The move is innocent looking, almost childlike, and reminds me of an eight-year-old girl sitting beside me when I was ten, reading books with adventure in them to me.

Genie was certainly adept at reading, and her reading to me was a highlight of each week that school year.

The year the reality of my mother's death seemed to have a chokehold on my father and strangle the light out of his eyes. The year he no longer saw his children as a blessing *with* his late wife but a constant, painful reminder of her absence. An absence he resented and blamed on his children.

"I'd be honored if you stayed," I admit, offering her a soft smile. "Help yourself to anything in the fridge or bar. I should be back around midnight."

From her seat on the stool, Genie continues to watch me. The gleam in her eyes still exists but a haze wavers around that spark. A look I cannot recognize.

I should stay. But I have to go. "Want to come with me?" A rush runs up my center. Would she watch me fight? Would she cheer me on?

Genie looks away, pursing her lips. "I think I'll pass." Disapproval forms in that haze.

Disappointment fills me. It'd be nice to have someone ring side at a fight. Someone there to support me.

Glancing back at me, she says, "I respect your passion, Judd. But I also, respectfully, disagree with it." Her brows pinch, asking me a question once more without speaking.

Why do I fight? The answer is so complex, and again, not something I want to discuss right now.

Plus, I'm running late.

Everything in me pulls me toward Genie. Wanting to kiss her temple. Reassure her somehow. But I hold back.

Instead, I nod once. "See you later then?" I'm the one needing reassurance now.

"I'll be here." Her feet kick again, and she offers a warmer smile before I leave.

Once on my Harley, I have time to reflect. Ten days doesn't feel like enough time to get back in Genie's good graces. To re-spark an old friendship. To re-kindle what I once hoped could be more.

However, I've been given a second chance. Somehow. Some-way. And I've learned to fight. This pretendship, as Genie called it, is a match I could not, would not, lose. I'd already lost Genie once before.

I have ten days to prove myself. Ten days to date my fake fiancée.

I haven't felt this fire inside me since I was eighteen years old. This desire to claim what I want. To believe in a future for the first time in a long time. A future that involved more than simply existing but living.

When I arrive at Mack's, I'm primed for my match this evening. I'm looking forward to the battle. The adrenaline rush and the endorphin high. That moment my body turns into a machine. One I control.

My movements are practiced; my skills honed. Nothing feels like the swift release of a left hook or a right uppercut. The contact of glove to glove doesn't spur me on as much as the mental challenge. The unknown of my opponent's moves. The anticipation of it. The excitement rises from counteracting him. A war rages within me, and the win is always bittersweet.

But tonight, it's not about bringing someone else down as much as pulling myself up.

Victory feels a little sweeter this evening.

Genie Webster is in my home, waiting for me. This time, I won't disappoint her.

9

———

[Genie]

"Now what?" I mutter to the emptiness after the soft click of the entrance to Judd's garage announces he's left the building.

I remember saying to Judd I'm better at making messes than cleaning them up and I've certainly made a mess of things now.

I'm wearing his mother's ring.

I'm hiding from my mother in his home.

And I've agreed to dating him, pretending we're engaged for ten days.

What the eff-ity are you doing, Genie?

"Marching to the beat of my own drum," I say to the empty room. "And now I'm talking to myself."

I clamp my lips shut, realizing I'm still doing it. As I slip off the highbacked stool, I finally kick off the shoes that match this ridiculous *costume* of a dress I wore today.

"How did I get myself into that mess?" I mutter once more to the cavernous space deciding what difference does it make if I talk to myself. The point is no one is here to hear me.

How did I get into this dress and how will I get out of it? Then I'm hit with the reality that I don't have a change of clothes. I don't even have my phone.

I should call my mom. Just fess up to the truth. Judd isn't mine. But my thumb tucks into my palm and rolls the gold band from the underside, righting it so the purple gemstone stands proudly on my finger.

It really is pretty.

Quickly, I glance away from the ring and decide I should eat. That whiskey I slammed earlier has gone to my head and a woman can't survive on cinnamon rolls alone.

Circling the large island, I open Judd's industrial-looking, double-door fridge to find it stocked full of fresh vegetables and fruits, plus an array of electrolyte drinks and protein juices. The selections are too healthy, and I'd need to be creative to compile a meal.

My day has been complicated enough.

"Wine it is, then." I reach across the counter for my glass, then pick up Judd's and pour his into mine. Holding the very full stemless glass to my chest, I wander the great room, taking it all in a second time.

The soft looking couches. The over-sized fireplace. The view of the lake.

The late-afternoon-slash-early-evening remains light a little longer as the season creeps toward summer, roughly halfway between the official start of spring and the end. The trees surrounding the lake are mostly awake, the green appears dusty in the fading light of another day.

I'm not certain how long I stand there, staring out at the silvery ripples on the distance lake but I finish my double glass of wine.

Wandering toward the dining room, I easily find the bar Judd referenced and the bottle of wine he opened.

"Engagement party for one?" I snark, lifting the bottle and setting down my glass.

I'm not *really* engaged. I've simply agreed to pretend I am.

When I'd normally be the first to demand honesty in a relationship, I'll be living a lie for the next ten days. And I don't feel as guilty as I should.

Judd Sylver is a mystery to me, and one I'd like to solve.

The fights. The mansion in the woods. The reserve still beneath the surface and yet, he seemed open enough.

He *did* save me from my mother. Rescued me from Heather. Brought me to his lair. I'm making it sound more sinister than it is. He did offer to take me back to my mom's, and I have my reasons for not wanting to rush.

Janet Hurley is a complicated woman. One I've learned to navigate with great exhaustion at times. I love my mother, but I don't always like her. And that in and of itself makes me feel guilty as well.

I miss my dad. He understood me. He appreciated me. And for the next ten days, Judd could be a good distraction from bad memories.

Not that Judd and I will be doing anything physical. Getting lost in one another's bodies. We'll just be . . . dating.

I internally groan. I'm a professional dater. Within minutes, I can tell how things will, or rather won't, go and it's all been daunting the past few years.

Still, I'm firmly against marriage which means I must firmly be in favor of singlehood. Unfortunately, I'm not embracing being alone as well as I once did.

"You'll keep me company tonight, though, won't you?" I say to the bottle of red and take a sip directly from it.

I could have gone with Judd. Maybe I should have gone

with him. Maybe it would crack the code of sorrow around him. But I can't witness someone pummeling Judd. Or Judd punching someone back.

I understand boxing is a sport, but the principle of it is where I'm stuck.

Wandering back into the great room, a chill ripples over my bare arms, and I pause near the couch with Judd's suit jacket draped over the back. Hesitantly, I run my fingertips along the lapel as Judd had neatly folded the jacket so the back panels tuck beneath the sides. Next, I pinch the outer edge of the sleeve and skim my fingers along the silky material.

Closing my eyes, I envision my fingers running down the length of Judd's arms. His skin warm beneath my touch. The ink vibrant and telling a story. What exactly is that unicorn beneath faded lines?

I set the wine bottle on the floor, and I pick up the jacket, holding it to my nose. Winter mint and sunshine lingers at the collar. I'd caught the scent as I pressed into his back while seated on his bike, but then the freshness of spring and the fragrance of pine mingled into our ride.

Holding up the jacket, the color reminiscent of Judd's eyes, I wrap the material around me and tug at the opposite sides, tucking myself inside the silk lining and the hint of heat from Judd wearing this earlier.

If I were bolder, I'd remove my dress and only wear the jacket.

Instead, I pick up the wine bottle and pad on bare feet over the hardwood floor in the direction of the garage. This wing of the house has several doors and it's time to explore.

My travels are short when I quickly come upon two closed pocket doors. Pressing them open, I pause on the pleasing whoosh they make, then I stare, wide eyed, mouth agape into the room.

Cue a Beauty and the Beast montage.

With my mouth still open, I enter the darkish room with bookshelves from floor to ceiling. Suddenly, I'm Belle standing in the gifted library. This one is even complete with a sliding ladder.

"Holy books, Batman," I whisper, twirling in a slow circle, trying to take it all in while not able to grasp everything at once. An etched glass window with X-patterned mullions. Rich, mahogany shelves. The extensive number of books. A deep-purple velvet chaise lounge in the middle of the room. If women could have wet dreams, I'm experiencing one.

Stepping closer to the bookshelves, I scan the eclectic mix of titles. A combination of old and new. A blend of gilded gold on leather spines and worn-creased bindings on modern paperbacks. Judd has everything from atlases to romance novels, and I tug a familiar book off the shelf.

Taking the treasured novel and my wine bottle to the lounger, I lean back against the raised arm panel, feeling like royalty. And an imposter.

Glancing down at the pretty ring on my finger, I wonder what the story is behind this piece of jewelry. Despite the significance of it being his mother's, I sense there is more to the story. *Why* has Judd been wearing it since he was eighteen? The age feels significant, but my memory wavers. I can't recall if he wore a chain during the time I knew him.

Maybe it's simply a keepsake of his mom.

I wish I had something that belonged to my dad.

After his passing, my mother quickly cleared out his belongings. Then it was on to husband number two. Denny, then Henry, and finally Lester.

I tip back my head and consider again how I'm in Judd's home and compare it to my mother's place.

The house I grew up in changed with each of my mom's

marriages. Like a new husband warranted an entire renovation to the place.

There was Denny and the industrial kitchen. Henry and a new den with the addition of a game room. And finally, Lester and bedroom makeovers.

The only room that remained untouched was mine, which stands exactly as it looked when I was a child and last lived with my mom. The same ruffly curtains and childish furniture. A collection of dolls, that come to think of it, are not mine, and a pile of stuffed animals. The room is more museum than sleeping quarters, and I did not want to sleep in it.

I wonder if Judd would let me stay here. *We are engaged.* I laugh without humor. I'm never getting married. I'd be shit at it, as I'd told Judd. It's not that I'd be disloyal or lack commitment, it's that I don't trust in the institution. Look how easily my mother has divorced and remarried? Nothing lasts forever.

I lift my head and reach for the bottle of wine I'd set on the floor. Taking another glance around the room, I speak to it.

"Have I entered *Bridgerton*?" The space is reminiscent of Regency England. A writing desk stands in the corner. A slim wooden chair behind it. Plus, this chaise lounge despite its contemporary flair. Then, I recall the book in my hand, and I'm reminded I'm very much in the modern era.

"I bet you're a kinky bastard, aren't you, Judd Sylver?"

I open the familiar book by one of my favorite authors, but don't get very far before my lids droop. The excitement and confusion of the day catches up to me. The whiskey and wine on only a cinnamon roll-filled belly might also have something to do with my sudden lethargy.

As I tip my head to the side, supported by the raised corner, I tell myself *just for a few minutes.*

Or maybe I speak to the empty room. It's becoming a habit.

Eventually, something brushes my cheek, and I startle

awake. The room is dark. The window is illuminated by an exterior light highlighting the X-pattern. Clutching the book to my chest, I shift and find Judd sitting in the wooden desk chair, now placed beside the chaise lounge.

"You're back."

Judd retracts his hand. It's difficult to fully see him in the dim light.

His chuckle is quiet, like he's afraid to break the silence. "I always thought when I finally brought a woman here, she'd be sleeping in my bed, not the library."

I stare at Judd a second before I shift on the chaise. The kink in my neck is a reminder I'd fallen asleep in this quiet, dark space in an awkward position.

Has he never brought Heather here? I don't ask. He said he didn't want to talk about her anymore, and I really don't either.

"I had my brothers pick up your car. It's parked in the drive. They also retrieved your suitcase and other belongings from your mom's place. I hope you don't mind that I took the liberty."

I chuckle. "Which brothers?" If I recall, the Sylvers are plentiful.

"Well." Judd stutters and clears his throat. "My brother Sebastian didn't always do things legally when he was younger. He owns the Curmudgeon Bakery. You might have seen him earlier."

During the breakup scene. When the man behind the counter and I caught eyes a moment, both feeling trapped by the tension coming from the front corner of said bakery.

"And then Knox can be quite the charmer. He's younger than me by two years but was a year ahead of you in school. He's a firefighter and works at Sylver Seed & Soil like me."

I remember Knox. He dated a girl from my grade named Halle Reynolds at the time.

Judd pauses again. "But I think the real smokescreen in

retrieving your things might have been Ford. Who doesn't want a professional sports star and hometown hero to show up at a local garden party?"

My mother would have absolutely been starstruck by the famous baseball player.

Judd clears his throat again. "That might have been when the not-quite-legal activities took place. Sebastian collected your things."

I laugh at the thought of three grown men distracting my mother and guests to *steal* my belongings out of her home.

"What did you tell them about me?" How did he convince his brothers to gather my things?

"I said I had a friend in need of assistance."

His silence after his simple explanation speaks volumes. He didn't tell them more. Perhaps they didn't ask.

"Anyway, I set you up in the guest room." Despite the low light in the room, Judd looks wary a moment and he bows his head, fiddling with something in his hand. "And I have this for you."

He holds up the item which I quickly see is a folded piece of paper between his forefinger and the middle one. Cautiously, I take it from him, but I don't open it.

I hardly move. The way Judd is looking at me, I'm trapped in the corner of this chaise lounge. Or maybe it's that I feel safer than I've ever felt. The energy around us crackles again and I lick my lips, watching him watch my mouth. I clutch the book in hand, which presses on his jacket which I'm still wearing, and each item feels like a layer I want Judd to unwrap and set me free.

I blink against the thought.

I'm not caged. I'm single and at liberty to do as I please. Which means I have the free will to leave . . . or stay.

"Thank you," I whisper, finding my voice rough and low, and also afraid to crack this new silent tension surrounding us.

One that feels like it could snap at any second, and yet I don't want it to break.

I don't want to want Judd Sylver.

My heart cannot take the possibility he might reject me again.

Even with this kindness. Even with this act. I remind myself Judd has wrecked me in the past.

"Sleep on it," Judd whispers eventually, his voice deep like his throat is clogged. "And sleep well."

"You too," I whisper, still struggling as I watch him stand. His full height could feel imposing and yet I suddenly want nothing more than Judd to climb up on this chaise and cover me. Blanket me in *his* warmth instead of his suit jacket. Remove this awful dress and lay me bare on the velvety seat.

And those thoughts should not be filling my head.

Judd nods once, slips his hands into his pockets, and turns to walk away, while I glance down at the book in my arms and slip the folded paper he handed me into the pages, like a bookmark.

Then I curse the book for the fantasy it placed in my mind.

The one where Judd would not have left but picked me up like his future-bride-to-be and carried me to his room.

Silly romance novels.

I swing my legs over the side of the chaise and stand, escorting myself to the assigned guest room.

IN THE MORNING, I better appreciate this room. The four-poster bed is made of dark mahogany but delicately carved and antique-looking. Across the room is a low dresser that appears to match the bed set and beside it is an overstuffed bedroom chair and ottoman with violets on the fabric. The room is painted light purple, corresponding with the lightest shade of violet on the chair. The space is pretty, feminine and sweet, and for half a minute, I wonder if it was intended for someone else.

Not wishing to think about Heather, I sit upright and toss off the thick white duvet. Last night, I hadn't bothered to unpack my suitcase or wrestle into pajamas. Instead, I simply stripped out of the custard-colored creation, shedding it like I'd scrape the inside of anything holding such a filling, and left the dress in a heap on the floor. I climbed into this bed, which might be the most luxurious mattress I've ever slept on, and fell into a restful sleep.

In only my underwear, I turn toward the nightstand where a small violet plant sits in a milk-glass pot. Beside it is the paperback from last night and the note peeking above the edge, reminding me I'd never read it.

I easily pull the sheet free and unfold it.

*W*ILL *you date me for ten days?* Check yes or no.

I GIGGLE. Like a schoolgirl receiving a note from her secret crush, passed across the desks in the back of a classroom. Covering my mouth, as if to contain the childlike sound, I snort next.

Oh my gosh. Judd Sylver actually wrote me a note similar in fashion to the ones I once wrote him. And . . . I do a double take at the paper.

The four-by-six sheet has light blue lines like traditionally lined notebooks, but it's the unicorn beneath the lines that catches my eyes. The one with a pastel swirl of color on its unique horn and the likeness of a white stallion that takes my breath away.

The paper is exactly the same as the one I once used to ask Judd if he'd be my friend on National Make a New Friend Day.

And it's the exact same unicorn with faded lines over it that is inked on Judd's bicep.

Suddenly, I'm leaping from bed, rustling through my suitcase and rushing into the bathroom to quickly take care of business. Then I'm marching into Judd's great room prepared to demand answers when I'm stopped in my tracks.

Judd stands in his kitchen with his back to the hallway I exit. He's wearing a black wife-*pleaser* tank and low-slung gray sweats that accentuate the firmness of his ass. His legs look long but thick in the loose pants. His upper body a sculpture of perfection. And those brightly colored arms remind me why I stomped out of my room.

As I near the island, Judd spins and flinches. "Jesus."

"No. Genie." I choke on my own joke. "Did you forget I was here?"

But then I remember why *I'm* standing here. The thoughts colliding in my head. *Why? What? How?* I don't know if I'm irritated or aroused, and I hate that I can't distinguish between the two. Maybe I'm both.

"Explain." I hold up the note and rustle the paper. Then I point forcefully at his upper arm. "And explain."

"Good morning, Genie. How did you sleep?" Judd's mouth turns up on one side. A devilish smirk if I've ever seen one, and yet, I'm not certain I've ever seen that look on anyone. Nor reacted to the curve of someone's lips the way I am right now.

"Judd," I moan. "Do not good morning me." I wave the paper in my hands again.

"You answer my question, and I'll answer yours."

"That bed was heaven." I give him my own smirk and cross my arms, arching a brow. *Your turn.*

Judd ducks his head and smiles a little wider. Just a sliver. Then his mouth twists, and he looks back at me. His cheeks turn a vibrant shade of pink and he tilts his face away from me. His lips move. The sound incoherent.

"What?" I chuckle, holding my hand cupped around my ear.

Judd clears his throat and looks directly at me. "I might have a notebook with unicorn paper in it."

I laugh loud and spastic, choking on the sound. "Why?" Maybe he has nieces and nephews who love unicorns.

"Because you had one."

My laughter sputters out. I blink a few times uncertain I've heard him correctly. I'm definitely confused. "When I was, like . . . eight?"

"And I was ten." Judd continues to hold his gaze on me, but sadness pinches his brows and dulls those bright eyes. "You asked me to be your friend then."

I huff out a laugh. "You remember that?" I uncross my arms and grip the back of a highbacked stool, suddenly feeling like I need something to anchor me.

"No one has ever asked me to be their friend like that." He doesn't look away from me. Although his words are soft, his focus is hard on me.

"With unicorn paper?" I lift the sheet once more.

Judd shakes his head and drops his gaze.

I wait out an explanation, thoroughly frustrated, before reminding him of one more detail. "You said you couldn't be friends with a girl."

His head snaps upright and Judd braces his hands on the kitchen island. "I was wrong to say that." His face morphs from distress at the memory to something darker before he closes his eyes and shuts me out a second. When he opens them again, those same eyes shift once more, pleading with me. "I'd like a second chance."

"At friendship?" I confirm, my shoulders lowering, my voice still tight.

"At everything." His gaze remains fixed on me, but his voice is low.

I want to ask what's everything. What does he mean? What does he want? Then, his phone rings, vibrating almost violently on the countertop.

"Shit," Judd mutters, closing his eyes for another second, before reaching for the phone and answering it. "Yep."

That single growled word is not the friendliest greeting, but then Judd hangs his head, going from irritated to tortured within seconds. He leans forward, bending at the waist and bracing his forearms on the island, then removes the phone from near his ear and taps it against his forehead a few times, while closing his eyes one more time.

Suddenly, he stands to his full height, puts the phone back to his ear and glances at me and holds. "Yep." Still watching me, he says. "We'll be there."

He clicks off the call and tosses the phone to the countertop.

"We've been summoned to the weekly family meal at my brother's house."

"Which brother?" I ask, trying to keep track of who is who.

"My eldest one, Stone. He's the town sheriff. But the call was from Clay. Next in line. He runs the Sylver Seed & Soil."

Sylver Seed & Soil had been a major sponsor of the Buttercup Society Garden Party.

"Is that why you were at the garden party?"

Judd shakes his head. "I *do* work for the Seed & Soil. They call me the chief financial officer, but I'm really just the accountant. But that's not why I was at the party."

"Then why were you there?"

Judd continues to stare at me and the answer feels like a slow breeze. A tickle against my skin. A sudden chill that's equal parts refreshing and a bit frightening.

Judd was there for me.

I clear my throat. "So, you need to go to your brother's house for lunch."

"*We* need to go to my brother's."

"We?" I choke.

He licks his lips and slides his hands closer together on the surface of the island while continuing to watch me.

"They want to meet my fiancée."

10

——————

[Judd]

After apologizing profusely to Genie for the demand—*er, request*—to attend the weekly family meal, we eat the French toast and fresh fruit I've prepared for her.

I've rarely made an appearance at the meal every Sunday that my eldest brother established as a weekly check-in on the siblings he was raising. By the time Stone took over the family, I was in college and not involved in this system of checks and balances. Balancing schedules and finances. Checking homework and work calendars. My oldest brother gave up a lot and I hate to disappoint him, especially when Clay tossed in that Stone would really like to see me.

My family. I swear they are worse than a bunch of old ladies sometimes. And the rumor mill is circulating fast with this new news.

I can picture the headline. *Judd Sylver is engaged, but who's the girl?*

She's still a mystery to me, as well, but I want to learn all I can, and I'm a little disgruntled I'm giving up precious time with Genie to be with my family. Then again, Genie is going with me, and I've never taken anyone else home. Ever.

"To be fair, my family might have already heard our news." *I have a fiancée.* "Because rumors and small towns."

"Such a nasty combination," Genie chides, tucking her chin onto her fist as she sits along the side of the island while I sit at the end, so we are perpendicular to one another. I like this position because I can see her when she talks and hear the little hums she makes with every bite she takes of what I made for her.

"So, we can just set them straight," she adds.

"Or . . ." I clear my throat. "We could continue the ruse. Ten days, remember?"

"Yes but dating and being engaged are not the same thing," Genie counters.

"No," I draw out, then think quick on my feet. "And you're against marriage, but what if you give me these ten days to prove it might not be so bad? Engagement is the middle ground between dating and marriage anyway."

"Like purgatory is between heaven and hell?" she quips.

"Assuming marriage is heaven." *Dating can be hell.* "Ten days of engagement to prove you are worth more." *And ten days to show her who I am now.*

Genie blinks, staring at me like I've said something that isn't possibly true. And that look is exactly what I want to wipe from her face.

"How would we play this with your family, then?"

"I'll figure something out." Because right now I'm too wrapped up in her agreeing with me, and sitting across from me, and staring occasionally at my mouth.

Genie clears her throat, breaking this magnetic spell

between us. "So, let me get this straight." She pauses to take a bite of French toast. "Stone is the oldest, and the sheriff."

I sigh in relief at the change in topic. "Yes."

She waves her fork in the air. "Then Clay, who runs the Sylver Seed & Soil. Then you."

I nod and take another bite of French toast.

"Then after you is Knox. The firefighter."

"And a bricklayer with the Seed & Soil. He specializes in designing patios and retaining walls."

Genie makes a face like she's impressed, and I wonder if she'd be impressed by the garden I have on the side of my house.

"Then Ford. Baseball player."

"Former centerfielder for the Chicago Anchors."

Wow, Genie mouths. "Then Sebastian, who runs Curmudgeon Bakery. I love that name."

"He's very . . . curmudgeonly. Well, he was until he married Enya." What a miraculous shift from grumpy Sebastian to a sunnier one. Is that all it took to absolve the hurts of the past? The love of a good woman?

"Huh. It might run in the family," she teases, arching a brow.

"I'm not a curmudgeon."

"Oh, please. You had this whole broody, soulful poet vibe going on in high school."

I choke. "I didn't have anything going on in high school. I was a loner." And a loser according to a few people. My head was always down in a book, and I kept to myself.

"But you were part of Math Club."

I don't know how many truths Genie can handle in a day. I can't believe I've already admitted I have the same notebook she had when she was a child. I'd rediscovered it stashed in my dresser at Stone's house years later when I officially moved out.

Then the tattoo which is a constant reminder of what she asked me.

One look also told her I attended the garden party to see her.

Not certain I have much pride left, so I decide to just let it all hang out. "I followed a girl into a classroom after school one day and suddenly I was a member."

Genie's face goes blank. "What girl?"

I tilt my head, implying the obvious. "What were *you* doing in Math Club?"

She blinks a few times and then clears her throat. "I needed extra credit in Geometry."

"From Mr. Martin?"

"Exactly." She points her fork at me. "Math and I are not friends. Neither were Mr. Martin and me."

I huff. "Didn't all the girls have the hots for him?" He'd been a young guy teaching math to high school girls only a few years younger than him.

"Not me." Genie fakes a gag. "So back to your family, who did I leave out?"

"Vale. My sister is the youngest." Vale tries so hard to keep me in the family fold, like she's the mother hen when she's the baby chick. "She's a physical therapist. And a single mom."

From there, I detail all my nieces and nephews, who goes with whom, and who has life partners.

"Stone, Vale, and you are the only ones single."

I nod toward her left hand. "I'm not single. For ten days, at least." I'm holding true to my promise which reminds me Genie never answered my note. The one she clutched in her hand, hellbent on wanting answers until Clay's call interrupted us.

I swallow thickly and set down my fork. Pushing my plate away from me, I fold my arms on the island. "You didn't answer my question. From my note."

Genie stares at me. Her eyes are so expressive. The brown

color is rich but not deep with flecks of gold that sparkle when the light hits just right. *Fireflies in the night.*

She sits taller on the stool and sets down her fork. Mirroring my position, she pushes her plate back as well.

"I check yes, Judd." Yes, to dating me for ten days. But then, her gaze lingers on me, like she wants to tell me more. Like she *is* telling me more, but I'll never master mental telepathy.

Instead, I just stare back at her, this weird tension building between us. A vibe I don't recognize, but don't mind. In fact, the energy seems to fuel me. Or it might be the sensual pull I feel toward her. From the moment I saw her in that yellow contraption I've had a hard-on. It might have happened sooner except for the ice pooling in my lap when I saw her in the bakery.

Then I consider seeing her with that douchebag Ralson outside The Boxer. I haven't asked her about him. It was clear she wasn't leaving with him that night, much to my relief. I wanted to go home with her. To follow her. To hang out with her. But she was gone in an instant. Like the firefly I first thought of upon seeing her. Flickering bright for only a flash and then disappearing back into the dark.

"Done?" I nod toward her plate, dispelling the momentary sizzle between us because I'm growing hard just looking at her and my gray sweatpants hide nothing. If I thought I'd get away with it, I'd clear these plates in one swoop, pull her up on the island, and make a meal of her.

But patience will be required when it comes to Genie. I owe her time, and while I don't have much, I don't want to waste any of it, which is another reason I do not want to go to my brother's later today.

"We don't really have to go to Stone's, if you don't want to." I stand and reach for Genie's plate.

She grabs it back from me. "I'm not done." Her eyes meet mine for a second. Another flash of gold in them before she looks away. "And going to your brother's is fine. It might be fun. And I'm curious about all your secrets."

She hums humorously, but the last thing I want Genie to know is *all* my secrets.

~

WHEN I ENTER the great room after cleaning up breakfast and giving Genie and me both time to shower, separately unfortunately, I find her standing with her back to the room. She's admiring the view of the lake again, and I'm admiring her.

She turns and my breath hitches.

"Do I look okay?"

"You look pretty." The words are not adequate. The sunlight is filtering into the room, haloing her in a warm glow. Although magical and bright, the moment is more than her appearance. There's a sense of rightness to Genie standing here, in my house. Like she's the remaining piece of a puzzle I've struggled to put together on my own.

She feels like home, and a sensation I haven't felt for a long, long time returns to me. One I'm not ready to define for fear Genie won't feel the same way. Thus, the need for more time.

Genie pulls at the sides of her dress, looking down at herself and distracting me from my thoughts. The Kelly-green skirt with small polka dots flares from her hips. The strapless dress is more flattering than the yellow thing she wore only yesterday. It accentuates her curves, making her breasts look even more voluptuous.

I'm in so much trouble.

"You clean up nice, too." She glances up at me.

I scoff at my dark jeans and an untucked dress shirt. It's been forever since I've attended a Sunday dinner, I honestly didn't know what to wear. I'd ask if I met her approval, but the way she's looking at me, my cheeks heat. She has no idea what she does to me when she looks at me like that. How it gives me hope, a feeling I don't think I've ever fully experienced.

"Shall we?" She waves toward the garage, breaking the spell.

When we enter, she takes in my motorcycle, pickup truck, and the Ford.

"What is *that*?" Genie stares at the shiny black, mean machine.

"A GT500 Ford Shelby." A total impulse buy, but I love my toys.

"Can I drive it?" Her eyes are wide as she glances back at me. Then she pouts her lips and folds her hands beneath her chin, batting her eyelids.

Oh my God, how can I say no to her?

I turn for the lock box of keys just inside the door and then toss the Ford set to her. The keys fall at her feet and Genie bursts into laughter. "I swear I don't drive as bad as I catch."

"You didn't catch them at all," I remind her, my mouth pulling up on one side. She's so adorable and refreshing. Fucking thunderstorm in a summer draught refreshing. "And I'm a little worried about your eye-hand coordination."

"Why?"

"It's a manual." When she tilts her head, I clarify by motioning my hand like I'm working a gear shift. "Stick shift."

"Ugh." She drops her head back. "Okay, you can drive." She stomps her feet as she moves toward me with the keys in hand, and I want to pull her in for a hug. I want to press her to me and kiss her head, then move on to her lips, and her throat and that cleavage.

"Judd."

I snap out of it as Genie dangles the keys in front of me. "Our chariot awaits."

"Well, you did have that whole princess thing going on yesterday."

I'd like to promise I'd treat her like a queen, if she'd only give me the chance.

11

[Judd]

By the time we reach my brother's house, the playfulness of the morning is gone. I can feel myself shutting down. The tightness of my skin. The swell of my throat. The vise-grip sensation around my chest. I almost can't breathe as I pull into the driveway.

"You okay?" Genie asks. One quick glance over at her, plus her hand on my forearm and most of the panic washes out of me. Like a dam broke free.

"Yeah. I will be." I exhale

I park beside a pickup truck, one of several in the drive which now looks like a small parking lot.

For the longest time, only four out of seven of us remained in Sterling Falls. Stone, Clay, Vale, and me. A decade ago, Sebastian was in jail, but when he got out less than a handful of years ago, he returned and started his bakery. Around that time, Knox retired from his long-time career in the Navy. And most recently, Ford retired from professional baseball and moved back here with his three little girls.

Other than Sebastian's wedding eighteen months ago, I haven't been to the house.

The place looks different than when I was a kid. The white clapboard is freshly painted. The old roof replaced with a green tin one. The front porch is newish. Still, all the improvements in the world cannot erase the ghosts inside.

The haunting memories are the main reason I don't attend Sunday dinner as often as Stone would like. The insults and abuse at my father's hands live in my mind as if they occurred only yesterday, and still exist within every crevice of this house. Even though the place has been renovated over the years, from the efforts of Stone who inherited it upon our father's death, I will always view this house for what it represented.

Hell.

Widowed father. Town drunk. The harm he caused his children was on a sliding scale from verbal assaults to physical punches. Most days, and nights, you didn't know which slice of the spectrum you'd get.

"Judd?" Genie's voice pulls me from my thoughts again. Her hand is back on my arm.

Offering her a tight smile, I pop open my door and get out, then make my way to Genie's side, giving her a hand to help her up from the low seat.

"It's so picturesque," she says glancing at the house, unable to see the haunting dings and dents hidden within.

I don't answer. A new wave of panic hits. I'm introducing Genie to my family.

As if reading my mind, she says, "I hope I make a good impression." Her gaze has dropped down to her white tennis shoes.

Unable to help myself, I squeeze the back of her neck and run my thumb along the column of her throat. "They're going to love you." How could they not? It's impossible not to love Genie and everything about her.

I've never actually experienced it—love—, but I *thought* I'd come close. Once. A long time ago. Hopefully, I'm not too late to regain that feeling.

I release Genie's neck and hold out my hand. Genie slaps her palm into mine, but then weaves our fingers together. I love the fit and I tighten my grip as we walk around the side of the house. As we breach the backyard, Genie grabs my bicep with her other hand and squeezes my arm. Like it isn't enough to hold my hand, but she needs to clasp onto more of me.

Maybe I'm wishful thinking.

"Hi . . . everyone." I stumble over my greeting and awkwardly wave like I'm still ten instead of forty-two. I had a whole speech prepared in my head, having run over it again and again as Genie and I rode in silence to the house. Now, I've got nothing. "Um . . . I'd like you all to meet Genie. My fiancée."

Spoken like I told Janet Hurley I was Genie's fiancé, I just sort of blurted it out like I can't contain the phrase. The idea is almost too big to keep to myself.

At first, no one reacts. I glance from the burly, silver beard-edness of Stone to the playful, weathered face of Clay. Then I look at Knox, who doesn't contain his surprise any better than the stoic Ford standing beside him. Despite helping in my ploy to get Genie's car and belongings from her mom's place, they both react with shock. Finally, I peer at Sebastian who has a gleam in his typically mischievous eyes, almost like he's proud of me. I'm never impulsive.

As Stone takes a hesitant step toward us, Vale rushes past him and leaps for me. Her hug is so fast and strong, she almost knocks me over. I release Genie's hand to prevent my sister and me from falling backward. The embrace takes my breath away, but I also panic for another second at the loss of contact with Genie. I hadn't realized how much she was grounding me.

As if sensing my unease, Genie rests her hand on my lower back.

"What a surprise." Vale's voice is a little too high as she glances from me to Genie and back. "I heard a rumor, but you know I like to dismiss them."

Then her gaze falls to Genie's finger, as if needing confirmation to *negate* what she heard. Her eyes suddenly well with tears and she clasps her hands beneath her chin. "Is that . . ." She swallows hard. "Is that Mom's ring?"

Most might think the precious family jewelry should go to the only girl, but at one point, Vale and I talked about the ring. She knows the significance to me, and considering she never knew our mother, she was happy to let me keep it.

Clay is the one I glance up at while nodding at Vale. They all know the story behind how I acquired the ring, but he's the one I'm closest to in the family. It's no secret I've been wearing the ring since I was eighteen, adding my father's wedding band to my chain when I was almost twenty.

"Let me see," someone female says.

In the past two and a half years, I've witnessed several of my brothers fall in love and get married or move in with the love of their life. A few of them even had children or bonded with the children of their significant other.

I'm pleased when Genie holds out her hand, admiring the amethyst gemstone and the small diamonds. If our engagement were real, I could afford something larger. *She* should have something bigger. She deserves something that expresses her worth. But there is also something in the way Genie stares at the ring, gushing over it herself as the others admire it on her hand.

Her smile is wide while sweetly shy. Her cheeks flush, and those brown eyes dance.

"Uncle Judd." Mavis's little boy, Dutton, rushes toward me and I bend to pick him up. I don't consider myself great with kids, but I'm protective of my nieces and nephews. Dutton is the newest member of our next generation, and he holds a special place in my heart. Last Halloween, there was an unacceptable incident where the then-six-year-old was bullied by an adult. My left hook made its first appearance in front of my family that night and my brother Clay discovered that I'd learned to fight. He doesn't know even half of the story though.

And I realize I'd forgotten to tell Genie not to mention the fighting in front of my family. I live by a need-to-know basis with them, and they haven't needed to know I box.

With Dutton in my arms, despite his lanky, seven-year-old size, he tugs the chain at my throat forward, exposing the remaining ring. He likes to slip his finger into one and then the other. One dainty. One large.

"Where's the other ring?" Dutton asks, noticing the smaller of the two missing.

"I gave it to Genie."

"Because you love her?" Dutton looks at me, eyes innocent and wide.

Shit. I'm not exactly certain how to explain the situation to my nephew. Nor to the rest of my family.

"I . . . uh . . ."

"He's letting me borrow it for a little while," Genie says, coming to my rescue. Although I'm not loving her answer. An engagement ring is for keeps.

"Are you buying her a different one?" Vale glances up at me with concern.

Genie is quick again. "Yes." But I can almost hear the swallow in her throat. She doesn't like lying to them any more than I do.

Thankfully, Sebastian saves both of us. "Never knew you to be so impulsive." He claps my shoulder. "I like it."

"When did you two reconnect?" Clay asks. I counted on him being the nosiest one and he isn't going to disappoint.

"I've had a crush on Genie for years."

Her head swivels so fast in my direction, a piece of her hair gets caught on her lashes, and I reach up to push it aside.

"What?" Genie whispers, glaring at me like I'm going rogue again. Which I am. Something I can't seem to stop in her presence.

I set Dutton on the ground and shrug before I begin. "When I was in fifth grade, Genie was my reading buddy." I side-eye her.

"Who needs a reading buddy in fifth grade?" Knox questions, especially as most of my siblings consider me the smartest in the bunch.

"Genie was in third grade. She's younger than me."

"Oh," he deadpans.

"Shh," Vale demands, waving at our brother. "Let Judd explain." She beams at me like I'm about to narrate the most romantic tale.

I don't want to disappoint her, but there isn't much to share. "Genie asked me to be her friend."

"Judd." Genie's voice is quiet, confused.

I feel her gaze on the side of my face, but I know I won't get this out if I look at her. I'll blurt out more truths than she can handle in a day. More than I care to share all at once.

"She always had these braids in her hair." I wave over my head like my hair is woven together. Finally, I turn to Genie. "And I thought she was the cutest girl I'd ever seen."

Genie quietly scoffs while her brows deeply crease.

"It was love at first braid tug." I reach for the end of her now shorter hair and tug a curl, then turn back to my family, unable to look Genie in the eye after admitting the moment I fell for her. Like I told her this morning, no one had ever asked to be my friend. In truth, I didn't have many. My older brothers were best friends with one another. I'd been especially close to my mother as a child, and as my younger siblings came along, I became her 'special helper'. She was my best friend until I was eight. Until she was gone.

"I never knew," Genie whispers, as if playing along with an act when what I've said is the truth.

I've had a crush on her since I was ten.

"And what about you?" Vale asks a bit suspiciously, her tone suddenly protective. "When did you fall for Judd?"

Genie looks at me a long minute, and then turns toward Vale, giving her a warm smile. "I don't think it was love at first braid tug for me. I pushed him off a chair after he pulled my hair."

My family collectively chuckles, and I'm hopeful that's the end of grill Genie-and-Judd time.

But Genie continues. "When I was in middle school, though, I had the biggest crush on him." She pauses and turns to me. "But of course, eighth graders were too cool to look at sixth graders."

She must be lying. I was never too cool for anything in middle school. But I remember meeting those eyes of hers across the middle school library. When she'd be waiting for her mom to pick her up after school, and I'd just be hanging out, avoiding my home and my dad until the last possible minute.

"Can I be a flower girl in your wedding?" Ford's oldest daughter, Zelle asks, breaking into the stare Genie and I share. I hadn't seen Zelle's approach.

"Can I be one, too?" Winnie asks next. The now-seven-year-old isn't much for stereotypical girl things. She's mischievous as hell but where Winnie is, Dutton is sure to follow, so I'm not surprised when he asks next.

"Me too," he adds enthusiastically.

"I want to be a flower girl," June, Ford's youngest states, so as not to be left out of the mix.

Oh boy. "Um . . . we aren't exactly to the wedding planning stage yet." The engagement was only established yesterday, and as it isn't real, I don't want to get too far ahead of myself. Plus, I'm sensing the panic starting to swirl around Genie.

"I'm starving," I announce, rubbing at my belly like a child to distract everyone.

"Why don't you help me with the burgers, Judd?" Stone asks, after having remained silent throughout this exchange.

Truth is, no one helps Stone with the burgers. He's a grill master and takes the position of feeding his family every Sunday very seriously. So, I know what Stone really wants. A chat.

"I don't want to leave Genie." She's new to this madness. Seven siblings plus significant others and the ever-expanding second-generation hoard. It's a lot to take in.

Or maybe I'm the one who wants her to remain by my side.

Stone glances at her and offers a kind smile. "Something tells me she can handle herself."

"Go," Genie whispers, placing her comforting hand on my back again. "Now I can get the real gossip on you." She nods toward my sister. "And maybe see a baby picture or two."

"No pictures," I counter, knowing how I looked when I was younger. Buckteeth and big ears. Then the awkward glasses stage. The skinny phase with ill-fitting clothes. And the hungry years.

"Oh, I have pictures." Vale wiggles her brows and slips her arm through Genie's, pulling her away from me. They are going to be fast friends.

With my head down, I follow Stone to the grill.

12

———————

[Genie]

While Judd and I passed the first test relatively unscathed, a second round comes up when the family lines the two wooden picnic tables pushed together to accommodate such a large group of people.

"So, Genie, what do you do?"

As much as I love my job, I'm also very protective of it. I'm hesitant to share at times.

As Ralson so lovingly pointed out, said tongue in cheek, my mother thinks my professional life is a hobby. As a woman who has never worked a day in her life, she wouldn't understand the ins and outs of working independently or self-employment.

"I design calendars."

Judd offers me a warm smile, as I've already told him what I do.

I clear my throat. "Actually, I run my own business called Quirky Girl Calendars."

Clay's head pops forward as he's on the same bench as me but down the way. I've surmised the basics about how Sylver Seed & Soil, family owned and operated, was once a small business but is now more of a medium-sized corporation with divisions and specialties underneath their company umbrella.

Which is what I want for my small business one day. Growth.

"As I'm the artist plus marketing director and chief financial officer," I glance at Judd and wink. "I'm looking to expand."

"Why does Quirky Girl Calendars sound familiar?" Enya asks. She's seated on the opposite side of the table where her husband Sebastian is practically glued to her side and holding their three-month-old baby girl, Annabelle.

Judd and I got separated in the seating arrangement, so we sit across from one another, and somehow, at the head of the table.

I hesitate again, feeling most eyes on me. This is the point where I either shut down conversation, sensing listeners will think my work is simplistic or play up my creative designs.

I take a chance on the Sylvers.

Flatting my hand and pushing up the ends of my short hair in a flirty way, I state, "I'm Quirky Girl, so I sketch lots of women in different colors, shapes, and sizes with a variety of outfits. Gardening. Reading. The like. Then I fill the calendar with fun, unique specialty dates."

"Like what?" Halle, Knox's wife asks. The red-haired mother of two teens is seated beside me.

I glance at Sebastian. "Like World Baking Day, coming up on May seventeenth."

He offers me a crooked smile and Enya turns her head to look lovingly at him.

"Wait." She pauses and swivels back to me. "I *have* one of your calendars. I love it." She glances back to Sebastian. "It's the one on my desk."

"The one that told us which day was National Sex Toy Day?" he questions, keeping his gaze firmly on his wife.

"What?" Judd chokes across from me and I look over at him to see him reaching for his beer.

"That's the one." Enya smiles sheepishly at Sebastian before looking back at me.

"I want to know more about a calendar that honors sex toys," Cadence, Ford's pregnant fiancée announces from the other side of Sebastian. I'm still a little star-struck that the country music icon is seated casually at this table with the rest of us adoring fans.

She lifts her phone and says, "What day is National Sex Toy Day? I want to mark my calendar."

"November fourth," I state.

"Don't mark your calendar, buy one from Genie," Judd interjects, and I turn toward him. No one has ever sounded so adamant about purchasing my calendars.

"What's a sex toy?" Winnie asks from somewhere behind Cadence and Ford who are seated together.

"A toy for adults and one you won't need," Ford explains to his eight-year-old, while twisting on the bench seat to free himself from the table. "Ever."

"Now, cowboy," Cadence chides, her mouth falling open as if to explain, but Ford is quick to cover her lips with his hand. She chuckles beneath his palm.

Ford stands. "Who wants to play catch?" After a quick hand-rub over Cadence's belly and a kiss to her head, he's off to wrangle the kids old enough to toss a ball.

Couple goals whispers through my head.

Wait? What? I don't have couple goals. I don't plan to be a couple. I'm party of one. Numéro uno. Only me.

Then I glance back at Judd, who, like me, was just watching Ford interact with Cadence. Slowly, he glances back at me and then lowers his eyes.

"Anyway, I'd like to grow my brand."

"What would that look like?" Clay asks.

"Merchandise. Notepads. Stickers. Pens. Office supplies to start." I wave around me. *Dream big*, my dad would say. "But I'm a one-woman show, so I'm looking for help."

"Like what?" Judd asks, his eyes trained on me again, like he's fully invested in learning more.

"I've accepted I can't grow alone. I need suppliers and purchasing. Pricing and marketing. Production alone is daunting. So, a large-scale greeting card company is interested in buying my brand."

As exciting as it should sound, my gut sours at the thought. I've worked so hard to develop Quirky Girl Calendars, but I have so much more I want to do with her. As I've said, I need help.

"What does that mean for you?" Judd asks.

I shrug as the sourness begins to burn a little. "Greetings Ambassador said they'd keep me on as a designer, after they purchase existing designs. Essentially, they'll own my brand, but I'll get to keep working on it."

"Your basic mergers and acquisitions," Judd states, his tone matter of fact. His gaze lowers to his plate and he tosses his napkin on it before glancing up at Clay. "Do we use Greetings Ambassador?"

Clay scoffs. "They're kind of a conglomerate in the greeting card industry. We appreciate the little guys. Or gals." Clay winks.

For some reason, I feel like I need to defend myself and the possible purchase of my *little* company, but my voice is small when I say, "They promised to still honor the Quirky Girl Calendar vision."

The truth is they could decide after purchasing that they hate my existing designs or my future ideas, and I'd be screwed.

I couldn't continue to create Quirky Girl products. I'd have to start all over again at square one.

I worked for a large paper production company before branching out on my own to design my calendars and finding my niche with the specialty dates. I've always loved calendars, having five at any given time, hanging in my home-office back in my apartment. For twelve years, I've been on my own, designing and creating, scrambling and fixating, and I just want a little relief. Some help.

Greetings Ambassador could be a big break. They could really elevate and elaborate on what I've started.

The idea is thrilling while throat-choking.

Judd and Clay exchange a look before Clay asks, "Is the sale a done deal?"

"I have a meeting in mid-June. Calendars are cyclical, every pun intended, and they'd like to get me so I can be in their fall release for the December-January market which is one of the hottest times for new calendar purchases."

There are two times in a year that calendars sell the most: the end of a year and late-third quarter when students return to schools. I'll miss the closer date due to the lateness of our appointment, but there's hope to meet Greetings Ambassador's fall lineup.

"They're old school. The meeting is in New York." I wiggle in my seat, sounding bougie about the location.

"Would you need to move to New York?" Judd's voice sounds strained.

"No. Most of my work is remote, so despite the daunting meeting in the big city, I can still work from my home in Knoxville."

The table goes quiet.

Oops.

"Are you moving to Knoxville?" Clay asks Judd

"No." His answer comes a bit too adamant.

"How is this going to—" Clay continues, pointing between Judd and me.

"Who wants dessert?" Vale asks, glancing at me from her position at the opposite end of the table. She stands rather quickly, bumping her knee beneath the table, and I'm grateful for the distraction despite the narrowed, questioning gaze in Vale's eyes.

Halle pats my leg, and I turn toward her. "Don't worry. We love a good second chance romance around here. And these things have a way of working out."

Halle offers me a compassionate smile and I'm certain there's a story between her and Knox I don't know yet.

Glancing back at Judd, I'm worried I might never hear their tale. He won't look at me. Instead, he picks up a bowl of potato salad and stands, helping his sister clear the table without speaking to anyone, including me. I don't like the slump in his shoulders as I watch his back while he walks away.

As for Halle's second chance romance comment, Judd and I would have had to be romantic in the first place, and that never happened.

13

[Genie]

"**I** messed up."

Judd's head snaps in my direction as he drives us to his home. "How did you mess up?"

"I mentioned living in Knoxville."

He's silent a second. He's been quiet most of the afternoon after I explained what I do and where. But Judd had also been attentive. He rarely left me alone unless he sensed I was comfortable with the brood of women suddenly in his family.

Enya is married to Sebastian. Her sister, Cadence, engaged to Ford. Halle and Knox are a second chance romance as reunited high school sweethearts, and I learn they are newly married. And Mavis is engaged to Clay.

"Don't sweat it." Judd pauses another second and shifts in the driver's seat. "Your business sounds really cool." He lets another beat pass. "Are you sure you want to sell?"

I'm not, but I've weighed other options.

"Have you talked to a financial advisor?" Judd asks next.

"Not really." I hate how I sound so sheepish, like I haven't done my homework. Licking my lips, I turn toward him. "Judd, please don't make me feel stupid about my own business."

"What?" His head jerks toward me again, pausing a little longer than he should considering he's driving.

"My mother thinks my *job* is just a hobby. I like to draw, she says, like it isn't creative or artistic to make graphic designs. And she's shocked that I *know* anything about calendars, assuming I must be copying my ideas from someone else."

In some ways, I guess I do copy others. I research novelty dates, but also customs and cultures and religions to know what dates are important to them and why. My calendars are meant for people to embrace the day.

Suddenly, Judd is pulling over onto the very narrow shoulder of the road. He shifts into Park, hits his hazard lights, and abruptly turns his entire body to face me.

"First, I call bullshit with your mother. It's not a *hobby*. It's your fucking livelihood, and I think you love it. You glow when you talk about it."

My cheeks heat at the mere mention of glowing. I do love designing. The creative outlet. The quirkiness of the dates. The *fun* in them.

"And second, I don't *ever* want you to feel like I'm belittling you. Like I'm putting you down for who you are or what you do or think or say. I'm sorry if you felt that way." He swipes through his hair and then dangles his arm over the steering wheel. "I respect what you do, and *respectfully*, I want to help."

Judd might be mocking me and the way I spoke to him about his fights only last night, but the raw fear in his eyes that he might have hurt my feelings has me believing he's sincere.

"I just want to understand why you'd sell," he continues. "There's something in your voice that sounds uncertain. But you're right, I don't know your industry. Maybe you could tell me more about it."

I'm so shocked I suddenly can't think of anything to say. Not many people ask so directly for information, nor hold my gaze as if truly interested in knowing more about what I do.

"As you might have picked up, Sylver Seed & Soil was our parents' dream. Our mother's, actually. She loved plants and animals, especially horses, and even if we are a small town, there was a farm-and-fleet business in need of some TLC. My parents bought it and turned it into Sylver Seed & Soil. My father nearly ran it into the ground after my mother died, though." Judd swallows thickly, lowering his eyes a second.

"I'm so sorry, Judd." I knew his mother had died. I even know his father is dead as well. There were rumors about his dad, but I don't remember them exactly. Some of them, I really hope weren't true. For Judd and his amazing siblings' sake.

Unable to help myself I reach for his thigh. Judd's eyes track the movement and then pause on my fingers against his leg.

"I just don't want you to give up a dream, unless part of your dream *is* to have Greetings Ambassador own Quirky Girl Calendars."

I don't want anyone to own my dreams. No one else can, really. But I understand what Judd is saying. "I just want to hear them out. The offer isn't sealed yet." Although an estimated amount for the purchase has been suggested. The money is a lot and Greetings Ambassador has resources, but still . . .

"I appreciate your concern."

Judd lifts his head. "I only have your best interest in mind. Your peace of mind in mind. And now I've just said mind too often."

His comment breaks the tension in the car, and I chuckle, releasing the breath I'd been struggling to control.

Judd sounds like he really means it. His only concern is for me.

"I don't have to worry about anything until mid-June. June eleventh, actually. National Making Life Beautiful Day. It feels appropriate."

The corner of Judd's mouth curls, like he's fighting a smile, but not just humoring me and my quirky dates. Like maybe he finds me cute, and I wouldn't be fully insulted at the childlike endearment.

Judd continues to watch me, and for a second, I think he's going to lean toward me. Your classic first kiss in the front seat of a car moment. I lick my lips in anticipation, finding I'm more excited for this potential kiss than I should be. I definitely want Judd to kiss me.

The abrupt gleam of headlights flashes through the back window, and Judd and I both turn our heads like we've been caught having sex in the backseat instead of just sharing this innocent moment.

Judd clears his throat, as the car breezes past us fast enough to jostle the Ford. He turns his head toward the darkening road outside the windshield and rights his body in the driver's seat. "We should probably get home."

"Yeah." I cough, glancing around us at the barely-there shoulder and the deep ditch to the right of the car.

Judd shifts the gear stick to take us back onto the road and clicks off his hazards.

The moment feels prophetic. Marked safe from the danger of Judd Sylver kissing me.

14

[Judd]

When we return to my house, I'm not ready for Genie and me to go to our separate corners. In my head, I hear the *ding-ding-ding* of the boxing ring bell. *Let the fight begin.* Or maybe it's the click of a stopwatch. The countdown starts.

Whatever metaphor I want to use, I sense how little time I have remaining to reconnect with Genie, and I don't want to waste a minute.

"Want to hang out in the great room," I ask once we enter. "How about a glass of wine?" We need to celebrate that we made it through the family dinner rather unscathed. Other than the conversation with Stone, where he expressed his concerns for me—*Where's my head? How's my heart?*—Genie and I did pretty well pretending to be a couple.

Only I'm a terrible liar, so the times I couldn't help myself and reached out to touch her were not an act. And the times she touched me felt real as well. Her hand was a comfort on my arm. Or placed on my back. Her encouraging smile. We were separated while eating but eventually she sat beside me on the picnic bench and my thigh pressed against hers, like my body was magnetically drawn to her.

"I could have another glass," she accepts with a smile and follows me into the great room.

As the sun is relatively low in the sky, Genie helps herself to one of the two swivel chairs while I pour us each a drink.

"These chairs are so cool," she says, rocking one side to side after I hand her the stemless wineglass. "I like how you can be part of the conversation square but swing yourself around to gaze out the windows without hefting the furniture around."

Conversation square? Hefting furniture? I chuckle at how her mind works and take the opposite chair which Genie already turned for me.

The view is peaceful, and a huge reason I bought this property. The lake is aglow with reflection of the setting sun, mirroring the sky in pastel oranges, pinks, and yellows, the final color reminding me a little bit of her dress yesterday, but much prettier. The budding trees are almost gold in color, despite their green base. The coming of night feels almost magical.

A time when fireflies come to life.

"So, you're an accountant," Genie says after sipping her wine and shifting her chair slightly so she can look at me.

We've already covered my occupation, and Genie adds, "I really thought poet."

"Are we back to those broody vibes in high school you mentioned earlier?" I chuckle and sip my own wine.

"You had them in college, too."

"What?" I choke on the peppery flavor in my mouth, the aftertaste of this particular red. I stare at Genie in shock.

"University of Tennessee." She stares back at me like I should understand.

I do understand. Orange and white. The Volunteers. Knoxville. But . . . "Did you go to Tennessee?" I'm going to hate myself is she says—

"Yes."

I close my eyes and want the room to swallow me. Wait, no I don't. My lids ping open. "How did I miss you there?" Somehow, I feel I should have been able to see only her, even in the midst of twenty-eight thousand students.

Genie shrugs and glances down at the wineglass in her hands. "I worked in the library." She gazes back up at me. "I'd see you there, late at night. On Saturday nights," she adds, her tone somber. "Nose in a book."

How had I not known? Not sensed her, seen her? She's a fucking firefly, bright and beautiful. Then again, only a flash of light and I'd missed it. "Why didn't you ever talk to me?" Why didn't she approach me?

Genie licks her lips then lifts her glass to her mouth, taking a drink like she needs time to think before answering. "I just figured you wouldn't want to talk to me."

"Why wouldn't I want to talk to you?" What am I missing here?

Genie exhales deeply and looks at me. "Because you stood me up for prom."

"That doesn't mean I didn't want to talk to you." I swipe a hand through my hair and glance toward the lake.

Shit, shit, shit. This isn't what I want to talk about tonight. I just want to get to know her as we are now, but Genie needs to understand something.

"Firefly, I never meant to stand you up." The strain in my voice isn't enough of an apology.

Her head flinches at the nickname, eyes blinking rapidly.

"I waited for hours, Judd. Even if no one else was present

except my mother"—she shakes her head like that was an issue —"it was still humiliating to be wearing that dress and waiting, waiting, waiting."

Janet Hurley's attitude is haughty at best, and I imagine her behavior can be intimidating, especially when I remember her glaring at Genie only yesterday, demanding to see a ring as proof of my announcement.

"I'm so sorry."

Genie swallows thickly. "And I get it if you changed your mind. I mean, *I* asked *you* to *your* prom. Pretty bold for a sophomore to a senior."

"Genie," I whisper, my heart racing as I set my wineglass on the table near the swivel chairs and then lean forward, bracing my elbows on my knees and steepling my fingers at my lips.

"You didn't even want to go in the first place, but I—"

"I wanted to go with you, Genie. Everything in me wanted to go. To be there with you. To see you in that dress you wouldn't describe to me."

Blue, she'd told me. *It's the same color as your eyes. For reference*, she clarified. No one had ever said anything like that to me before or since. No one.

"Why didn't you just call me and tell me you changed your mind?" Genie's voice is strong but the hurt rings through every syllable. The pain of waiting on someone who wasn't showing up for her. The embarrassment. Somehow, I picture her mother staring at her, not with compassion but with criticism.

I'd been willing to risk everything to be there with Genie. I hadn't changed my mind about attending. Someone else changed everything for me.

"My father beat me up," I murmur to the tips of my fingers, pressed against my lips. The memory so sharp. So quick, like the flick of his fist that I never saw coming at me.

Genie gasps. Her eyes wide. Her bright cheeks suddenly draining of color. "Oh, my God. Judd."

"I was dressed in my rented tux. A cummerbund I hoped would match your dress. I knew I was cutting the time close." I'd had to work at the Seed & Soil earlier in the day, doing manual labor at the time and slowly building up my strength. I was never athletic as a kid, not like most of my siblings, but I wanted to be stronger. I wanted to be tougher.

Where is it, you fucking pansy? My father's words typically hurt more than his fist, but he'd gotten me good. Right in the nose. Blood spurted everywhere. My white shirt. My rented tux. The bow tie.

I was too stunned to answer him at first. He'd hit me before but nothing so direct. I was certain my nose was broken.

I don't know what you're talking about, I'd lied through the blood suddenly filling my mouth. I'd wanted to insult him as well. Call him a weak man.

Be the bigger man, Clay told me when I complained things were getting difficult at home. He'd already moved out and I didn't have the same rapport with our father. I didn't have the cutting banter the two of them had. The one where Clay could blow off insults, and my father didn't appear half as offended when Clay did mouth back.

Plus, my father *was* bigger than me. I'd been small as a child. Third smallest in my class. I'd had a growth spurt in high school, but I was still thin as a stick, lanky and willowy, back then.

"I couldn't show up after what he'd done," I admit, choking as if I can still taste the blood. Still feel the crack in my nose and the pain in my eyes. Holy hell, it had felt like my eyes were going to pop out of their sockets.

One hit hadn't been enough. He went in for another and another, not believing me. He'd been right not to. I had been lying but I wasn't going to tell him the truth.

"Not like that," I clarify about my appearance. I did not

want Genie to see me in the ruined clothes with my battered flesh.

"What happened?" Genie asks, setting down her own glass of wine and scooting to the edge of her chair. Our knees almost touch as we face one another. My elbows still balance on mine. My fingertips are still near my lips. Genie almost mirrors my position, but her hands reach toward my knees. Her fingertips are so close she could touch me, and yet not close enough that she does.

After all the insults and punches I took from my father, this woman could break me more than he ever did.

I'd deserve her rejection. I'd deserve her resentment. But I still want a fucking second chance to right the wrong.

I didn't want to leave her waiting. I didn't want to disappoint her.

I close my eyes.

Genie's voice lowers to almost a whisper. "Why didn't you call me? Or send me a note? Have someone else reach out? God, Judd, if I'd only known—"

"You'd what?" My lids ping open, and I lower my hands, my fingertips breaching that distance between us and finally touching hers. At first, just the tips brush, but then Genie is linking our fingers together, and suddenly, we're palm to palm, our hands clamped together.

"I could have been there for you."

The shock of the thought has me lifting my head. She'd have felt sorry for me. Pitied me. And that wasn't the setup I wanted when I had something important to ask her back then. When I'd wanted so much more between us. I wanted us to be together but not out of sympathy, not because of my father's behavior.

"You disappeared," she reminds me. "You didn't even come back for your graduation."

"I stayed with Clay for a while." I'd needed time to heal. My nose was busted. My eyes were black and blue. My teeth ached for weeks.

The high school administration was understanding. I'd been in a car crash, I told them. I'd been near the top of the class with my grades and finished out my exams remotely when that was hardly a thing then. When my diploma came in the mail, I left for Knoxville with the intention of never returning to Sterling Falls again.

"I'm so, so sorry that happened to you," Genie whispers, before scooting forward a little more and I spread my knees to accommodate hers between my legs.

"Judd," her voice is hesitant and thick. "May I hug you?"

I almost shatter. Like a clay pot tossed to the ground, I'm practically breaking apart at the idea of Genie holding me.

"I'd like that," I whisper, my voice shaky with the truth. I can't remember the last time someone hugged me.

Genie comes forward, and she's suddenly in my lap. Arms around my neck, tucking my head beneath her chin. Her knees pull up beneath my arm that wraps around her waist, and she settles into my chest.

And I realize this isn't just a hug. This is an embrace. This is a full body cocoon.

She is light, and warmth, and a spark of hope in the darkness of my past, and she's holding onto me like she might never let me go.

15

———

[Genie]

Last night, Judd looked like he'd been watching a horror film when he told me about his father. He'd gone sheet white, and my heart broke into a million pieces. *If only I'd known*. But now I did, and it was one more piece of what I was learning was a complex puzzle named Judd.

I sat in his lap, feeling too comfortable, before I finally pulled myself from him and sat in my own chair again.

"Thank you for telling me," I eventually said when there wasn't much else to say.

We finished our wine. The sky outside was a deep black. The silence between us heavy.

Eventually, Judd excused himself. Between the time with his family and his confession it'd been a long day.

His siblings and their significant others were amazing but there had been a ribbon of tension around Judd and I the entire time we were present. Like we needed to keep up an act, when I didn't feel like I was pretending anything.

Which surprised me. I'd been myself around the Sylvers. I am an affectionate person by nature, but selective in whom I touch. Touching Judd came easily. His family was funny and accepting. They seemed genuinely curious about me, my business, and Judd and I. Protective of him, rightfully so, but willing to give us a chance. I sensed that protectiveness was like a web, spanning wide over all the Sylver members, young and old, and I was curious what it would feel like to have someone else concerned about me.

I tossed and turned all night.

When I wake, I realize I cannot put off calling my mom. Not that I think she's worried. Not that I think she's concerned. I just feel like I owe her an explanation.

Daughter's guilt. It's a pre-requisite of being Janet Hurley's child.

When I enter the great room, I instantly notice Judd's absence but spy a note on the island countertop.

GOOD MORNING. *Went for a swim. Wait for me for breakfast?* Check yes or no.

WITH A SMILE ON MY FACE, I plop down on a highbacked stool. My fingers lightly caress the childlike paper, recalling Judd's other note about dating him for ten days and the tattoo on his arm we still have not discussed.

With a heavy sigh, I realize Judd's absence is the best time to call my mom. Like pulling off a bandage, I just need to get the sting over. My palms are clammy as I click on her contact and set the phone on speaker mode, laying it flat on the countertop. My heartbeat becomes erratic. I almost hope she doesn't pick up, but not answering my call would only prolong the inevitable.

My mother answers on the fourth ring. "Hi, Mom."

"Oh, you remember who I am?" Sarcasm is my mother's favorite language.

"How could I forget you." I clench my teeth, instantly wondering once more why I thought coming to Sterling Falls was a good decision. How on earth had I been talked into attending the Buttercup Society Garden Party or wearing that ridiculous dress?

But that guilt I feel is the answer to all my questions.

"Well, it's nice of you to finally grace me with a call after your behavior on Saturday."

My behavior? Spoken like I am an errant child instead of a nearly forty-year-old woman.

"I didn't see *that* coming." Vitriol laces with venom. I can picture her tight jaw. Her narrowed, frigid eyes.

While I'd like to joke that I hadn't seen Judd's announcement coming either, admitting my own surprise only plays into her cynicism. She doesn't believe Judd and I are together, and there are any number of reasons why she'd doubt it.

Someone like Judd, established, wealthy, and maybe even a pillar of this community couldn't possibly be interested in me because I'm . . .

Someone wayward and flighty, with my own rhythm and a slightly different approach to relationships than her.

Or someone who is distinctly not Heather Remington.

Instead of concern for me, my gut says my mother feels sorry for Heather.

"I cannot believe you did this to me."

"What did I do to you, Mom?"

"Embarrassed me like that."

How did I embarrass her? By announcing I was engaged. Okay, there wasn't really an announcement.

"And hurting Heather's feelings."

Ah, there it is.

I don't bother to mention that *I* didn't directly do anything to her precious best friend's daughter. And neither did Judd. Judd and Heather are no longer together. Judd and I aren't officially anything, but maybe becoming friends.

I also don't feel the need to defend myself, or my relationship with Judd, to her, real, fake, or otherwise.

"I didn't know you were acquainted with Judd Sylver." She pauses a beat. "Wasn't he the one who dumped you on prom night?"

"I wouldn't say dumped—"

"It's a good thing he left town. You don't need the likes of a man like him."

"Like him?" Wasn't he good enough to be with Heather? I don't bother asking. It's a double-edged sword with my mother. She always *jeers* both sides of a chess board, wanting neither side to win. She's simply never happy.

"You know, Virginia, if I've taught you anything it's that men don't appreciate easy women. They find them *easy*. To love and then leave."

"What the fuck?" The startling snarl comes from behind me, and I spin on the stool to find a beast of a man behind me.

Judd is a vision, wearing a striped pool towel around his waist, chest exposed and notable for the number of ripples along his abdomen. A patch of hair decorates his pecs along with the glistening silver chain around his neck with a thick, masculine ring dangling from it. His hair is slicked back, dark as night, but his eyes are flames of blue. With his hands on his hips, his broad shoulders look even broader, and the dark expression on his face is frightening.

He points at my phone lying flat on the countertop in speaker mode, but before he can say more, my mother continues.

"Being a slut will not result in a solid relationship."

Judd's entire body tightens. His shoulders appear to expand in front of me. His chest heaves as he draws in a long breath. His nostrils flare. Smoke might actually burst from his ears next.

With a steady hand, he reaches around me and presses his thick fingertip to the bright red End Call button.

"Judd," I whisper. Hanging up on my mother will fire her up more.

"What the fuck was that?" He glaringly points at the suddenly black screen.

"It's just my mother." Not exactly complimentary of her and certainly embarrassing to me to have someone witness her opinion. That because I haven't married, I must be spreading my thighs for every Tom and Harry's dick, and giving away what Mother believes men should pay for.

The irony in her statement is she doesn't know anything about a solid relationship. She's on marriage number four!

And there isn't a price tag on love.

"Fuck that," Judd states so sharply I flinch in my seat.

"She doesn't mean anything by it," I defend, but I don't know why I'm standing up for her. She means exactly what she's saying, and the hurt runs deep. I've heard comments like the one she just made all my life.

"She shouldn't speak to you like that," he emphasizes, his irritation continuing.

"It's just who she is."

"It's unacceptable." Judd crosses his thick arms. The colorful ink on his arms is a sharp contrast to his chest flesh, which looks chilled and pink from his swim in the lake.

My eyes suddenly burn with tears, and I don't know if the sting is the dagger of my mother's words, Judd hearing her say such a thing to me, or Judd himself. He's clearly upset, bordering murderous, and it's in my defense. How my mom spoke to me. What she implied.

I don't know why she's like she is toward me, but a niggling sensation in my gut always reminds me, even if my mother hasn't, it's my fault my dad is no longer with us. Over the years, I've told myself my mother is simply bitter and angry about something she couldn't control, because my mother needs to control the narrative.

My phone rings, vibrating against the countertop and star-tling me. Judd and I both glance at the screen. MOTHER lights up the caller ID. Janet Hurley and technology do not go hand and hand, so I know she assumes we were disconnected by a fluke. If I were to answer, disconnection is the excuse I'd use for the dropped call.

However, Judd reaches around me again and clicks Dismiss Call on the screen. Then he powers off my phone.

"Do you have a bathing suit?"

"What?" I sputter, glancing back at him, uncertain how swimwear is relevant right now.

"Put your suit on. We're going swimming."

"I am *not* swimming." I don't feel like doing much of anything and that's what I hate most about phone calls with my mother. She can squelch my energy and dull my creativity.

You can't control everything that happens to you, but you can control how you react to it. My reaction is to take a little time to quell my immediate response to her and erase her temporary damage. The older I get the easier I bounce back. Still, I need processing time.

"Put on your suit. I'll wait." Judd doesn't budge, standing like a palace guard, stone still and glaring at me to move along.

When he doesn't back down, I slink from the stool, taking my time to enter the guest room and rummage through my suitcase for the bathing suit I'd tossed in last minute. I hadn't planned to swim anywhere, but packing the suit is like bringing along that little black dress you can wear for any occasion. One should always be prepared when traveling.

In some respects, I should just go home. Accept that this was a lost cause trip and return to where I'm familiar. My apartment awaits. But my apartment is also lonely at times, especially as I work in such an isolating industry. Being a creative is a solitary job, and another reason working with Greetings Ambassador sounds appealing.

I wouldn't be alone day in and day out anymore.

Slipping into my bathing suit, I don't bother looking at myself in the mirror. I'll only be critical of my appearance in the Kelly-green two-piece tankini. I'll only see what my mother called me and not a proudly single person, embracing her sexual freedom as a woman of the modern era. The damning insult insinuates that I'm not particular about who I converse with, or date, or sleep with. I *am* selective because the last thing I want to become is her, desperate and vying for a man's attention to replace the man before him. Or bitter and angry because no one lives up to her standards.

I toss on a coverup and reenter the great room where Judd is waiting, staring down at my phone from his seat in a high-backed stool. The device looks small in his larger hand.

"I want to smash this to pieces." He looks up at me. "No one should ever speak to you like that, firefly. I don't give a fuck if she is your mother."

"Firefly?" He called me the same name last night.

"Genie, you're a bright light even in broad daylight. Don't let anyone diminish that spark."

Okay then.

Judd sets the phone face down on the counter as he stands up. Then, he holds out his hand. When I take his offering, he tugs me forward and I stumble into him. Wrapping his arms around me, he tucks my head against him. The position is dangerous. Cheek to bare chest. His heart hammers beneath my ear. His winter mint and lake water scent is strangely intoxicating.

I could get lost in Judd. Or maybe I'd feel found.

I shake the thought as we linger in this position. My arms wrap around his cool flesh, and I flatten my hands on his shoulder blades. Judd hisses at the contact, so I loosen my arms, thinking he doesn't want me to touch him there, but he tightens his grasp, pinning me to him.

I swear he kisses the top of my head, but I can't be certain. Then he releases me.

"So . . . um . . . swimming." He swipes a broad hand down his face and clears his throat.

My gaze drifts lower on his body, noticing our closeness has an effect; however, I don't want to turn this moment sexual. I don't want to feel like the *slut* my mother called me.

Judd waves toward a door to the right of the fireplace, and I lead the way until we step out onto his back deck. He reaches into an outdoor wardrobe to retrieve additional towels and tucks them beneath his arm, then he guides us across the grass to the dock jutting into the lake.

The late morning is beautiful. The sky is crystal clear, and the water reflects the brightness, giving off a silvery sheen.

"How deep is this thing?" I question, not a fan of spaces where I can't see what's below me.

Judd has dropped the excess towels to the dock, plus the one at his waist, to reveal a Euro cut swim trunk that rivals fitted boxer briefs.

Sweet succulents. Judd's body is sinful. The muscles in his legs are apparent. Those abs still on display. He's just too much.

"Maybe six feet closest to the perimeter." He points vaguely at the space closest to the dock. "But don't worry, I'd never let anything happen to you."

His gaze catches on my eyes, and I sense he means something deeper than letting me drown or be attacked by the unknown.

Slipping off my coverup, I glance self-consciously at Judd. His eyes are wide and bright, blending with the sky behind him.

"Your body is downright deadly."

I tilt my head. "Is that a compliment?"

"Yes." The answer is strained. "You steal my breath, firefly." His voice is rough as he drinks in every curve and dip of my body. The subtle swell of my hips. The short length of my legs. The hourglass shape of my waist and breasts. I'm not flat-bellied and toned, but Judd's appraising gaze makes me feel like a supermodel.

"That sounds a little like a pickup line," I joke, feeling a slight relief after the tension of the call with my mother.

"Really?" Judd tilts his head and steps closer to me. "This feels more like a pickup." Instantly, I'm swept up into his arms.

"You wouldn't," I shriek, wrapping my arms around his neck.

"No line required," he finishes his joke.

Then he hops off the dock and we plunge into the water.

16

[Judd]

I'd been raging with anger.

Then Genie revealed that sweet body of hers and teased me about pickup lines and it's like someone released a filled balloon. The pressure squeaks out of me.

Genie shrieks as I hop off the dock and drop us into the lake. The sudden blast of frigid water is a shock to my system. One I relish.

Instantly, I calm, awash in the numbing relief of the crisp lake.

Just what the fuck was *that* with her mother?

Her mother's tone and the damning words reminded me so much of my father. His cutting comments. His malicious intentions. Only a weak man keeps his children down, but it took me years to accept that truth. And I realize it doesn't matter if you're a pillar of the community or the town drunk; an asshole is an asshole.

I don't want to let Genie out of my arms. As I've promised, I'll never let anything happen to her. If we need to live in a cocoon of just one another and my home as a bubble to protect us, that's what I'll do for her. However, I don't think Genie wants that kind of seclusion in her life.

I also don't want to weigh her down beneath the water, so I release her.

She pushes herself upward, breaching through the surface, and I follow, hearing her laughing before she shoves water at me.

"It's freezing," she shrieks again, the tension from her mother's words instantly washed away, as I'd hoped.

"It's refreshing." *So are you.* Her laugh. Her smile. The tease in her eyes.

She continues to shove water in my direction before I lunge forward and capture her wrist. Tugging her to me, our bodies collide. My bare chest against her covered breasts. Her bathing suit leaves nothing to the imagination, other than if her nipples are dusty rose or cinnamon brown. Does she taste like sweetness or is she spicy? She's all subtle curves and soft edges, and I want to outline every dip and curl with my hands, and my mouth, and my teeth.

However, our swim is about distraction, not attraction. I want her out of her head and away from that bullshit her mother spewed on the phone.

Genie wraps an arm loosely around my neck. Our bodies continue to tap. Legs brush beneath the water. Hips knock together. Despite the cold, I'm hard as the planks on the dock, and any second Genie is going to discover how deeply my body craves hers.

"I don't think I can stand here." She giggles, skimming her other arm across the surface of the water.

"Try." With my hands at her hips, I hold onto her as she lowers her body, feet reaching for the lake bottom.

When her head dips underneath the water, she quickly pops back up and spits. "Nope."

"No worries. I've got you." I'll keep her safe. From her mother and any other person who wants to speak to her in such a condescending manner.

Genie glances around, taking in the budding greenery, and the silver glow of the lake water, rippling beneath the vibrant sunshine.

"I don't see other docks. Where are the other houses?" She squints into the distance as if focusing will reveal hidden homes that don't exist.

"There aren't any. This is private property. The house. The woods. The pond. It's all mine."

"Pond?" she chuckles. "This is a lake."

"It's technically a pond," I clarify of the spring-fed body of water.

"And all of this is yours?" She turns her head.

Our faces are so close, I could rub my nose against hers, or better yet, I could run it along her chin and down her neck. Inhale the perfume she wears that's a strange combination of floral and spice, and completely intoxicating.

"All of it." I hum, attempting to keep my arm loose around her lower back. My other hand is on her hip, keeping her lower half distant from mine.

"Are you rich?" The question is asked with curiosity.

"I'm good at investing."

Genie twists her lips, questioning my non-answer. The poor kid inside me, the boy who was once hungry and wearing clothes that didn't fit him as he grew, wonders if money matters.

"What happened first, investing or accounting?"

"Definitely accounting."

"Because you like money," she teases.

"Because I never wanted to be poor again." My sharp answer wipes the smile off her face. *Shit.*

Her mom's call still lingers in my head. Her words a trigger for the voice of my father's in mine.

What a fucking runt. You weakling. Pathetic coward.

"Sorry," I mutter, brushing back a clump of wet hair plastered to the side of Genie's face.

Genie nods once, accepting my apology.

"Tell me more about the special dates you put on your calendars. Tell me more quirky ones." I need to shift this lingering anger to something that makes Genie happy.

Genie is thoughtful for a moment. I can touch the bottom of the lake where we are but Genie drifts beside me. My hand is still on her hip, but she slips away from me, so she's only holding onto my shoulder, anchoring her from floating away.

"Let's see. There's World Kiss Day, on July six."

My gaze instantly drops to her mouth, and I roll my lips inward, as if the motion will quell the instant desire to kiss her.

"And as Sebastian pointed out yesterday, National Sex Toy Day is in early November."

Internally, I groan. Is she telling me these dates on purpose?

"Might not want to talk about that date around here." I snort. "The Sterlets will make you their newest member and demand a festival."

"The Sterlets?" Genie tips her head. "Vale told me something about them. It's a book club that meets on Thursdays."

I chuckle. "If that's what they're calling it."

"It isn't a book club?" Genie's brows lift. Her eyes flicker from the sunshine reflected in them.

"I think I'll leave it up to Vale to explain the details." I do not want to discuss how the book club has a secret side that involves self-pleasing toys.

"Well, Vale invited me to attend on Thursday, and it's not even National Book Lovers Day, which takes place in August."

I laugh. "I think you're making some of these dates up."

"I'm not," Genie says emphatically, dragging her body

closer to mine beneath the water and then drifting away from me. "That's the beauty of calendar design. A calendar practically fills itself. The world is full of diverse traditions, various cultures, different nations, and tons of religions. Plus, there are themed calendars, like library-related ones. Or teacher ones."

"Is there an accountant calendar?"

"I don't know." Genie's head pops upright and her eyes widen. "But there is World Savings Day, strangely on Halloween. National Dollar Day in August. And of course, Tax Day, April fifteenth."

"Of course." I arch a brow.

Genie snaps her wet fingers and a bit of water sprays toward me. "Oh, and there's National Lucky Penny Day at the end of May, not to be confused with National Lost Penny Day, which happens on February twelfth. Ironic how the lost penny day is the day after Make a New Friend Day."

The mention reminds me once again that I turned her down to be her friend when we were both children, and how I'm enjoying becoming her friend on a new level as an adult. At least, I hope we're becoming friends.

I'm struggling to have friendly thoughts with my hands on her hips and her body gently swaying closer to mine underneath the surface.

"There should be a National Judd Day," I state.

Genie tilts her head, smiling at the inventiveness. "And what would National Judd Day involve?"

"Doing whatever Judd says."

"Like the game Simon Says?"

I hum. "Something like that."

"And what is it Judd would demand on National Judd Day?"

I dig my teeth into my lower lip and roam my gaze over her face. Then I lower my eyes to take in the column of her throat and the curve of her shoulders.

"I'll come up with a list of bylaws and get back to you."

"You do that." She swallows, as her gaze drops to my lips, then along my neck and to my shoulders. "And I'll come up with a National Genie Day."

"You mean there isn't one already?"

"That's National Make a Wish Day on April twenty-ninth, but that celebrates the beginning of the Make-a-Wish foundation. So nope. No official Genie Day, and if you get a day, I want a day."

"Deal." I hold up my hand to high-five her in agreement. Genie's gaze catches on my forearm a moment before she slaps my hand in response, but then I capture her fingers. Without thinking, I bring her hand to my mouth and kiss her palm.

Genie's eyes widen. The water on her eyelashes glitters. Her lips are wet.

Damn, I want to kiss her. Instead, I ask, "Tell me how you get Genie out of Virginia."

"My dad gave me the nickname. He said he'd made a wish for a beautiful daughter and there I was." Genie wiggles her head and smiles wide, batting her eyelashes, like she was the answer to such a request. "We even had this golden lamp looking thing, that my mother later told me was just a gold-colored gravy boat, and my dad would rub the side of it to show me how he wished for me."

Genie's expression slowly sobers, and she squints toward the distant trees to the side of us. "He said I was his wish-granter."

"Huh. Your dad might have been onto something." It feels too soon to tell her how many wishes I'd had pertaining to her, and how getting this second chance feels like one come true.

If a genie only grants three wishes, though, I've already used one and I better be cautious what I ask for next.

"Of course, my dad used to warn me to be careful what I wished for. Sometimes you can have negative wishes, and those might come true as well. Or you might wish for something that doesn't quite turn out as you'd hoped."

I understand that one. I'd wished not to be alone any longer and stumbled into a relationship that wasn't quite how I'd envisioned ending my solitude.

"What would you wish for, Judd?" Her gaze falls to my mouth again and her body drifts closer to me.

I risk bending my arms and allowing her body to fill the distance I'd been carefully keeping between us. Her pelvis taps mine and Genie's breath hitches.

"Do you mean right now or just in general?" My voice drops, my focus falling to her mouth as well.

"Either one you want to share."

"Hmm." I don't want to lose a wish.

Genie wraps both arms around my shoulders. Her gaze is still aimed at my lips. I slide my hands from her hips to her lower back, pressing her to me. Her mouth opens and I lean in.

"Wait." Her hands slip to my shoulders and her body tenses against mine.

Fuck. "What?" I whisper choke.

"I . . . This probably . . ." Genie swallows and pushes back from me, and I let her go. "I'm cold." She moves further away from me, and I spin only to watch her swim to the ladder on the side of the dock. Then she's scrambling up the metal rungs like the water has caught fire.

I should call after her, but I can't seem to find my voice. What the hell just happened?

Too quickly, Genie has picked up her coverup and a towel, and she's thundering down the dock, like kissing me is the last thing *she'd* wish to happen.

17

[Judd]

As Genie disappears down the dock, I slip beneath the water, needing a moment to cool off and allowing her the space she wants between us.

Eventually, I enter the house, deciding Genie and I should talk. I'd like a shower first, then I'll seek her out. Once inside my bedroom, my cell phone rings on my nightstand, and I hang my head.

"Hey," I answer.

"Judd? You okay?" My brother Clay's concern comes from a good place. He has a large heart. He's the one credited with being the most intuitive out of our family and he seems to read the room correctly.

"Yeah. Why?" I quietly ask, squinting toward a window.

"You didn't come in today."

"I don't come in most days." I stop in the Seed & Soil once a week and gather anything I might need, although most things we do are electronic. For the most part, I work from home. I like my solitude, and I'm considered a bit reclusive.

For the past few years, though, I've been itching for more. More color. More sound.

In forty-eight hours, Genie has been both of these things.

"Yeah, but you typically pop in on Monday mornings." He pauses a second. "Just checking in on the newly engaged."

"We're . . . good." I stammer, swiping a hand through my hair.

"Only good?" Clay teases. He's in his all-in-love era after finally getting the girl *he* crushed on last fall. His situation was a little more complicated than mine with Genie but no less daunting.

It's difficult to desire someone who doesn't reciprocate the feeling. And Genie does not want me.

"No, Genie and I are great." My voice cracks. I'm not good at lying, or even pretending. We aren't great, but she's amazing. She took my apology last night and offered compassion after what happened when we were in high school. When she thought I'd purposely stood her up.

She doesn't know there's even more to the story, but what she knows is enough.

"Are you taking today off?" Clay teases while inquisitive.

"What is this? Twenty questions?"

"Nope. Just four."

"I think you're only at three," I correct.

"And that's why we have you as our accountant. Good with those numbers."

I scoff.

Clay is amazing with numbers in a different way. Instead of spread sheets, he has spatial vision, like Knox does. Our resident bricklayer makes beautiful patios, and I need to get him over to my place to remove the deck and set a stone patio. However, we rarely make ourselves the priority.

"Math Club paid off for you," Clay continues.

The memory rushes back to me of how I had to ask Clay to give me every Thursday after school off from working at the Seed & Soil, back when I did grunt work instead of office work.

"Yeah." I pause a second. "Now, if you don't need me, I should probably get to work."

"You know it's okay to take a day off."

"Says the man who never takes days off himself."

"I do now," he reminds me. "Because some people are more important."

I could correct him, that he means *some things* are more important than work, but I understand what he is saying. The people in his life are Mavis and Dutton, and he's a lucky man. He's richer because of them. Happier.

"I know." I whisper, wanting the same for myself. I want my person. The one promised to every other person.

After what happened in the lake with Genie, I'm worried I'm too cracked, battered and damaged for someone as shiny as her to love. And thinking of love might be getting ahead of myself.

After hanging up with Clay, I hop in the shower, hoping to clear my thoughts. Only they fill again the second I'm soaping up my dick. Images of Genie in that bathing suit. The swell of her breasts. The flare of her hips. Her skin.

I hum as I stroke the growing length.

We'd almost kissed, and I concentrate on how her lips might taste. Sweet. Soft. As hard as I am, I envision that softness around me, slowly sucking up and down my heavy cock.

I tip forward catching myself with my hand against the steamy tile. With visions of Genie on her knees before me, taking me into her mouth, I squeeze, imagining her mouth has me in her grasp. She hollows her cheeks, increasing the suction. Her tongue swirls around me until she tugs me to the back of her throat and then—

"Fuck," I grunt into the tiled space, the sound reverberating around me. I slap the hand bracing me upright against the tile, while I spill into the shower over my fist. My breath comes fast and sharp. I blink several times, attempting to wipe away the silver stars suddenly dancing before my eyes.

Holy shit. I've never come so quickly.

What would you wish for, Judd? If only I could tell Genie what I really want from her, but if the idea of kissing me is too much, she isn't going to want to know more.

With a deep exhale, I step out of the shower and dress in dark jeans and a fresh T-shirt. Then I head to the guest bedroom, shaking out my hands before lightly rapping my knuckles on the door. I'm typically not the one to open communication but I don't want any misunderstandings between us. We've already had too many.

If friendship is all she desires, I'm here for her.

When she doesn't answer the door after a second knock, I risk invading her privacy and open the bedroom door.

Instantly, I notice how neatly the bed is made. Not a trace of Genie's belongings are present. No clothes strewn on the chair. No shoes on the floor. Nothing on the dresser. I rush to the closet and let out a deep sigh of relief. Several dresses are neatly hung on hangers. Her suitcase is tucked in a corner.

My heart hammers with relief after skyrocketing with fear that she's left.

Still, I wonder where she is. With the ensuite bathroom door open, she isn't in there. I check the library next door, then traipse through the great room, trying not to let panic settle in.

I call out her name, but the silence echoes eerily back to me.

I scope out the garage and find relief once more when I notice her car still parked in my driveway.

A different kind of fear settles in. I head to the back deck, calling Genie's name again with a little more urgency. She isn't familiar with the woods surrounding my property, and a cold sweat covers my skin.

My concern becomes panic when two hours later, she still hasn't answered her phone or shown her face.

18

[Genie]

Just what was I thinking? *I almost kissed Judd.* Judd Sylver.
After stomping away from him, I needed some space, and while his home is plenty large enough to put distance between us, I need even more space. The outdoors was the answer. A walk was the best way to burn off this pent-up energy.

My mind races faster than my feet can carry me.

I almost kissed Judd.

A man I now know had a crush on me when he was ten and didn't purposely stand me up for his prom.

The same man who put his mother's ring on my finger *and* has a unicorn tattoo that matches the lined paper I once wrote him notes on.

I stop dead in my tracks at this point in my walk. Then I make a turn, knowing in the back of my head, I might get lost.

Strangely, being lost feels appropriate because I do not

know how to navigate what I'm feeling inside me and what is actually happening between Judd and me, because something is happening.

Something unfamiliar and frightening and thrilling and his body alone is just everything.

I'm flipping from emotion to emotion in a flash. Maybe I am a slut. *Is this lust?*

I consider what Judd told me last night. The pain in his eyes as he shared what happened to him when he was only eighteen. My heart aches for him, but he'd never want my pity.

And here I'd been worried he'd think *I* was pitiful. Nearly forty, needing a date to appease my mother for ten days.

And there's Judd offering to do it for me.

*W*ILL *you date me for ten days? Check yes or no.*
Will you be my new friend? Check yes or no.

T*HE* T*WO* N*OTES* merge together in my head and then I visualize the writing in another manner. In another place.

My memory rattles around until I have the answer.

Judd's skin.

When Judd held up his hand to high-five me, I'd noticed lettering on the underside of his arm. In bold script lettering was inked: Check yes or no, with a box beside each word and a giant checkmark in the yes-box. More lettering was underneath, but I couldn't make out the rest of it that quickly.

Judd had *my* question inked on his skin. And his answer, at least one time.

I didn't understand any of it. I'd played a dangerous game asking him what he'd wish for because as his body came closer to mine and he leaned in, it was apparent what he wanted.

I wanted it, too. Yet, it felt wrong. Not that Judd feels wrong. He feels right, so very right. And that's why I'm freaking out.

He's Judd. He shouldn't feel this good. It's too much too soon.

What did *I* want? What is my wish? I'll be forty soon. Shouldn't I be entering my no-fucks era? Shouldn't I feel a change coming? Accept singlehood. Sell my company.

These were big. *Huge.* Yet, why did they feel so small, like I was giving up instead of embracing life?

And, if I was entering my no-fucks era, I should have let Judd kiss me.

"Gah!" I yell at the trees along the empty road, coming to a full stop. My legs ache and my brain is fried, and that's when I realize . . .

I'm actually lost.

My phone shows I've been gone a few hours, and I try using the map app to redirect me, but I don't have Judd's address nor do I have good reception. I can't even figure out where I am.

Suddenly, everything hits me at once. The physical activity. The mental exhaustion. Tears burn the back of my eyes.

I'm left with no choice. I press the contact for Judd which mysteriously wound up on my phone.

"Genie?" My name is said with a deep exhale, like he'd been exerting himself before answering.

"Hey." I swallow and squint up at the bright noon sky. "I'm lost."

"Where are you?"

"I don't exactly know. I went for a walk, but I got turned around."

Judd takes another sharp inhale before saying, "Drop a pin in your location. I'll find you."

"How?" There are apps to follow your friends, and as a single woman, my friends and I often share our location with one another. Safety first, especially when one accepts random dates.

"I'll be there." Judd hangs up without further explanation and my breath hitches.

I've heard those words before, and they weren't spoken by Judd. The innocuous phrase could be said by anyone at any time and yet a haunting memory mingles with Judd's promise.

Quickly, I shake my head, not needing that memory while I wait on the side of an empty road.

Instead, I consider how I haven't been on a date in a long time other than Ralson, which I don't count. While I'm still in a mingle-phase, dating is getting tiresome. The getting-to-know you process. The finding out we don't fit disappointment. I've been duped enough that I'm good at deciphering compatibility with another person within five minutes of meeting him.

Which is another reason Judd is so confusing.

We seem to fit.

Within minutes, I hear the telltale roar of a motorcycle engine and then one is breaching the subtle hill in the road.

Judd slows as he nears me. Dressed in jeans and a leather jacket, he wears a helmet on his head. He rolls up alongside me and stops. The engine revs. The heat of the machine warms my bare legs. Judd frees the helmet he had attached to the back and holds it out.

With shaky hands, I set the protection on my head and fumble with the chin strap I can't see. Judd reaches out and clicks the latch into place. Setting my hands on his shoulders, I hitch myself onto the back of his bike but hesitate.

I'm the one who ran. I'm the one who killed the kiss.

Judd answers my reservations by cupping the back of my knees and tugging on both of them at the same time. Without further hesitation, I wrap my arms around Judd's waist.

He takes off faster than I expected, and I tighten my hold, so I don't fall backward. We race in the opposite direction from which he arrived, and I realize after a few minutes, we're going for a drive.

Eventually, Judd pulls off the road into a small parking lot that marks a scenic viewing point. The mountains are breathtaking from this vantage with the blue sky overhead, and the green-brown of early spring in rolling peaks and valleys. With equal parts of fear Judd will leave me here in the middle of nowhere and afraid to let him go, I remain on the bike.

I don't have a good reason for not kissing him earlier.

After a minute, Judd shifts, cuts the engine and removes his helmet. I do the same and slide off his Harley with shaky legs. Judd slings his leg over the bike in one smooth move and faces me.

"If anything had happened to you—" He swallows thickly, his eyes roaming down my body as if looking for signs of injury. Still, anger wavers around him like the haze on a hot day over blacktop. He slams his fists into his pockets and stares at me long enough I look away, uneasy from his glare.

"Do you have any idea how worried I've been?" Judd's voice is low and harsh. A shiver-inducing rumble that's more intimidating than if he'd yelled at me.

I lick my lips, preparing to apologize, when he speaks again.

"Just what the fuck were you thinking?" he continues, stepping closer to me. His jaw is tight. His shoulders stiff. He swipes a hand through his thick hair before those fiery eyes shudder closed. He takes a deep breath and when he opens his eyes again, fear fills them.

And suddenly, I understand. I know what he's feeling. That drop-in-your-gut sensation when you expect someone to be there, and they aren't. When you expect them to show up and they don't.

This has nothing to do with our prom night, and I feel terrible for making Judd worry.

"I'm sorry," I whisper.

"I don't know what's going on between us," he begins, blowing out a breath. "And frankly, it scares the hell out of me."

I agree with his sentiment.

"But I'm standing here, wanting you." He points to his boot-covered feet. "And if that's not something you want, I respect that. Nothing needs to happen between us. Nothing."

He exhales again. "Just, please, don't run away."

"I wasn't. I just . . ." *got lost in my head and then got lost on the road*. For some reason, I can't tell him that, though. Self-doubt and past experiences have taken over.

His voice quiets. "Don't let me think you've simply disappeared." As his voice grows quieter, I realize what I've done.

The panic. The fear. The anger. Judd was truly scared I was gone *forever*, and I know the feeling.

Only I'm right here. Standing before him. Wanting him, too.

I rush at him, wrapping my arms around his midsection, locking my hands against his back. I bury my head in his chest, feeling the heat of the day and the warmth of the road on him. His pounding heart hammers through the tough exterior of his leather jacket. And Judd stands with his arms outward, not touching me.

I squeeze him once before accepting he won't hug me back, but just as I attempt to pull away, he closes his arms around me.

His lips come to my head, and he lingers there, breathing me in like I'm breathing in him. Winter mint and sunshine. And something that feels so right, it scares the hell out of me.

19

———

[Genie]

After Judd drives us back to his place, he makes me lunch, and we sit on his deck discussing everything and nothing while we eat.

I like the color green. He likes purple.

His favorite number is 3.14159265359. Mine is simply 13.

He can multiply large numbers in his head, which has never been my specialty. We discuss Mr. Martin and Math Club. Mrs. Chapman and the middle school library.

I explain how I once had a friend who thought *antidisestablishmentarianism* was the longest word in the English dictionary, however, *supercalifragilisticexpialidocious* is actually longer and officially a word according to Merriam-Webster.

Judd tells me how he loves to garden, growing as much as he can for himself.

I tell him more random calendar dates.

When our conversation settles into silence, Judd excuses

himself, suggesting he should check in on a few things for work. After he heads to his home office, I step into the library. I don't know how it goes for him, but I cannot concentrate and eventually wander back into the great room where I find him behind the island counter working on dinner.

"Can I help?" I sidle up next to Judd, who has taken chicken breasts out of his refrigerator along with an array of fresh vegetables.

"Sure. I was going to grill all this, if you want to chop up some of these veggies."

"Hand me a knife, chef master." I'm not great in the kitchen but I can chop a carrot.

Only Judd doesn't seem to like how I'm cutting the long, thick vegetable, so he steps up behind me. "Like this." He cups the back of my hand and positions my other one a safe distance away, then moves our collective hands in a steady rhythm. Up and down. Up and down. In a measured beat. In an even spacing, until I'm no longer certain who is doing the slicing.

I'm too focused on his hand over mine. The heat of his touch. The tenderness of his instruction. The patience and pace.

"Good girl," Judd whispers near my ear, his voice low, sending a shiver down my spine. Why is that praise phrase so freaking hot?

I clear my throat, realizing that I was leaning into him. "You're a good teacher."

"I still have a lot to learn." His tone remains quiet.

I don't turn toward him, keeping my focus on the now slivered carrot. "Like what?"

"Like how to better express myself."

I drop the knife and spin to face Judd. Our bodies close. When he doesn't step back, I'm pinned between the warmth of his chest and the counter at my back.

"I think you're doing just fine expressing yourself."

I'm standing here wanting you. You don't get more direct than that, but Judd also gave me an out. Telling me if I didn't want the same thing as him, feel the same way as he does, nothing has to happen between us.

Suddenly, my hands tingle, a need to touch his chest and soothe his heart.

Judd offers me a half smile. His eyes meeting mine only briefly before he notes our proximity. If he leaned forward just the slightest, my breasts would brush against him. My nipples are already erect and tingling. Something unfamiliar but not unpleasant rushes up my middle. If I tipped up on my toes, I could kiss him and—

"I should probably get the chicken on the grill." Judd reaches around me, his arm brushing mine. We aren't finished cutting vegetables, but he rushes for the back door, and I need a minute myself.

Throughout dinner, we eat as if the crackle between us isn't like a third person seated at the kitchen island. Once we finish, we clean up in silence, washing dishes and putting away leftovers like an established couple.

The moment feels . . . nice.

Eventually, Judd asks, "Want to watch a movie?" Strangely, he sounds nervous.

"Sure. What do you typically watch?"

Judd shrugs, and I'm puzzled.

"Well, when you've gone to the movies, what did you pick?"

"I didn't pick." Judd quickly glances at me and away, tucking his hands into the front pockets of his jeans while we stand in the great room.

"What do you mean you didn't—" I stop myself, sensing Judd's discomfort and the possibility that Judd didn't ever get to decide on a movie. When he had dates. Or when he was with a certain someone.

"Okay. Let's see." I hold out his remote, nodding toward the television for him to find the streaming service, and then we scroll through some options.

"I love this one," I pause on *The Adjustment Bureau*. A little intrigue. A little romance. A little fantasy. Basically, a movie about free will and fate and the choice to love whomever you wish. "Want to watch it?"

I want Judd to feel he has a choice as he focuses on the preview. "Sure."

We settle in on the couch that faces the fireplace and television head on, sitting not exactly next to one another, but not necessarily tucked into opposite corners. It's a relief that I've seen this movie before because this anxious electricity is circling around me again due to the closeness of Judd's body.

To break the tension, I slump to the side and rest my head on a throw pillow, tucking my knees to my chest and my feet in the space between Judd and me.

Judd picks up my ankles and moves my feet to his lap, rubbing his thumb deeply into the bottom of my bare foot. The strength of his thumb. The pressure in the arch of my foot. I flinch.

"Ticklish?" Judd teases.

"Wouldn't you like to know?" There are places I *am* ticklish. Areas that are sensitive. But I can't share that with Judd, and I don't know why I said what I said. My zero filter is zero-filtering.

Still, the *snap-crackle-pop* exists.

Judd hums in response and I close my eyes a second as the purr in his throat shoots straight to a part of me that wants to feel the vibration of his mouth.

And suddenly, I think I've made a grave mistake.

I should be kissing my fake fiancé.

∼

THE NEXT MORNING, I enter the great room and see Judd dressed and moving about his kitchen like he has plans for the day. A bag rests on the floor near the large island. Two travel coffee mugs sit on the surface. Two water bottles rest beside it.

"Are you going out?" Judd hasn't left my side other than Saturday night for his fight.

He pauses after filling the first mug with coffee. "I was hoping I could take you somewhere today."

"Really?" I'm surprised and thrilled that he'd like to take me out.

Judd looks up at the crack in my voice. His eyes assess me. Like he can see inside me and wants to. I'd love a better understanding of myself as well.

"How do you take your coffee?" He watches me. "I feel like, as we're dating, I should know."

"Oh, black is fine."

Judd tilts his head. "But is that how you really take it?"

My cheeks heat. "Actually, I love a splash of almond milk and honey but that's complicated and—"

Judd turns away from me, miraculously producing both products. "Do it for me once. I want to learn."

Has any man ever said that to me? He not only wants to learn my coffee order, he wants to learn how to make it himself.

Don't swoon. I rejected him yesterday. I cannot play wishy-washy. Less than ten days now. That's all we have.

I step up to the counter and make my morning drink. Judd watches with meticulous attention. When I finish, I take sip to measure my perfection.

"Ah," I groan, and Judd's bright eyes dilate.

He clears his throat. "Dress comfortable. Shorts. Gym shoes. Whatever." Then his gaze roams down my body. "Is that my shirt?"

Busted. I'm wearing his Sylver Seed & Soil tee I found in a basket in his laundry room.

"How much time do I have?"

"Maybe fifteen minutes."

"Fifteen?" I gape, needing at least twenty to shower and shave all the important bits. Dry my hair. Do my makeup.

Judd sets the coffee carafe back in the machine and glances at me. "You look beautiful."

"I'm wearing your T-shirt," I remind him, tugging at the hem that ends just above my knees.

"Like I said. Beautiful." Judd continues to stare at me, while lifting one of the travel mugs like he's going to take a sip.

That pause does me in, like he's contemplating something. Like when he stalled and considered being my friend when I was eight. Only now, he looks like he's considering things that are very much adult and very inappropriate, and I want to know more.

What do you wish for, Judd?

PULLING up in front of a single-story house I don't recognize is not where I expected Judd to take us. He was exceptionally quiet on the ride here and he appears nervous as he pops open the driver's side door and exits his pickup.

I'm about to exit the truck when Judd meets me on the passenger side and holds out his hand.

"The people inside this house are important to me." He isn't warning me to behave, he's simply making a statement. Like meeting his family, I want to make a good impression, for Judd.

He knocks on the fiberglass doorframe on the screen door and a beautiful woman answers. With ebony-colored skin and soulful gray eyes, her smile is wide and exposes a set of perfectly white teeth when she sees Judd.

"Hey Trudy," Judd greets her. "This is Genie Webster. My fiancée."

Trudy's eyes widen as she glances from Judd to me. "Well, *my, my, my.* Sounds like you have some explaining to do, Judd Sylver." Her tone is friendly and playful as she reaches out for him and hugs him.

She holds out a hand for me next and covers the top of our hands as we shake. "Trudy Wallace. And it's a pleasure to meet you girl."

My mind is reeling, wondering what the connection between this woman and Judd could be, when a boy around nine, ten, eleven—I'm terrible with guesstimating ages—saunters up to Judd and hugs his waist.

"What's up, little man?" Judd greets him and the two bump fists. "Heard you weren't feeling well today?"

Trudy chuckles and runs her hand over the thin boy's dark brown hair that flops over his forehead like Judd's does. "I think he has a case of summeritis, as in wishing it was here." She winks at me over the boy's head. "I told him just this one time." The warning is clear in her voice. She's letting him play hooky today only.

"I really appreciate this, Judd," Trudy states, glancing at him.

"Any time. You know that."

I have so many questions, but I smile back at Trudy and then glance down at big blue eyes behind dark-rimmed glasses that are watching me. The resemblance to Judd is almost uncanny, and a bit unnerving.

"Simon." Judd speaks directly to the boy as he squats to his level. "This is my fiancée, Genie."

"Fiancée?" Simon chokes, eyeing me before staring wide-eyed at Judd. "You getting' hitched?"

"Someday." Judd glances at me before looking back at Simon. "I thought she could hang out with us today."

Simon looks me up and down once more. "What happened to that other lady?"

What *other lady?* Oh, he means Heather.

Before Judd answers about the *other lady*, I extend my hand toward Simon. "Nice to meet you, Simon."

"Remember what we talked about," Judd questions. "Shaking hands is a polite way to greet others."

Simon clasps his hand in mine. "Nice to meet you." He enthusiastically pumps my hand once and offers an extra-large grin. I can't read kids, so I don't know if he's being genuine or sarcastic, but I follow Judd's lead. This boy is important to him, and I can't help my next thought. *Is he Judd's son?*

We haven't discussed children. Not as in *us* having them, but rather, if Judd has any. My heart is racing at either thought.

Judd stands and Simon is patting Judd's pockets. "You bring me anything?"

"Simon," Trudy chides.

Judd chuckles while affectionately rubbing his hand over the boy's head and then gently cupping his chin. "I told you, not every visit comes with a gift." Judd pats his firm chest. "Today, I'm the present."

Simon *phffts*, but his smile says he's just as happy to see Judd as receive something from him.

"Simon, show Judd your new summer clothes, and then outside with the two of you." Her voice is kind while direct. She isn't taking any nonsense from anyone. "Us ladies will step into the kitchen and grab a cool drink."

Judd runs a hand up my back before kissing my temple and I relax a little bit. Simon takes off for somewhere in the house, but Trudy places her hand on Judd's arm, halting him from following Simon.

"You still doing that thing."

Judd side-eyes me and he slowly lowers his head like a chastised child. "Yeah."

Instantly, I understand that Trudy Wallace knows Judd has

been fighting but strangely the topic never came up with his family.

"When you gonna quit?" Her tone is soft with concern.

Judd shrugs, keeping his eyes lowered.

Trudy purses her lips like she has more to say about *that thing* he's doing but won't speak of it in front of me. She releases his arm with a gentle pat, and he heads toward wherever Simon went.

Trudy leads me to a kitchen that is small but bright, with stainless-steel appliances and fresh white cabinets.

"Finally got myself a cozy cottage just for me and now I got Simon." She chuckles unbegrudgingly as she opens her refrigerator. "Lemonade okay or would you prefer sweet tea?"

"Sweet tea would be great."

As she busies herself retrieving a pitcher from the fridge and removing glasses from an upper cabinet, I notice pictures of Judd and Simon on a bulletin board near a door that exits to the yard. The collection appears to be recent. Both boys are wearing Chicago Anchor gear in one image. In another, they are inside what looks like a tree fort. Another picture includes a beautiful woman with tan skin and silvery eyes like Trudy. Her and Judd have Simon between them, the camera close to their faces and all three are smiling.

Suddenly, my throat is tight, and I blink a few times, certain I'm missing something. Did Judd love someone else before Heather? Did they have a baby? I stare at the picture of Simon, trying to see a connection between Judd and this beautiful woman.

"That's my niece. Tallulah Alexander."

I turn to find Trudy standing close behind me, staring lovingly at the picture.

"They make a beautiful couple," I say. *A beautiful family.* Instantly, I'm jealous, when I have no right to be. Judd could have loved someone once upon a time. He should have a lovely partner and adorable offspring. Maybe I'm only hurt that he hasn't mentioned her or Simon before today.

Trudy chuckles and grimaces. "Judd and Tallulah would never be a couple." She laughs harder. "He's too reserved for her over-the-top personality."

"Oh." I can't explain the rush of relief that washes through me. The gratitude that Judd wasn't with *this* other woman.

"They've made a beautiful child, though," I continue, certain Simon is theirs.

Trudy laughs loudly, like I've told the funniest joke.

"Simon is my grandson of sorts but doesn't belong to either Tallulah or Judd. I used to foster children. Most of them my own kin. Nieces and nephews. But then I took in a few stranglers." She smiles with a fond memory. "And Simon belongs to one of them."

Strange relief that Judd did not love this Tallulah person, nor is he's the father of such a sweet looking boy, swims through me. Then I realize, as Judd's fiancée, I should know these things about him. All his secrets.

"Would have taken in all those Sylvers if that dang fool daddy of theirs hadn't been against it." Trudy lowers her voice. "Violet would have been so disappointed."

Violet is Judd's mother, and I glance down at the ring on my finger.

"Hmm," Trudy hums. "He finally gave it up."

Looking up at her, my brows pinch in confusion.

"That ring was her mama's. She'd been pleased as punch when Flint proposed. She had big dreams, and that man intended to give her everything. Then the Lord took her away from all of us, and Flint . . ." Trudy shakes her head. "He just lost his head when he lost his heart."

After what I'd learned last night about Judd's father, my heart aches all over again for him and his siblings.

"Anyway, Simon belongs to one of my foster kids. Babies

having babies." Her pursed lips show her displeasure at the concept. "And now, I've got him. And he's got me."

I pause thinking they are one in the same thing, before accepting they are not.

"And Simon has Judd. Judd needed him as well."

"What do you mean?"

"Let's take our drinks outside. We can chat there." She offers another smile, and I take the glass of sweet tea she offers me, then follow her into the backyard. The space is vast with a fence around a freshly cut lawn. A large wooden playset stands near one corner and the picture of Judd with Simon in a tree fort makes sense.

"Judd built that thing himself." Trudy states with pride before taking a sip of her sweet tea.

"Being Judd's fiancée," Trudy exaggerates the term, "I suppose you know a thing or two about his daddy. His beautiful mother, Violet, was one of my best friends." Trudy smiles fondly. "And her man treated her well."

Trudy shakes her head once, pursing her lips again, and squints toward the yard. "I'll never make excuses for him. He had seven beautiful children, each a spitting image of his lovely wife. He should have done right *by her* by loving them."

She nods, almost like she's deep in her own thoughts. "But the only person who could save Flint Sylver was Flint."

I don't know what to say. Judd's clearly only given me a sliver of the abuse he endured from his dad and that truth is as weighty as a boulder sitting on my heart.

"Anyway." Trudy shivers like the body shimmy will clear her mind. "I've known Judd since he was in diapers. Timid thing. *Tiny* thing. Loved his mama hard." Trudy shakes her head again, and I'm realizing that shake is a thousand unsaid words. "Been hard on all of them growing up without Violet. I know. I raised a handful of kids who'd gone without their mothers."

"But they had you," I finally speak knowing how special being a foster parent is.

"And I had them." She smiles. "There's healing in love, girl."

I sit with that thought a second while Trudy adds, "One day Judd will find acceptance in himself and stop fighting his demons. Stop fighting period." Her gaze lands on me. "And I'm hoping that day is soon with you here."

I don't know what to say, but I agree. I don't want Judd fighting, demons or otherwise.

"Judd is fortunate to have you in his life," I offer, knowing whatever their shared history, Judd already admitted Trudy is important to him. He loves her without saying the words.

"And I'm fortunate to have him. He helps me out with Simon. The boy needs a man in his life and Judd has stepped in to take that role when he can. When he had that *other lady* he couldn't come around as easily."

I tilt my head. "What do you mean?"

Trudy waves her hand. "Heather wasn't a fan of children, and she's a demanding thing." Trudy scoffs, shaking her head once more with disapproval. Then she smiles warmly at me.

"Let me see the ring again." She holds out her hand and wiggles her fingers, and I hold out my hand for inspection. "He must really love you, child."

My head pops up. I want to ask her what makes her say that, but then I remember I'm supposed to be his fiancée and I'm wearing his mother's ring. The two items in combination should say enough, but it's only make-believe. And I feel a little queasy lying to this woman who means so much to Judd.

A cold trickle runs down my spine. I can't make Judd any false promises. I don't plan to marry. I don't plan to have children. And the last thing I want to do is hurt Judd, or have Judd hurt me.

I'm almost forty. Even *if* I did plan to marry Judd, I don't know that children could be a possibility, and I wouldn't want to disappoint him. The inability to have children would be another reason Judd wouldn't want to marry me for real.

The thought of children collides with a rumble of emotions I don't recognize. Visions of Judd with his nephew Dutton the other day flit through my head. Then the tender moment between him and Simon. Judd would be a great dad.

And I don't want Judd to have children with someone else.

Suddenly, my heart is racing and I'm struggling to find my breath. I reach for my sweet tea as if that will help regulate the hammering in my chest or restore my lungs which feel like they are constricting. I'm such a contradiction, which is another reason it was best I didn't kiss Judd yesterday. I don't want to cross fragile lines and complicate things.

We're pretending.

But then Judd steps out of the house, his smile wide and his too-often sad eyes are filled with love and contentment as he watches Simon, and I realize lines have already been crossed.

Things are getting complicated.

And that's the reality of pretending.

20

[Judd]

Simon Gilbert is nine years old and a little spitfire of energy. He's also a foster kid, although Trudy calls him her grandchild. She was delegated next of kin even though she doesn't have any direct blood relation to him.

Much like my brother Clay, Trudy has trouble turning away strays, and that's how she ended up with a number of her nieces and nephews over the years.

She tried to take in most of us Sylvers as well when our mother passed. Stone was only twelve. Vale a newborn. Our dad's addiction to alcohol happened rapidly and Trudy saw what was happening. She'd call him out on his behavior, but Dad didn't want to listen.

"I find one of my kids at your home again I'll have you arrested for kidnapping." He'd threatened Trudy in our front yard one afternoon when she was dropping me off after spending time at her place. She also came bearing groceries that we desperately

needed. In hindsight, I suspect she could hardly afford them as she had her own brood of kids to feed.

"You hush yourself, Flint." Trudy could glare like no one I've ever seen, but then her shoulders lowered, and she shook her head. *"Violet would be so disappointed in you."*

The string of swear words strung together after that comment had me running toward the old stable that stood empty because my dad sold off my mother's beloved horses.

While Trudy didn't come across as someone who'd take to idle threats, I'm not certain my father was joking when he added in that he'd kill her if she stepped on his property again.

Somehow, she snuck in help however she could, especially teaching Stone and Clay how to change diapers and potty train Sebastian.

"Babies raising babies," she called it.

Between Mary Haven and Trudy Wallace, our mother's best friends found little ways to be surrogate mothers that made a big impact. When I was older, I'd sneak over to Trudy's house, despite my dad's warning, but then I'd feel guilty being there. She had her own set of kids to raise, and I hated feeling like I was freeloading off her kindness.

In some ways, hanging out with Simon was my way of repaying Trudy for her compassion. Simon was sprung at her later in life. It wasn't that Trudy didn't want him; she was just done raising children when he arrived a year ago.

As for me, he felt like my redemption. I didn't want the young boy feeling like he didn't have a man in his life to support him, model for him. I demanded Trudy call me when she needed something for him or someone to watch him, like today, when she has an important meeting to attend.

Clay's fiancée, Mavis, owned a house in the historic district which had a fire nearly two years ago. She eventually sold the property as is. A private investor purchased the space, and a new house will be built to replicate the original home. Unfortunately for the builder, design requirements are in place to match the aesthetic of the historic boulevard outside the business district. Trudy is on the approval board for the future build.

Trudy's small home suits her. She had a larger property when her husband was alive but once her kids were gone and he passed from a sudden heart attack, Trudy wanted something that was just for her. That's also when she went into real estate sales.

Simon finishes showing me his collection of summer clothes, the ones I financed after arguing with Trudy about it. He's growing like a weed right now, and I know all too well about the discomfort of wearing clothes that are too small or too short, or shoes that are too tight. Hand-me-downs were a staple of my upbringing. Simon deserves better and he can have better because of me.

I adore Trudy and I'm so grateful to have her in my life. Being my mother's best friend, she often shares little tidbits about my mom with me. About their childhood together and my mother's love of plants and animals. She also taught me how to garden. I like to think Trudy is a good reflection of what my mom embodied. Kindness. Laughter. Compassion.

"Want to play catch?" I ask Simon. After years of tossing balls to Ford for his practice, I'm decent at the simple game, and Simon loves baseball.

He rushes to his closet for a baseball cap. Chicago Anchors, of course. My brother's former major league team. With the cap on his head, he trots toward the kitchen with a spring in his step.

"You really have a stomachache?" I chuckle as I follow him.

"Nah, I just hate school."

When we reach the kitchen, I stop and pull Trudy's cookie jar on the counter toward me. I can never pass up one of her homemade snickerdoodles, and I remove one from the jar for me, and another for Simon.

"No telling," I state as I hand him the cookie.

Simon motions zipping his lips and tossing the key over his shoulder. Then he turns around, pretending like he's looking for something on the floor, pinches at the invisible item, and stands. He places his pinched fingers near the corner of his mouth and twists them like he's uncaging his lips.

"Can't keep my lips locked if I want to eat this thing." He raises the prized cookie and takes an exaggerated bite.

I adore this kid. He's quirky and spunky while introspective and smart. So freakin' smart. He hates school because he's bored, and I've talked to Trudy about him taking more advanced classes, possibly even skipping a grade.

For a little man, he has big concerns. *What if Trudy dies next?* Like me, both his parents are dead.

I've promised Simon I'll always be here for him, and I intend to keep that promise, in whatever form that takes. He knows Trudy loves him. We've talked about it, but his fears run deeper. Without Trudy, who else will love him?

In my own way, I love him although I haven't said the words. I've never said the words to anyone before, minus mumbling a shortened version back to Stone or Clay or Vale as they so freely offer them to me.

I smile at the boy chomping on his contraband cookie, and I take a bite of my own before heading outside where Trudy and Genie have taken a seat in the shaded section of her patio.

My eyes instantly seek out Genie, who is watching me with a puzzled expression on her face. Then she smiles, slow and lazy, before her cheeks flush. She's so pretty. Like a sunflower that seeks the sun, only the sun wants to worship her like I do.

When Simon's hand slips into mine, I'm drawn to him. He tugs me over to a plastic bin kept beneath the shaded overhang where a collection of balls, a variety of bats, and two mitts are kept. Simon hands me one leather glove before finding his, and we step into the grass.

"Don't be telling my girl any secrets," I tease Trudy, as I toss the ball to Simon.

"You only got one secret worth telling, Judd Sylver, and that seems to be this pretty thing sitting here staring at you like you set the sun in the sky."

The ball Simon tosses to me hits me in the arm, because I turn to see what *someone looking at me like I set the sun in the sky* would look like. All I see is Genie watching me.

"She's the one who set the sun in the sky." I wink at Genie and return my attention to Simon.

"Woo-wee," Trudy hums. "There's a fire on my lawn. You two are scorching a line through the grass."

I grunt and Genie laughs.

"Seriously, why didn't you mention Genie before? You're the one keeping secrets."

"Wasn't anything to tell until a few days ago," I admit, lobbing the ball lightly into the air for Simon to catch. "But I've been waiting years for Genie to come back to me."

I hear the soft clink of a plastic cup settling on a glass-topped table.

"I wasn't the one who disappeared," Genie counters, reminding me that I had. I didn't show the night of prom, and I went away to college as soon as I could leave. A college we'd both attended, and I've been beating myself up ever since learning that fact. I've lost so much time I could have had with her.

"Well, you shouldn't have been waiting, boy. You should have been chasing." Trudy hums teasingly.

She's right. What have I been waiting for? I should have sought Genie out years ago. Hell, I'd been around Janet Hurley often enough I should have asked about Genie. Where was she? How was she?

But I can't dwell on the past, at least not on these concerns. What matters is Genie is present now and I won't waste a minute.

Trudy announces she needs to go and proceeds to tick off a list of items. Lunch options for Simon. Time she'll be back. Reminding me I have her number for an emergency.

"Go," I reassure her. "I've got this."

I've watched Simon often enough and spent enough time with him to know peanut butter and bananas on wheat is Simon's favorite meal when lunchtime comes around.

As I slather peanut butter on one piece of bread, placing the bananas on the other piece, I glance up to see Genie watching me.

"What?" My mouth slowly curls, my face heating from her looking at me like she is.

Her eyes glisten. Those flecks of gold in them sparkling like pinpricks of light. "You'd make a great dad."

My brows lift. I don't trust myself to be a father. I didn't have the best role model. I had Stone, though. He did what he could to keep me in the fold, but he hadn't been able to protect me from the insults and injury of my dad every second of every day, especially when he went off to college.

I don't know what to say to Genie's compliment, because I don't know how I feel about being a dad. *If* I'd ever be a dad. It's just one more thing I've been thinking about lately. How I've not only been in solitude and wanting a partner, but maybe I want more. Like a family of my own.

The possibility feels too big to wish for.

At her comment, I offer Genie a shy smile and then proceed to make myself a classic PB and J, while Genie opts for peanut butter only.

The three of us picnic on a blanket in Trudy's backyard.

Genie learns Simon loves all things *Star Wars* and she does a perfect imitation of Yoda speak.

We play three rounds of Uno before chasing each other around his playset.

Simon asks to play catch again, and we include Genie, who I quickly discover is hopeless.

"It's that hand-eye coordination thingy," she jokes about herself.

Unable to help myself, I wrap my arm around her shoulders and tug her to me, pressing a kiss to her temple. "You're perfect."

She doesn't need to be able to catch a ball or win at Uno. She's amazing as she is, and I'd like to tell her that every day.

When Trudy returns, Genie does a quick sketch of Simon. Skinny, long body, a bit distorted but a strong likeness of him complete with his floppy hair and dark rimmed glasses.

"For a quirky boy," she tells him. "Thank you for making today a special day."

"Even though it's National Poem on a Pillow Day?" Simon chuckles, shaking his head like Trudy does. Genie told Simon about her job designing calendars and he asked her what made today's date special. Besides National Roasted Leg of Lamb which made Simon snort, Genie told him about Poem on a Pillow Day.

"*You've* made today extra special."

Simon's face beams with pleasure, while staring down at his gift. "Can you draw a picture of Judd and me?"

"Next time," I suggest as Trudy stands nearby. Genie and I really should get in some hours of work today. Plus, I want there to be a next time, when Genie is here with Simon and me.

"Definitely," Genie assures him, and Simon surprises all of us by hugging her around her hips.

When he tips back his head, Genie runs her hands through his hair. The way Simon gazes at her, it's love at first hair tug.

I know the feeling, kid.

When we enter my truck, Genie is quiet a second while

waving out the open window at Trudy and Simon who stand on their front stoop.

Then she turns to me. "That kid was awesome."

"I know, right?" Pride warms my chest at how easily Genie and Simon took to one another.

"Today was a great day, like I told him."

I agree. I want all the days with Genie. They'd all be great.

We're both silent a second, letting the warm breeze of late afternoon filter through the open windows of my truck.

"Do you want kids?" Genie asks sheepishly, toying with the shredded hem of her denim shorts. "I mean, one day. Maybe?"

I risk a quick glance at her and then stare out the window. "I didn't dare to dream about having kids. For a long time, I thought I'd be a terrible father, and I didn't see myself finding a life partner anyway. When I learned to fight, I found an outlet for all this anger inside me." I wave around my belly. "I started to feel better. About myself. About a future."

"You aren't your father," Genie whispers.

I glance briefly over at her again. "Oh, I know I'm not. I couldn't even create half the insults he conjured. Nor could I speak the way he did. It's not in me to be that crude or rude or condescending." Most likely *because* of how my father was toward me. "He said a lot of things that put me down, made me think negatively about myself."

You're weak. What a fucking coward.

"I've only had Stone as a role model," I continue. "But more so Clay was an example of how to be with kids."

"Why? What's the difference?"

"Clay is just more easygoing. Stone isn't a hard man. Just quiet and reserved like me, so he isn't the best person to emulate." I chuckle to myself. "He's a good man, though. The best brother. They both are."

"It must be nice to have siblings."

I side-eye her, knowing she doesn't have any.

"When my mother's husbands come and go, so did any stepsiblings I might have had."

I don't recall anyone being her stepbrother or stepsister.

"Most of them lived with their moms, more than their dads," she clarifies as if reading my thoughts. "Anyway, I just always thought it'd be nice to have a big family. A loving set of parents, who went the distance with each other." Genie pauses a second. "But it's one reason I don't plan to marry."

"Ever?" I question.

"I don't trust the institution. Look at my mom."

"You aren't your mother," I remind her, swallowing a sudden lump in my throat. "Remind me what happened to your dad."

"He died." Her quiet tone suggests that's the end of the subject. "He was everything to me."

"I'm so sorry, Genie." I cup the back of her neck, needing to touch her.

"My mom was like that for me," I whisper, giving us each a moment while my thumb still rubs along the column of her throat.

Then I clear my throat. "So no to marriage, huh, fiancée?" I attempt to tease her, but the words sound more like I'm being strangled.

"It's so weird being called that" she states, adjusting the ring on her finger.

"For a few more days." The idea makes my stomach instantly sour. Like I told Genie yesterday, I want her. Like I also told her, there is no pressure to be more, if she doesn't want that from me.

I just want her time and a new friendship.

When Genie doesn't speak, I ask, "What about you? You might be against marriage, but what about kids? Lots of women decide to have babies on their own, by choice. Enya did."

Genie turns her head but doesn't ask for details, and I'm glad as that's not my story to tell.

"I guess I hadn't really thought about it much. Sometimes, I feel like I've let too much time pass and maybe missed out on something special but now it's too late. Other times, I consider that dream for a big family, and realize I'd like a life partner, *if* I believed in marriage. Kids would be part of the package."

Genie goes quiet again.

"For what it's worth, I think you'd make a great mom, if you ever wanted to be one." The way she interacted with Simon was priceless and she'd been amazing this weekend with my nieces and nephews. I know it's not the same when a child is your own, but Genie has the loving, nurturing skills one needs to be a mom.

I stand by what I said earlier.

She's perfect.

21

[Judd]

That night, I'm seated in the library when Genie enters. I'd decided to read after dinner, needing space with my thoughts about Genie. Only, I've read the same page twice and still don't know what it says.

"Mind if I join you?" she asks, taking her time to wander amid the shelves in the dimly lit room.

"Sure." While I keep my eyes aimed at the page, I sense Genie's movement along the shelves. The curve of her hips. The reach of her arm. The soft hum as she peruses the back of a book.

Suddenly, she's rounding the chaise where I sit tucked into the corner. The only other seat option in the room is the desk chair which is not comfortable for casual reading.

Genie pauses beside me. Her knee almost brushing mine. "May I sit?"

I nod, acknowledging her question but unable to find my voice.

She sort of falls onto the cushion instead of folding down to it. She also sits very close to me as the back of the chaise does not run the full length of the cushioned seat.

Time moves in slow motion as Genie opens her selected book and flips to pages in the middle instead of starting at the beginning.

My legs spread a little wider than necessary. Her thigh presses against my mine.

Sensing her close proximity might be on purpose, I'm not certain I'm breathing. She teased me last night about wanting to know the ticklish places on her body. And I certainly would like to know every dip and corner that responds to a tickle. Every swell and curve that molds against my hand.

Eventually, Genie shifts, but her thigh only presses tighter to mine. A quick side-eye toward her shows a deep blush on her cheeks.

"You okay over there?" My voice is caught in my throat.

"I'm good." Her voice is almost as strained as mine.

I realize I haven't turned a page in my book, so I flip the paper, not certain what's happening on the page. Hell, I can hardly remember the title of the book at this point.

Genie suddenly fans her face once with her open book and then glances back at the page.

"Whatcha readin'?" I tip my head to catch a look at the back cover, but I can't seem to place the title of her book either.

"It's a romance novel." She flips the book to the front cover, keeping her finger in place to mark her spot. "You have quite the eclectic selection of books."

"I like to read a variety of things."

"Ever read this one?" Still holding the book cover upward, finger as a bookmark, I glance at the title.

"I don't recall," I lie, having vivid memories of reading the erotic romance. "Maybe you should read me a section. See if it jars my memory."

"Hmm," Genie hums. "Okay."

What? *Dear God, no.* I hold my breath again, hoping to stop my heart from racing, because as Genie begins reading, I remember exactly which passage she's stuck on.

" . . . and then he spreads her thighs, running his hands up the insides. Her flesh is soft, but his destination is fire, calling to him. Blazing with heat and want and a musky scent that—"

I abruptly stand, slamming my own book shut. I scrub a hand down my face and risk a brief glance at Genie before averting my eyes. "Yeah, I don't think I remember that one."

"You sure?" Her eyes dip down my body and if it weren't for the precarious position of the book I'm holding, dangling it in front of my zipper, Genie would know just how familiar I am with that passage, and just how much her reading it in that smokey voice has turned me on.

Friends. Not really my fiancée. We are friends. I remind myself on repeat, but I've never wanted to be only friends with Genie.

I've always wanted more.

Quickly, I excuse myself but not before leaning forward and pressing a lingering kiss to her forehead. Closing my eyes, I inhale her scent, drawing it into my nose and holding the fragrance, knowing she's going to play out in my mind in the exact fantasy she was reading.

Only I don't want the fantasy. I want the reality of Genie.

Touching her flesh. Inhaling her heat. Breathing her in every night beside me.

~

"WELL, WELL, WELL," Clay sings the following day, as he enters my designated office at Sylver Seed & Soil which I hardly ever visit. "First you take a day off on Monday. Then you enter the office on a Wednesday. Who are you and what have you done with my brother?"

He's all tease but I don't appreciate the humor. "Funny."

Clay's eyes are kind. His face lined with age, reminding me just how long and hard he has worked to save the sinking ship of our parents' dream and turn it into a legacy for all of us.

With my head bowed, attempting to focus on my laptop and projections for the third quarter which begins in July, I don't look up at my brother. His official title is Chief Executive Officer and Manager, which essentially makes him my boss, but I don't give a shit.

"What's going on?" His tone turns more serious when I don't respond, and he helps himself to a spare office chair on wheels that has no purpose in this office. However, the addition of a desk pad calendar and a plant near the window shows someone has been working in here.

Clay parks himself on the opposite side of the desk, leans forward and taps his fingers to the surface. "Judd. Talk to me." He pauses a beat. "Are you hiding out here?"

I quickly glance at my brother then look away, as if the spread sheet on the screen holds my interest when I've been staring at it for twenty minutes without reading a single number.

The same thing is happening in my home office.

"I'm not hiding out. I just can't seem to concentrate at home."

With Genie in another room, her presence haunts me in the most tempting way. I want to be near her. I want to talk to her. I want to hear her laughter.

And I don't want to get into a discussion with Clay. He has always been good at reading me. Staring a little too long. Digging a little too deep. Out of us older three Sylver siblings, he's the jovial one. The one with a joke, a smile, or a laugh. I long to be that easygoing when I know for a fact his life hasn't been easy in the least.

"I see you," Clay states, reminding me he's watching out for me. I am not alone.

I hadn't needed looking after like Knox, Ford, Sebastian, and Vale had when they were younger. I was more independent and aloof, trying to keep a low profile and be invisible to our father. Clay hadn't always been present when altercations with Dad happened. When physical fights occurred with either Knox or Sebastian. Or insulting words were tossed at Ford and me. Still, Clay didn't miss how bad things had gotten before I left for college. I'll always be grateful that he took me in for a few weeks before I left for Tennessee.

"I'm not hiding," I snap, a little too aggressively.

Clay is taken aback, and I brace my elbows on the desk, pressing my fingertips against my closed eyes.

"Fucking Genie," I mutter with more desperation than bite.

Clay chuckles. "You're fucking Genie? Well, that doesn't sound so bad."

"I'm not *fucking* Genie." I drop my arms to the desktop. "I'm fucking up with her." I must be doing something wrong because there's this wall between us and I can't climb over it. I just want her to curl up in my lap like she did the night I explained about prom. I want to hold her to my chest and breathe her in, and I feel like a fucking creep.

I've been turned on since seeing her again and nothing I do relieves the pressure. Despite jacking off in the shower like a randy teen, I'm hard as a stone even after the relief.

"Well," Clay clears his throat, fighting another round of laughter. "If you were fucking her, that would be okay. She *is* your fiancée."

"She's not," I mumble.

Clay's brows arch. "Excuse me."

I hang my head and tuck my hands behind it, squeezing the

back of my neck. I suck at lying. And I quickly glance back up at my brother. "She's not my fiancée."

"But—"

"I attended that fucking garden party like you asked."

Clay twists his mouth, and I instantly feel bad. He so rarely asks me for anything, and now that he has a sweet family of his own, he deserves time off to be with them. He deserves them. I am so happy for my brother that he's found someone like Mavis, and her son, Dutton, to teach him how to slow down and enjoy the simpler things in life.

I'm envious.

And I attended that party for Genie.

"Anyway, there was a little bit of a misunderstanding. Genie wanted a date. I said I was her fiancé. Heather saw me holding Mom's ring . . ." The rest is history.

"Did you *ask* Genie to marry you?"

"No." That question never crossed my lips, and I hate myself a little more.

"But . . . you're introducing her as your fiancée." Clay's voice is all question.

"I know." I blow out a breath and cover my eyes again as if the position will actually hide me.

"Judd," Clay's voice softens. He knows that tone gets me every time. "Do you want to marry Genie?"

Yes. It's hardly been four days, but I want all the specialty dates and official holidays and all the days in between. I've known since I was ten how I felt about her, and at fourteen I knew I wanted only her, and when I was eighteen that I needed to make her mine.

She's wearing the ring I always intended to give her.

"It's too fast, right?" I argue even though I've answered in my head. "It's wrong to want her so much."

Clay's brows lift and he blinks once. "Wrong? I don't think it's ever wrong to love someone."

Are we discussing love? Marriage and love should go hand in hand. They do. I'm clearly ahead of myself.

"I just can't concentrate at home," I circle back to how this conversation started.

Clay chuckles again. "Good to see you opening up."

"About my feelings?"

"Well, that too. But I just meant to me." The gaze in my brother's eyes is full of adoration and pride. He's happy for me, even if I'm befuddled. "Now, get to work."

He's kidding. I work almost as hard as he does.

Clay stands and moves the mystery chair back to the corner of the office. "But don't work here too long. Your fiancée awaits you at home."

"I told you she's not—"

"Not yet," Clay interjects, holding up a hand. "But if you want her to be, that's a different kind of work. One more important than this place." He waves around, meaning the Seed & Soil.

I could argue, *how can he say that*, but I know his reasons for changing his outlook.

I want those same kinds of reasons to change mine.

TO AVOID the couch and the chaise lounge, I suggest Genie and I play a game. We can sit perpendicular to one another at the dining room table. No close proximity. No tickling feet. No touching thighs and no torturous reading passages.

Only with the just a chess board between us, my concentration is shot as Genie's foot continues to meet mine beneath the table. Once by accident. But when it happened a second time, I wondered if the move was intentional.

Suddenly, it's a battle of toes more than pawns on the chess board. Her delicate ones brushing over the top of my foot. My stronger ones capturing hers and pinning them to the floor. Every swipe is like a current up my leg and straight to my dick, straining beneath the table like a schoolboy trying to contain his erection behind a desk.

Genie has me so wound up I can't think straight.

Eventually, Genie sets a piece in line to take my queen and calls out, "Checkmate, baby."

My head shoots upward at the softness in her tone. She didn't say the endearment in any other way than to claim her victory and yet it sounds like a win to my ears.

The coo of her voice. The glee in it. And the spark in her eyes as she looks at me. As seconds tick by, I'm holding my breath again, desperate for Genie to make a move. To give me a sign that she wants more from me.

For three nights in a row, we've danced around one another. Fumbled touches. Purposeful caresses. Fingers and toes. Thighs and hands.

Tonight, Genie is the one to pull back, though not as abruptly as I did last night. With her eyes still on mine, she says, "I think I'll read again."

If only it were an invitation to join her, or better yet, act out that scene she read to me last night.

Instead, I say, "Good night, firefly," hoping to hide the disappointment in my throat.

"Good night," she says, standing up while keeping her eyes on me like she has something more she wants to say.

When she doesn't speak, I drag out the moment. "Sweet dreams, firefly."

Her smile is gentle, like she might like the nickname. She is the brightest thing in this room, and the brightest thing in my life.

And I watch as she takes that light with her, out of the dining nook, and across the living room until I can't see her anymore.

Suddenly, the need to expel energy hits me hard.

Quickly, I'm in workout shorts, gloves on, and at the punching bag in my home gym, running through a routine I've already practiced this morning.

Right. Right. Left.

Left. Left. Right.

Hooks and jabs. Upper cuts.

Time passes as I dance around the heavy bag.

On and on and on, I go through the rhythm, stretching my muscles, sweat beading on my skin, as I work to numb my mind.

To rid myself of the dangerous dream of love and marriage and children with Genie.

To quell the desire to kiss her and hold her and learn every part of her that's ticklish or sensitive.

To taste her and breathe her in and hear her sounds when my hands cover her skin.

Having her in my house is too much. Calling her my fiancée is too close to what I want from her. All these things feel like wishes I shouldn't be making.

Then I hear a scream.

22

[Genie]

In the middle of the night, I leave my room to get a drink of water from the kitchen. Judd's house feels exceptionally dark, and I hear the slight rhythmic sound of something being tapped somewhere down the hall leading to Judd's portion of the house.

Tap. Tap. Pause. *Tap. Tap.* Pause.

I consider investigating but I don't want to intrude on Judd at such a late hour. For the third night in a row, he hasn't made a move to kiss me, and it's been all my fault. I blocked him the other day, then sent him into a tailspin of worry, and now we're flirting in the friendzone when all I want to do is crush over the invisible boundary.

After retrieving a glass from an upper cabinet, I'm just about to set the container beneath the waterspout on his refrigerator when a violent crack of bright lightning illuminates the enter great room and scares the hell out of me.

I drop the glass and scream.

As my heart hammers like it wants out of the cage of my ribs, I flatten my palm against my chest and suck in a deep breath. I'm wearing sleep shorts and a tank top, and my exposed flesh is clammy. I'd giggle at my sudden panic if I didn't feel struck dumb from the sudden flash or the deep roar of thunder that quickly follows.

I've also broken the glass, which shattered as it hit the strip of tile between the kitchen island and the sink slash work area, and in the darkness, I can't tell where the shards of glass rest. My feet are bare.

"What happened?" The heavy exhale in Judd's questions suggests he sprang from bed but when I glance up at him, he's wearing a pair of shiny athletic shorts and tight-fitting shoes on his feet. His chest is bare and heaving from exertion. Tape covers his knuckles and hands.

"I was getting a drink of water, but the lightning struck and startled me."

Judd makes to move closer, but I hold up a hand which would be difficult to see if it wasn't for another flash of electric volts lighting up the sky.

I flinch, then anxiously giggle.

Judd takes another step forward, but with my hand still lifted, I warn him, "Stop. I broke a glass."

He ignores my caution and takes the final steps to close the distance between us. Glass crunches beneath his feet as he sweeps in and scoops me up, setting me on the island countertop.

"Your feet," I state, concerned that despite his shoes, the glass will puncture them.

"Are covered. What about yours? Did you step in anything?" Judd awkwardly lifts one ankle to inspect my foot but there isn't enough light to see.

Lightning bolts through the sky again and I flinch, sharply

turning my head toward the windows, where the lightning exposes the lake.

"Are you afraid of storms?"

"A little. I think it just caught me off guard." I hadn't been aware rain was rolling in. I've been so consumed with thoughts of Judd and spending time with him that I didn't pay attention to the weather.

Lightning flashes vibrant and angry once more. I glance back at Judd who is watching me. He stands at the edge of my knees, my feet brushing his legs. He lifts one hand, digging his teeth into the edge of the tape near his wrist and pulls back, then uses his other hand to begin unwinding the long strip.

With one hand free, he uses the other to repeat the action, removing the protective strand around his knuckles. He tosses the spent tape on the counter beside me, then braces his arms on either side of my legs which spread a little allowing him to stand between my knees.

The entire scene is a bit barbaric and yet I'm completely turned on. The rip of that tape. The strength of his teeth. The sharp fling of the discarded equipment. Visions of him treating me in the same manner rush through my head. My shirt ripped down the center like in a historical romance. His teeth digging into the flesh of my neck, and then him pressing me to my back on this countertop.

My core is already thumping, the pulse pounding ridiculously hard.

Lightning strikes again. Then thunder rumbles. I flinch, all fantasy bopped out of my head.

"You're safe here, firefly. I'm not going to let anything happen to you."

"Why do you call me firefly?" I've never been a nickname girl and yet every time he calls me the term, something flutters in my belly, like a flock of the magical insects in flight.

"Seems fitting. You're brightness in the dark."

I swallow thickly. The summery bug only blinks once, like something mystical. A star on earth. Then its light is gone. "But for only a flash, like lightning." Am I only a momentary spark for Judd?

"You seem to be some kind of anomaly. You even light up during the sunniest day."

This man. His words. His actions. He's so much and yet I cannot get enough of him. I've been toying with that *snap-crackle-pop* between us. Skirting a line when I can no longer know why I've drawn it.

I want him to kiss me. I want to be closer to him.

I also don't want to hurt him, and I don't want to be hurt by him.

Still, the energy swirling around us cannot be denied. Like the storm brewing outside, Judd and I are on the precipice of something explosive. The tension between us escalating from simmer to boil.

We stare at one another despite the blackness around us. As another ripple of lightning hits, illuminating Judd's face. His eyes are a mixture of hesitation and desire. A crease in his brows expresses his internal conflict.

Another roar of thunder booms, but the hammering of my heart suddenly rings louder in my ears.

"When I was little, I was afraid of thunderstorms," he tells me, his voice low, like speaking to a frightened child. "Stone taught me this trick. Count between the lightning's strike and the thunder's rumble to know the distance of the storm from wherever you are."

I nod, keeping my eyes on his.

Lightning hits and we count, getting to eight before thunder grumbles.

"The storm is eight miles away," Judd clarifies.

My brows lift, skeptical, as the storm feels like it's over our heads, but I like that Judd is trying to soothe me when he's admitted storms used to frighten him. Still, my heart hammers, echoing the pulse between my spread thighs.

"Your turn," he says when the next current of lightning brightens the room.

My count only makes it to five.

The storm is coming closer. Our eyes lock together.

Another strike of lightning and the thunder sounds like it's dancing with the bolt.

Judd ticks off. "One. Two. Three."

Our eyes remain on one another until an explosion, so fluorescent and aggressive, shakes the windows and has me turning my head. My voice trembles, "One. Two—"

Judd's mouth is on mine, cutting off my count and blindsiding me, but I welcome this flash. The warmth of his lips. The tenderness of his touch. The distraction of his mouth covering mine.

I pull back and we stare at one another, chests pitching, breaths heavy.

Another wave of light. The entire house feels like it's trembling.

"One—" Judd only gets out that first count before I'm holding his jaw and kissing him. My hands slide over his warm shoulders and around to his back, clasping at his corded muscles, that strain as if he's still holding himself back while kissing me. He's sweaty, and there is something primal and addictive about it. His arms remain outspread, hands braced on the counter another second, but I cling to him. The strength of his posture. The heat coming off him. The calm that comes from touching him.

Finally, he wraps his arms around me, palms cupping my lower back to tug me forward, spreading my legs wider to embrace his hips.

We kiss and kiss until I can't remember there is a storm outside. The thunder and lightning are clashing in this dark kitchen instead.

Moving my head to the side deepens the kiss and Judd groans into my mouth, then his tongue joins the mix. He tugs me tighter against him and my center meets his abs, desperate for friction with other places on him.

My skin crackles. My heart jolts. I am the storm. One of desire and lust for this man kissing me like no man ever has and no man ever will again.

"Firefly," he moans, dragging at my lower lip before pulling away. His forehead rests on mine. "I thought you didn't want this."

"I do," I whisper. "I don't want to complicate things, but I really want you to keep kissing me."

"Your wish is my command." His mouth returns to mine, and I feel as if a special wish has been granted.

Judd is the untold riches and the ability to fly and the secrets of the unknown. All impossible wishes rolled into reality.

I hitch my knees higher, tucking my feet around the back of Judd's thighs. He leans forward, pressing me back a bit. And we kiss like this storm will destroy us. We kiss like it's the end and a beginning. There is no more pretending. Something is happening between us. Something electric and magnetic, and frightening. Something special and unique like unicorn stationery and yes checkmarks. Judd tastes familiar although I've never kissed him before. He tastes like friendship and flirtation and anticipation of more.

As the rage of the storm outside eventually recedes, and the patter of rain becomes more distinct, Judd slows our kisses until they are only soft suction. Then his forehead comes to mine again.

"I don't think the storm is over," his voice is thick.

I don't know that I ever want it to end.

Heavy raindrops pelt the windows distracting me for only a second before Judd hikes me off the counter. I squeak, tightening my legs around his waist and wrapping my arms around his neck. Fragile glass crunches beneath his feet.

"I'll get it in the morning," he mutters near my ear, anticipating what I was about to ask. *Shouldn't we clean that up?* Instead, he carries me toward his room.

Judd sets me on his bed and then stands upright beside it. "I've been working out and I stink. I need a shower."

He smells good to me. Winter mint and all man.

"Stay put?" Those eyes flicker with concern that I'll disappear like I hadn't meant to do the other day.

"I'll be right here." My voice is low and shy.

Judd disappears through a door off his room but returns rather quickly. His hair wet. His chest damp. A fresh pair of shorts.

He tugs back the covers on his bed, and I follow suit on the side he laid me. Once beneath the light blankets, Judd scoots closer to me and we mirror one another, resting on our sides facing each other. He brushes back hair that's falling toward my face.

"What are we doing?" I whisper, suddenly uncertain of everything. I'm not a one-night-stand kind of woman anymore. I also can't remember the last time I slept in a bed with a man.

With my hands tucked beneath the pillow, Judd reaches for my left hand and pulls it to him, kissing my palm before covering the back of my hand.

"We're weathering the storm. Together." His voice is deep while quiet, eyes seeking mine in the dim light of his bedroom. A nightlight glows from somewhere in a wall outlet.

Judd leans forward, kissing me once more, like a hesitant teen experiencing his first brush with a crush. We kiss a few more minutes, hands never roaming, no body parts rubbing, and I've never been so turned on in my life.

But I'm also at peace. A strange balance of electric energy and calm.

Judd is both those things, and I don't think I'll recover from the storm.

Once again, the kisses subside, and Judd and I stare at one another. Like we don't want the night to end. We don't want to sleep despite the rain acting as a lullaby against the roof.

"Tell me a secret, Judd Sylver. Something no one else might know," I ask, like I want to hold onto a little piece of him. Something just for me.

Judd stares back at me, thinking before speaking. "I did want to be a poet."

My eyes widen, both shocked while pleased that vibe coming off him wasn't just an act.

"When my mom died, I wrote poems to help with my emotions. The agony of losing my mother. The distress of dealing with my father." Judd pauses.

He is a tortured soul, one deeply repressing his feelings while needing a creative outlet to release them.

"I thought writing would somehow relieve this ache inside me," he continues. "Eventually, my father found one of my poems. Something rudimentary about missing my mother. He ridiculed my words, then slapped me for crying over the loss of her. I was eleven."

"Judd," I whisper, feeling tormented for him.

He shrugs as if it was nothing, so used to the abuse he endured, so locked in the existence of it as a part of him.

"Now you. Tell me a secret." He leans forward and kisses my knuckles, right over the ring.

Something inside me tells me to share my darkest secret with Judd. To tell him the guilt I carry with me day in and day out. The reason I take my mother's condescending words and question my worth.

But this moment feels too fragile for such a secret, so I offer Judd something else.

"I noticed your tattoo earlier," I whisper.

"Which one?" Judd scoffs, knowing he has so many.

"The one on your forearm that says check yes in bold script."

"How is this a secret of yours?" Judd tease, his tone quiet but easygoing.

"My secret is that I want to check yes to you, Judd." In every way, I want to be that YES for him, but I still don't think marriage or kids is in the cards for me.

And it's too bad because some lucky woman is going to check all the yeses for him someday. She'll be his wife and she'll be the mother of his children, and I hate her already when I have no right to dislike her.

Judd Sylver deserves all his wishes to be granted and his dreams to be fulfilled.

And I wish it could be me to give him those things.

"You already do check all my yeses," he whispers and something in me cracks open. The sliver in a shell that spreads down the delicate shield, allowing in oxygen, providing a glimmer of light.

Could I really be all those things to Judd? Could he want me as I am? Fragile and a bit tarnished. Perhaps I'm the one afraid to check yes to unasked questions, despite thinking I'm a free-spirit and open-minded.

Would I really be a caged bird in marriage?

When Judd scoops my hair around my ear, eyes on me as if he knows my mind is racing, I settle under his patient gaze.

His hand lowers for my left one once more and then he squeezes. "Come closer."

The command could mean so many things, but for now, I

scoot closer to his body, calmed once more by the heat of his skin and strength of his presence. Judd slips his arm around me, tugging me even closer and tucking me underneath his chin, my forehead against his chest, and I breathe him in.

Weathering the storm together.

23

———

[Genie]

I once read an article that said Thursdays were the sexiest day of the week. Some study showed that cortisol levels are highest on the fourth day of the seven, and thus sex hormones elevate.

First, I'd like to know who runs these studies and how.

Second, I don't think they've met Judd Sylver because being around him, I feel like my cortisol levels and sex hormones have been pinging all over the place *every day* leading up to this day.

Which happens to be a Thursday, and my first Sterlet meeting.

Minutes before I'm set to leave, accepting an invitation from Vale to meet her and several of her sisters-in-law at Milton Roadhouse for a drink, Judd comes to stand outside the guest room door.

"Hey." My voice comes out shy. Even though, we shared

kisses and a night of only sleep together, I feel even more uncertain about where Judd and I stand. When I woke early this morning, he'd already left his bed. He also left me a note explaining he went for a run, and I decided to spend the day outside.

After the storm, the vegetation around Judd's place looked like it sprang to full summer bloom overnight. Green was everywhere from the deep forest color to the brightest lime shade, and I could not concentrate again, although an idea had sparked.

A mountain adventure Quirky Girl Calendar had a rough beginning.

Now, Judd sheepishly smiles before lifting his hand and twirling a set of keys around his finger. "I'm giving you a ride."

"Oh, I can drive myself." I wave, tugging my crossbody bag over my shoulder. I'm wearing another green dress that ruffles along the collarbone and dips between my breasts. Judd's gaze follows the line of ruffles before his eyes leap back to my face.

"I don't want you drinking and driving, so I'll be your chauffeur for the evening." The intention is rather thoughtful and sweet, and while I don't want to put him out, I do appreciate the gesture.

"If you are sure," I counter.

"I'm sure." His sheepish smile grows into a crooked grin, and I wonder if he's been thinking about our night like I have.

The way he kissed me. The way he held my hand as we slept. The secret he shared with me.

The day has not been awkward, but I've been a bit anxious around him. The nervous energy more likely a result of the lingering effects of the storm and my continued confusion.

Once we arrive at Milton Roadhouse, Judd parks down the street and comes around to the passenger side to help me out of his truck. He tucks my arm into the crook of his elbow as he walks me the few feet to Milton's front door.

"Text me about fifteen minutes before you want to come home, and I'll pick you up at The She Shed."

Home. He so casually tosses out the word and I glance up at him. The curve of his jaw. The heat in his eyes. The softness of those lips that kisses me last night.

He pauses and I spin before him. When we face one another, he tucks my hair around my ear again and says, "Have a great night."

Too quickly, he's releasing my hair and drawing back from me. And I stare after him as he takes one step back and then another while still looking at me.

We don't separate with a parting kiss which feels like it should naturally happen, and yet everything feels so new, itchy and uncertain.

Couple goals. Always kiss for greetings and goodbyes.

The thought hits me so hard, I stumble on my high heel when I haven't even moved my foot.

Judd rushes forward again, catching my elbow as if I'm still unsteady on my feet. "You okay?"

I give him a thumbs up because my voice is trapped deep inside me, along with a lot of emotions I'm not ready to evaluate.

With a questioning smile, Judd pulls back again and something inside me says not to let him go. To reach for him and tug him back to me. Give him that kiss. But I don't. I watch as Judd once again steps back, nodding at the door of Milton's, like he'll wait for me to enter the bar before he'll leave.

The inside of Milton Roadhouse reminds me of an old-time saloon and rumor claims that eons ago this former hotel was once a popular watering hole on Milton Peak. With thick beams in dark wood and the occasional wagon wheel chandelier, the space is large but dimly lit. A square bar is off to the right, with an empty space around it like a wood-floor moat. A smattering of high-top tables made from barrels crowned with oak planks fill the space, while regular tables are scattered around a dance floor and small stage tucked into a corner.

Instantly, I find Vale. Her cornstalk-blonde hair is the lightest color on the spectrum of Sylvers which run from a heavy silver mix to still dark brown with sprinkles of gray. As the youngest, she is roughly mid-thirties. With her tonight is the pregnant Cadence, and her sister, Enya. The sisters look like sisters despite Cadence's acorn-brown hair being lighter than her sister's slightly darker tresses. Cadence's stage hair is blonde.

We'll meet up with Halle and Mavis a little later at The She Shed, a knitting shop owned by Meredith Mulligan.

"I know Ford said a sex toy wasn't something necessary, but there's nothing wrong with toys-as-tools to enhance things," Cadence is saying as I step up to the table.

Vale groans but having seen me, slides off her stool to hug me.

"Don't tell me you don't have sexy Sylver superpowers as well, girl," Cadence teases Vale.

"Just ignore them. I do when they start discussing the men in their lives, forgetting the sexy superpowers she's referring to are from my *brother's*."

"Cadence," Enya chides her younger sister.

"I'm just saying, I'm as horny as the day is long with this little one inside me." She rubs her hand over her baby bump. "And with three little ducks already running around, we need to be creative."

Vale shakes her head before nodding at a stool next to her to take a seat. The waitress arrives quickly, taking my order for a gin martini.

"Anyway," Enya groans, cutting off her sister, and turning toward Vale. "How was your last date?"

Vale groans next. "They're always the same. Same questions. Same answers. I don't know why I torture myself."

"I know the feeling," I chime in.

"But not anymore," Vale sighs, and I realize my mistake. They all believe Judd and I are engaged, and I glance down at his mother's ring, remembering our kisses from last night.

"There just isn't much of a dating pool in this town or the next town over or the next after that." Her shoulders fall in defeat before she lifts her glass of white wine. "Which is why *I* need tonight."

Book club? I'm all in favor of books assisting in the bedroom, especially for a party of one which describes Vale's relationship status. But a book isn't the only thing to help stimulate *superpowers.*

"We aren't really attending a book club, are we?" I ask the ladies.

Vale looks shocked. Enya only smiles. Cadence laughs, then addresses Vale. "Honey, I keep telling you, the best kept secret in this town is not a kept secret. The best kept secret is what Stone and Emerson Milton are doing with one another."

"What's the unkept secret?" I demand playfully. "And Stone and Emerson Milton?" I'm confused and rightfully so as I don't live here, but I know the Milton family. Everyone knows them. Their family laid claim to this mountain top, and the entire county was named for them. The Miltons have been the ruling government of this town in some form or another for almost a century.

"Emerson is the mayor. Stone's the town sheriff. It's a simple equation," Enya states.

"But are they really just friends with benefits?" Cadence leans in like inquiring minds want to know.

Vale shakes her head. "I live with the man. You'd think I would know but I just don't. Sure, they are seen together, and seen leaving places together, but I'm not convinced they are more than friends. No benefits."

Stone Sylver is a good-looking man, and any woman would

be a fool not to want benefits with him, but Emerson might have her reasons. Stone might have excuses as well.

"So the secret club?" I want to circle back to my initial question as the waitress returns with something resembling a gin and tonic.

"Meredith Mulligan sells sex toys to supplement her yarn shop," Enya explains, and I take a hasty sip of my drink. Definitely more gin and tonic than martini, but it will do.

"Oh my." I sound like a ninny, but I'm eager to learn more. My favorite toy is back in my apartment.

"The book club"—Vale air quotes—"is invite only. Consider yourself invited." She winks at me.

"Girls Night Out before book club? How quaint." The blonde bombshell suddenly standing beside our table is none other than Heather.

"Call it like it is, though, ladies. A dildo is a dildo." Heather's icy blue eyes latch onto me. "You'll need one to deal with Judd's frigidity."

My mouth falls open, shocked by Heather's audacity and blatant insult of Judd.

"Tone down your jealousy, darlin'," Cadence snaps, spinning on her stool. "It's unbecoming."

With Heather's gaze still trained on me, she says, "I have nothing to be jealous of." She lifts her martini glass like she's toasting me and takes a sip of a drink I'd like to splash in her face. I hope her martini is actually a gin and tonic as well, and she chokes on the lime.

"You're OWD is showing, girl," Cadence adds. "And you *were* the other woman."

I chew my lip, both surprised at Cadence's brazen speech and her lack of fucks.

However, I don't want an altercation with Heather. Being my mother's best friend's daughter has nothing to do with my hesitancy. I'd been hopeful that Heather would come to terms with losing Judd, maybe even realize she didn't want him. They are so different from one another.

From my history with Heather, there is no way she's been sympathetic toward Judd's past, if she even knows the half of it. I might not know all his secrets, but I know some dark details that make my skin crawl and make me believe Judd doesn't share those stories easily or with just anyone.

Making a derogatory comment about his sexuality so publicly is not appropriate and couldn't be further from the truth.

Sometimes a bully is a bully, and that's calling it like it is.

With Heather put in her place by a world-famous music superstar, she huffs and spins on her heels, but not before a final jab at Cadence.

"And to think I *used to be* your biggest fan."

Cadence waits a beat for Heather to walk away before she says, "I'm certain one of the nine-hundred ninety-nine thousand and nine-nine-nine behind her will be happy to step forward and claim her crown."

"Careful." Enya nudges her sister. "Your stardom is showing."

Cadence laughs. "Every once in a while, it doesn't hurt to let your ego glow." Cadence tosses her hair over her shoulder in a mocking manner. "No one has time for that." Yet Cadence glances after Heather with a twinge of sympathy on her face.

"How did they ever get together?" I mutter, more to myself than to the group collectively. Plus, Judd told me what happened, so my question is more rhetorical.

"Judd doesn't want to admit it but he's more a lover than a fighter," Vale states nonchalantly.

I choke on a sip of my gin and tonic, reminded once more that Judd eventually told me his family was on a need-to-know basis about his fights, and he didn't feel they needed to know.

"He's craved the same deep connection all my brothers, and me, want but have struggled to find," Vale continues.

"You didn't have that connection with Hudson's father?" I ask.

Vale's son, Hudson, is nearly twelve. From my understanding, Vale has raised him since birth on her own, with mainly Stone's help.

Vale turns her head and looks longingly across the bar. "No. It doesn't take deep connection to make a baby."

I nod feebly, sorry I brought up such a sore subject.

"Making babies can be so much fun, though," Cadence breaks in, trying to turn the frown on Vale's face into a smile.

"Who's that?" I ask, hoping to change the subject as I glance in the direction Vale once did. A broad shouldered, thick armed man sits on a stool at the bar, nursing something dark in a short glass. His hair is dirty blond. His beard thick. He looks like a Viking in modern-day flannel.

Enya twists on her stool. "Isn't that Cortland Haven?"

Vale doesn't look back up, almost purposely keeping her head down, but I don't miss her side-eye the guy for a second before she says, "I don't know. I don't think so."

There's another story here but I already put my foot in my mouth about Hudson's dad, so I don't ask.

The waitress returns to the table with a shot topped with whip cream and sets it before Vale.

"What's this?" Vale asks, glancing up at the young server.

"The message is 'bees like something sweet'." She nods at the mystery man in flannel, who isn't looking at our table, but keeping his eyes trained on the large screen television with a baseball game on it.

"*What* is that?" Enya asks, staring at the concoction.

"A blow job shot."

I wrinkle my nose. "A bit assumptive, don't you think?"

I'm ready to defend Vale's honor but Vale is already shaking her head, fighting the twitch of her lips. Her hand covers mine and stills the sudden desire to cross this bar and give flannel-man a what-for and a fuck-you.

Vale keeps her eyes on the shot, contemplating something, before whispering, "I'll kill him." She sets the glass before her, places her hands behind her back, and opens her mouth wide. Leaning forward, she wraps her lips around the shot glass then she tips up her head, swallows down the shot, and then grips the short glass, slamming it down on the table.

"Any responding remarks." The waitress tweaks her brow, almost enjoying her position as messenger.

Vale hands the shot glass back to the waitress. "Bees sting. That's all."

Then Vale focuses on our table. "Let's get back to that discussion about toys-as-tools for companionship."

Enya cranes her neck, head swinging from Vale to flannel-man and back, like she knows a bit more about the longing in Vale's eyes and the mystery behind the man at the bar.

"Yes," Cadence smacks the table, drawing all of us back to our circle. "I heard sex might motivate this little love to move out." Cadence runs her hand over her swollen belly once more.

"You're only five months along. Don't rush it." A gentle warning graces Enya's tone.

"Right. Okay. I just want to have sex with my hot future husband." Cadence winks at me, as if I understand the super-power of the Sylver males.

Vale groans.

"And you," she points at Vale. "We need to get you all *sexed* up."

"Set up," Enya corrects.

"That's what I said," Cadence smiles, tossing me a wink.

Vale groans again but lifts her glass of wine in a mocking toast.

"God, I miss tequila," Cadence grouses, but lifts her glass of water to knock against Vale's.

And I wonder what it would be like to be *sexed* up for a certain sexy Sylver.

WHEN JUDD PICKS me up at The She Shed, he offers Vale a ride home as well. She's had a few too many glasses of wine to complement her earlier shot.

Judd opens both the front and back passenger door of his pickup truck, and Vale motions for me to climb into the front seat while she lugs herself into the back.

"I see it's been a good night," Judd chuckles, helping me into the front.

"I think she's a little overserved," I stage-whisper.

"I'm *under*served," Vale announces. "That's my problem. Under-*serviced.*"

Judd arches a brow at me before closing my door and then closing his sister's once he confirms she's fastened her seat belt. He rounds his truck, effortlessly hopping in, and drives toward his family's home where Vale lives with Stone.

"Judd," she leans forward, then falls back at the constriction of the seat belt. She wrestles to release the latch despite Judd's protesting tone, and then slides herself forward so her head can slip between the front two seats.

"Judd, listen to me. Friendly, sisterly, womanly advice." She's tapping his shoulder like an annoying sister might do, wanting his full attention.

"Jesus, Vale. Sit back. Buckle your seat belt," he chides, giving her a stern look.

"Judd," she continues, ignoring him. "Make her pleasure your pleasure." She points between Judd and me. "Make sure she's pleased before you're pleased. You get my meaning?"

Judd coughs, shifting in the driver's seat and keeping his eyes forward. "Got it."

I fight a smile at how uncomfortable Judd suddenly looks but also how seriously he answers his sister.

"And another thing," Vale continues. "Make sure she finishes. It isn't a race. Not a sprint. No circle, circle, fifty-yard dash. Complete the process. Finish line." While Vale speaks, she motions two fingers in a circular motion, then shoves her arm forward, imitating a dash.

The laugh I want to contain breaks free and Judd tips his head to the side window, shaking it slowly.

"Someone should have cut her off," Judd mutters.

"That's the problem. I've been cut off too quickly. Men don't know how to finish what they start. Finish, Judd. Make it worth your Genie's while. Don't just rub the lamp. Show her the love."

I full on snort, covering my mouth with my hand at Vale's advice to her brother, who looks like he'd like to crawl underneath the seat.

"Okay, now sit back," Judd says, glancing briefly at his sister who still has her head between the seats, leaning on the edge of mine. "Don't make me pull over."

His voice is all tease.

Vale groans and slips backward, refastening the seat belt, and tipping her head to the window like all the steam went out of her.

When we reach Stone's home, Judd helps his sister out of the truck and walks her up to the door. There, Vale wraps her arms around Judd's waist, and he hugs her back a second before she pats his back and pulls away to enter the house.

The exchange is sweet and makes me wish for siblings again. A whole brood of them that care about one another and want the best for each other.

When Judd returns to the truck, he glances back at the front porch making certain his sister is in the house even though he just watched her enter.

"Have fun tonight?"

I roll my head on the headrest and stare at him as he reverses his truck. In the reflection of the dashboard lights, I admire his profile. A strong nose. Full lips. Those bright eyes.

"Vale is my new best friend."

Judd's mouth curls in a soft way. Not a full smile but a hint that he's pleased. "I want to be your new best friend."

"You are my fiancé," I remind him, stating the word all fancy in a fake French accent, and adding a poke to his arm like his sister had been giving him.

"They can be the same thing."

I hadn't really thought about that. I mean, couple goals—*be friends with your betrothed*—but only days ago, I'd thought friends and fiancé were two separate words, when they really should be synonymous.

"So, what did you do tonight?" He's had hours of relief from me in his home.

"Waited for you."

I snort. "Seriously?"

"Seriously. I met Stone for dinner, and we hung out until I got your call."

That's strangely sweet.

"I saw Heather tonight," I report quietly, not really wanting to bring her up and yet still bothered by what she said about Judd.

He turns his head toward me, brows pinching with concern. "Did she say something to you?"

I chew on my lower lip. Heather didn't so much speak to me as she insulted Judd, and now I'm sorry I mentioned her because I don't want to share with him the hurtful things she said.

Judd must sense my unease, and he glances at me again before pulling into his gated driveway. "What did she *do*?"

I shrug. "Nothing worth repeating."

"Tell me anyway."

"It wasn't nice, Judd. Nor necessary." She's just jealous, as Cadence said.

Judd parks in his garage, cuts the engine and turns toward me in his seat. "Tell me."

"Judd." I sigh, the sound an admission that I don't want to tell him.

"Did she call you names? Threaten you in any way?" His voice rises, his agitation growing as he reaches for my hand, his thumb instantly finding the amethyst on his mother's ring and toying with it.

"No, nothing like that."

"Just tell me then." His tone grows sharper, and I glance up at him.

"I don't want to hurt your feelings."

Judd continues to stare at me, willing me to speak.

With a heavy sigh, I admit, "She said you were frigid. It was absolutely uncalled for and unnecessary. And before I could defend your honor or pride, Cadence was shooing Heather off like an annoying insect." I should have said something. *I'm* his fiancée. I should have been arguing to the contrary.

Judd purses his lips and rocks his head a few times, then releases my hand and pops open the driver's side door. He rounds his truck as I'm exiting my side and he takes my hand in his again, helping me out of the truck before leading me into the house.

We bypass the guest room and library and then stop inside the great room. Only undercabinet lights in the kitchen area are on, giving the room a warm glow.

Judd and I face off a second, and I'm worried revealing Heather's jab has hurt Judd's feelings.

"Did you buy anything tonight?" he asks, noticing a bag in my other hand. His eyes are trained on the paper sack. The blue in them like the bright flame at the first light of a burner.

"Judd," I whisper, my throat growing dry.

"Can I see it?" He looks me directly in the eye. The heat in them scorching me. The desire a sudden inferno.

With shaky hands, I pull out my new purchase. "It's called The Pickler."

Judd stares at the item that I'm holding up like a magic wand and takes in the bulbous wedge and the surprising likeness to both a vegetable and the male anatomy.

"Not a very appealing name," he mutters as we both stare at the device.

Meredith gave a very detailed and convincing sales job on how to use this product and what it can do to enhance my *sex*perience.

"Want to show me how it works?" Judd adds, focusing on me.

My head whips in his direction, my heart galloping as well. His question is a cross between asking for permission and an assumption I'd show him how I'd use this product.

I'm also instantly turned on. *Darn Thursdays.*

"Want to help me?" Toys-as-tools, Cadence said.

"Checking yes." Judd's breathless reply has my thighs clenching and another part of me pulsing. Touching myself with this product, while Judd watches or participates or whatever will happen, involves a layer of trust, and instantly, I realize I do trust him.

Snap-crackle-pop. The sexual tension is palpable between us, almost more intense than the thunderstorm last night.

Judd stares at me for another long minute before he demands, "Lose your panties."

24

———————

[Judd]

"You haven't kissed me today," Genie says quietly, lowering her eyes while still holding that damn purple pleaser in her hand.

"What?" I don't mean to sound obtuse, because I've been *thinking* about kissing her all day. But I also know Genie is like a skittish cat, and I don't want to see claws when I want to hear her purr.

Last night, she hummed with my mouth on hers, distracting us both from the storm, but in the light of a new day, I'm worried I've crossed a boundary that Genie set. She hadn't wanted to kiss me only days ago, although she was certainly willing last night.

Our situation is only days old and I'm trying to navigate it as best I can without scaring her off.

Then again, it isn't every day the woman of your dreams

stands before you with a sex toy in her hand, looking all innocent while sinfully seductive at the same time.

"You haven't kissed me," Genie repeats, slowly looking up at me.

I rush forward, taking her face in my hands and kissing her fast and deep. If this woman wants kisses before I can touch her, so be it. I'll give her anything.

She pulls back first, and I swear those dark eyes are the brightest gem I've ever seen. Polished onyx.

Genie steps back and back again, until she's seated on the edge of one leather couch. She sets The Pickler beside her and reaches demurely beneath the skirt of her dress to remove her underwear as I requested. Then she dramatically holds it up and I snatch it from her hands, bringing it to my nose.

"Sweet as I suspected," I hum, keeping my eyes on hers while I inhale deeply.

I fold down to my knees and press at hers, forcing them apart. The skirt of her dress falls between her thighs, covering what I long to see. Every reserved movement is an additional tease.

I kiss her again and bunch up the material of her dress. When I pull back, Genie's knees are wide, her center exposed to me.

"Beautiful," I hum, reaching for her new purchase. With a flick of my finger, the item vibrates in my fist. Genie's eyes light up and she watches as I lower it to her inner thigh, taking my time to run it up and down the inside of her leg. Her hips start to rock. She scoots closer to the edge of the couch, hinting that she wants more from this thing.

"Need something, firefly?"

She casually leans back on her arms, keeping her gaze on where I'm teasing her.

"You," she whispers.

Her answer has me rushing to her center, letting this toy

give her pleasure. Pleasing her pleases me. Watching Genie's eyes flutter closed and her mouth softly open, I'm as hard as this mechanism in my fist.

I circle her core until her breath hitches when I've hit my intended mark. I continue to watch her face as her expression softens. Her mouth a perfect little circle of surprise. Her nostrils flaring gently.

"Like that?" I don't really need an answer from her. Everything about her body language says she does, especially when her hips jut forward and her knees nearly kiss the edge of the couch, spreading as wide as her legs will allow.

"Judd," she whimpers.

"Is my fiancée in need of some relief?" I tease.

"Yes," she groans. "Checking yes. In all the boxes. On all the notes."

I chuckle as I move the vibrator in my hands lower and watch her body take it in.

Genie's eyes flip open, wide and staring directly at me with a hunger I've never seen before. "Yes, Judd. Yes."

Suddenly feral, I'm desperate in my own way. I'm not opposed to getting her where she wants but I want it to be me who takes care of her needs.

"Genie, let me taste you." I'm practically salivating.

"Yes," she cries. Her fingers clutch at the edge of the couch. Her legs tremble.

I pull the vibrator free from her, and Genie cries out with distress, but I won't disappoint her. I duck my head, latching onto her swollen folds and suck hard.

"Ahh," she preens, shoving her hand through my hair and cupping the back of my head. Her hips thrust upward, but I clamp her inner thighs to the couch, pinning her in place.

This. This is all I've ever wanted for her. To be the one who makes her feel good. Feel alive. Because she does that for me.

I slip my hands beneath her thighs and sling them over my

shoulders, angling her lower half like I'm drinking from a treasured chalice. Sipping from the magic lamp that will grant all my wishes.

A litany of thoughts stutter from me. "Spill for me, firefly. Mark this couch. Stain my tongue. Light up for me." Let me see that spark. That flash in the dark that's magical, almost mystical.

Genie screams my name, gripping my hair and pinning me to her center when there is no chance I'll pull away from her. Not until she is fully satisfied.

Eventually, she presses at my forehead. Her chest heaves. Her eyes are closed. She's spent but a sly grin curls her mouth.

"Judd Sylver, you are hot. Scorching flames. All the chili peppers. *The* hottest."

While her comment instantly reminds me of what she mentioned from she who shall not be named, I don't find a trace of my initial upset.

I'll warm this woman in every way.

"Stand up," she says breathlessly. "Lose your pants."

I chuckle until her gaze lands on me, a new fire in them.

"You don't need—"

"I need." She awkwardly presses herself upright and scrunches her fingers which could be frightening if I wasn't already so hard I could cut glass.

Slowly, I rise before her as Genie watches me stand to my full height. When I reach for the button on my jeans, Genie pushes my hands away and eagerly pulls down my zipper, setting me free from the confines of my boxer briefs.

With my jeans just below my hips, Genie strokes my hard length, and I hiss. "Sweet firefly," I croon, petting back her hair and glancing down at her.

When she lifts her eyes while dangling her tongue against my engorged tip, seeping with need for her, I swear I grow even harder. Still watching me with those eyes, she squeezes me.

Nothing wrong with her eye and hand coordination now.

Genie takes a long lick up my shaft then opens wide and sucks me deep, and my eyes roll back in my head.

"Oh God," I grunt, knowing nothing has ever felt like this. It isn't skill or talent or some strange witchcraft, this is pure ecstasy on a level I've never felt before.

"Genie. Baby. I think you've put a spell on me."

Her hand cups my balls, and she takes me as deep as she can and I gently rock forward, petting over her hair, holding myself back while melting under her attention to detail. A lick. A suck. A pump.

"Genie. I'm gonna—" I choke on what she does next. The depth. The roll of her throat against my tip.

It's too much and I picture marking that crease between her breasts, the one that's tempting between the sweet, green ruffles exposing her collarbone. As if reading my thoughts, she releases me and I spill on the column of her throat, watching as my seed drips down her sternum and between those lush breasts.

"Did you just read my mind?" I ask breathlessly, staring at where I've just painted her skin.

"Now, you've marked me." Her voice is sultry. Her eyes mischievous, and I lean down and kiss her flirty mouth.

With a sharp tug to pull up my jeans, I leave the mess on her chest, cup her ass and lift her to me, carrying her to my bed where I intend to sleep next to my *fiancée* and new best friend again.

I WAKE DRAPED over Genie like she's my personal body pillow. My cheek is on her chest. My arms tucked into her sides, and one of my legs drapes over both of hers. She's locked in like I was afraid she'd disappear in the night.

I press a kiss to her chest, instantly recalling what we did last night and how I marked her here. It's been a long time since anyone has done what she did to me last night, but it wasn't the act itself that was special. The moment is etched in my heart because of *this* woman. The pleasure heightened to a dizzying crescendo because of Genie.

Afterward, I cleaned her off with a warm washcloth before helping her into my Seed & Soil T-shirt.

"Good morning," she whispers, combing her fingers through my hair again.

"Mornin'," I mutter, unable to lift my head because of how good her scalp massage feels.

"What's on the agenda today?" Her voice is still quiet.

"Asks the calendar girl," I tease, rubbing my nose along her T-shirt covered breasts.

"I can't seem to help myself." She lightly chuckles, jostling my head.

"Well, I know you told me last weekend was Naked Gardening Day but how would you feel about commemorating the day today."

"You want me to be naked in your garden?"

I finally lift my head, pressing up on my forearms. "Now there's an idea."

She laughs. "Is this one of your wishes? Because a genie can only grant three."

I tilt my head. "I only get three?" I roll my eyes to the side and quirk my lips like I'm thinking. What would my wishes be? But the answers come easily.

Love. Marriage. Family. All with Genie.

Not wanting to frighten her, I say instead, "I'll have to think about those wishes. One must choose carefully."

"Yes, one must," she mocks playfully.

"What would your three wishes be?" I ask. "Can a Genie ask genie?"

Genie laughs deeper, her body shaking beneath me. "I don't exactly know the rules, I guess, but I'd say I'm allowed three wishes as well."

"And what would your wishes be?"

Genie stares back at me more a long minute. "I always thought I knew what my wishes were." She slides her fingers through my hair again. "But I think my wishes might be changing."

"Checking yes to a few new things?"

Her eyes momentarily cloud. I'd almost say fear flashes through them. She has her reasons for not wanting to get married and even some deep-seated concerns about her ability to parent. I never want to force her to do anything she doesn't want, so if I'd only get one of my wishes, it's that I'd want Genie to love me.

And if one of *her* wishes is to be loved, I can make that happen for her.

"Checking yes to a few new things," she says quietly. Then she tips her head so I can kiss her, and we start our day where we really do work in the garden, but unfortunately, keep all our clothes on.

25

[Genie]

I have never gardened before, and I had no idea how hard it could be. But also, how extremely satisfying it is to dig in the dirt, plant a baby seedling, and envision how the garden will grow.

And what it will look like all the months I might not be here.

The thought doesn't hit me until our second day working on Judd's extensive garden. He has a greenhouse and has begun some plants from seed. Tomatoes and peppers. Beans and a few cucumbers grow vertically up a thin wire. Judd appreciates the merits of farming and prefers to produce what he can, giving him the healthiest eating experience as food goes from ground to table.

Like he once told me he became an accountant, so he'd never be poor again, he tells me he learned to garden so he'd never go hungry again.

And my heart breaks all over for the struggles the Sylvers endured as children.

A collection of raised beds with a gravel path between them and rivaling an English garden is to the left of the greenhouse, and we spend the majority of our second day there.

"A happier memory is that my mother loved gardening as well. She had a real green thumb, and that's one reason she shifted the original farm and fleet to the Seed & Soil."

Judd has so much love for his mother, and as this weekend is Mother's Day it feels appropriate to celebrate her, even if she isn't here, by gardening.

Still, I'm exhausted and I'm looking forward to a night curled up on Judd's couch until he says, "I have a fight tonight." He isn't looking at me as he presses dirt around a plant in one of the raised boxes.

Instantly, the air shifts around us. "Another one?" My voice is quiet.

"Every Saturday night."

I pause where I've been tapping at my own plot of dirt and glance across the box at Judd. "Why?" I clear my throat of the sudden clog. "Why do you fight?"

Judd tips back so he sits on his haunches and looks at me. His face hardens a bit, the sweat from the heat of the day and the redness of the sun adding to the edge in his expression. "Why does the boy whose dad beat him up fight?"

I swallow at the sudden sharpness in Judd's tone. "Yeah."

"Because my father said I was weak. *A fucking runt.* He called me a coward because I never fought back, never talked back to him. And the truth is, I didn't know how. I didn't have the snark of Sebastian or the strength of Knox. Didn't have the invisible shield like Ford or quick comebacks like Clay."

He pauses and glances to his right. His sorrowful expression doesn't match his strident tone.

"Did you know I was supposed to be a girl? As if a baby's

gender can be predetermined." Judd scoffs. "And he'd tell me, if I'd only been the girl they'd wanted, then—"

Judd closes his eyes. His Adam's apple bobs once before those blue-sky eyes look at me again, suddenly stormy and tight.

"Then what?" I softly prompt.

"Then my parents might not have kept having babies, and the girl they eventually had wouldn't have killed our mother."

I gasp. "He couldn't have meant that." How does a father say such a thing to a child? Poor Knox, Ford, and Sebastian who came after Judd. Poor Vale, to have such blame thrust upon her.

"Oh, he did. And he'd say it often enough to me. To Vale." Judd looks away again. "He'd insult me in every way he could, implying maybe I *was* a girl. Too soft. Too emotional."

Judd swallows hard again. "And I swore after that night—" He pauses, and I know which night he means. Our prom night.

"I swore, he'd never hurt me again. I'd learn to fight back. I'd learn to fight." Judd's hands are fisted on his thick thighs and his gaze is pointedly on me, but unfocused, like he's looking back on the past instead of at me. "And now, it's just who I am."

Judd is more of a lover than a fighter, Vale had said. Was Judd trying to convince himself he was the opposite? He was more fighter than lover, as if being a loving human being somehow made him less.

"But you don't need to fight," I remind him quietly. "Your father isn't here."

"And now it's no longer about him." Judd's comment is the first real lie he's told me.

"Do you have a temper?" The question tastes acidic. It's like asking an alcoholic if he has a drinking problem. Judd might not be able to admit the truth.

He shakes his head. "It's not about controlling a violent side of myself. It's about controlling the narrative. I never want to *feel* weak again."

He never wants to be that helpless little boy, but he doesn't see how very capable he is as a man. How strong he is, in body and heart. Maybe his spirit isn't as full as I think.

In some ways, I know the feeling. I can't seem to fight my mother. Word to word might not be the same as fist to fist, but there's still a will in me to counteract my mother. Her negative attitude. Her toxic opinion. Even with age, I tell myself I can handle her better, but can I really?

Have I found the strength I need?

"You don't look weak to me," I attempt to tease him, eyeing his body. The sweat along his collar and down the sides of his tee. The thickness of his thighs as he sits back like he is. The sureness of his hands.

But no playfulness rests in Judd's eyes. He huffs, quiet and closed off, and returns to pressing at the dirt, a little more forcefully than necessary.

In some ways, I want him to ask me to attend his fight like he did last weekend. But deep down, I know I'll refuse the invitation, and Judd doesn't need that kind of rejection.

He's already rejecting himself when he's so wrong. He is a lover more than a fighter. He can even be both, but not if he's fighting demons that no longer exist.

His father is gone, and Judd should live in the relief of his absence. He should live in the present, not the past.

Too bad I don't always take my own advice.

AFTER A QUIET DINNER WITH JUDD, I take a long, warm bath. Sleep won't come easily tonight despite my aching body. Gardening is the most physical exercise I've had in months. With his garden in mind, I consider how I won't be present when the flowers bloom or the vegetables are harvested. A week has already come and gone, with only two days remaining in our arrangement. The clock is winding down.

I don't know if I'm ready to go home yet.

I also hide out in the bathtub because I don't want to be present when Judd leaves. I could not be a well-wishing fan for something I struggle to understand.

While I'd told him a week ago I respected his choice to fight, I'd also told him I respectfully disagreed with the concept of fighting. I stand by my opinion.

His fights shouldn't be my concern. But I am concerned because I care about Judd, and I don't want to see him hurting, physically or mentally.

After my bath, where I've re-evaluated all my life choices including Greetings Ambassador and the sale of my company, I enter the guest room and curl up on the bed which suddenly feels unfamiliar after only two nights sleeping with Judd. My position reminds me I'm a guest here, not his lover. Not his fiancée.

The thought makes my stomach ache, and I wonder if our chicken dinner wasn't cooked thoroughly enough. Food poisoning might be the explanation for this pain in my gut.

Definitely the chicken.

But the truth is I'm going to miss Judd. Missing someone is what hurts the most, which is another reason not to get overly involved with someone. Absence is definitely another hindrance to marriage.

What if you love someone and they die?

Look at Judd's father. He fell apart. Look at my mother. In her own way, she did the same.

The sad thoughts cause me to close my eyes, but they spring open when I hear the heavy thud of the garage door announcing Judd's entrance and then the soft thud of something against the hallway wall.

Bolting upright, I reach for my phone and check the time. After midnight. I toss the light blanket off my legs and slip out of the guest room, but don't wander far before seeing a sliver of light coming from the library. The pocket doors are haphazardly closed, and I hesitate outside them when I notice Judd on the velvet chaise. His head is tipped back, eyes closed. His shirt is unbuttoned to his waist. One hand holds a glass of amber liquid. The other holds an ice pack against his left side, on his lower abdomen.

Pressing open the pocket doors, the soft rolling sound of their movement doesn't startle Judd. With his eyes still closed, he mumbles, "You should be asleep."

"Are you drunk?" The accusation is tightly spoken. Panic takes over, my tone shrill when I ask, "Did you drink and drive?"

Judd slowly lifts his head, eyes dull as they seek mine. He lifts the half-full glass in his hands. "I never drink it. It's only a reminder of why I fight."

His father was an alcoholic. His father beat him.

"Judd, this is sick torture." I rush to stand before him, examining him closer. His right cheek looks red and raw. The beginning stages of a bruise shades his eye. His knuckles are swollen on both hands.

Gingerly, I take the glass from him and place in on the floor near the corner of the chaise.

Judd lets his head fall back. He doesn't look drunk. He looks exhausted.

I bite my lip. I don't want to ask how was the fight? Win or lose, he's suffered injury.

My gaze falls to his left side, and I brush back his shirt. Judd lifts his head again and moves the ice bag, revealing a welt on his side.

"Judd," I gasp.

"I lost tonight. Couldn't keep my head in the ring."

"Where was your head?" I whisper, my fingers trailing above the redness along his side but afraid to touch him.

"Here. Home." His voice is rough.

Instantly, I'm angry. He told me earlier he fights the demons of his past, but his answer implies he didn't fight well because he was thinking of the present. Of me. *Damned if he does, damned if he doesn't.* Neither makes me happy, and mostly because it's hurting Judd.

"I don't want to fight with you," he whispers.

"We aren't fighting." I tilt my head, looking down at him, splayed out and worn out.

"You don't approve."

"I don't understand." A heavy pause filters between us. "Your father is dead, Judd. He isn't here. You don't need to defend yourself."

"I do." He snaps back. "Even arguing with you, I'm defending myself."

I clamp my lips shut and swallow at the sudden sting in my eyes. "I just don't want to see you hurting."

"I'm not hurt."

Another lie. And I'm making it worse.

For me, this is where my flight or fight comes in. I either flee and leave him to himself or fight for what I want. The issue is, I'm not a clean fighter. I might not necessarily play fair, but I want Judd to know there is another way.

A way to prove his father wrong. To fight the past by living the present to its fullest.

Slowly, I lower to my knees. I'm wearing a silky nightie I'd brought with me. Not necessarily the sexiest thing I own but something that brings me comfort. Kneeling at Judd's feet, I remove his shoes and press his knees apart so I can wedge myself between his legs.

His head is tilted to the side. His temple resting on his fist. He squints at me with the eye that's bruised.

"What are you doing, firefly?" he grumbles, not stopping me, hardly moving except for his chest which lifts and lowers a little faster. The ice bag on his side slides off his wound, exposing his bare abdomen. The ripples of his muscles. The firmness of his pecs. The trail of hair leading below his waistband.

"I can fight, too."

Judd dressed up again for his fight. A crisp shirt. Slick pants. And I reach for his belt, loosening it.

Sex isn't a substitute, but it's one way to burn off energy, and while I don't think Judd has it in him to engage in sex tonight, there are other ways to relieve his mind.

After lowering the zipper of his pants, I wrestle the sides and his boxer briefs below his hips. Tipped up on my knees, I curl my hand around his thick shaft and tug. Judd has the nicest penis. Honestly, the best dick I've ever seen, and while I don't normally love the whole oral thing, tasting him has become a new obsession.

I lick up the length of him and then press a kiss to the leaking tip. I swipe my thumb over the engorged end and Judd hisses.

Don't fight, Judd, my thoughts whisper. My wishes wish. Fight for me instead.

The thought comes out of nowhere, almost like a sucker punch at me, and to distract myself I open wide and drag Judd into my mouth. His abs contract. He hisses again.

I pull off him. "Am I hurting you?"

"No, baby. No." His eyes focus on me, and he reaches for my cheek. This tender touch is in such sharp contrast to his swollen knuckles. Hands he so recently used to punch someone else. The thought should still my process, but I want Judd focused on me.

Opening wide once more, I take him deep, dragging up and dropping down his length, until Judd is digging his fingers in my hair and gripping the short waves. He isn't controlling me as much as it feels like he's holding on for dear life.

And I recall how he spilled over me last night. So possessive. So intimate.

That *snap-crackle-pop* between Judd and me is about to become an explosion of wills.

Who will win? What's the prize?

My fear is that hearts are on the line.

For now, my mission is to cleanse his thoughts and relax his body, and I've quickly achieved my goal when Judd tips back his head and groans, like a beast unleashed. He comes down my throat tonight and I swallow the salty mix, feeling powerful and victorious.

When I pull off him, Judd gives me a sultry glance before he shifts faster than I'd think him capable. He winces once but doesn't stop, hoisting me to the chaise and slipping off the seat to kneel between my knees.

"Judd, you don't need to." Tonight wasn't about tit-for-tat, or even me. I only want him out of his head, and here, at home, like he said.

His hands are already beneath my nightie, though, slipping my underwear to my feet. He doesn't take a dramatic inhale like he did last night, but he stuffs the panty into his shirt pocket. Then his face is between my thighs and his thick tongue takes a lap up my seam. I cry out and cup his face.

Judd is relentless, diving in with his tongue. Nipping with his teeth. Then soothing the bite with a deep kiss.

Holy hibiscus, I've never been taken care of like this. I'm his victory feast.

Judd curls his tongue and then adds fingers, and every touch adds to my sensory overload. Even more than the other night, when he started with The Pickler and ended with his mouth. I'm wound tight, and ready to spring. The anticipation is almost as thrilling as the release which hits me so hard, I double over Judd's head, curling around him as if I can keep him between my thighs for eternity.

"Judd, Judd, Judd," I moan, like a prayer and a promise. Yes, yes, yes. He only has to ask, and I might give him anything.

My body *and* my heart, which scares me more than anything.

26

———

[Judd]

"**E**nough." Genie's soft command pulls me from my head, and I press a kiss to her center. Then I glance up at her from my position on my knees.

What am I doing? I wasted another night. One where I could have had her on my couch, cuddled under my arm, or in my bed, snuggled up against me. We could have had time together, like we'd spent gardening for two days, but as the clock ticked closer to Saturday evening, I felt like a beast inside me wanted to be released.

Then that creature couldn't be contained in the ring. My thoughts kept drifting to Genie. What was she doing? What was she thinking? Was she worrying? Was she angry?

We hadn't fought directly, but a shift happened, and I didn't know how to shift back.

For the moment, all feels right again. Genie staring down at me, those expressive eyes sated. The fire in them more of a smoldering gleam.

Picking her up like I did the other night, she wraps herself around me, like a bear cub in a pine tree.

Then she lifts her head. "Your side."

"Feels nothing." It's a lie. My lower abdomen is screaming. My opponent got me good tonight. I also have a no face policy, not wanting my family to visibly see what I'm doing, and yet tonight, my opposition got me in the cheek.

The blistering punch was a reminder of my father's from decades ago.

And yet all I could think about was Genie. She wouldn't like the mark. She'd be concerned for me.

Genie wiggles in my arms, forcing me to set her down.

"Come to bed with me?" She'd been in the guest room, but I don't want her sleeping in there. I don't want her sleeping anywhere except with me.

She nods and I take her hand, leading her to my bedroom, envisioning us doing this every night. Going to bed together. Sharing the nights together. Being here for each other.

Which I can't do if I'm not present. If I'm off fighting. I want to argue that she's wrong. I do need the fight. The thrill. The relief.

But she's just drained me in a new way, and I'm reminded once more that I have something good at the tip of my fingers. I don't want to waste it, and I only have a few days left to convince Genie to stay longer.

My wish? Eternity for Genie and me.

I lead Genie directly to the shower, pulling her in behind me and turning on the spray. She squeals at the initial rush of cold water.

"What are you doing?" Then she laughs. Deep and rich, and full of glee. She's so bright and vivid. My firefly.

Her spark is leading me out of the darkness, and I need to keep following her lead.

As the water heats, I slip off her night dress and then remove my shirt. I don't want to fuck her. I just want to hold her. Chest to chest. Cheek to cheek. Bare skin to bare skin.

So once my pants are removed, and we're both naked, I pull Genie in for a hug, and then just hold her as the shower heats our flesh.

And my heart feels like it's melting, moving from a cold state of numbness to the low heat of a springtime campfire.

This feels like love.

IN THE MORNING, I leave Genie in bed as she slept fitfully. I couldn't imagine what kept her shifting and rustling within my bed, but I clung to her until she clung to me.

When she rushes into the great room, while I'm preparing a cup of coffee in the kitchen, she startles me. "Hey."

"Hi." I smile wider than I think I ever have and adjust my glasses. I don't typically wear them but today my eye socket is screaming.

Genie looks extra adorable, especially as her hair has a lump on one side. The other side is more limp. She went to bed with wet hair. *My* bed.

She stills and toys with the hem of the T-shirt I slipped over her head last night. The same Seed & Soil one I continue to put on her, liking how she looks in my things.

"So, today is Mother's Day."

"Oh." In the recesses of my mind, I'm certain I knew the date. Second Sunday in May. This weekend is also officially planting season, and why I've had Genie helping me the past two days.

So, yes, on some level I know the date, but I typically try to ignore it. I don't have a mother to celebrate, and while I could meet my family for an annual remember-Mom celebration, I find them too painful to attend.

"My mom has asked me to meet her for brunch."

My brows pinch. "Okay." I pause a beat. "I hadn't known you were in contact with your mom." After last weekend's hang up, I'd hoped Genie hadn't had any other interaction with her mother.

Genie shrugs. "She left me a message." She glances to the wall of windows. "More like a demand."

"All the more reason not to attend." The instant I say the words, I sense my error.

Genie turns her head back toward me. Her eyes are soft, sad even. "She's still my mom."

And Janet Hurley treats her daughter like shit, but I don't comment. Biting my tongue is hard, though. I know all too well about never speaking up. Never fighting back. Genie has a backbone in every other aspect, but her mother makes her believe that she's weak.

The similarities to how my father made me feel are all too familiar and the last thing I want for my brave, strong girl. Genie comes across like she knows her own worth, but has this one sliver of hesitation, and I don't want her to ever doubt herself. She's beautiful, capable, powerful.

"Okay," I whisper, acquiescing, understanding again that struggle to appease someone you despise.

"Would you . . ." Genie licks her lips and glances down at the hem of the tee. "Would you come with me?"

My eyes widen as surprise and elation wrap around me. "You want me to be there for you?" Because that's what she's essentially asking and I'm all for supporting her. "Heck yes."

She giggles. "You mean, check yes."

"That too, firefly." I set the coffee mug on the countertop and step around the island to pull her to me.

Last night feels like lightyears away, and yet I know I was a bit aggressive with her. Eager to please her.

"You okay today?"

She tips back her head and looks up at me. "Yeah. Think you can wear these glasses later today and we can play dirty accountant and naughty secretary. I could play with your calculator."

I laugh a little harder, squeezing her tighter. "Fuck. You into role playing?"

"I could be with those glasses on you."

I shake my head before resting my forehead against hers.

"But seriously, thank you in advance for doing this today."

"Whatever you wish, Genie." I kiss the tip of her nose but then she leans up to kiss me, and with that kind of morning greeting, I'll never deny her anything.

Even brunch with her wicked mother.

Or wearing my glasses while she pretends to be my naughty secretary.

When we arrive at Evergreen Terrace, a sickening sensation in my belly rears, and it isn't the ache in my lower left abdomen screaming in warning.

Being here has bad idea written all over it, but I'm present for Genie.

The first hit comes when the hostess recognizes me when Genie and I enter the lobby. "Mr. Sylver, great to see you again."

At the recognition of my name, Genie bristles beside me, perhaps knowing *who* I've been here with before, and I run my hand up her spine, cupping the back of her neck.

"The Remingtons are already seated. May I lead you to their table?" The young girl's smile is friendly, her intention well-meaning.

"Actually." Genie clears her throat. "We're here for brunch with Janet Hurley. My mother."

"Oh." The hostess glances between us. "Perfect. She's seated with the Remingtons."

"What?" Genie snaps, her mouth falling open.

What the fuck?

"Brunch was supposed to be a party of three," Genie explains to the high school-aged girl. "My mother, Lester, and me."

A fourth chair would have been easily added for me.

"She entered at the same time as the Remingtons, and they decided to be seated together. There's space for another chair." The hostess glances anxiously between Genie and me.

Everything in me says run. Hike Genie over my shoulder and just get out of here, but the gleam in Genie's eyes was dim this morning, caught between anxiety and obligation. She wants to do right by a woman who doesn't deserve her concern, and I remind myself I'm here for Genie.

27

———

[Genie]

I cannot believe my mother did this to me—*to us*—by accepting an invitation to sit with the Remingtons.

Since Judd hung up on my mother last week, guilt hit me hard, and I sent her a text telling her I had bad reception. I promised to call her later in the week. I hadn't called. She sent me a text requesting—no demanding—we meet for brunch.

I remind myself this is what I'd wanted. I'd originally planned to arrive on Friday, spend four days with my mother and celebrate *her* day on Mother's Day, in hopes she'd celebrate a special day with me on Monday.

Spending an hour or two with the Remingtons is the last thing I want to do, and I don't want to put Judd through this torture either.

"We can leave," I turn toward him as the hostess steps into the main dining room.

Judd cups my cheeks, his eyes tender, his touch light. "Is

this meal important to you?" Somehow, he's sensed that it is. I wouldn't have accepted being here otherwise, I guess.

"Yes," I whisper.

"Then we weather it together." He takes my hand, and lifts it to his lips, kissing my knuckles near his mother's ring and then slipping his fingers between mine.

I like the fit, and the strength of his hand boosts my confidence as I turn to face the dining room and instantly see Heather standing a few feet from us. Her face dumbstruck. Mouth agape. Then her icy eyes narrow and she glares at Judd, killing him with a glance before stalking away.

Is it wrong to be hopeful she's leaving?

The hostess remains stationary, waiting on Judd and me, and I finally force my leaden feet to move into the dining room.

As we near the table, I catch the eye of my stepfather. Lester Hurley isn't a bad man, I just don't know him very well. He arches a brow and musters a weary smile. If he has any sympathy for me, he doesn't dare show it, especially when I meet my mother's eye next.

Disapproval wavers around her like a dark aura. She scans down my dress, the look not appraising but critical. As I lean forward to press a kiss to her cold cheek, she mutters to me.

"I've never seen you look so *full*, Virginia. Perhaps a strapless dress wasn't the best choice for brunch."

"Excuse me," Judd growls beside me but I squeeze his hand. We might be in this together, but I need to face my mother on my own terms.

"She looks radiant," Judd adds, and I catch him looking at me. His eyes bright and full of something I can't read but I'm grateful for him standing beside me.

Judd pulls out an empty chair for me beside my mother and then helps himself to the vacant seat beside me at the round table.

"That was Heather's spot," Carl Remington states. The

sixty-something, gray-haired man with a mustache narrows his eyes at Judd. "What happened to your eye?"

Judd's cheek is swollen and the telltale sign of a black-eye is present despite the rim of his dark glasses attempting to cover the bruise.

"We're getting another chair," Cheyanne quickly interjects, preventing Judd from answering. The poor girl. The tension surrounding this table could not be cut with a machete.

My mother leans toward me although she doesn't lower her voice. "Was bringing *him* really necessary?"

I lift my left hand, flashing my ring finger at her. The one she demanded to see a week ago. "Yes. He's my fiancé."

In many ways, my mother started this whole thing. Despite Judd announcing I was his fiancée, my mother was the one who demanded to see a ring. So here it is.

I'm playing into the fib, and yet, so many pieces of our lie don't feel like a lie.

Judd's hand finds my thigh beneath the table, emphasizing one of those things that make our situation feel a little too real. I cover the back of his hand, squeezing tightly, like I don't intend to let him go.

"Funny how that happened so quickly," Carl Remington states, glaring at Judd.

"Are you pregnant?" my mother blurts.

"Janet." Gloria Remington chides, glancing over her each of her shoulders like someone nearby might hear. As if the idea of pregnancy is shameful. Her blond hair doesn't ruffle with the sudden movement due to a helmet of hair spray.

"No," I defend, my brows pinching. "Would that be the only reason Judd would marry me?"

I'm certain my mother has a list of reasons why *I'm* not good enough for Judd. Or maybe she's had a change of heart and now Judd isn't good enough period while he might have once been perfect for Heather. My mother's heart is fickle like that.

Judd squeezes my thigh tighter.

"You'd have to have sex to get pregnant." All heads turn toward Heather's voice as she returns to the table with a man beside her who instantly looks uncomfortable.

"Could this get any worse?" Judd mutters beside me while I'm narrowing my eyes, assessing the man next to Heather, trying to figure out why he looks familiar.

"Tate Haven." He clears his throat and holds up a hand in a weak greeting.

"Tate," I whisper, instantly recognizing the name.

The Havens are another Sterling Falls family with a deep history. One once closely linked to the Sylvers but the details are fuzzy to me. Tate is the second son in the family and the same age as Judd.

In contrast to the Sylvers, who are primarily a dark-haired, blue-eyed family, the Havens have more of a Viking look about them, with a range of blond hair and a mix of eye colors.

Judd stiffens beside me, and I turn toward him, whispering, "What is it?"

Judd numbly shakes his head and stares forward into the room.

Heather cannot take her eyes off Judd. "Seems you weren't the only one sneaking around."

"First," I counter, my irritation instant. "We were not sneaking around." The second after I speak, I clamp my lips shut. Of course, Heather might think that happened. An engagement on the same day as Judd breaks up with Heather look suspicious. But the engagement was also a misunderstanding. Words said to keep my mother off my back. Then an assumption when Judd was holding out the ring and Heather caught us on the side of the house.

But Judd has been playing into the misinterpretation, introducing me as his fiancée, and I haven't been denying it either.

Even if we promised we'd date for ten days, everything feels a little more real and a whole lot unfinished.

Suddenly lingering over my head is our end date—*tomorrow*.

Heather Remington does not need to know the truth, though. I don't owe her anything and her statement implies *she's* the one who has some explaining to do.

Judd looks like he's going to be sick, and I can't decide if he's jealous of Tate, or if something else is going on here.

Two more chairs are brought to the table, and I scoot left, causing Judd to do the same.

Tate takes the seat beside Judd, Heather on the other side of him. The additional seating arrangement makes the round table tighter and the tension tenser. I've completely lost my appetite and the last place I want to be is in this restaurant. I seek Judd's thigh beneath the table, and he covers my hand this round, shifting us so our palms meet and our fingers twine together.

Then Judd shifts again. The seating arrangement *is* close.

"Sorry," Tate mumbles through gritted teeth, without a hint of sincerity in his apology.

Judd only tips up his chin, letting the brush of Tate's shoulder against him go, but his jaw is tight. He reaches for his glass of water at the same time Tate stretches for the sugar packets when he could have asked for them to be passed.

Judd and Tate bump arms again.

"Nope," Judd states, glaring at Tate, a warning coming off Judd that's nearly frightening. His hand covering mine squeezes tighter.

"It's a tight fit," Tate mutters.

"Show some table manners, ask for the sugar to be passed."

"And risk you tossing it in my face," Tate scoffs. His low voice carries across Judd's tense body.

"That isn't the type of shit I'd do. That's more your MO."

Oh God. Is Judd sitting next to someone who used to bully him?

"Judd," I whisper. "Why don't we just leave?" There isn't room at this table for us anyway and the tension is stifling. My mother had to have known this would happen.

This type of bullshit is the exact reason I've stayed away for so many years.

"No." Judd whips his head toward me. "You wanted to see your mother."

He's here to support me. We're weathering this together, but is it worth weathering?

I'm about to say such a thing when Heather slips her left arm around Tate's shoulder and wiggles her fingers. A glaringly large and rather gaudy ring with a round diamond-like gem beams on her finger.

"Are you getting married?" I blurt, distracted by the ring and the position of Heather's hand on Tate's shoulder.

Tate turns his head, craning his neck so he can better see what's on Heather's finger. Then his head whips in the direction of Heather.

"Whoa, whoa, whoa," he grunts as Heather removes her hand and holds it out over the table, staring at the garish piece of jewelry.

"This is *my* mother's ring," she emphasizes, pride filling her voice. "Mama gave it to me for when we're ready to take our relationship to the next level." She hitches her left shoulder and turns the tightest smile I've ever seen at Tate before she glares at Judd. "I'm leveling up."

The insult is like an arrow, but the shot misses the bull's eye. Heather isn't leveling anything but her reputation as a cheater. And Tate looks struck dumb, having missed the memo that he's engaged to Heather.

"Perhaps you'd like to go after Tate next," my mother says

beside me, and both Judd and I swing our heads in her direction.

"What?" I choke, disbelief blooming. Is my mother implying I'd *go after* another woman's man?

"That's enough," Judd barks at my mom.

Lester bows his head while Mom holds hers higher. "It's a joke. I was kidding."

"It isn't funny," I state, my voice weak. *You look like a slut, Virginia.* No man likes an easy woman.

With a shaky hand I reach for a white wine that magically appeared before me when I don't even like white wine.

Judd catches my wrist before I touch the glass. "That's it. *Now*, we're leaving."

"What?" My mother and I say in unison.

"You're ruining Mother's Day brunch," she directs at Judd.

"You ruined Mother's Day brunch, Janet," Judd says, pushing back his chair, tossing his napkin over his empty plate, and standing. He helps me shift my chair out of the tight seating arrangement and holds out his hand. Once our palms clasp, he presses a kiss to my knuckles.

"You're making a scene," my mother grouses. "Sit down, Virginia," she demands through gritted teeth.

With my hand in Judd's, I lift my other hand and flick my wrist like I'm tapping at an imaginary drum. "Just marching to my own beat, Mom."

"I don't even know what that means," she retorts as Judd leads me away from the table.

She should know. She said it often enough to me as a child. *A little less rhythm, Virginia.*

And I prefer the rhythm of Judd's hand in mine, and the racing of my heart, as no one has ever defended me in front of my mother.

No. One. Until Judd.

~

"Fuck," Judd shouts as we hastily exit Evergreen Terrace and enter the bright sunlight of late morning. He removes his eyeglasses a second and scrubs a hand down his face in frustration.

The parking lot is packed, and we need to wait for the valet service to bring Judd's car to us.

"I'm sorry about all that." My voice is timid while Judd replaces his glasses and turns toward me, cupping my shoulders.

"You have nothing to apologize for," he says a bit too gruffly, pointing toward the double door entrance and adding, "*That* was total bullshit."

I agree. My mother. Heather. Even Tate Haven.

"Genie," Judd sighs, still holding my shoulders. "You are fucking amazing. I'm spellbound by your goodness, and I know you want to believe because she's your mother you owe her something, but that is not how a parent should speak to her adult child. *I know*." He jabs at his chest. "It's not acceptable."

I squint up at Judd. "She doesn't respect me." It's the first time I've ever voiced the words aloud. *Admitted* them out loud. "I'm an accomplished woman and I think she . . . resents me."

I've done more than my mother ever will and admitting she might be jealous feels like I'm being egotistical. But then I remember she does have reason to resent me, and I'm not ready to face that truth today. Not after what just happened in Evergreen Terrace.

Judd nods. "Exactly. She should be proud of you, not demeaning you." His gaze roams down my dress. The same green one with polka dots I wore the first time I met his family. "You radiate. Fucking brighter than the brightest firefly."

I chuckle weakly, knowing that still isn't very bright but Judd's meaning is well-intended. He thinks I glow.

"What was all that with Tate?" I ask as the Ford Shelby is brought to where we wait.

Judd sighs. "Let's get in the car and then I'll talk." Judd reaches for the passenger side door handle before the valet can assist me and he waits until I'm seated before closing the door. He tips the valet as they cross paths, and then he enters the car. With a rev of the engine, Judd pulls forward as if he can't get us out of the parking lot and away from Evergreen Terrace fast enough.

"Tate," Judd groans. "Such a man child, but once upon a time, Stone and Cortland Haven were best friends. So were our mothers. Stone and Cort grew up together. Were high school football superstars. Went to the same college. And both were NFL hopefuls."

Judd releases a huge breath. "Then our dad died." He turns his head, wiggling his brows. "And there was a girl."

I laugh, intrigued. "There's always a girl."

But Judd's face sobers. "Without going into all the dirty details, Stone and Cortland were no longer friends. The riff divided the families. Sebastian and the youngest Haven, Clint, decided not to speak to each other, choosing loyalty to their brothers over their friendship. However, Tate and I were *never* friends." Judd stares out the windshield a moment, reflective. "Taunts and jabs in middle school, when the mean years really kicked in. An unkind word here. A poke there. Minor moments to some that added up to years and years of torment for me."

"Judd." I reach for his forearm. "I'm so sorry that happened to you." As if his younger years weren't bad enough, throw in a family friend's son being a bully, and the layers just build.

"I tried to tell Stone what was going on when I was around thirteen or fourteen years, but he told me to ignore Tate. Said Tate struggled being in the shadow of his older, more successful brother. Stone wanted me to offer compassion when what I really wanted was to throat punch Tate. I never brought up our strained situation again."

Strained situation was a nice way of saying Judd was bullied.

Judd has held a lot inside over the years and this example adds another brick to the wall of reasons he fights. He has so much to let out and hasn't had an outlet for it. The toxicity. The negativity.

"Think Tate knew he was getting engaged to Heather?"

Judd's chuckle is bitter and raw. "He absolutely did not get *that* message in whatever scheme they were planning."

I watch as he loosens his hand on the steering wheel and then grips it once more. "Are you upset?"

"I'm fucking livid. If I ever hear your mom—"

"Not about my mom." Although, I appreciate his avid insistence and irritation. "About Heather. She all but admitted she'd been with Tate before you two separated."

Judd twists his lips. "Honestly, it wouldn't surprise me. I thought we were exclusive but one day Heather said to me, if I wanted exclusivity, I should put a ring on her, and I think that's when it really hit me that we weren't meant for one another."

Judd reaches over the gear shift and takes my hand in his. His thumb finds his mother's ring, flicking over it like he does. "You are meant for me, firefly. And I know that scares you a bit, but I'm willing to do whatever it takes. I'll wait until we're on the same lined page with unicorns. Patience is one of my best virtues." He grins wide, exposes his white teeth, like that will lessen the *wham* of what he said.

He'll wait for me? "I'm supposed to go home tomorrow."

Judd's head turns so quickly I'm afraid the car will shift as well. His expression suggests he'd forgotten. Our ten days are almost up, and while I'd like to complain the trip was a bust from my original intention, this visit has turned out to be so much more than I'd expected.

Judd's shoulders lower and his hand loosens on the steering

wheel again, fingers flexing before he regrips the control. He doesn't respond to what I've said.

For some reason, I don't want us to be alone yet. Today should be about family. "We should go to Stone's."

"What? Why?" Judd asks, glancing briefly at me again before returning his attention to the road.

"Because it's Sylver Sunday. And it is Mother's Day," I soften my voice. "Do it for your mom, Judd. Because she'd want you to be with them."

He might no longer have his mother, but he has siblings. Some remember his mom. Some don't. Judd should be with them in memory of her. *For her*. Violet Sylver's children turned out to be amazing despite their father.

Judd rocks his head once and then says, "I'll do it for you, firefly. Your wish is my command."

28

[Judd]

If Stone is surprised to see me for the second weekend in a row, he doesn't say a word. However, he does eye me suspiciously, noticing my glasses and the black and blue bruise they hardly disguise.

My family appears to be just the chaos Genie needs after that shitshow at Evergreen Terrace, but I need a moment to myself and wander into the house.

Fuck Tate Haven. Fuck Heather. Fuck Genie's mother.

As I walk through the lower half of the house, I try to find my mother in corners of the rooms. Her scent. Her touch. Something that says she was here. But this house has been changed so much, it belongs to Stone and Vale collectively now. My mother's rocking chair is long gone, broken by my father's rage. Her stack of gardening books once tossed in the fireplace. All that remained were a few pictures, most of them stolen off the wall or taken from photo albums for fear our father would destroy them as well. Those framed pictures now grace the fireplace mantel, but the memories are so distant, they don't even feel real.

It's been so long since I've been inside this house that I stumble when I see an image of my father and mother together, tucked at the end of the montage of frames highlighting my siblings. I step closer to the photograph, noting my father's arms around my mother from behind, his head turned so he's looking at my mother while she's laughing toward the person taking the picture. They look so happy, so in love, and I never understood what went wrong.

"Hard to remember there were good times." Stone's low tenor from behind me startles me.

I turn only my head to glance at him over my shoulder.

"He hurt all of us." Stone pauses. "Might have been easier if he'd been an asshole from the beginning." He stops again. "But he wasn't, and that's what hurts the most."

I snort, glancing back at the photo of my parents, and unable to recall a single good time with my father. "I think he resented me from birth." Not being that girl my mother desired. Being close to her. A real mama's boy, much to my dad's disgust.

"He resented God for taking his wife too soon. He resented having to live without the love of his life. But deep, deep down, he did not resent his children, contrary to his behavior."

"Funny way of showing it," I mutter.

"Difficult to appreciate the man was hurting as well."

I stare back at that picture, unable to recall a single smile on my father's face but looking at my mother it's clear he had them. Looking at her, she was the sunshine of his life.

And a brief memory flashes through my head. Our family playing baseball when I was young in the meadow on some summer day. Stone tagging Dad out at first base and my mother sweetly laughing. All of us, including my father, basked in her light.

Then I think about Genie being my firefly. The comparison might seem inconsequential. A tiny blip of light compared to the entire world being lit up by a star, and yet the feeling inside me is no different. Genie is brightness.

My father's love-light was snuffed out too soon, plunging him into blackness. My life has felt like only darkness, but a sliver of light is leading me in a different direction.

"I've tried long and hard to forgive him," Stone states, interjecting into my thoughts.

"How's that working out for you?" Sarcasm isn't typically my language but I'm still feeling brittle after the encounter with Genie's mother and the supporting characters at that brunch.

"Hard." Stone chuckles. "Forgiveness is a daily battle."

"Forgiveness?" I twist to look at Stone again.

"Yep. I need to forgive him, or my resentment will eat at me just like it ate at him."

Stone has so much to resent my father for, too. Our dad took the cowardly-for-him way out and left our eldest brother with a brood of kids when he was too damn young for the responsibility. Stone worked his ass off, along with Clay, to keep this family together. To remind us every day that we could count on each other. At the very least, we could rely on Stone.

It didn't always work in Stone's favor. Sebastian had been particularly difficult, Vale tempted to follow his path. Ford disappeared into baseball and Knox just left the family, pursuing his career in the Navy. Even though I work for the Seed & Soil, I've kept to myself as much as I can.

The most unwavering constant among us has been Stone.

"Is resentment eating you?" Stone asks. He isn't mentioning the swollen cheek and black eye, but he might as well have.

"I can take care of myself." *I've learned to fight.*

"That's not what I asked," Stone clarifies.

I lower my head, not wanting to answer, not wanting to disappoint my brother.

"I know you've always felt like you are outside the family, but you are part of us. I love you, Judd."

Suddenly, my throat is thick, and my eyes are flooding. Three simple words. So difficult to say. And yet, for all Stone has been through, he says them so easily, with so much emphasis. Love is the only reason he would have come back for everyone else. To take care of everyone. To try to keep us together.

"I know," I whisper. "Love you, too." My voice is thick, the words clunky on my tongue. This is where I feel weakest. I don't say the words with the strength they deserve.

Suddenly, Stone is cupping the back of my neck and squeezing. "You ever get to that moment you can forgive him, I promise it will feel so freeing," he says close to me. "And when you can accept that love is more powerful than hate, an entire world of possibility will open up for you."

Genie. Her whispered name in my head is the possibility I want. Yet earlier, she reminded me she's scheduled to leave tomorrow. I hadn't forgotten but I also hadn't let the countdown weigh on me. I've been too engrossed in enjoying the time we have.

I nod, acknowledging what Stone has said, although I'm not certain forgiveness is part of my vocabulary.

"I'm gonna step upstairs a second," I say, needing another minute for a new reason. I need to get my head back into this day.

Genie is scheduled to leave tomorrow night, which means I don't have much time left with her.

∼

"ARE YOU OKAY?" Genie asks, stepping into my childhood bedroom and closing the door behind her. As I've been laying on the double bed in my old room, I realize I might have been up here a little too long.

"This used to be my room. The one I shared with Knox." I continue to stare up at the ceiling. The space is entirely different from our old twin beds and posters on the wall. A dark navy-blue color covers one wall while the others are a sandy brown. The spread on the bed is a deep plaid, keeping the room masculine while void of any other personal affects.

"Each of us boys had a roommate. Stone and Clay. Me and Knox. Sebastian and Ford." I chuckle recalling the antics of my younger brothers. "Ford and Sebastian never got along as kids. Funny how they married sisters."

Genie only smiles when I glance over at her, but her eyes are aimed at the floor. "Has today been too difficult?" Slowly, she lifts her gaze. "My mother might be saucy, but she's alive to be saucy."

And my mother is gone.

"Which is all the more reason *your* mother should appreciate you, Genie. You're smart and talented. Creative. You have a strong sense of what you want." I've been doing some research on her company. "And you're beautiful and kind."

"Still, I'm sorry she behaved how she did. I'm sorry for all of it."

"Don't apologize for them. Please, nothing earlier was your fault."

Forgiveness, Stone said. I'm not ready to forgive Genie's mother or Heather or Tate. Resentment is a battle. Right now, it is winning.

I watch as Genie glances around the room as if looking for something.

"Ghosts in every corner," I state, but then realize how wrong I am. This new, improved room is another reminder that this house has changed. My siblings' opinions have changed, or at least Stone's has. Love is also running a victory lap around many of my brothers.

Genie steps closer to the bed where I remain sprawled out like an angsty teen, having tossed myself down on the mattress. She lifts a knee to the edge of the bed but doesn't sit.

I continue to ramble. "Flint and Violet. My parents' names. Appropriate as he was hot under the collar and quick to spark. But my mother? She was soft and gentle. Sweet. God, she loved to laugh." My brows crease. "Like you."

Instantly, I envision my mother running her hand around my younger face, much like Mavis does to Dutton or Halle does to her son, Tim. And next, I see Genie doing the same thing to a little boy that looks like her. Large brown eyes, expressive and carefree. His laughter contagious. His smile wide.

Blinking, I shake the thought, reminded Genie is convinced she'll never have children.

"There once was a woman named Violet," she says softly, reaching for my hand. "Her favorite material was eyelet."

My brows press together. *What's eyelet?*

"She was sweet and kind. Miss her all the time."

My eyes widen at the rhyme in Genie's words. A strange rhythm to them.

"Now she's a heavenly starlet."

"Firefly," I whisper, feeling my shoulders relax, the tension seeping from my limbs.

"It's a limerick, almost. In honor of your mother." Genie watches me a second. "Don't make her into a ghost haunting you, baby. She's an angel. That's what I tell myself about my father."

Other than her story about her father and the gravy boat, Genie doesn't mention him much.

"Tell me more about your dad." Still holding her hand, I squeeze her fingers. Genie only jostles my arm and shakes her head, dismissing *that* conversation.

"As for your father." She sighs. "Don't let him win, Judd. You are not him. Or anything he said you were. Or whatever it is about him that keeps you to yourself."

In my home. Separated from my family. Afraid to love.

I nod, hearing what she's saying but not ready to process it. Between Stone and Genie, I'm all over the place.

"Let's think about something else today." *Mother's Day be damned.*

"What would you like to think about?"

"You." I narrow in on Genie's face. The pertness of her nose. The sweet puff of her lips. The gleam in her eyes.

"What about me?" she asks, her face blushing sweetly.

"Honestly?" I arch a brow as my thoughts rapidly shift to something dirty that will instantly change my mood.

"Of course."

"I want to go down on you."

"What?" Genie chokes, the atmosphere of the room going from depressing to desperate. My mouth is already watering at the idea of tasting her sweetness. Hearing her moans. Feeling her tug my hair as she loses control.

"You consume my thoughts, firefly. Your scent. Your sounds. The taste of you." And I want to get lost in the reality of her body, not just the fantasies in my head.

"Judd." Genie fans her face, signaling I need to stop talking, but I have more instructions to give.

"Lock the door, firefly," I say, jackknifing up on the bed and removing my glasses. "Then I want you to sit on my face." I want to feel the weight of her around me. Be smothered in her fragrance. Taste all her essence.

"Here? Now?" Genie chokes on a laugh while I lay back down, placing my hands behind my head.

"I've never had sex in this room." Never kissed a girl in here either. The only girl who's been present was Genie Webster in my head with fantasies of doing just what I'm asking of her.

"Judd Sylver, as tempting as you are, I am not sitting on your face with your family downstairs." Her tone is stern but laced with strangled laughter

I pout. "How would you feel about making out?" Maybe I can live out at least one fantasy. All those nights dreaming of sharing a bed with Genie, kissing her dizzy.

"Ever do that in this room as a boy?"

"Never." The honesty seeps out with my exhale.

"So, this would be a first?" Genie tips her head, teasing me.

"Only ever fantasized about you in this room with me," I admit, staring directly at her. She's been many firsts for me.

My girl is suddenly crossing the room and locking the door, then climbing onto the bed, curling up next to me and letting me kiss her until we're both dizzy.

And all the ghosts disappear.

29

[Genie]

Later, back at Judd's, I take a shower and then search for him, finding him in the library seated at the antique writing desk. His large frame looks a little disproportionate behind the delicate furniture. Or it might be the image of a modern man wearing a white T-shirt and a backwards baseball cap sitting behind such an ornate desk.

As I enter, Judd glances up like he'd been concentrating hard on something. His large hand flattens over the paper on the desk.

"What's that?" I ask, attempting to see around his spread fingers which cover most of the page underneath them. Several balls of paper are crumpled and dropped on the floor around the desk.

"Just a little something I've been toying with." He shrugs but his voice betrays any innocence.

"Just a little something-*something*," I tease. "Let me see."

I reach forward, catching the tip of his fingers, attempting to pry them upward but Judd is stronger than me, even in his fingertips. His palm remains flat. His fingers don't budge.

My curiosity doubles down.

"Judd," I whine like a simpering child. "Let me see."

With my lip pouting and my eyelids batting, Judd finally relents.

"Earlier, you spouted off a limerick about my mother, and I wanted to repay the favor. Did you know today is National Limerick Day?"

I'm surprised that *he* knows the occasion. Edward Lear is credited with popularizing the limerick poem and May twelfth is his birthday. Typically, the five-line poems are whimsical, and a bit raunchy, and sometimes even nonsense.

And Judd is writing one for me.

"Can I read it?" A touch of warmth fills me. *Judd wrote me a poem.*

"It's not very good," he defends, keeping his voice low and gaze downward.

"But it's about me," I flirt. "So, it must be great."

My playful comment brings Judd's head upward and his lips tip up in a hint of a smile. His eyes flash like the crackle before a summer shower. One welcome and refreshing and desperately needed after a long dry spell.

Judd will be my undoing.

Cautiously, he lifts one finger at a time, as if pulled upward by an invisible string, before removing his hand.

I snatch up the unicorn lined paper, smiling to myself.

He wrote me a poem *and* it's on this special paper. I read the poem once, then a second time more slowly.

. . .

THERE ONCE WAS a woman named Firefly.
*   Her spirit was bubbly and spry.*
*   Her presence, shiny and bright,*
*   She lit up my loneliest nights.*
*   Now, I don't want to say goodbye.*

"I'M A BIT RUSTY. I haven't attempted a poem since I was eleven," he says, reminding me of his past poem-writing experience.

Clutching the paper to my chest, I stare over the desk at him, sensing what this means for him while expressing my own sentiments.

"No one has ever written me a poem."

No one has ever looked at me the way he does.

No one has ever made me feel the things I do when I'm around him.

And I'm not certain *I* can say goodbye.

"It's beautiful." My eyes prickle with tears brought on over-whelming emotions. I don't want to leave him.

As I round the desk, Judd scoots back the chair. I slip onto his lap, circling my arms around his neck while he casually wraps his arms around my waist.

"Let me see." I hum. "There once was a man named Judd." I focus my eyes on his.

"He made my heart go thud-thud."

The corner of Judd's mouth quirks upward again.

"He is handsome and strong. And his beep-beep is long."

"*Beep-beep*," Judd mouths before he chuckles, the sound jostling me on his lap.

"And he knows how to blossom my bud." I laugh, knowing the line doesn't make sense, but not a bad limerick for off the cuff.

Suddenly, I'm lifted when Judd stands. He spins us and my back hits the sliding ladder leaning against the bookshelves. My backside balances on a rung while my feet rest on a lower one.

When Judd pulls away, I cling to him, afraid I'll fall forward.

Then his mouth is on mine, pressing me back. The poem is still in my hand, and I release it, letting the paper drift to the floor while Judd pins me to the ladder. His broad body holds me in place as my breasts crush against his chest. My hands are in his hair. His palms cup my face. And he kisses me like it's his superpower.

"You make my heart go thud-thud, too, firefly."

I hum as his mouth meets mine again, scattering my thoughts. His lower body wedges between my legs, spreading them farther apart. Judd bends a little, lining us up so his thickness meets my core but too many layers of clothing separate us.

Why haven't we had sex yet?

He shifts his hips, rocking against me, and I purr against his mouth. Back and forth he moves, until he's hastily lifting the hem of his T-shirt which I wear and swiping his knuckles over the damp center of my underwear. I hadn't bothered with shorts after my shower, thinking we'd curl up on the couch together. This is ultimately better.

"I don't want you to go," Judd hums in my ear before moving to my neck, sucking at my jaw, nipping at my chin. "Stay with me a little longer."

Longer than ten days? Longer than tomorrow? Could Judd want forever? The thought hits me so hard, I gasp, but he's also slid his fingers around my boy-cut panty and runs his knuckles over bare skin, sensitive and damp with desire.

"Judd." I whimper. How does this man take me from zero to sixty in less than a minute? "I want you inside me." Give me something to always remember you by. Give me *more*.

Judd pauses on his kissing spree, stopping at my collarbone a second before lifting his head. His fiery blue eyes stare into mine. "Not yet, firefly."

Before I can protest, he kisses me hard again, sweeping swiftly into my mouth with his tongue. He moves to my neck, sucking and nipping at the tender flesh once more.

I tip back my head, tapping it lightly against a ladder rung behind me.

"Hold on, firefly," he whispers, removing my arms from his neck and setting my hands above me to cling to a higher rung. Then Judd drops to his knees, taking my underwear with him as he lowers.

Precariously stretched on this library ladder, I'm too blissed out to move.

Judd's head is between my thighs, one leg draped over his shoulder. His tongue against that nub of nerves. His mouth sucks at me. I'm completely at Judd's whim in this position, and I never want to move. Like a flower pressed into a book, I'm pinned in place, preserved forever in this moment.

Except, Judd is my keepsake.

This man has given me so much in such a short time. The answers to long-held questions and new truths. He's shared me with his family and other important people in his life. He's proud of me and what I've accomplished, and he's taken me to new levels of arousal.

Couple goals. Never lose one another.

Tears well again. The combination of his mouth on me and the fullness of my heart. It's too much and yet I selfishly want more.

Judd's tongue flicks and I'm drawn back to the moment. He hums against me, and I fall apart.

My orgasm comes on like the snap of a book closing at the end of a chapter. When you're anxious to continue the story but just need another minute to process what's happened so far. I cry out as I shatter, clinging to the ladder and Judd takes me over the edge and into unchartered waters.

I've never felt like this before.

Exposed in an unfamiliar way, the sensation is not just my current position, spread wide and dripping, legs trembling, but with Judd overall. The things he does to me. How I feel about him. I want . . .

More. More. More.

The thudding rhythm plays on repeat. An exciting, frightening, marching beat. One I'm afraid to get comfortable hearing.

With a final kiss to my core, one that's tender, almost loving, Judd leans away.

I cup his chin as he stands, kiss him quick and thoroughly, then release the ladder and glide down to the floor.

"Genie?" Judd chokes around my name as I spread my knees wide around his feet and hastily tug down his jeans. With the denim and his boxer briefs pooled at his ankles, I squeeze Judd's thick shaft, marveling at the length and weight of such a magnificent cock. He hisses when I lick up the shaft, and he catches himself on the ladder rung above my head when I suck at only the tip.

Then I swallow him against my throat. With one hand on his hip, I steady myself and work him in and out of my mouth.

More. More. More.

With both his hands on the ladder, Judd gently rocks forward, using my mouth like I envision him entering me. Filling me up. Making me whole.

Not yet, he'd said.

Why wait? Tomorrow might be our last day, but I can't think about that yet.

With Judd in my mouth, the winter mint fragrance of him mingles with a sexy, musky scent that surrounds me. I breathe him in. Drink him in. Until he surges forward, tapping the back of my throat and then pulls back only enough to give me a breath.

Then Judd is spilling down my throat with a loud groan. Glancing up at his strained neck, his face pinched in ecstasy, I wonder if I can stay.

What would *more* look like?

30

———

[Genie]

Today is the big day. The reason I came to Sterling Falls in the first place. While I'd hoped for a better outcome with my mother, giving in to her request to attend the Buttercup Society Garden Party and lingering for an entire week to spend Mother's Day with her, the real purpose of my visit is today.

And my mother didn't bother to remember.

While Judd and I spent the night in his bed, learning ticklish places and exploring other ways to please one another, I feel off in the morning. The day feels like any other day when it shouldn't and it's going to be a long one. The energy around me is a spiral of melancholy.

"Good morning," I greet Judd as he stands in his kitchen making coffee. He's perfected my almond milk and honey mixture better than even I make the morning brew. He woke early, running through a workout regime that complements his boxing practice. He's very disciplined.

"Hello, firefly." He steps over to me, cupping the side of my neck and kissing me.

Couple goals. This.

Only, today, I have somewhere I need to be. "I'm going to head into town for a little while this morning. I have . . . something to do." The explanation is vague even to my ears but I'm not ready to share this date's significance. I don't want Judd to pity me.

"Want company?"

Yes. "Thanks, but I won't be long."

Judd watches me, his gaze assessing. "You'll be back, right?" The question is meant as a tease but there's a tremor to his voice. I promised I wouldn't disappear. I'd never leave without saying goodbye.

"I'll be back." I offer him a reassuring smile.

Today is the day I'm supposed to head back to Knoxville, and we haven't discussed what Judd asked last night.

Stay with me a little longer.

I don't know how that would work and it's not something I can tackle yet.

When I enter the Curmudgeon Bakery, I hadn't considered Sebastian Sylver might be present as the owner and head baker of this small-town establishment. He does a double take upon seeing me and greets me before I reach the display counter.

"Hey, Genie." Sebastian wipes his hands on the apron tied around his waist. "What can I get you?"

The bakery is bustling but I'm quick to spot what I'd hoped he'd have at the ready.

"I'll take one of those." I point at a vanilla cupcake with a thick swirl of white frosting on top plus an overload of confetti sprinkles. "To go, please."

"Birthday cake cupcake, coming up." Sebastian retrieves the delicacy and gingerly sets it in a plastic container.

"Is it *your* birthday?" His tone is all tease.

When I don't answer, he glances up, catching me chewing on my lower lip. His expression turns stern. "If it's your birthday, why are you buying *one* cupcake? Better question is, why isn't Judd picking this up?"

I hold the intensity of Sebastian's stare only so long before I sheepishly glance to the side. "Uhm. He doesn't know it's my birthday."

Sebastian folds his arms over his chest and narrows his eyes. He looks like a man who has led a hard life before turning into a big softy for bakery items, and his wife and children. His jaw ticks once before he says, "You and Judd keeping birthdays from one another for some reason?"

I won't admit I don't know when Judd's birthday is, so I shrug. "It's not a big deal."

"Every birthday is a big deal." Sebastian continues to eye me, as if reading the truth. "Even if it isn't the happiest."

He's guessed correctly. My birthday doesn't hold the fondest of memories. The date is a reminder of one of my biggest mistakes.

"How much do I owe you?" I ask, while retrieving my wallet from my bag.

"Happy Birthday." Sebastian slides the plastic container closer to me, implying this is his gift.

"Thanks," I whisper, picking up the package. I turn toward the door and then turn back to Sebastian, needing one more favor from him. "Promise me you won't tell Judd."

Sebastian tips up his chin. "Not good at keeping secrets anymore. They cause too much trouble."

From what I've learned, Sebastian knows a thing or two about trouble, so I won't ask him to go against his principles.

Instead, I nod and leave.

WHEN I ARRIVE at a roadside scenic viewpoint, I take a seat on the short stone wall lining the gravel parking spaces. Taking a deep breath, I glance out at the mountain view. The forest is awake in a variety of vibrant greens. The air is crisp with the scent of pine and wood and the fresh scent of something bursting from the earth. Life is blooming all around me.

With no one else present, I'm able to hold a private conversation with the trees.

"It's my birthday, Dad. The big four-oh." Still in its container, I hold the cupcake in my lap and stare down at the generous swirl of frosting. "I think you'd be proud of me. I've accomplished so much."

I reflect on attending business school and taking art classes on the side, finding my true passion and a place for my quirky girl designs and my love of organization. At least, the organization of dates.

"Big day today," I whisper. "But an even bigger date is coming." The potential sale of my company. For twelve years, I've been my own boss, and it's been rewarding in so many ways. My time is mine. My schedule, too. However, I don't know what's next, or at least, how to handle working beneath others again as I will no longer fully be in charge. I'll be a creative designer, and nothing more. The idea is bittersweet.

"Anyway, I just wanted to share the news," I explain.

And tell you, again, how sorry I am, Daddy.

Sorry that you aren't here. That you didn't see me march to my own beat.

"I met someone," I announce to the trees because my dad isn't buried in one place. His ashes were dust in the wind over this peak. "You'd really like him." I swallow hard. "For me."

Judd is patient and kind. He respects me and defends me. He wants me on some level, cherishing me when we're together. Maybe, he even thinks of me when we're apart.

If I kept people in my life, I'd keep him. Instead, I tend to lose them, like my father. Like my mother.

I'm forty and alone, and a bit iffy about my future. Then, I glance at the amethyst ring on my left hand.

Would being married be that bad? Not every day would be perfect, but overall, marriage might be nice. Having a partner in life. Sharing the days, both specialty ones and the mundane. Cuddling with someone at night and continuing to discover what makes each of us happy. Growing together, like Judd's garden. Weathering any storm hand-in-hand.

Perhaps that's been the issue for my mother. She never found a hand that fit hers. Maybe my father hadn't even been it for her. Her numerous marriages might have been the desperate search to find a love that doesn't sour; however, her rigid expectations have made everyone fall short. She is hard and bitter, and everything I don't want to become.

And I am *not* her. Love doesn't come with a manual or guidelines. It doesn't fit in a box, or march to less rhythm, or force itself into an atrocious yellow dress. Love does not restrict or belittle.

Love is being tossed into a cool lake or found when lost or cuddled in a storm. Love is quiet nights reading and warm afternoons talking. Love is being honest and ink on skin and hearts marked with memories that can never be replaced.

Love is . . . Judd.

The revelation isn't shocking. Like the flicker of a candle, it's enlightening.

"Happy birthday to me," I whisper and lift the cupcake container, like an offering to the sky, like a toast when I don't drink champagne because of this day.

"My wish would be that you were here to celebrate." I blow a kiss to the sky, hopeful that heaven exists and my dad is up there hanging with the entity that created the universe.

Then I bow my head and smile weakly to myself. I don't know that I've ever believed in fate until ten days ago when Judd Sylver stood in the corner of my mother's living room, a bit anxious, a lot handsome, and waiting on me when I didn't even know he'd be present.

Could Judd Sylver be my destiny?

Sitting on the side of a different mountain pass, I open the plastic container and take a bite of the birthday cake cupcake, humming at Sebastian Sylver's ability to create such a treat.

Then I make a second birthday wish.

Couple goals. Keeping Judd as my other half in a couple.

When I return to Judd's place, I school my expression and try to tap into a happier place inside me. I'm forty. I've reached a milestone some people don't see.

Judd sent me a text that he went to see Simon. Earlier, he didn't mention asking me to stay, and I didn't want to bring it up, afraid he didn't mean to say it. Between the poem and the moments of passion afterward, maybe he simply misspoke. Asking him would resolve my doubt but my mind is already mush because of the date. Initially, I intended to leave Sterling Falls after a birthday celebration with my mother; however, as that moment didn't happen, I find I'm stalling.

Taking a seat at Judd's dining room table, I decide to work through the day, getting lost in some art. I have a good mental picture of my new Quirky Adventure Girl, the one who appreciates the outdoors a little more than my original girls who are more into plants and books. I'm eager to get started on some sketches.

With my laptop open and the sunlight streaming into the room, Judd enters the space with his laptop in hand.

"Simon missed you today," Judd says, his gaze lowered, like he has more to say but doesn't know where to start.

"I'm so sorry *I* missed him." I mean it. Simon is important to Judd. They often text one another and Judd checks in with Trudy to see if Simon needs anything. He's told me more about what he does for the young boy and how he feels about him, and I'm sorry I missed out on time spent with him.

However, I had a reason to be alone for a while.

"Mind if I join you?"

The rectangular table is dark wood with six dining chairs but suddenly I'm reminded of library tables. The arrangement of tables between the mass of bookshelves.

"This seat is open," I announce, pointing to the one to my left as I sit at the head of the table.

Judd takes the chair, his back to the bright windows, and opens his laptop. Hardly a minute passes before he's glancing at my paper sketch pad and some notes I've made.

"What are you working on?"

"Another Quirky Girl." I hear the lift in my voice as I sit straighter in my chair and wiggle my shoulders. The one thing I love to talk about most are my calendars. Knowing Judd will listen, fully engaged, I explain my vision, share my initial sketches, and tell him a few of my ideas for specialty dates.

"National Love a Tree Day is coming soon. May sixteenth. And National Tree Day is in early August which is different from National Arbor Day which takes place in April." I continue to tell him additional dates related to the great outdoors and explain my research for even more novelty dates to include.

At one point, Judd's bare toes connected with mine beneath the table and we hold that hidden connection throughout my chattering.

Judd is attentive as I suspected he'd be, asking questions, offering suggestions, until finally he says, "I don't think you should sell."

"What?" I stammer. I could instantly be on the defense. *It's my company, I can do what I want with it,* but I'm also curious why Judd is saying such a thing.

"You have great ideas, and you can do this on your own."

"I can't—"

"You just need help. Some assistance and maybe some financial resources."

I'm already shaking my head, but Judd is holding up a hand. "I can help."

"I'm not taking your money." The moment I speak, I realize he isn't actually offering.

Judd simply smiles, though. "Let me look at your financials. We can form a budget and make a plan. You might not have that lump payout Greetings Ambassador is promising but you'd still have control, and over time, you might benefit more from that. You'd have longevity. Maybe even a legacy."

His suggestion isn't about money but about keeping my brand. Plus, Judd has told me how he's good at investing. He helped Sebastian set up his bakery and he keeps Sylver Seed & Soil in good financial standing. He's mentioned helping other small businesses in the area as well, even a non-profit one called Art's Studio.

"I don't know." I set my elbow on the table and drag my fingers through my short hair, before holding them on the back of my head. It's a lot to consider, and today I just want to draw.

Sensing my frustration or hesitation, Judd sits back, watching me. "Okay. Well, I'm here for whatever you need." The way he continues to look at me, I sense he means more than just looking at my business spread sheets. Judd could be the moral support I want, both in business and beyond.

Eventually, he glances back at his open laptop. "When we were in high school, I pictured us like this."

I press off my elbow and stare back at him.

"Hanging out in the library together. Studying or talking. Just anything."

"Anything?" I quirk a brow.

"Well, I also might have thought about clearing the books off the table and ravishing you on top of it like I am now, but—"

"I'm open to ravishing," I blurt, glancing at the sketch pad and laptops between us.

Judd leans forward again, while forcing his chair backwards. He's reflective another minute. "Laptops are expensive."

Then he stands, takes my hand and walks me to the other end of the table.

"Would it sound strange if I told you how turned I am by how rational you just were?" I ask, as he takes my hips and lifts me to the table.

"Only if I can tell you I've had a hard on since listening to you talk about national days on a calendar."

Oh my God, I could love this man.

And when his mouth lands on mine, and he presses my body back, I forget my name and the significance of this date for a little while, especially when his fingers and lips work their magic.

His tongue dips and his fingers spread me. Every time Judd touches me is an adventure. Although his mouth has been on me before, his tongue will move in a different way or his lips will add new pressure, and I'm taken over the edge in a manner I haven't experienced before.

Judd is voracious today and as soon as I'm crying out, he's tugging me to the edge of the table and flipping me over.

With my breasts pressed to the warm wooden tabletop,

heated from the sunlight streaming into the dining nook, my nipples are hard peaks. My palms streak against the surface as Judd tugs me backward, then hitches my leg upward so one knee rests on the table. My other foot is tiptoed on the floor. I'm open and exposed to Judd in a new way, and I hold my breath anticipating what he'll do next to me.

What I do not expect is the heat of his length suddenly pressed between the crease of my backside. His stiffness wedged in place, then sliding up and down until he positions himself between my legs.

"So wet for me, firefly," he hums near my ear as his hand slips around to my front and his fingertips flick my clit.

"Judd," I cry out.

I can feel the tip of him near my entrance as his fingers circle that sensitive nub, already ripe and swollen from his mouth moments ago.

"God, Genie," he grunts, running his length back and forth against damp folds. He's so close and I tip my hips, wanting him closer. Wanting him to fill me.

"Come inside me," I cry out, wanting him to enter me.

Judd groans, fisting himself to prevent his dick from diving in. "Not yet."

Frustration hits me, and I whimper, "No!"

He's so close. He could just slip inside me. Complete me.

But Judd doubles down his attention, using the tip of his cock at my clit, teasing me, torturing me, until soon enough, I'm crying out his name again, thumping my palm against the table as I let go.

I preen as I release against his tip, arching my back and jutting up my backside, until Judd quickly pulls himself from between my legs, laying his length against my lower back and jetting over me.

Sprawled out on the table, cheek pressed to the top, I breath heavily. My body relaxed. My mind a void.

"You look so beautiful with me spilled on your skin." He runs his fingertip through the mess, like he's painting a tattoo on my back. Admiring a masterpiece.

Oddly, the motion feels like the shape of a heart is being drawn on my flesh. He's marked me again.

Happy birthday to me after all.

31

[Genie]

"We should go out tonight," Judd eventually states, after our round of oral tag on the dining room table and a shower that included naked hugs.

I'm still puzzled why Judd and I aren't having sex. The final act. The full enchilada. But I don't complain as I'm more or less completely satisfied by the attention he's given my private parts.

However, I am surprised when he suggests we go out when I was looking forward to possibly snuggling into his side and eating my body weight in popcorn while we watched a movie.

We still haven't discussed how I should be leaving tonight.

He isn't asking me to stay. I'm not suggesting I go.

"We haven't had a proper date," he adds.

A proper date? Judd and I have had tons of private moments. Memory-making moments. But a date implies he wants to take me out in public. He wants to be seen with me.

"What did you have in mind?" I ask as Judd runs a towel

over my overly-sensitive body, then wraps the soft terry cloth around me, tucking it tight above my breasts.

"Just something casual." He purses his lips.

If I knew Judd better, I'd say he's playing at something. But I can't read his expression. His stoic reserve is firmly in place.

"But wear something that makes you feel pretty. I'm partial to the green dress with polka dots but wear *your* favorite."

I smile at the suggestion Judd has a favorite out of my clothing.

"Okay," I whisper, suddenly shy while thrilled at the prospect of a date with Judd. Maybe he's simply making up for that failed prom date all those years ago.

Somehow, I doubt this thought, especially when Judd parks in downtown Sterling Falls and walks us hand-in-hand to Milton Roadhouse. He opens the door like the gentleman he is, but then he body-blocks me, which I find rather strange, and almost plow into him.

"Judd." I chuckle as I catch myself, feeling the strength of his back muscles and heat of his skin through his shirt. He's actually a little sweaty through the fabric when it isn't that hot outside.

He steps to the side, and I'm hit with a resounding, "Surprise!" A chorus of cheers and clapping follows, and I'm stunned into silence, staring wide-eyed at the display before me.

Several tables are pressed together, surrounded by the adults in Judd's family. Sebastian and Enya. Knox and Halle. Ford and Cadence. Clay and Mavis. Vale. Stone in his sheriff's uniform.

And a giant pair of balloons in a four and a zero in bright green, my favorite color.

I blink back the well of tears blurring my vision, both shocked by this amazing surprise and guilty that I hadn't told Judd.

"What did you do?" I whisper, turning toward him.

"Happy birthday, firefly." He leans down and kisses the corner of my mouth without pressing for answers about why I hadn't told him.

Turning back to the group, I clasp my hands beneath my chin and stare. "This is too much." And yet I'm overjoyed. My heart is too full.

I spin back toward Judd. "Thank you, baby." *Thank you for everything.* I tip up on my toes and wrap my arms around his neck, tugging him to me and holding on for dear life. Judd hugs me back in the same manner, squeezing me hard to his chest.

"I love—" I choke on what almost popped out of my mouth. Pulling back, I look Judd directly in the eyes. "I love this. This is amazing."

If Judd is disappointed, he doesn't say, but his body language suggests otherwise. His shoulders fall while his hand comes to my lower back.

"Make all the birthday wishes, Genie. I hope every one of them comes true."

Ask me to stay. Say that you love me. Say you can't live without me.

Three wishes. Each a tall order.

Breaking free from Judd, I step up to each of the girls, hugging them all in turn along with Judd's brothers.

I'm pointed to a seat at the head of the table and two servers bring pitchers of margaritas and beer to the table.

I point at Sebastian. "You have some explaining to do." It's the only reason Judd would have discovered the significance of the day.

Judd's hand slips up my back and squeezes my nape. "*You* have some explaining to do. Why didn't you tell me?"

I shrug as I look over at him. His chair touches mine. "I didn't want to make a big deal of the day."

"But every day *is* a big deal to you. This one should have been the biggest. You're forty."

I cover Judd's mouth with my fingers. "Shh. We aren't discussing how I'm old."

"You're hardly old," he murmurs against my hand, and then moves it so he can nip at my fingertips before leaning closer to me. "And that move on the dining room table tells me you're still quite agile."

I cover his mouth again, while giggling at the reminder of how Judd satisfied my body earlier. His fingertip heart feels like it's actually etched into my lower back. His words still whisper on repeat in my head.

The memory makes me squirm.

"Okay," Cadence calls out. "Who's ready to karaoke?"

"Why would she need karaoke?" I tease, asking Judd. Cadence is a mega superstar and the last person I'd sing in front of.

However, hours later I'm on the stage, a bit blurry eyed and feeling a little loose, and deciding I can sing when I know I cannot carry a tune.

"This song is a duet," Cadence announces to the group from her position beside me in the area blocked out for a band. Today, the karaoke machine is the entertainment. "Judd?"

"I'm good from here," he calls to his future sister-in-law, and I'd call him a chicken if I didn't know it would hurt him on a deep level, even in jest.

"I got this," I state, like I know what I'm doing when I don't. I know enough about karaoke to follow the words on the prompter but that doesn't mean I can sing.

Thankfully, the song Cadence picked is more speaking-ish than singing at first, so I muddle through the lines about a country singer on the road, wandering into a bar, and latching her eyes on a cowboy. Which is when I narrow in on Judd.

In the chorus, the singer tells the cowboy he looks like he

loves her and wants to take her home, and the words hit me hard in the chest. Like I've knocked the microphone against myself.

Judd *does* look at me that way. Like he might love me. And right now, he's definitely giving me fiery eyes like he wants to take me home. Having his way with me again on the dining room table or the library ladder.

When the song finishes, I make an exaggerated curtsy and hand the microphone to Cadence. Then I skip toward Judd who stands as I near the table. I leap for him, wrapping my arms around his neck, and Judd catches me around the waist, swinging me side to side.

The motion sloshes the margaritas in my belly, and I sway a bit when he sets me on my feet. Thankfully, Judd keeps his hands on my hips to steady me.

"Looks like she wants you to take her home," someone calls out behind Judd. Sounds like Knox.

"Did you hear me, Judd?" Although I'm not certain I've asked a coherent question.

"I heard ya', beautiful." He laughs.

"Did I sing well?"

"Like a lark."

"Did I seduce you?" *Why won't he have sex with me?*

"Every day with you is a seduction."

I break into a fit of giggles and dip my head to his chest. I should put that on a calendar. Quirky Girl Seduction Calendar.

"You okay?" Judd whispers near my ear, brushing my hair around it.

"It's my birthday." I lift my head a little too fast and the room warbles.

"Yes, it is, firefly."

Yes. And firefly. Check yes, Judd.

"Want me to take you home? Or do you want to stay a little longer?"

Home. Stay longer. Checking yes.

"Would you mind if we stayed a little longer?" I'm practically dangling from Judd's neck, arms still around him but my body suddenly feels heavy, weighed down by both the day and the date.

The anniversary of my father's death. My fortieth birthday. My mother never called me.

But Judd threw me a surprise party.

"How long have you known?" I whisper. Or I think I whisper.

"Sebastian is horrible at keeping secrets."

"So, since this morning?" I'm definitely slurring. And Sebastian is a tattletale.

Judd looks at me. *Both of him.*

"We need champagne for the birthday girl," a female voice says somewhere near the table. Sounds like Vale.

And the thought of champagne, the bubbles exploding in my mouth, the acidic aftertaste of cheap liquor. The burn going down *and* coming back up.

I burst into tears.

"Aw, fuck," someone mutters as I slip my arms from Judd's neck to cover my face.

"Looks like we're going with plan A, baby," Judd says, swooping me up. "I'm taking you home."

And that's the last I remember of the night.

∾

"Hey," I hear as my eyelids ping open. Sunlight slips into the room through the slanted blinds.

I turn my head a bit too quickly and notice Judd sitting in a black leather chair that typically rests in the corner of his room. He shifts like he slept there all night.

"How are you feeling?"

"Like the world needs to stop spinning. I want off the ride." I scrub my forehead, finding my fingers shaky. My mouth feels like I licked a cat's tail, and my skin is clammy. Slower this time, I roll my head on the pillow and stare up at the ceiling.

Judd chuckles. "Quite a party."

I turn my head in his direction again. I should thank him. The party was generous, and kind, and unwarranted, especially when I hadn't mentioned it was my birthday yesterday.

"Why didn't you tell me it was your birthday?" Judd's eyes hold that melancholy I witnessed too often upon first seeing him ten days ago.

Today marks day eleven.

I shrug, but even that motion feels like too much effort. "I just didn't want to make a big deal of it."

"But you're forty. That is a big deal."

"I'm officially over the hill, right?"

Judd's brows cinch. "What hill? You're currently on a mountain with peaks and valleys. Keep climbing or coasting."

"I meant figuratively," I snort.

"I don't." Judd slowly sits forward. "And you aren't answering my question." He pauses a second. "Did you want to be alone on your birthday?"

"I don't think anyone ever *wants* to be alone on their birthday."

"Then did you just not want to celebrate the day with me?" There's a rawness in Judd's voice as he lowers his eyes. Like he really believes I'd rather be by myself than with him.

We did spend the day together. A glorious afternoon where I drew new designs, discussed my business, and had two orgasms on his very sturdy dining room table. Plus, he threw me a surprise party.

"Judd, look at me," I whisper, my voice shaky as my throat is dry.

He lifts his head, his expression weary. He looks almost

boyish with his wide blue eyes. Caution is etched in the fine lines of his face.

"My birthday is always a difficult day," I begin, not really wanting to share this story, especially as I'm hungover. But I don't want Judd thinking my decision yesterday was about him.

My birthday is a me-problem.

Slowly, I press myself upright and shift the pillows to prop up my back.

"The night before I turned thirteen, I went to a sleepover at Heather's house. I wouldn't say we were friends. We were never friends, but we do have our mothers' friendship in common and that meant sometimes we were forced together. This particular night, I hadn't wanted to go to Heather's. My birthday was the following day. My mom pushed the agenda, and I'd had a bad feeling about it all day. Not like a stomachache but a persistent, gnawing sensation in my gut."

I fist my hand near my belly and swallow, feeling the lump in my throat from both the sadness this tale brings, and the awful reminder of all I drank *last* night.

"My parents had been fighting a lot. At first, I don't think I paid enough attention or thought the arguments were out of the norm. My mother told me couples disagreed. But the *disagreements* seemed to grow more consistent."

I lower my eyes and pluck at the blanket over my legs. My skin feels clammy for a new reason. I rarely tell this story. I've never dated someone long enough to delve this deeply into my past. Into the recesses of my history and my broken heart.

"That night, our dining room table was set with candles and flowers. I assumed my parents were planning to have a romantic evening with me away. Maybe they'd talk to each other instead of fight."

I swallow heavily as the thickness in my throat grows.

"At Heather's house, she'd stolen a bottle of champagne from her parents' bar area. She said it was for my birthday. It wasn't like she held the bottle to my lips and made me drink, but she did make me feel small when I said I didn't want to try the stuff." I toss my voice to mimic Heather's. "*But you're becoming a teen. You didn't want to be a baby anymore, do you?*"

Judd's eyes narrow as if he knows exactly how Heather made me feel. *Like a coward.*

I shrug. "I didn't really care what she thought of me, but I was also twelve. There were other girls present. Turning thirteen *is* a huge deal, so I drank. And drank. And drank."

I swallow thickly as if I can feel the bubbles on my tongue and taste the slightly acrid aftertaste of champagne. "I can't blame Heather. She didn't force me but . . . peer pressure, I guess."

I risk a glance at Judd, who leans forward with his elbows braced on his knees and his fingers steepled at his lips.

"Anyway." I exhale, blinking at the burn in my eyes. "I didn't feel well. I wanted to go home. I called my mom first, but she didn't answer. Then, I called my dad."

I turn my head and stare at the window where the blinds are partially open, allowing filtered morning light into the room. "He sounded tired. He also sounded like he'd been drinking." The slur in his voice only comes into my memories when I look back. That night, I'm not certain I could identify the sound.

I glance back at Judd. His shoulders are stiff. His eyes wide.

"He said he'd pick me up." The worn-down whisper of his voice floats through my head. His promise sluggish. *I'll be there, Genie.*

With my eyes focused on Judd, he blurs before me. "He never made it."

Suddenly, I'm encompassed by Judd's arms and pressed into his chest. Only, his closeness overwhelms me. The hangover. The memory of champagne in my throat. The slosh of margaritas in my belly.

I press Judd back, needing space. I'm suddenly too warm and if I don't get some air, I'm going to be revisiting my fortieth-birthday drinks.

Judd leans away, slipping his hands down my arms before resting them on either side of my legs.

"I'm so sorry, firefly."

I peer up at him. "There's more."

Judd runs his thumb beneath my eye, catching a lone tear.

"At the funeral, Heather found me in the ladies' room, sitting alone, crying. She told me she didn't know why I was upset. My father was leaving my mother anyway. He was leaving me."

"Son of a bitch." Judd hisses.

I choke. "A twelve-year-old whom I was never friends with was telling me my parents planned to divorce."

The bile in my throat reaches dangerous levels and I swallow hard. "My parents never had that romantic dinner. They had a fight. My dad left. He might have told my mother he was leaving her. She denies it. I don't even know where he was when I called him, but he'd answered his phone, and he said he would come pick me up."

I whisper, "Or was he only saying that? Was he really leaving?" I glance back up at Judd. "I'll never know because he crashed into a tree that night. His car was found on a road leading out of town, not in the direction of Heather's house."

Rumors circulated that my father *had* been drinking. Others suggested he swerved to miss an animal on the darkened road. The gossip about my father's intention to leave my mother trickled around us.

Maybe he'd been coming to get me after all.

Maybe his car spun in the opposite direction.

Maybe he'd have gone home and changed his mind about leaving.

But deep down, I know the truth. In my gut. In my heart.

"He didn't want me." *Or my marching beat*. My voice breaks and I'm in Judd's arms again.

This time, I melt into him. I'm tired, so very tired, and it wasn't only the hangover and turning forty that drained me. All these years later, the events on the eve of my birthday are still a mystery and have forever marred the date. Every other date on the calendar is special, except my birthday.

"I can't stand the taste of champagne," I whisper into Judd's shoulder. "Even looking at a bottle of it makes me shaky."

And I hate Heather Remington. I shouldn't have heard what everyone else already seemed to know at my father's funeral. I shouldn't have heard it from her of all people.

And if I hadn't gone to Heather's house. If I hadn't drank champagne. If I hadn't called my dad . . . he might still be alive, even if he left us behind.

I don't have tears left for something that happened twenty-seven years ago, but a soul-crushing sorrow fills me.

"I'm sorry, Judd," I say. "But I'm gonna be worthless today." I pull out of his arms and slip down beneath the covers.

Which Judd sweetly pulls up over my shoulders and tucks around me.

"Can I get you anything? Do anything for you?" He hesitates. "I could stay. We don't have to talk. I'll just be here for you."

I shake my head and close my eyes. "I just need to sleep this off." I attempt a soggy smile. "Can't handle my liquor anymore. I hear it's a sign of getting old."

Judd swipes his hand over my hair and cups the back of my neck. "You'll never grow old, firefly."

I huff. Everyone grows older.

I can only hope I grow bolder, and wiser.

Like telling Judd Sylver how I feel. I think I love him.

32

[Genie]

At some point during the day, I woke to find a glass of water and some Tylenol on the nightstand. Later, I found Judd napping beside me, holding my hand. I hated myself for the scene I'd made the night of my birthday—bursting into tears like a drunk sorority girl—and learning about my outburst from concerned texts from the women in Judd's family. I also hate how I'd wasted a day away from Judd.

The day *after* my birthday hangover, a note on lined unicorn paper rests on my bedside table when I wake.

You are cordially invited to May fifteenth which celebrates:

World Stationery Day (yay for lined paper with unicorns)

National Bring Someone Flowers Day (please enter the kitchen)
National I Love My State Parks Week – get dressed for adventure
National (surprise to be revealed later) Day
National Chocolate Chip Day

I GIGGLE at the idea that Judd has planned out a day that celebrates the novelty of the day. His love language must include quality time together, and I'm grateful for the action. At some point, we really need to talk but, apparently, today will not be that day.

His thoughtfulness astounds me. A surprise birthday party and now this.

Rushing to the kitchen like a child eager for Christmas morning, the largest bouquet I've ever seen rests on the island countertop. The floral collection contains white roses, light chrysanthemums, and lily of the valley plus green eucalyptus and something else green and feathery.

"Did you know lilies of the valley are the flower for the month of May?"

As I'm kneeling on a stool to sniff the flowers displayed in the large vase, I almost fall off it when Judd startles me with this information. I somehow missed him seated on the couch in an athletic shirt and loose-fitting hiking shorts. He looks delicious as ever, while he casually hitches his arm along the back of the couch.

Lilies of the valley are also known as forget-me-nots. I will never ever forget Judd and the incredible time we've had together.

I swivel on my knees, clutching his handwritten invitation to my chest. "What is all this?" He has already turned my birthday upside down, hosting a surprise party when I hadn't even told him it was my birthday. He took a day that started sad and lonely into a family affair where I felt more love than I feel I deserve.

"You didn't have a proper birthday."

More birthday surprises? I'm nearly giddy, but still I ask, "Why May fifteenth?"

"Why *not* May fifteenth?" he teases, pressing himself up to stand next to the couch. "I spelled out all we'll celebrate today." He points to the invitation I'm still holding to my chest. "Let's just celebrate a day."

"Celebrate a day," I whisper. "I like that."

Judd steps around the couch, coming close enough he leans over me and grasps the back of the high back stool. "And I . . . like you."

Judd's smile forms against my mouth, and he kisses me, sweet and long, reminding me that we didn't kiss yesterday. I missed his kisses, and I slowly came to the realization I don't think I want to go a day without kissing him.

Couple goals. Kiss Judd every day.

When Judd pulls back, his eyes are heated. His gaze roams down my chin to my chest. I eventually showered yesterday and changed into my own pajamas which include a silky set with a thin-strapped tank top and shorts.

Judd runs a fingertip along my collarbone. "There's room for addendums to the day, of course." His voice lowers, turning husky and deep. "I only want to please you, Genie."

I hum. "I can think of several ways that can be done."

"Let's start the day with breakfast."

Assuming he means food, I deflate a little bit while definitely hungry for something healthy. Until I'm hoisted off the stool and into Judd's arms, forcing me to wrap around him like a vine up a pole. I squeal as he takes a giant step over the back of his couch, while still holding onto me, and then we lower to the soft leather.

Judd shifts until he's on top of me and his weight blankets

me as he kisses me senseless. Moving down to my neck and over to my shoulder, his large hand covers my breasts over the silky material of my tank. He plucks at one pebbled nipple while tugging down the other side of my tank top to suck at my breast.

I arch my back, sighing at the rush of excitement his tongue causes while swirling around the peaked nub and flirting with me.

"I thought we were having breakfast," I tease as Judd shoves my tank top up and lowers his head for my belly, sucking lazily at my skin.

"I *am* having breakfast." His fingers curl into the waistband of my pajama shorts and with a swift tug, he has them down to my knees.

"Firefly," he groans, instantly noting I am not wearing underwear.

With the pajama bottoms at my knees, I bend my legs, forcing the material to my ankles, and Judd lowers down my body. He lifts one leg and hitches my ankle against the back of the couch. My other leg is gently forced to the opposite side. I'm spread wide and Judd drinks me in with his eyes before he swipes over me with a thick lap.

"I'll never have my fill of you."

I feel the same way, and I gasp in response as he dives in. Teasing me with his tongue. Flicking me with his fingers. Quickly, I'm dripping, certain to be making a mess on the leather.

"We're going to stain your couch," I warn.

"You've already made your mark. On me."

I exhale at his honesty, but I'm quickly distracted as Judd returns to his mission.

In no time, my hips are thrusting upward, and my head is tipping back. I clutch the edge of the couch cushions and let out an appreciative moan as I shatter against Judd's mouth.

May fifteenth is starting out as a very good day.

Judd startles me when he hops up to his knees and hastily works at shoving down his shorts and boxer briefs. Before me, his dick is thick, long and proudly on display with an angry vein and seeping tip.

This is it. We're going to start the day with him finally entering me, filling me whole, making us one.

Judd falls forward, catching himself with one hand beside my hip while the other fists his length. He tugs several times before dipping his lower half closer to mine.

"I want you to hold still, Genie."

I nod as I chew my lip, wondering what he intends to do to me.

"I'm still not going to enter you." His voice strains as he watches himself come closer to my center. "But I want to be close to you. Want to feel your wetness on me. I want you to soak my dick again."

Sweet succulents. For half a second, I don't know how he means that to happen other than climbing up my body for my mouth. But then, he lowers even more, lining up his thickness to press against my slick skin. Judd moves back and forth, dragging his heavy cock against sensitive folds and knocking at my tender nub like he did on my birthday, and my eyes roll back.

I move instinctively and Judd halts. His head lifts and his eyes catch on mine. I want him to enter me so badly I could cry.

"Not yet, baby. But soon. Let me have this today."

I chew my lip again and nod, letting him lead as he moves against me. The weight of his cock. The firmness of it. The tease each time he rubs against that trigger point.

"Judd," I whimper, feeling the build inside me again.

"Gonna come like this?" There's shock in his voice as he moves his gaze from my face to where he presses against me. "Gonna come with my balls kissing your clit?"

"Oh God," I groan while he drags himself higher, doing

exactly what he said, before swiping his length down my seam again.

He grunts. "Petals after a rain shower."

"You did this to me." He's the summer storm I hadn't expected.

I clutch at his lower back, desperate for him to complete the deed. "Judd," I groan again, in warning.

"Let go, Genie. Rain down on me."

I've never been one to come on command, but I break apart as Judd catches his tip on my clit. My hips thrust upward, wanting more of him, but he's quick to move.

Then he's lying his length against me, and as I'm still reveling in the high of a release, I feel the pulse of him as he lets go on my lower belly. Hot and sticky, he marks me in a delicious way. Like the ink on his skin, he's permanently etching himself on me.

Judd kisses me, sweeping his tongue inside my mouth, which is a delicious connection to distract from the disappointment of him not slipping inside me in other ways.

Eventually, he pulls back and glances down at the mess he's made. "Showering together?"

"Two birds, one bird bath?" I tease.

Judd's mouth slowly curls, hitching higher on one side before the other follows. His full smile is simply spellbinding.

"Exactly." He kisses me again, once and quick, and then presses upward, standing awkwardly with his shorts at his thighs. He helps me upright before tugging up his shorts but not latching them. Then he lifts me like he did the other night at the bar and carries me like his *future* bride to the shower.

33

[Judd]

I had not anticipated the morning going as it went, but I am not complaining about one second of exploring Genie's body, both on the couch and in the shower. The shower was more of a torturous flirtation. Genie took her damn time with the soap on my dick and around my ass. Then she hummed like she does when she breaks while I simply washed her hair.

I swear I almost gave into my *not yet* rule but I have my reasons to wait.

And I have the rest of this day planned. I want Genie to enjoy it, and I also want a do-over of her birthday. Today will be all about her, even if it is a random Wednesday in the middle of May. The day has its own significance, and as I told Genie, I plan to celebrate some of the novelties of this day, making the time extra special for her.

I want every day with her.

The adventure for this date might be a risk. I don't recall if Genie is much of a hiker but there are easy trails in the area.

As we pull into the parking lot of the local park, Genie turns in her seat. "We're going to Sterling Falls?"

The scenic falls is our claim to fame and the namesake of this town. Several legends surround the mystical water. One such tale includes drinking the water with your lover to confirm *if* they are your true love. Other legends involve a taboo relationship more than a century ago, where star-crossed lovers died in the lower river. Rumor has it her family disapproved of him, and her older brother killed her lover. She killed herself in retaliation. Some people believe you can see those fated lovers in the falls when the light hits the cascading water just right. Others say the sterling sheen is simply a mirage as silver isn't a metal found in West Virginia. Whatever you believe, the falls are beautiful and peaceful. They can be viewed by climbing to the top and looking down from a ridge, or seen from below, which is how I intend to view them with Genie.

"Yep. When was the last time you were here?"

Genie blinks. "Gosh, I don't even remember. Sometime in high school, I guess."

Whatever her forgotten memory is, I want to make a new one for her with me.

After I hop out of my truck, I retrieve a backpack filled with items for a picnic. Taking Genie's hand, I admire her once more in a pair of calf-cut leggings and a racerback tank top.

"So, we've covered World Stationery Day," I begin as we start toward the lower trail.

"Because one must celebrate lined paper with unicorns," she teases.

"Exactly." I nod, then continue. "And you received flowers this morning from somebody."

"And that *somebody* is so sweet." Genie leans into me and cups my bicep while holding my hand.

"And now, we're here to enjoy a national park."

"Is Sterling Falls in a national park?"

I shrug. *Probably not.* "Let's pretend it is." I wink.

Genie beams a smile at me, and I swear I feel like a god. She's looking at me like I created this landform just for her. If it was within my power, I'd make her a waterfall.

We chat about nothing and everything as we take the easy trail around the falls toward the base. The water spray makes the surrounding boulders slick and the giant rocks in the lower river are dangerous to cross. Still, we find a place to sit and stare at the cascade for a few minutes.

"Sometimes I forget about the hidden gems around here," Genie says.

"The falls are hardly hidden." Reaching for my backpack, I start removing items, which includes food carefully prepared in compartmentalized containers for ease in a tight space. I wish my garden was in bloom, but we've only just passed the official planting date. Still, I have cheese and meats, grapes and apple slices, plus sweet tea and water.

Genie squints into the sunshine, watching the water drop from the higher elevation. "I think you're a hidden gem, Judd."

I quickly spin to look at her. "That was . . . nice of you to say."

"You're thoughtful and considerate. You're patient and sweet. You're a rarity." She hesitates as if she has more to say but then thinks twice.

"I think you're a rarity, too, firefly."

We eat in silence as the falls can be loud while soothing. I like Genie doesn't always feel the need to fill the quiet. As a man who has lived alone a long time, I'm used to silence, but I've enjoyed her breaking the sound barrier around me. Filling it with her noises. She's like a favorite tune I want to hear on repeat.

"My parents got engaged at the base of the falls," I eventually say.

Genie's head turns sharply, and she blinks. An anxious giggle fills her throat when she says, "Judd, if you're about to propose, might I remind you I'm already wearing your ring."

"And I never officially asked you to marry me." I hadn't. I was holding out the ring, asking Genie what she thought, after I'd called her my fiancée. But I never asked *will you marry me?*

"It would be important to me to get it right." To ask her the actual question. To have her permission to ask because as far as I know Genie is still against the idea of marriage. "I want forever." With her.

But when her eyes widen and her shoulders stiffen, I worry I've frightened her.

"I just sort of settled before." I don't reference she who shall not be named. "But now, I'm much clearer on what I want." How is it a firefly in a dark room has given me such illumination? It's simple. It's Genie.

"Genie, I—"

She covers my mouth with the hand wearing my mother's ring. The fear in her eyes say everything. *Don't ask a question I don't want to know the answer to.* Or better yet, don't ask a question she doesn't want to answer.

I mumble against her palm, shifting gears. "I just want to thank you for giving me these ten days. Well, now twelve." A dozen days do not make up for decades of absence. Or even that night I didn't show up for her. Still, I'm grateful for this sliver of a second chance.

"You're welcome." She takes a deep breath and smiles. "I'm really glad I stayed as well." She clears her throat. "But I don't want to overstay my welcome. We agreed on ten days and now we're at twelve."

"You can stay as long as you like." *Stay forever*, if you wish.

Genie rubs her hands down her thighs. "I was thinking maybe I want . . . I mean, *would* . . . stay a little longer."

While I'd love a clear definition of what 'longer' means, I take it. "What's mine is yours." My home. My heart. Which hammers in my chest. Genie is staying and I heave a sigh of relief. A breath I hadn't known I'd been holding since her birthday.

After a few more minutes of silence, Genie says, "Tell me how you got named Judd. After Stone and Clay, I don't understand."

I huff and stare out at the water. "My mom tried to name everyone after something related to landscape. Stone and Clay are obvious. Knox means hill. Ford is a take on fjord, a body of water, and Sebastian means earth. Valentine was shortened to Vale, like a valley."

I narrow my eyes. "I've told you how I was supposed to be a girl, according to my father. I would have been named Judy after my mother's mother. Not necessarily a landform, and then, *surprise*, it's a boy," I mock. "My mom didn't like the name Jude, so she picked Judd."

I blow out a breath, lifting my knees and wrapping my arms around my shins. "When I was really young, Stone and Clay would tease me, saying my parents meant to name me mud." I snort dismissively. "I've just always been the outlier."

"You're not an outlier, Judd. You just march to your own beat, and I like the sound."

Genie wraps both her hands around my bicep and rests her head on my shoulder. And I lean into her, enjoying the rhythm of our hearts.

34

[Genie]

Today has been a perfect day. The invitation. The morning orgasm. The picnic. The hike.

Judd nearly gave me a heart attack when he mentioned proposals, though. Within seconds, my heart hammered, and my palms were sweaty because I wasn't certain I would say no to him.

A resounding check yes was caught in my throat.

Before, I hadn't ever found someone with staying power. I sensed a loss before a relationship had been found, and I always skated out first, before I could be hurt.

Judd has been different. He's been patient and kind, thoughtful at every turn. He's also sexy as hell, even if we haven't officially had sex.

The longer I wear his ring, the longer I want to *keep* wearing his ring, but one step at a time. Staying a little longer is an unspoken test. We've had twelve wonderful days, but I don't want that to be the honeymoon period. I still have a large decision to make with Greetings Ambassador, and although that doesn't involve a move to New York, it would involve changes.

I can only handle one shift in my life at a time.

Judd and I finish our lunch, sticking to easier topics, then we pack up and hike back to his car. I quickly learn the day isn't over as he drives us into town.

I haven't been to Sterling Falls other than my short visits to the Curmudgeon Bakery and Milton Roadhouse, so I'm a little surprised by the array of boutiques lining the main streets. However, two staples are still present: Frederick's Ice Cream Parlor and the diner which stand on opposite corners from one another.

As Judd and I walk hand-in-hand, fingers easily linked together, I pause before a women's apparel shop where a pretty, royal blue dress hangs on a mannikin in the window. Judd stops beside me.

"It kind of reminds me of my prom dress." I wistfully recall the strapless dress I'd selected with a full skirt and dismiss the heartache that dress eventually represented, especially now that I know the truth of what happened to Judd and why he didn't show.

"You should try it on," Judd prompts.

I huff a laugh. "I think I'm a little old for prom dresses."

"Is that a prom dress?" Judd eyes the strapless dress with a heart-shaped bodice and a shorter skirt that's still full at the bottom but not as whimsical as my original prom dress.

"No. It's just a special occasion dress." Simple yet fun. Not necessarily appropriate for something formal like prom, but definitely a dress for an important day.

"Today is the perfect day to get it then," Judd says.

With surprise, I glance at him, but his tone suggests he's dead serious. Tugging me toward the boutique door confirms his suggestion.

"Judd, I don't need a special occasion dress." I really don't.

"Just try it on anyway." He's already opening the door, and a tiny bell tinkles overhead to signal our entrance.

Within minutes, I'm wearing a dress I don't need, but kind of love. The heart-shape neckline and cinched waist emphasizes my breasts. I love the fullness of the skirt and that the color matches Judd's eyes.

To my surprise, Judd enters the fitting room while I'm admiring myself in the mirror.

"Judd," I whisper. "You probably shouldn't be in here."

"I just want a peek." He meets my gaze in our reflection in the mirror. "I already know what I missed, but now I can really envision it." His eyes don't leave my body, taking in the fit of the dress.

His hands join the exploration when he sets them on my hips first, coasting them down my thighs before skimming back up and along my sides, brushing at the side of my breasts.

"Looks like a good fit."

"And suddenly you're a dressmaker," I tease.

"I'm a dress expert. Especially when it comes to you in one." He runs his knuckles down my back along the zipper which sends a shiver up my spine and goosebumps erupt on my skin. He covers my shoulders next, rubbing his hands down my arms to warm me up. His mouth comes to the side of my neck, and he kisses me once before running his nose up to my ear.

"You are so beautiful," he whispers, giving me more goosebumps and visions of Judd removing this dress from me.

With that, he steps back and slips through the curtain covering the fitting room. I hadn't realized I'd been holding my breath, turned on by his appraisal and his tender caress, until he exits. He didn't touch me anywhere special and yet everywhere is humming. My flesh. My clit. My heart.

I admire the curvy fit one final time, admitting that I *feel* beautiful in a dress like this. Then I carefully remove it and hang it back on the hanger.

As I open the curtain, a salesgirl surprises me by holding out her hand. "I'll take it to the counter and wrap it up for you."

"Oh, I'm not—"

"Your fiancé already paid for it. Judd is so sweet." Whoever the girl is, she recognizes Judd like the hostess at Evergreen Terrace had, and a tiny pinch pierces my chest. But I remind myself Judd is spending this day with me. *He's* made this extra special.

I smile timidly as the girl delicately folds the dress between tissue paper and tucks it into a paper bag before handing me the new purchase. "Enjoy."

While uncertain when I'd wear such a dress, I thank the salesgirl and step out of the store to find Judd standing on the sidewalk looking at his phone. He glances up the second I hit the pavement and slips the device into his pocket.

"You didn't need to buy me a new dress."

"I wanted to." He shrugs and takes the bag from my hand, then grabs my other one to lead us down the street.

The next spot we visit is the local pharmacy that's more of an all-goods store. They have everything from a greeting card section to Sterling Falls T-shirts, plus your basic houseware needs and pharmaceutical products. The superstores are located near larger cities, so this pharmacy is for immediate needs.

Judd leads me to a hat rack covered in an array of sun hats and baseball caps, plus a few straw ones. He picks up a grass-woven cowboy hat and sets it on my head. I laugh while he sets a similarly made rancher's hat on his own.

"Perfect," he mutters, watching me as I watch him. "Happy National Straw Hat Day."

I laugh. "You're making that up."

"Nope. That's the surprise mentioned on the invitation." He

takes my hand and walks me over to the counter, where he promptly pays for two straw hats to celebrate the special day.

I'm still giddy when we walk out of the store wearing our new hats.

"One more stop to celebrate May Fifteenth Day." Judd opens the door to Frederick's Ice Cream Parlor on the corner of Main and Corner.

"Ice cream?" I question as the cool air conditioning hits us, and we saunter to the freezer counter to examine the flavor options.

Fredericks is famous for seasonal flavors like purple-tinted blackberry and pumpkin spice, but Judd has our order ready.

"Pick between chocolate chip cookie dough or mint chocolate chip. Your choice on National Chocolate Chip Day."

My smile is so wide it might actually break my cheeks. "Mint chocolate chip, of course." I hum.

"Of course. Two, please," he says to the clerk.

Despite it being late afternoon on a Wednesday, the bench outside the shop is taken. We could re-enter the place to enjoy our frozen treat at their bistro tables, but Judd leads us down the street again and out of the business district to the green square off the main streets. Once there, he plops down in the grass, and I follow.

After taking a lick of my ice cream cone, I thank him. "Today has been amazing."

"Thank you," he emphasizes. "For being amazing. It's been really fun. I've never planned a day before. Or a date, for that matter."

I still my tongue on the next lap around my ice cream. "Seriously?"

Judd told me how he and Heather often went to functions or fundraisers. Situations that were more of a collective event than an intimate activity. He'd never picked a movie or a meal, at least not in the last two and a half years.

"Seriously," Judd states before swiping at his ice cream cone with a long lick. He winks at me and the gleam in his eyes says everything. He's pleased with himself, and I'm honored to be the recipient of the meticulous planning and effort on his part to make today such a special day. He catered to my quirks and interests, celebrating them, appreciating them.

"Another first," I state, thinking back to making out in his childhood bedroom.

"Another first," Judd confirms, staring at me as he licks his ice cream. The grin on his face is easy and relaxed. His body posture matches the ease as he leans on one arm in the grass, enjoying a day in the middle of the week instead of working.

He's been many firsts for me as well.

That tongue is on the list.

But I'm certain the overwhelming possibility that I love him is at the tippy-top.

OUR CELEBRATE-THE-DAY DOESN'T END with ice cream.

At night, Judd grills us a steak dinner with fresh asparagus, and we open another bottle of sweet red wine. Judd and I hang out on his deck, sitting in lounge chairs that he pulled next to each other. I'm leaning on my side looking at him, while he sits with his back pressed into the cushion. And we talk for hours, sharing more stories about growing up in Sterling Falls. I mention my limited adventures as an only child and Judd tells me a hilarious story about his brothers and sister when they were younger.

Eventually, the sun sets, and Judd says, "You should put on that dress again."

"What? Why?" I giggle. My birthday hangover is long gone, but getting drunk is the last thing I want to do tonight.

However, I am relaxed and full to bursting on a rich dinner, good wine, and excellent company.

"I just want to see you in it one more time."

Slowly, he turns his head to look at me, and everything rushes to my belly.

He really wants to see me in the dress one more time, so . . . *what the heck*. I stand while keeping my eyes on him and drain the remainder of my wine.

"I'll be back in a sec."

Judd stares back at me as if he can't believe I'm going to put on a dress for five minutes, but then he gives me that half-smile. The crooked one that makes my heart go *thud-thud-thud*, and I race off to change.

I'm giddy as I step into the guest room and slip into the silky fabric. I fluff up my hair, reapply my lipstick and even spritz myself with perfume just for fun. As I don't have the right shoes for this kind of dress, I skip footwear and walk out to the great room barefoot. From the middle of the room, I can see Judd is no longer seated on the deck and I spin in a slow circle wondering where he went.

"Judd?" I call out.

"I'll be right out," he hollers from his side of the house.

I wait until he calls again. "Firefly, meet me in the library."

For a half a second, I think I've heard him from the wrong direction of the house, and I practically skip toward the library expecting Judd to be inside.

Instead, I see the flowers from earlier have been moved to the desk in the room. The lights are dim, and music plays over a hidden speaker. The song is familiar, very 1990s, but I cannot place it because Judd enters the room . . . wearing a tux.

My mouth drops as I stare at the man who was once a boy intended to be my prom date. Now, he's dressed in a stunning, fitted black tux with a circa 1990s cummerbund and bow tie in royal blue.

A perfect match to the dress I'm wearing.

35

[Judd]

"Judd." Genie's breathless whisper of my name causes me to look up at her. She is beautiful in that dress which accentuates her curves and emphasizes her breasts. A thousand percent better than the yellow contraption she wore at the garden party.

She leaves me breathless.

And yet the way she's looking at me, I'm not certain she's breathing either.

"I was a hell of a lot thinner the last time I put this on." I smooth a hand over the silky cummerbund I found in the back of a closet years after moving out of the house. A specialty dry cleaner was able to restore it.

My comment is meant to break the crackle of anxiety around us. I'm recreating our failed prom night, and I'm suddenly nervous.

"Which was when?" Genie whispers, her voice lower than the music.

"When I was eighteen."

"And you kept it all this time?"

"Rented the tux then. Had to purchase the set." The cummerbund and bow tie. "Now, I own this suit."

Genie's face is full of surprise. "Is today . . ." She swallows hard.

"The anniversary of our prom." A date burned into my memory like a hot branding iron to my skin, and yet, spending time with Genie today has changed everything about this date.

And I do not want to think about my father right now.

"You look absolutely gorgeous," I say, stepping closer to her and brazenly admiring her in that dress. I twirl a finger in the air, suggesting I want her to spin in a circle so I can see every angle and curve of her.

"I'm not wearing shoes."

"I don't care." She could also be wearing an ugly yellow costume, and I'd still love her.

Because I do love her. Call it too soon. Say it's too fast. But I've had twenty plus years to hate what *never* happened between Genie and me, and I've only had twelve days to make it up to her.

"Your turn," she says, once she finishes twirling. "You are stunning."

My ears heat and my cheeks burn but I spin as well, arms out at my side. Once I finish and catch the appraising look in Genie's eyes, I close the distance between us and pull her close.

"I know I'm twenty-four years late, but Genie Webster, will you dance with me?"

"That would be a check-yes." Her smile is extra wide. "I'd love to dance with you, Judd Sylver."

At first, we sway like middle schoolers. Just a little hip

action side to side, but eventually I take her hand, keeping the other on the small of her back.

"I didn't even know how to dance back then," I admit. "I was so scared I'd mess up that night."

Clay tried to teach me a few moves. Knox said just hold her tight.

"I'd dance with you any day, Judd. Couple goals." The second she speaks she clamps her lips tight.

"Couple goals?" I ask, halting our dance.

"Forget I said that."

"No, explain."

Genie looks to the side, and I restart our dance, hoping the movement of our bodies will loosen her tongue.

"Since I've been . . . hanging out with you . . . I started making a mental list of couple goals. Things I'd like to do as a couple."

Intrigued and thinking the list would be simple, I ask, "Like what?"

"Always kiss as a greeting and goodbye."

I stop again, anticipation racing through my veins. *What is she saying?*

"Never lose one another."

My heart begins to beat faster.

"Comfort in the little things. Soft touches and warm smiles." Genie looks up at me with eyes that gleam with flecks of light. Fireflies in the night.

She runs her hand up the back of my neck and whispers, "Kiss you every day."

Something in me shatters. This woman. A cage around my heart has been opened. I'm not a beast unleashed as much as a bird set free. A firefly myself, released from a jar.

The last secret I've kept from her is on my tongue. With her hand in mine, I lift it for my mouth and kiss the ring on her finger. My mother's ring. The cause of everything.

"That night," I exhale, finding the courage to admit the rest of the story. "The reason my father beat me up." I blow out a breath. "I'd stolen this ring from him."

The memory rushes back at me. His thundering voice. The sharp point of his finger.

Where the fuck is it?

"He'd accused me of taking it from him, and I lied. I told him I hadn't." He'd caught me admiring her ring often enough. Often picking on me for missing her so much. He even threatened to toss the ring in the trash and that's when I took it. I didn't doubt he might throw it away. My last memory of her.

"Why?" Genie whispers.

"I'd planned to ask you to be my girlfriend."

Genie stops moving, staring up at me with wide, sad eyes and severely pinched brows.

"I'd been wanting you, yet never admitting my feelings. I hadn't ever checked yes until *you* asked me to that dance. It gave me hope that you might want me the way I wanted you."

"Judd," she whispers, still holding my hand but staring at me with wonder and fear in her gaze.

"I wanted to do it right. Make a grand gesture. You wouldn't have simply been my first girlfriend, you'd have been my first everything."

My first and last. I knew it then as I know it now. She is the perfect woman to wear this gift, and I don't want her to take it off. I want her to wear it for real as a bond between us, as a promise of a future.

"Baby," she says softly, cupping my cheek.

"You were younger than me and it would have been a big ask to ask you to wait for me, me going away to college while you were still in school. I wanted the ring to be a promise. A statement of my feelings."

Genie glances at her hand.

I swallow, almost embarrassed by how backwards my question will sound, but I ask my fake fiancée anyway, "Genie Webster, will you be my girlfriend, for real?"

I'm met with the most soulful eyes I've ever seen. A black so deep I could get lost in her and yet I know she'd find me.

Never lose one another. *Again*. Never, ever again.

"Yes," Genie whispers, then clears her throat. "Yes, yes." Then she tips up on her toes and kisses me, sweet and hesitant, like a first kiss might be.

"You would have been my first kiss," she admits. "First date. First boyfriend."

I release her hands and cup her face, kissing her with all the passion of missed kisses and all the promises of future ones.

Kiss every day. With her in Knoxville, and me here, I don't know how I'll make that happen, but I'll figure something out.

Suddenly, I'm moving us, pressing Genie to walk backwards until her legs hit the edge of the velvet lounger. Our kissing has grown heavier, needier, and I'm starving for more from her. I spin her to face the chaise and pepper kisses along her shoulders and across her shoulder blades. Only two days ago I had her bent over the dining room table, my dick at the ready and so tempted to be inside her.

Tonight, I have other fantasies to act out.

"Remember how I asked you to sit on my face at my brother's place the other day."

Genie giggles beneath the kisses I continue to cover her skin with. "What about it?"

"I'd like to do that now. Only I want you to take me in your mouth at the same time."

Genie spins to face me, her gaze darting all over my face and for a moment I worry I've asked for too much.

"Here?" she questions, her eyes puzzled like she isn't certain how that would work.

I nod. "I'll lay on the settee, and you climb over me."

"I don't want to crush you."

"You won't." My voice is too sharp, my answer so quick. My heart is hammering, and I loosen my bow tie, then strip off the cummerbund.

"Unbutton my shirt?" I ask, as I shrug off my jacket next and kick off my shoes. I just want Genie's hands on me.

When my shirt is open and untucked, she reaches awkwardly behind her back, like she intends to unzip her dress, but I gently catch her arm.

"Would it sound weird if I asked you to leave your dress on?"

"Not as weird as how turned on I am at the prospect of you burying your head beneath my skirt."

She tugs at the side of her dress and smiles seductively.

I lay down on the chaise with my head where my feet should be. Hastily, I unlatch the tux pants and shove them down to free my heavy cock. I'm rock hard with anticipation. I don't think I'll last more than thirty seconds in Genie's mouth, but I want this moment.

With my hand on her hip, I guide her to straddle my face, tucking her dress up over her back. Within seconds, Genie has her hand wrapped around my shaft.

I lick up her seam. She takes me in her mouth.

And my mind is blown.

I rim her folds and tickle her clit with my tongue and all the while she drags up and down my dick. This is a million times better than any fantasy I've ever had of this woman.

This woman who lets me play her body and strings out mine.

This woman who smiles at me like I light up the world. And I want to.

I'd give her everything and anything she asked of me.

I lap while she sucks.

Her hips rock, mine buck, and too soon my balls tighten and my back spasms. *Dammit.* I come hard and fast. My dick betraying me, jolting in the warmth of her mouth, and shooting off down her throat.

"Fuck," I mutter pulling back from Genie. "I was too worked up. And you didn't yet."

"I'm okay," she says, glancing at me over her shoulder.

"Fuck that." Awkwardly, I assist Genie off me and sit upright, shifting my position so the top of my head is pressed against the raised arm of the chaise. "Back on my face, firefly."

Genie chuckles anxiously, and I see her shutting down, but I won't let that happen. Her pleasure is my pleasure, that's on *my* couple goal list. With my hand at her hip, I guide her back over me, lifting her skirt and burying my head beneath it. Genie holds up the front, while her other hand catches on the raised arm of the chaise.

"My God, this is better than any romance novel."

I smile against her slick skin. My girl has her own fantasies, and I want to bring all of them to life.

With another lick of her folds and a twirl of my tongue on that sacred nub, I add two fingers to the mix. Working in and out of her heat. Letting her essence drip over my cheeks. I want to drown in her scent and her sounds.

"Judd," she cries out. Her hips gently rock and I feel myself growing stiff again.

As she breaks around me, I sigh with relief.

I'm so full of love for this woman I don't know how to contain myself. And she said yes to being mine.

Fantasies are now a reality. Once dreams are now completed goals. Another wish has come true.

As Genie comes down from the high, she slowly pulls back and I scoot over, wanting her to slip in beside me. Breathless, I want to hold her a moment, and we squeeze together in the space made for one.

With her head on my chest, she draws on my skin where I'm free from ink. As if reading my thoughts, she sits up and tugs at the sides of my shirt and I slip out of it, then lay back on the chaise lounge.

Genie eyes my bicep where she's seen the obvious mark of a unicorn with a rainbow horn covered in with faint blue lines. Then the giant words, check yes or no with the box for yes marked, and the smaller words beneath it which read: always check yes.

Her eyes scan for other signs, catching on the violet flower for my mother and a giant sunflower beside it.

"You reminded me of a sunflower when we were younger," I admit. "So bright, the sun worshiped you."

"I think the flowers worship the sun," she corrects.

"Not when it comes to you." I smile, settling an arm behind my head.

"You marked your skin with memories of me," she whispers, tracing over other lines of ink.

The symbol for pi as a reminder of Math Club.

The small genie lamp with a drop of blood shaped like a heart near my wrist.

"You marked my soul the moment you asked me to be your friend."

Genie meets my eyes a second before folding back into the cradle of my shoulder and we stay wrapped around one another for a long while.

The perfect end to an amazing day.

36

[Genie]

My mind is spinning. My heart cyclones in my chest.

Judd stole this ring from his father. He took a beating for it. And his intention had been to give it to me. As a promise. Would I be his girlfriend? Would I wait for him?

So much wasted time has passed. If only the younger Judd had come to me when he was lost and hurting. I'd have been his years ago, but such was not our path.

And now we are here, curled around one another tighter than the red and white swirls on a candy cane.

"Is this how you envisioned our prom night? Did you have visions of us sixty-nine-ing?" I snort into his skin, giggling like a schoolgirl at the mere mention of such a position, despite having just performed it.

Judd scoffs. "Are you kidding me? I thought I'd be lucky

enough to kiss you. Then I'd go home and whack off to the thought of your mouth on mine. This"—he chokes—"far surpasses any lame prom night fantasy I had at eighteen."

At eighteen years old, when he suffered because he wanted me to have something of his. To be his.

"Judd," I shift to glance up at him, my tone more serious. "I'm so sorry all that happened to you. Back then." His father. The results. "I'm not worth it."

Judd takes my left hand on his chest and lifts my arm upright, admiring the ring on my finger, before linking his fingers with mine.

"You are worth *everything*." He sighs. "And now, you're mine."

"I'm your girlfriend," I repeat.

Judd hums, noncommittally.

"Can I ask you something then?" My voice goes small. "Why haven't we had sex?"

Judd shifts his head to glance at me. His eyes turn soft. "Because I don't want to just fill you, Genie. I want to *fulfill* you. I want to make your wishes come true, however that may look."

This man.

Still quiet, hesitantly I ask, "What if I don't want to get married?" Although, I've been slowly changing my mind about the institution. Maybe it isn't just that my mother is doing it wrong, as much as that *I* haven't found the person who is right for me.

And Judd feels right. Too right.

"Then I'll be your boyfriend." He answers so quickly, so confidently.

"Forever?"

Judd continues to watch me. "If that's what you want." He presses a kiss to my forehead and pulls back. "Look, boyfriend, fiancé . . . husband. I don't need a label as long as you lov—" He stops short, biting back words that might be coming too soon. "As long as we just stick together." He tightens his hold on my hand.

Weathering any storm.

"But my couple goals include us living together. Otherwise, how can I make the kissing every day happen?" He squeezes my body underneath his arm.

Couple goals. I press a kiss to Judd's chest, almost feeling the thump of his heart beneath my lips.

"As for sex, I'm in no rush, despite wanting to take you on every surface inside *and outside* this house."

"Outside?" I chide.

"The greenhouse. The dock. The lake."

Here, there, and everywhere. My body hums to life at the possibilities.

"The point is, I want you to be confident in our future first."

He wants me to love him. Because he loves me. It's in every look, every touch, every unspoken word.

I nod against him, lost to the rhythm of his heart and the patience in his voice. He'll wait for me to be on the same page of lined paper with unicorns.

And I'm not far off from being where he wants me to be, but talking about love is more than we need to say tonight.

Once more I settle into his chest, while the soundtrack that's been playing in Judd's library flips to another song. When the new one starts, my head pops up at the familiar tune.

"I love this song."

""Just Like Heaven"," Judd states the title.

I slip over his body and start singing into my fist about running away with him. My body takes over, my feet kicking, left, right, left to the beat. My hips rock, arms flapping forward and back.

Then I hold out my hands to Judd when the song asks, why are you so far away.

I drag Judd upright. He groans at my enthusiasm. But eventually, he gives in and dances, albeit awkwardly, when he said he didn't know how.

And I fall in love with him when I don't know how to do that either.

37

———

[Genie]

Judd and I linger in bed the day after our prom-revival, but on the following morning, I beg off another day in bed.

"I'm going into town." A little separation might refocus my mind. With Judd nearby, all I can think about is orgasms and the perfection of his body.

Judd is almost insatiable about giving them to me.

He pretends to pout when I make my announcement. He's taken a seat at his dining room table, set up like he'd hoped we'd spend the day in the space, working side by side like we did earlier in the week, and as much as I'd like to do that too, I have work to do.

If something were to happen and Greetings Ambassador didn't come through with their proposal, I'll still need to produce fresh, new calendars for the upcoming year. I need to concentrate. For at least a day. Maybe half. Even just a few hours.

I groan when Judd wraps his arm around my hips and tugs me close to him.

"I have something for you, though." Digging my hands into his hair, I kiss the top of his head before pulling back. "Check your email."

"What is it?" He glances up at me from his seated position. His hair mussed. His eyes cautious.

I want to permanently wipe away the sadness that creeps back into his sky-blues. I want Judd to be confident in our new commitment to each other, in my commitment to him.

"I've sent you my financials for Quirky Girl Calendar. Maybe you could take a look after all." It's a big ask and a bit frightening. I don't make the kind of money he does, but it isn't about comparison. I feel like I'm opening a piece of my soul to him. This is me. My business and my plan.

And I'm open-minded to his thoughts. Trusting his opinion. Trusting in him.

Judd's eyes widen and his head turns toward his laptop, like he can already see the email I've sent. Then he glances back at me. "I'll look at it right away."

"No rush." I chuckle, swiping his hair back again. My meeting with Greetings Ambassador isn't for two more weeks.

Which reminds me, I should really go back to Knoxville and collect more of my belongings. The thought of home is daunting, though, as I don't want to be away from Judd.

The emotions growing between us have happened gradually and yet all at once, and I need to accept my stay is not a vacation from life, but the possibility of a new life.

With these thoughts in mind, I step back from Judd, but he catches me by the hips again and slowly stands, filling any space between us. Cupping my jaw, he kisses me soundly. A deep sweep into my mouth and a playful suck at my lower lip before releasing me.

"Couple goals," he whispers, dropping his forehead to mine. "We kiss goodbye and hello."

I tip up on my toes, my smile nearly too wide to properly kiss him back but I do.

Because, couple goals.

~

WHEN I TAKE my corner seat in Curmudgeon Bakery, the last person I expect to see enter the place is Clay.

"Hey, birthday girl," he teases although days have passed since my birthday. He could pick on me for being a *drunk* birthday girl, but the outpouring of concern from the Sylver clan has been compassionate. No judgment. Just gentle worries. Turning forty is a big deal.

"Hi there." I lift my coffee to salute Clay before he places an order with the young man behind the counter. Sebastian is out somewhere on a delivery.

After Clay picks up his coffee and a berry-mix scone, he grabs a seat at my table. "I've been meaning to talk to you and wonder if now is a good time?"

"Shoot." I wave toward him, a little apprehensive about what he'd want to talk to me about.

"You mentioned your meeting with Greetings Ambassador."

I roll my eyes and chuckle, considering Judd's concerns. "What is this, a Sylver ambush?"

Clay smiles, his eyes crinkling with delight. "What do you mean?"

"First Judd, now you."

"Ah, well, I was hoping Judd would talk to you."

I tilt my head. "Now I want to know what *you* mean."

"Just that Judd has a way about him." Clay places his hand near his ear and twists it back and forth. "A real way with numbers. Finances. And I've been hoping he might help you find an alternative to selling."

I could be offended that this family isn't in favor of me giving up my business. Instead, I'm flattered they just want what they think is best for me.

"Our mother had a dream," Clay continues. "She wanted to turn the local feed and farm supply store into something greater, and my parents were on their way to making that dream happen when she passed away." He offers a sad smile. "Our father ran the place into the ground instead of honoring her dream, and it's taken primarily me and Judd to turn the business around. To grow our mama's vision into something bigger."

He smiles again, warm and proud of their accomplishments. "I hate to see anyone give up their dream, and you seem like someone who still has a vision for yours. Direction for it. You're young and talented. Very fun. Very fresh, and very relatable to garden and book lovers."

"Clay Sylver, have you been investigating me?" I twist my lips, giving him a wry grin.

"Just looking into Quirky Girl Calendars, and I like what I see. I'd really like for Sylver Seed & Soil to carry your line."

My mouth pops open. "Through Greetings Ambassador?" I've earned a customer before even starting with their company.

"Through Quirky Girl Calendars directly."

"Clay," I groan, setting my elbow on the bistro table and placing my forehead in my hand. "I don't have the merchandise I want to expand the line."

"And I could help you with that."

"You're already running an empire," I joke.

"And what's wrong with adding more to the galaxy?"

"Was that a *Star Wars* reference?"

Clay smiles. "Dutton is a fan. He also likes Power Princesses. It changes every day." The affection he has for his son is amazing and the twinkle in his eye as he speaks about his child is exactly how I envision Judd speaking about a child he loves. Heck, I've seen that gleam in Judd's eyes when he talks about Simon.

"I'll think about it," I state, although I've already been thinking about Quirky Girl Calendars and if I'm taking my company in the right direction.

"Let me know if you need anything." He raps his knuckles on the table and stands, picking up his uneaten scone and to-go coffee cup.

"Actually, there is something I'd like to talk to you about." I lick my lips, nervous about what's on my mind. My concern isn't what I came into town to discuss, but with Clay suddenly in front of me, I can't hold back. "It's about Judd."

I don't want to betray him, but I also need help in supporting him.

Clay slowly sits back down, his hand tightening around his coffee cup. "Is everything alright?"

I shake my head and explain what I can.

WHILE RIDDLED WITH guilt after speaking with Clay, I also have a plan. An actionable one.

So, when Judd exits his bedroom, dressed for his evening fight, because he took a Friday slot due to family obligations for the remainder of the weekend, I'm also dressed. And extremely nervous.

Judd looks up at me standing in his great room wearing the green dress with ruffles along the neckline. The one I hope he remembers fondly.

"Hey, beautiful. What's going on?" He eyes my outfit, noting my face lightly made up and my hair curled. His head tilts, and I can already see the gears clicking in his brain. He's wondering why I'm going out and where I'm going without him.

Only, I'm not going anywhere alone.

"I thought I'd go with you tonight."

"To the fight?" He blinks.

"Unless I can convince you to skip the fight entirely." I shove at the shoulder of my dress, pushing it downward and hitching my shoulder up, giving Judd my best sensual pout as I glance at him over said shoulder.

He smiles. His face flushing pink. "Don't tempt me."

I tug the shoulder panel back upright and straighten. "I didn't think that would work." I clear my throat, fighting down the hit of rejection. "So, I thought I'd go with you."

Judd continues to stare at me while fiddling with the cuff of his dress shirt. "I thought you didn't want to watch *that* happen to me."

I don't. Still don't, but . . . "I want to support you. I want to understand."

Judd stares at me again. Really looks at me. The intensity is so strong, I feel raw. Naked. Exposed. Then he closes the distance between us and takes my face in his hands, lowering to kiss me, long and deep and breathless.

For a minute there, I almost think I have him reconsidering his fight. But when he pulls back, he lowers his forehead to mine.

"Thank you," he whispers.

His gratitude reminds me why I'm attending. Judd doesn't believe anyone will support his decision to fight. That no one supports him.

I'm out to prove him wrong.

38

[Judd]

Mack's is located outside of Charleston. With a pub-like feel in the front, similar to The Boxer near Knoxville, the place is dimly lit with dark wood accents. Behind a swing door is a functioning boxing circuit that caters to local enthusiasts in the know.

As I'd told Genie, my family was on a need-to-know basis, and I hadn't wanted them to know.

Mainly, I hadn't wanted their judgement. Stone might worry it's not legal. Clay would definitely find reasons I should not participate. Knox might even think I'm imitating our father.

None of these things could be further than the truth.

My rage is internalized, and I manage it in this controlled environment. In the ring is where I release the lingering anger for my father. In the ring is where I release the frustration toward myself for ever being weak. In the ring is where I explode before everything else consumes me.

And tonight, I have Genie by my side. Or at least, holding my hand as we enter Mack's. We hang out in the pub, not saying much, until it's almost time for my match. Too quickly, I'm leaving her seated at a table near the ring and disappearing to change into my silky purple shorts with a thick black waistband.

For a moment, I hesitate, knowing Genie is out there among drunken men. She'll be sitting alone amid men hyped up on adrenaline. The excitement of competition. The thrill of a bet. The rush of alcohol. And she's doing this for me.

I'm not worth it.

The energy around me is a clash of emotions. I'm thrilled to have Genie present. I'm concerned about her thoughts. I want to impress her. I do not want to disappoint her. I'm worried she'll still be upset by my fighting, and I wish I could form the words to clearly explain myself. Why I do what I do.

The idea of talking through my emotions in therapy did not appeal to me. Talking in general often wasn't high on my list of things to do. Boxing felt like a good alternative.

With Genie, it'd been different, though. We talk but we are also good in silence.

Fighting got me out of my head. In the ring, the sweat and exhaustion freed any pent-up anger and cleared my mind for a little while. From week to week, I could manage any memories or doubts, fears or frustrations. The fight took it all out of me.

Then again, Genie does the same thing for me.

Spending time with her is a comfort. And now that she's officially my girlfriend, hope of making things even more permanent between us has sprung up and that settled some of the anger constantly swirling in my head.

I am not alone with Genie here.

Through the closed door of the locker room, which is more like an old supply closet emptied of everything other than a few hooks on the wall and a safe for personal belongings, I hear the thump-thump-thump of loud bass music.

My heart matches the rhythm.

He makes my heart go thud-thud-thud.

I shake away the whisper of Genie's limerick, knowing I need to get my head in the ring. Closing my eyes, I visualize the space. I picture my faceless opponent. My movements become clearer.

Left jab. Right hook. Left hook.

But then Genie's in my head again. Her eyes as she looked up at me after I kissed her at the table. The fear in them. She's truly scared for me, and deep down, she doesn't want to see someone hit me. She doesn't want to see me hurt.

As I'm seated on a folding chair, head bowed and right leg bouncing, I sit upright, roll my shoulders back and hold my head higher.

I won't be hurt. I am not weak. I am not a coward.

I'll win tonight and maybe renegotiate my time with Mack. He likes to keep guys that are good on a regular rotation. Keeps the patrons coming back and the crowd involved. Bets are up. Tips run heavy.

For me, it's not about the money.

Thinking of Genie again, I wonder what it is I'm fighting for, then?

The door swings open and a familiar young voice calls my name. "Sylver. You're up." The thumping beat roars louder with the door open. The crowd is raucous with shouts and chants echoing down the narrow hall to this even narrower space.

Typically, the sound seeps into my veins. The noise infuses me with more energy. More clarity.

I'm about to fight.

I'm also feeling a little off tonight.

A strange vibe buzzes around me. Nerves I haven't felt since my first fight years ago. When Harvey Mack asked why a pretty boy like me would want to box. He didn't like my answer. I said I had my reasons. Hoping to set me down a peg, he put me in the ring with a guy in the next higher weight class. I didn't win but I held my own, hellbent on proving myself. To Harvey. To me.

And I've become a fan favorite.

But now, who was I proving anything to? Genie didn't want to see this side of me, but she was also sitting out there waiting on me.

She'd be my reason to fight tonight.

I press off the cold metal chair and follow the kid into the dim arena. An area that is darker than the front bar, lighting aimed only on the twenty-by-twenty space. The air around the ring is smoky although smoking is not allowed in here. The surrounding tables are hard to make out, but I know exactly where Genie is seated.

As I slide through the ropes, I glance her way, noticing two men are also sitting at the table with her while two more stand behind her like bodyguards. Arms crossed over their chests. Stern looks on their faces.

Shit.

Knox and Ford both look stoic. Clay leans on the table, his face unreadable for once. Sebastian sits next to him, leaning forward against his thighs, one leg bouncing like mine had been only moments ago.

At first, anger spikes. *Genie.* What did she do? How could she do this to me? I feel betrayed. I'd trusted her with this secret, not wanting my family to know. Wanting something for me.

A new surge fills me. A fresh level of irritation.

Why am I only proving to myself I can fight? They should all see that I'm not a weakling. I'm stronger than they give me credit. I'm braver than they know.

So when the match is called and my opponent, some guy

from Wrightwood, another small town in West Virginia, steps forward, I easily fall into a better mindset.

Focus. Determination. Fight.

We dance, at first. A hop here, a bounce there, until the first punch is thrown. I'm not even certain who strikes first.

As the battle begins, I'm all in. The gathered crowd disappears. The murmur of the patrons mutes. Nothing outside the ring exists for me.

My mind goes blank.

Then, that unfamiliar buzz humming near me in the locker room returns. The energy crackling around me like a sudden summer storm. I shake it off again.

My opponent and I circle one another before a second round of hits happen. A right hook to his chest. A left jab to my shoulder.

Despite my no-face rule, my opposition gets a knock to my head, and I twist.

The sharp feminine gasp from just outside the ring breaks through the muting barrier in my head. My vision flips outside the perimeters of the ropes. In a matter of seconds, I take in everything.

Genie's hand covering her mouth. Clay sitting straighter. Sebastian leaning upright, holding up a fist. Knox has lowered his arms. Ford leans toward him, muttering something out the side of his mouth.

Then, I hear my name. "Get him, Judd."

I don't know who calls it, but it brings me back to the ring and the man standing opposite me, bouncing on his toes and taunting me.

"Pretty little thing you got there," he snarks, salacious and hungry for a taste of what's mine.

I lose my mind at the thought of anyone coming near Genie. Hurting her. Touching her. And I become a fury of fists.

Practiced punches and hammering hooks. Quick jabs and dancing feet.

The next few minutes are a whirlwind until someone is pulling me off my opponent and pressing me into the opposite corner.

My chest heaves. My heart thunders against my ribs.

I glance toward the table where my family remains, staring in shock and wonder and pride.

But Genie is missing.

"Where is she?" I've hopped the ropes, sweat blurring my vision. My chest feels constricted. I can't breathe. "Where did she go?"

"Take it easy," Sebastian says, his hand on my rising chest. "She only stepped outside for a breather."

I brush past my brother and race toward the pub, still wearing my shorts and gloves. Still breathing heavily.

"Hey," the bartender calls out as I rush into the outer bar, knowing all competitors need to be changed and presentable before entering this portion of Mack's.

I ignore him as I run toward the front door and out to the sidewalk, looking left then right before jogging to the parking lot.

There, among the darkness and parked cars, I find Genie pacing back and forth.

"Firefly," I call out and she stills. I close the distance between us, grateful that she leaps for me.

I'll catch her every time.

With her arms around my neck, I lift her off her feet and squeeze her to my sweaty chest. "Don't leave me."

One of my greatest fears seeps between us.

"Judd." Her hand comes to the side of my head. "Baby."

She squirms in my arms until I set her on her feet. Then, she's pressing back from me when I only want to hold her tighter. Reluctantly, I give her the space she seems to need.

Her cool hands cup my cheeks, and I risk looking her in the eyes. Those dark orbs with flecks of gold, pinpricks of light dancing in the blackness.

My firefly.

"You are so beautiful."

Her words bring me up short. "What?" I pull back a little more, uncertain I've heard her correctly.

Her hands skim down my sweat-coated arms and her gaze follows the trail she burns into my flesh. "All long limbs and powerhouse strength. Your body is incredible. And you have skill. Real talent." Her voice is full of awe.

"Then why did you leave?"

Genie is shaking her head, her gaze dropping. "I still can't watch, Judd." She looks up at me, sad while proud. "I cannot witness someone hitting you like that."

Her hands return to my face. "After all you've been through. *For me.*" She swallows thickly, remembering what I told her about our prom night. All those years ago and yet a memory so fresh in my head most days, until recently. Until her.

"Firefly, I—"

She covers my lips with her fingers. "You're amazing, Judd. Truly gifted. But that"—she nods toward the bar—"is too much for me."

She pauses again, her gaze darting all over my face. Sweat trickles down my temples and along my nose, but I don't dare break our stare. I'm afraid if I look away, she'll disappear.

"I'm here to support you, Judd. I'll be your biggest cheer-leader, as long as I don't have to watch you take a beating."

"I won." My voice is rough, scratchy and raw. I was *not* beat.

She shakes her head. "But you don't need a boxing match to prove to me you're a winner. You've won my heart, Judd. And I'll be by your side for whatever you need. Just . . . Please, don't ask me to sit ringside and watch that again."

I lift my hand for her cheek and then remember my boxing glove. I want to hold her hand, link our fingers. Together, we'll weather the storms. But I also want sunny days with her.

With my wrist at my mouth, I tug at the glove closure with my teeth. Then, I hold out my hand. "Tug," I gently demand.

Genie gives the bulky protection a yank, and then giggles when it hardly budges.

"I've got it."

I spin to face the masculine voice I'd recognize in my sleep. Behind me, Stone stands with his hands on his hips.

I lower my head, and Genie guides my gloved hand toward my eldest brother. With steady hands, Stone removes one glove and then the other, tucking them each beneath his armpits.

He glances at Genie standing partially behind me. "I'll give you another minute." Then he steps back but not far enough that I can run.

Not that I would, but I'd love nothing more than to pick up Genie and make a dash for my truck.

Instead, I turn back to her, brows pinching. Irritation creeping back into my veins. "What did you do?"

Her eyes widen, her hands coming up, palm out in defense. "I only spoke to Clay."

"That's like taking out a headline in the local paper." My tone is harsher than it needs to be, and my words aren't exactly true. Knox is the gossip.

"They needed to know."

"And it was my place to tell them when I was ready." I don't want to argue with Genie, but she had no right to tell my family what I was doing.

"They love you," she lowers both her head and her voice. "You're fortunate to have them."

It's a reminder that Genie is alone. An only child with a

revolving door of stepsiblings she never connected with, and three stepfathers plus an evil mother.

For me, I have five overbearing brothers present and one kid sister who is probably wearing a path into the wood floors back in her home.

This is what I didn't want.

"They're worried about you."

"Exactly," I snap.

"It's called love, Judd. Appreciate it." When she spins on her heels, I take a step to follow her, but a firm hand on my shoulder stops me. My gaze continues to track Genie until she's safely inside the bar again.

"We need to talk." Stone's voice rings serious and firm in my ear as I watch my girl walk away from me.

39

[Judd]

Dread fills me when I head to the locker room to change out of my sweaty shorts. I can almost hear the coming lecture. Words to dissuade me. Questions about why. I dress slowly into loose sweats and a tee, despite having arrived in a crisp shirt and suit pants.

Once I enter the pub-like area, I notice Stone, Clay, Knox and Sebastian seated at a low table.

"Where's Genie?" I ask again, fear clogging my throat.

"Ford took her home," Clay states.

"Want a drink?" Knox asks, holding up a glass of something dark and foamy near the top.

"Man, I wish I still drank," Sebastian states, having given up the pleasure after abusing drugs for years. He eyes me warily. "Where the fuck did you learn to do all that?"

Leave it to Sebastian not to hold back.

"Let's let him get a drink first." Stone points toward the

bartender, who leers at Stone like he knows he's a nearby sheriff despite the plain clothes he wears. Stone motions toward me. "Whatcha having?"

"Whiskey, neat."

Knox whistles low. Sebastian sucks in air. I can't look at my brothers. The order is my father's drink.

An inch-deep glass of whiskey is placed before me. The drink has become a ritual. A salute to my father. A *fuck you* to the old man and his choices.

"Let's start at the beginning," Stone says as the drink sits between all of us, a glaring reminder of our past.

"You really want to go that far back." I lift my head, almost challenging Stone when he is not my enemy.

"How about last Halloween?" Sebastian counters, reminding the table of when I punched a man for bullying *a child* at a family Halloween party.

Clay's eyes are on me, knowing he stopped me in his office to explain myself a few days later and I didn't. That was six months ago.

"What we just witnessed was more than a spontaneous, lucky punch," Knox clarifies. "Which might explain how you landed that other hit like an expert."

My mouth twists, fighting a desire to smile, a twinge of pride on my lips. Then the curve of my mouth straightens. My two *younger* brothers sitting at this table took more beatings than me. Sebastian as a scrapper and Knox as an interventionist. Neither should see me how they just saw me.

"When did this start?" Stone asks next, his voice still puzzled.

"College," I state and lift my head. "But I don't want y'all to think I'd ever use my skills outside the ring."

I glance from Knox to Sebastian, then Stone and Clay. I'd never intentionally hurt someone else. The boxing ring is a controlled environment. A cage of energy.

"We know that," Clay says, drawing my attention to him and offering his sympathetic support. "I think the question is why? Why now? Why here?"

I let out a deep exhale, uncertain I can put it into words. "I just wanted to prove to myself that I wasn't all the things he said."

"You're not," Clay quickly defends.

"And I know that." I tap my temple. "But sometimes, it's still hard to accept." I point at my chest, where my heart still beats faster than it should.

"I'm sorry you've let him be under your skin this long," Stone states, his voice low like he's disappointed in himself. Like he should have done something else to right the wrongs of our father when it wasn't his responsibility.

"You didn't need—"

"We all carry the demon with us," Sebastian cuts me off, staring at Stone. "No matter what you *think* you needed to do for us, you cannot take away what he did."

We sit in silence a second before Genie returns to my thoughts. "She's going to leave me."

Clay's head swivels toward me. "Who?"

"She's not," Knox adds.

I stare at my younger brother and former childhood roommate. "How do you know?"

"Because your heart has been calling out to that girl for years, and you aren't going to give her up so easily again."

"Again," I scoff.

"I was there, remember? I know what happened. What you did. The beating you took in order to protect that ring." Knox eyes me. "But you were also a kid, like me."

When Knox reached his final straw and fought back harder than any of us ever had. It hadn't even been his fist that ended our dad but cutting words.

We wish you were dead.

I hadn't been home when it happened, happy to leave Sterling Falls in the rearview mirror. Guilty but content to leave my three younger siblings behind with that man, knowing Clay was looking out for them, even if from a distance.

We all have our guilts and our crimes. Our demons.

"You have loved Genie since you were eighteen," Knox says.

"Ten," I correct."

"Then it's time to fight for the girl," he continues, keeping his eyes on me.

"She's not really my fiancée," I admit, glancing at Clay, knowing I've been lying to them about more than one thing.

Not one brother flinches, which means they all might know the truth. Guess I'm more of an open book than I think.

"But she loves you," Clay adds.

"I'm not so certain," I counter.

"The fuck she doesn't," Sebastian states, sitting straighter in his seat. "She told Clay about you and this." He waves toward the swing door leading to the backroom. "Because she's concerned about you. Worried for you."

"That's not love," I state. But Genie's words come back to me. *It's called love, Judd. Appreciate it.*

"The fuck it isn't," Sebastian continues. "When a girl like that is concerned for you, there is only one reason, especially when she knows how you might react. That's the definition of selfless love."

"When did he become the master," Stone chuckles, lifting the glass of water before him and taking a sip to hide the smile on his face. Stone knows the answer, but Knox clarifies.

"When he fell in *love* with Enya." Knox throws his voice like he's his fourteen-year-old stepson, Tim.

"Oh, and like you aren't whipped by Halle," Sebastian retorts.

"This isn't a love-pissing contest," Clay adds, glaring from brother to brother. "Judd is our focus here."

And the last thing I want to be is the center of attention, but four sets of eyes are on me.

"Is this going to continue?" Clay tips his head toward the boxing ring hidden in the back of the bar.

"And if it does?" I don't want to be saucy with my brother. He *does* care about me.

"I want your schedule," Sebastian states.

My head whips in his direction so fast my neck cracks. "What?"

"I can't promise to make every weekend, with the baby and all."

He means Annabelle, and Adara turning three, plus Enya.

"But when he can't be here, I will be," Knox says next, keeping his eyes on me.

"Why?" I ask, glancing from him to Sebastian and back at Knox.

"Because we're brothers, and that's what we do for each other. We're here for you." My younger brothers, who were often my saviors. Only now they aren't here to save me, just support me.

I glance over at Stone, who has his eyes lowered. "You know I can't make promises." The sheriff probably shouldn't be in a boxing arena, legal or not.

Clay clasps my shoulder. "Whatever you need. Just *tell* us."

Open up to them. It's a frightening concept, but as I'm learning with Genie, who has made it easy, maybe I should give my family a little more of me.

On that note, I need to get home, and I hope Genie is still there.

40

[Genie]

I've been sitting on the couch for what feels like hours, waiting for Judd's return.

My head has been a mess. The thought of losing Judd has been eating at me. The simple truth is, as big and scary as love and marriage might be, I cannot imagine a life without Judd. And knowing he would be willing to hold my hand through all the bumps and dips, I want to be holding his hand right back.

I want him to know I love him. Fights and flaws included. Because despite them, he has a huge heart and a good soul. He *is* the tortured poet, complicated and scarred, but a light exists in him. One that makes me happy and whole. One that strengthens me, and I want to be the light that strengthens him in return.

His firefly. Continually leading him from the darkness in his head and reminding him that we are the brightness he seeks.

When he enters through the garage, he's walking so fast toward his room, he nearly bypasses the great room without a glance in my direction.

He comes to an abrupt halt, does a double take, then circles around the couches. Slowly, I stand, afraid to rush him while desperate to touch him.

Instead, we stand a foot apart.

"Hey." Judd holds up his right hand in a weak semblance of a wave, and I hold up my left, catching his hand, pressing our palms together.

We stand with our fingers linked, just staring at our hands. His large knuckles are red and swollen. Mine smaller and wearing his mother's ring.

Slowly, I release his hand and skitter my fingers to the center of his palm, tracing the raised line across his lifeline, easily finding the scar I'd felt on our first day *unofficially* engaged. "Is this from fighting?" How many wounds on his body are from boxing?

"My dad."

My gaze leaps to his face. His heavy brows crease. "He warned me that night. The night I took the ring. He'd already gotten his initial hits then cracked a beer bottle against a table and came at me. As much as I tried to hold my ground, as much as I was willing to let him end me." Judd swallows, the motion harsh. "My hand flung upward to protect me. Flight or fight. My fight had finally kicked in and my hand took the wrath."

My heart stops. My mouth gapes. "Please don't ever say you are willing to let someone end you again." I stare at his face while he glances at his hand, rubbing his thumb on the mark.

His head lifts at my words. The fear in them. The sadness.

I step closer to him and wrap my arms around his waist as if I could hold onto him forever. Be tethered to him. I will not let him drown in the sorrows of his past.

Cautiously, Judd circles his arms around me, and we stand clinging to one another.

"Don't ask me to stop," he whispers.

"I won't." As much as it pains me, if he needs that boxing ring, I will not stop him. "Just don't ask me to watch."

"I won't." He presses his lips to the top of my head, and we hold tighter to one another before Judd scoops me up and carries me toward his room.

"Shower," I suggest, a sudden need to take care of him. Pamper him somehow.

"Two birds, one bird bath?"

I chuckle into his neck. "Something like that."

"How about an actual bath?"

Judd carries me to his bedroom before setting me on my feet. Next, he steps into the ensuite and starts the water in a soaker tub beside the glassed-in shower. We've spent plenty of time together in the shower stall, washing one another and hugging each other. Somehow, a bath feels even more intimate.

When the tub is full, Judd holds out a hand to help me inside, but when I take a seat, I scoot back, and Judd looks confused.

"Let me take care of you tonight." I spread my knees and motion to the space between my legs.

Judd lowers his head and steps in front of me, then folds down so his body is cradled between my thighs. He leans back, slipping a little lower beneath the water, and tips his head to my shoulder. For a long time, we just sit, while I gently swish water around his chest and over his shoulders. Eventually, I take the soap bar and lather my hands before squeezing tightly at Judd's shoulders and working down his arms. I use extra care near his knuckles but dig my thumbs into his palms.

Judd hums with every rub.

I press him forward a second to massage along his upper back before pulling him back to my chest.

Re-soaping my hands, I rub over his chest and dive deeper beneath the water, finding him hard and erect. With my hands on his thick length, I work up and down while Judd melts against me, humming and moaning with each tug and squeeze.

Suddenly, he flips to face me, then does a quick acrobatic shift where he's seated and I'm straddling his lap.

"This is a dangerous position," I tease him, as my throbbing center lands on his thick length.

Judd presses on my hips, moving me back and forth as his head tips back on the edge of the tub and his eyes close a second. He hums again.

"Just the tip," I joke as his crown catches on my clit.

Judd's eyes ping open. "I could never do that. One inch and I'd want the whole mile."

"Well, I don't know about a mile . . ." I jest.

Judd's mouth softly curls. The tension of earlier tonight slowly washing off both of us.

"Please don't be mad at me," I whisper, brushing back his hair with my wet hand as I rock over his thick dick.

"I'm not really mad, I'm just—"

I cut him off by covering his mouth with my wet fingers. "I violated your privacy, and I apologize."

Judd shakes his head. "Stone said he already knew. *You don't think I know what my siblings are doing, even as legal adults.*" He lowers his tone to mimic the ruggedness of his brother's.

"Why hadn't he mentioned it?" I'm still seated on his hardness, but this conversation feels more important.

"Said he was waiting for me to share. Figured I would when I was ready."

"And I forced your hand." My intentions were good, but I lower my gaze, unable to look at him. I wanted Judd to see his family supports him. They love him. "Did they try to stop you?"

I glance up and Judd shakes his head, his smile puzzled. "Actually, they want my schedule."

My spirits lift and I cup his cheek. "See. The family champion."

Judd chuckles, jostling me on his lap and reminding us both of our position. "I don't know about that but if you want to give me a victory *lap* dance, I won't complain."

I laugh, loud and light, feeling better than I have all night. Then I kiss him.

The lap dance follows until he's seated on the edge of the tub and I'm on my knees, taking him in my mouth, giving him all the congratulations he needs.

41

[Judd]

My brother Ford is opening an overnight summer baseball camp for kids outside of Sterling Falls. The location used to be an old hunting lodge. A very rustic, minimalist lodge. Now, the small cabins have been converted into bunkhouses and a main building has been built, doubling as both the dining hall and a meeting place. Located on a lake, the acres of land also include two new baseball diamonds.

And enough extra space to host a carnival-themed soft opening for locals and their families. Ford credits Cadence with the idea. He also faults her for this event getting out of hand. The original intent was some traditional games like a three-legged race and water balloon toss. A few concession stands. Maybe some food trucks. And a local firefighter versus law enforcement baseball game. But Cadence, along with Halle who is a seasoned event planner, has turned Ford's property into a mini fair, complete with a Ferris Wheel and Tilt-A-Whirl.

I was not too keen on helping staff simple lawn games, so I've been recruited to monitor the money. The event is also a fundraiser, building a reserve for scholarships for kids who can't afford to attend the future camp but have the talent to be present.

Even though Ford is retired from the game, he isn't abandoning the sport. He is looking to train future baseball hopefuls.

Genie, on the other hand, is all in for the festivities, working the sno-cone machine and handing out popcorn. From a distance, I eye her as she politely speaks to Tate Haven. Heather is nowhere in sight, but her father's auto sales company has generously donated a pickup truck as a grand raffle item.

The day is a perfectly sunny mid-May afternoon. Summer is on the horizon, and I relish being outdoors, enjoying the community of those who have gathered to support Ford and his endeavor. The excitement is not only a testament to Ford as a hometown superstar but also the desire for something unique and special in the area.

Throughout the day, Genie and I pass like yellow ducks in the Yellow Duck River, a game for younger children. Eventually, Simon and Trudy find me, and I enter the three-legged race and the water balloon toss with my young charge. We lose the water balloon toss. I almost think Simon pitched it to me like he did on purpose.

The scent of peanuts and popcorn and Cracker Jacks seem to permeate the air. Cadence nearly force feeds me a hot dog with my name written in mustard on it. Knox and Stone playfully razz each other as members of opposing teams during the baseball game later in the evening.

By nightfall, the lights of the rides illuminate in the darkening sky.

And all this is to say, it's been a great day.

Simon. My family. My girl.

Genie and I have breached a new level in our relationship, especially after last night. Internal wounds were tender. I'd been angry she told my family about my secret, but I also licked those wounds after their resounding support.

Then I licked Genie to show her how grateful I am that she pulled me from my shell.

I'd been keeping my boxing to myself, for myself, and yet sharing it with my brothers took the thrill of the sport to a higher level.

Speaking of heights, I finally get Genie alone on the Ferris Wheel, which starts and stops as the ride fills with enough new patrons to warrant a few trips around the metal spiral.

"Did you know that proposing on a Ferris Wheel did not make the list of top places to propose?" Genie blurts.

I love how she's so full of random information.

"Interesting." With my arm along the back of the seat, I twirl a piece of her short hair around my finger. Chocolate and strawberry blonde. She's my favorite flavor of the day.

"Proposing near a waterfall made the list, though," she continues. Her hand rests on my thigh as the ride jolts upward then comes to an abrupt stop to allow new riders to hop on. She isn't looking at me but out at the crowd of people lining up for the ride.

"Really?" I turn my head and arch a brow, reminded of how I told her my parents got engaged near Sterling Falls. "Cliché, right?"

Genie doesn't strike me as someone who'd do anything cliché, but rather something outside the norm. She told me how asking me to my prom with the unicorn paper was now called a promposal, and she claims she's a trendsetter for unique ways to ask someone to the high school dance.

"I always thought it was cliché to get engaged on the standard days. Christmas. Valentine's. And while Paris or Greece might be great locations, there are plenty of other amazing locations to pop the question."

My brows pinch, curious where she's going with all this information. The Ferris Wheel starts again but then pauses once more at the apex. The entire world looks like it's before us in the vibrant glow of carnival lights and the dim landscape of mountains in the background.

"I'm not fishing for a question to be asked," she states, suddenly embarrassed by the topic. "Of course." She shifts, straightening up a bit and setting both her hands on the safety bar.

"Of course," I repeat. "Says the woman who is adamant she's *never* getting married, but, also, already wears my ring."

Her eyes lower to her hands on the safety bar which she drags apart and then pulls back together. "I wouldn't say *never*."

"You wouldn't?" She has my full attention now.

"I mean, I can have a change of heart, right?" Genie finally turns her head and looks at me. Her eyes dance in the glow of the Ferris Wheel lights.

Has she had a change of heart? "Don't you mean, a change of mind?"

"Maybe it's both." She licks her lips, staring into my eyes.

"Firefly, what are you saying?" I need her to spell out what she means.

"I think, what I'm trying to say is . . ." She blows out a long breath. "I love you, Judd."

There are few times I've heard that phrase said to me, but never spoken with the emphasis and fear in Genie's voice. Afraid I won't reciprocate. Scared I don't feel the same.

But I have loved this girl since I was ten. Pined for her from afar for most of my life. And then made a bold decision to ask her to be mine, risking everything to make that moment special.

So, at first, I have no response. I'm too stunned to speak. Struck dumb myself by the possibility that she could love me.

Then my mouth is against hers and she's falling back in the bucket seat as the Wheel begins to drop, the ride fully beginning. I'm quick to catch her by the back of her neck and dig my fingers into her hair. And just kiss her silly. Kiss her with all the love I feel for her, too.

"I love you, too, firefly," I murmur against her mouth. "Always."

Always have. Always will.

Suddenly, Genie is kissing me back just as fiercely as I kissed her.

And we spin round and round on the Ferris Wheel until I almost feel dizzy with love.

～

"WHAT ARE YOU DOING?" Genie gasps, as I hitch her over my shoulder and smack her ass when we enter the house. It's been a long day, but I'm wound up, especially after she said she loved me.

And now I want to show her how much I love her in return.

I shift her on my shoulder, and she squeals again, gripping the back of my tee as I carry her to my room. *Our room.*

With a gentle drop, Genie falls to the bed, and I climb over her. "I want to worship you, firefly."

"You already do," she giggles as I nuzzle into her neck and pepper her with kisses before capturing her mouth, sweeping my tongue inside and swallowing her moans.

This woman. Sight and sound. Bright and vivacious. I never want to hear silence again.

Genie does not disappoint as she begins to squirm beneath me, working her body until we line up, but there are too many clothes in our way. Slowly, I pull away, standing to admire her a moment before tugging off my shirt.

"Your body." She hums next and sits up, running her hands over my stomach.

"I love how you touch me." Like she worships me as well.

Her smile is sweet, and I reach for the hem of her shirt, tugging it over her head before pressing her back again. My skin feels like it sizzles when we are chest to chest, and she isn't even naked, but still wearing her bra. Quickly, I rectify that and move down her smooth flesh to bring one heavy swell into my mouth.

Genie's hands dig into my hair as she purrs. I dangle my tongue around her pert nipple then nip.

She hisses at the sting but I'm quick to suck her breast once more to soften the bite.

Soon, we're in a tug-of-war of pants, shorts and underwear until nothing is in our way, and I coast my hands over her body, memorizing every inch. Genie and I have had a lot of oral exploration. A lot of fingers and touching. Tonight, I need the final act.

"I wanted to wait," I whisper as I watch my hand slip between her thighs. "Wanted to have you as my forever." I want her to be my wife. "But I don't think I can hold back any longer, Genie. I love you."

I glance up to find her watching me. Her hand cups my cheek. "I love you, too, baby."

With that, I'm over her, lining myself up, dragging my tip through her slick slit.

"We should talk about protection," I say, kissing her neck and her chin.

"Is it weird that I'm turned on by you wanting to discuss this?" she says, smiling up at me.

"Not as weird as I'd really like to enter you with nothing between us."

Genie continues to stare at me, knowing I haven't been with anyone in over six months, not even she who should not be named.

"Not as weird as I'd really like that, too." Her voice is quiet, breathless even. "And I'm on the pill."

As I slip forward, her breath notches again.

I've heard this feeling described as warmth, comfort, home, and love, but none of those words are enough for what I feel as my body joins Genie's.

It's an explosion of my heart and an opening of my soul and a completeness I never expected to feel.

"Firefly." My throat tightens as I slide to the hilt and pause, needing a moment.

Genie brushes back my hair and tips up to kiss me, tender and sweet until my hips thrust and Genie gasps. "Move, baby."

That's all the permission I need to slip back and then surge forward on repeat. I reach for her left hand and lift it over her head, clasping our fingers together as I fill her.

I meant what I said, I want to *fulfill* her. I want to be all her wishes come true, because she is my ultimate desire. Genie beneath me, me inside her, us as one.

As we rock together like we're both new with each other yet familiar as an old couple, I relish every thrust, every gasp. Wanting Genie to come around me, I reach between us, using my thumb at her clit, teasing her with more sensation.

Her head tips back. Her mouth pops open, eyes close, but I want to see her fall apart around me.

"Look at me, firefly. Give me that light."

Her lids flip open and the intensity in her gaze is almost too much. Specks of light in the darkness. So much love she's practically glowing and I feel that mythical warmth.

"God, I love you," I say, lowering for a kiss while rocking my hips and touching her. Then Genie's legs wrap over my hips and clutch at me like I'm not close enough.

"I love you, too."

Within seconds, we're frantic movements and desperate grunts. Genie clings to me as I fill her until she moans my name. Home and comfort wrap around me as I feel her clench and fall apart. Still holding onto me like she'll never let me go while slipping into the bliss of us being together.

"That's my girl. Glow for me."

Her fingers are in my hair, tugging at my head and I kiss her hard and fast before my own orgasm knocks, tightening my lower back and bringing up my balls. My dick is the stiffest I've ever been and then I'm pulsing inside her, making her truly mine

Couple goals. Make love to my girl.

42

——————

[Genie]

Judd and I have definitely entered a honeymoon phase, where between his working from home and mine, we hardly get anything done. We have sex on the dining room table and against his shower wall. We do it on a highbacked stool which took some skill, and even on the back deck. Every day is a new position, a new location, and I cannot get enough of him.

I don't know why I ever doubted this type of feeling. It wasn't that I was opposed to love, I just didn't see myself getting married, that final act of commitment. Now, I can't imagine *not* being with Judd forever.

I find him in the kitchen as I often do after waking. He hardly breaks his routine of a morning workout and a swim in the lake, but he lingers a little longer in bed these past couple days as we use each other's body as a private exercise program.

"Good morning," I murmur, slipping up behind him and

wrapping my arms around his waist, pressing my head against his strong back.

"Mornin', firefly." He quickly turns and cups my chin to kiss me, slow and deep.

When we eventually pull apart, he scoops my hair over my ear and says, "I have something for you."

"For me?" I press my fingers to my chest, feeling my face heat for some reason. Judd has already given me so many things.

A thoughtful day only last week. The sentimental ring on my finger. And so many honest moments.

Stepping around me, he opens a kitchen drawer and pulls out a square, white ring box.

My heart hammers. My thoughts leap. Is this another proposal? An actual one? As Judd clarified, he never officially asked me anything before we agreed to date for ten days. It's been three weeks. So little time. So much has happened.

I swallow hard, staring at the hinged box he holds out to me. "Do you have something to say?" Shouldn't he be asking me a question? Is it cliché to ask in the middle of a kitchen on a random Thursday?

Only no day is truly random, and I'm certain today is a specialty date of some sort, but my mind is short circuiting, and I can't think of a single special occasion for this day.

"Open it." Judd's voice is calm, not a whisper of apprehension. His quiet command is still not quite what I thought he'd say.

With shaky fingers, I lift the lid, holding my breath as it slowly reveals the contents. As I'm already wearing the precious ring from his mother on my finger, I've never imagined any other ring. In my head, I'm already processing the inside of this box might be an actual wedding band. One pretty and petite that would easily sidle up against the thin gold ring holding an amethyst.

Instead, I blink at the item inside. Then lift my head and question Judd. "It's a penny."

What's with the sinking sensation in my belly? My lips quiver as I force a smile.

"It's National Lucky Penny Day," Judd proudly announces. "So, I'm giving you a lucky penny."

I don't respond. I don't know what to say. I don't recognize this wrongful sense of disappointment.

Judd isn't asking me to marry him. He is making another sweet gesture to mark another specialty date on the calendar.

But my throat is thick, so I swallow hard again. "Is *this* penny lucky?" Did he find it on some random pavement somewhere? The shine of the copper is too polished to be a worn penny from a sidewalk.

"I might have cheated on this one. I went to the bank. I wanted a penny as shiny and bright as you are to me. It's not a polished genie lamp, or an old gravy bowl, but—"

"I love it." I snap the lid shut and tip up on my toes to offer him a quick kiss of gratitude. I do love it. The gift is thoughtful and he's romantic, comparing a lucky penny to a genie lamp. You make wishes on pennies and toss them into ponds.

And my wish on this one would be that Judd Sylver would propose to me for real.

As I pull back from the kiss, my phone rings on the kitchen counter. A quick glance at the caller ID and I know I can't avoid this call.

"Let me get this," I pat his chest. "I'll meet you by the lake." Maybe I'll toss in my lucky penny to officially make my wish.

Judd's brows lift in surprise as I never swim with him in the morning, but he presses a kiss to my cheek as I answer my phone before my voice mail will pick up.

I walk toward the library, taking my call, and fighting my stomach as it drops further.

Once I finish on the phone, I change clothes, but not into a bathing suit. My feet feel heavy as I cross the backyard and head down the dock. Judd is seated on the edge waiting for me, and I fold down beside him.

My heart is beating triple time. I don't know why I'm so worked up all of the sudden.

"Everything alright?" He turns his head toward me while his feet dangle in the cold water below.

I tuck my knees up beneath my chin and wrap my arms around my shins. "That was Greetings Ambassador."

"Oh-kay." The tone of Judd's voice matches the swirling pit in my belly.

"They have an opening and want to move our meeting up." I pause and turn my head to look at Judd. "They want to see me tomorrow in New York."

This shouldn't be a big deal. I just get myself to Charleston, hop on a plane, and have the meeting tomorrow as scheduled. But I'm off-kilter at the thought of leaving Judd. I'm stumbling with what this appointment might mean for me. For us. If I accept the offer from Greetings Ambassador, I'd be losing my company and I'd be at the whim of *theirs*. While I don't think they'll ask me to move to New York, it is a possibility.

"This is good, right?" Judd nudges my shoulder with his arm, trying to find the positive in the moment when he isn't always the most optimistic guy.

Suddenly, I'm not only nervous about my meeting but I'm anxious to leave Judd.

Judd watches me a moment, his Adam's apple bobbing while he glances down at the ring on my finger. "I could go with you."

"You'd do that?" I lift my head which I'd been resting on my knees. Would he really come with me?

I'll be there, Genie. For some reason, my father's quieted voice whispers through my head. His promise to pick me up, which ended fatally.

"Of course. I love you." Judd says is so casually, like he's been saying it all his life to me.

He runs his hand up my spine and cups the back of my neck, tugging me toward him for a promising kiss.

Only, the energy around us crackles, and suddenly, Judd is pressing me back to the deck.

I shove his swim trunks down his hips. He's wrestling with my jean shorts. Too soon, we're naked, Judd over me, slamming into me, and I cry out, desperate for him to do it again and again.

The boards at my back aren't comfortable but all I can think about is Judd above me, filling me up. The sunshine above him, the blue sky as a backdrop, and his eyes that match that vast space.

I'm swallowed whole by his love and intensity and an unexplainable fear.

I cling to Judd as I fall apart, screaming his name into the morning sunlight. Judd quickly follows, his signature grunt and that finishing wave of pulses becoming all too familiar.

Judd leans forward and kisses me. When he pulls back, bracing on his hands over me, sweat beads his brow.

"I love you," he says again, like he's puzzled by that love.

I want to reassure him we will be okay but, for now, we need to get moving. Plane tickets need to be purchased, and my sketches gathered, plus packing, and laptops, and . . .

Judd is hardly out of me and I'm already ten steps ahead. He pops upright, tugging up his swim trunks, before holding out a hand and pulling me upward as well. I slip into my underwear and shorts, and Judd takes my hand, linking our fingers together. I grip his bicep like I need the extra support to guide me up this dock and into the house.

"I'll get some plane tickets. You shower and start packing."

"Thank you, Judd. For doing this. For me." I'm stammering,

discombobulated a little from the rush of sex on the dock, and the switch to business mode.

We kiss again, too quick and short, before he smacks my ass, and I head to Judd's room to shower. One day my belongings were suddenly hung in his closet and moved to empty drawers in his dresser.

After my shower, I pick from the limited dresses I have with me and fold them into my suitcase which should have taken me home, to Knoxville, weeks ago.

How time has flown. The days on the calendar have flipped and three weeks have past, and yet my future is flashing before me. A blur of images I can't see.

Could I marry Judd? What about children? Should I sell my company? Should I keep it? Can I live in Sterling Falls again? My anxiety is in overdrive, and I rub my thumb over the palm of my left hand, seeking the edge of a gold band, straightening the petite ring on my finger.

The move has become a habit.

And my hand stills when there is nothing to right.

Glancing at my hand, I stretch my fingers, noticing how naked they look. My brain is slow to process what's missing when the reality hits like I've whacked my head.

The amethyst ring with its whisper of diamonds and gold band is missing.

Franticly, I glance down at the floor, dancing in a slow circle in hopes the ring simply slipped from my finger. I drop to my knees and look beneath the bed. I sit back and curl my hand, fisting it and then extending my fingers as if I can make the ring magically reappear.

Rushing back into the bathroom, my heart sinks when I consider the ring might have slid off in the shower or near the sink and been washed down a drain. The idea seems impossible. I would have heard the clink. I would have noticed the slide of the band against my knuckle. The gold circle has never been loose on my finger. I've never feared losing it. The fit was perfect, almost too perfect, like it had been made for me.

Hastily, I dress and run toward the great room where Judd is standing, holding his phone. A striped towel circles his hips as he has been waiting for the shower.

"Tell me you took it," I whisper, my voice harsh and rough with panic. "Tell me you slipped it off my finger without me knowing."

My heart breaks with the accusation. Logically, I know he wouldn't have done that.

"What?" Judd's eyes roam my face. "What are you talking about?"

I clutch my closed hand to my chest, covering my left with my right before finally revealing my naked fingers.

"Your mother's ring. It's gone." My voice breaks on a sob as I hold out my shaky hand which blurs from the tears in my eyes.

Judd remains stone still in front of me a second before I'm in his arms. My wet cheek sticks to his naked chest. His heart thuds as well but mine beats harder.

"I'm so sorry." I pull back. "We'll look for it. Two sets of eyes, one search." I don't even mean it as a joke. Two sets of eyes are always better than one.

Judd remains mute a second, slowly releasing me like thread pulled from a spool. I feel like I'm coming unraveled. "Tell me when you last saw it."

I recount glancing at it while on the phone and then righting it with my thumb. "I'd been in the library."

Judd heads there and I follow, searching the plush rug and even the cushion of the chaise though I hadn't sat down.

"What about on the dock?" Judd askes

"I don't know." I hadn't been focused on the ring, only on Judd's face but at one point, I thought I saw him glance at my fingers, like he often does. As if confirming the ring was still on me.

Judd nods, then takes off for the backyard, skipping off the deck with one hop without touching a single stair. Then he's running for the wooden planks that jut over the water and stops short at the end.

I'm quick to catch up as we both turn in circles, hoping the gold band or purple gem will gleam up at us.

Dread hits me hard with a question I can't voice. What if I lost the ring on the dock and it somehow rolled into the lake?

"I'm so sorry, Judd. We'll find it." I want to reach for him, and I do but he pulls back. His naked chest sucking in as if he's afraid of my touch.

"It's not important." The words are choked and he swallows hard, staring down at his feet.

"How can you say that? It was . . . is . . . very important to you." *His mother's ring.* The last item he has of her. A vivid reminder of who she was. Bright and beautiful. The purple gemstone matches her Violet name.

Nausea rushes up my throat.

"You're important to me," Judd says but his voice is distant, yet trembling uncharacteristically. His hands come to his hips, and he blows out a breath before he squints toward the house. "And you need to go."

"What?" Horror slaps my cheeks. *He wants me to leave?* I can't go now.

It was an accident. I haven't taken it off since he gave it to me, so I'm truly puzzled how it could so easily, so undetectably, slip free. And I can't leave him. He'll never forgive me for this infraction.

"I'll stay. We'll search everywhere. Maybe get a metal detector."

"No, firefly." He nods, the movement slow and methodic. "You can't miss your meeting."

Is he prioritizing my meeting over his loss?

"You'll come with me?" I wave toward him, but I already know the answer.

Judd is shaking his head, glancing back at his feet.

He'll stay. I'll go.

Don't leave me.

Those are the words he once asked of me.

I'm not leaving. Not really. I might be the one going to New York, but it feels like Judd has already left me.

I stare at his impassive features. His gaze staring straight through me rather than at me.

He can't mean it. He can't want me to leave. Alone. But he does.

My stomach drops, twisting in disbelief, as silent tears fall down my face unchecked. The bitter, salty taste collects on my lips.

He just promised he'd come with me.

I'll be there.

I should have known I wasn't worth any of it.

Suddenly, I'm crushed.

43

[Judd]

As Genie returns to the house alone, I take another moment to survey the surrounding dock. If the ring fell into the water, all might not be lost. I have a metal detector, but I also need help.

I'm numb as I retrace my steps to the house, recalling how I'd just seen the ring on her finger.

It had been there, right?

Genie looked devastated but I had no words. The ring had become my focus. I felt like fucking Golem. *My precious.*

So much was tied to that ring. My mother. My history. Genie herself.

I had to get it back.

Once inside, I put on some real clothes, and text in the family chat. Might be the first time I've initiated contact.

Emergency. Lost mom's ring. Need help searching.

I don't know who would show or when or how.

Genie is packed and standing in the great room when Vale arrives first.

"I don't want to go," Genie says, her voice hesitant, as she peers out at the lake.

I didn't want her to leave either, but her meeting is important. She'll be gone only one night, maybe two. "I'll be right here."

She steps up to me and leans against me, but I'm granite. To be anything otherwise would cause me to collapse.

I must find the ring.

It represents everything I've been through to become the man I am today.

No family member ever complained that I wore the rings around my neck. In many ways, I felt like the keeper of the rings. The last shreds of our parents, representing the good and bad in them. The yin and yang of the lightheartedness of our mother and the darkness of our father.

The loss feels irresponsible, and I feel responsible to right the loss.

As Vale enters my place, she says, "What can I do?" Her eyes search mine knowing what this means for me.

"Take Genie to the airport?"

"What?" Vale and Genie say in unison, glancing at each other and then back to me.

"Genie's meeting with Greetings Ambassador was moved up. I need you to take her to the airport. Someone else can help me look for the ring."

Vale steps closer to me. "Judd, it's only a ring."

"It's our mother's ring," I state loudly, feeling the edges of my composure begin to fray.

Vale briefly looks at Genie who has stepped away from us. "Some things are more important, Judd."

My heart hears her. Genie is the most precious person in my life. She is important to me. But my head, my thoughts, take over.

Vale looks between Genie and me once more, but Genie is no longer looking at me. Her eyes are aimed toward the open front door.

"Just go," I whisper to Vale, nodding at Genie.

Vale takes Genie's rolling suitcase by the handle and struts forward while Genie gives me a final glance. "Good luck, Judd." Then she's shutting the door with a soft click.

The words hold finality. *Goodbye.*

The soft nick of the door nearly echoes but it sounds like the metal clang of an iron gate closing around my heart.

She didn't kiss me. The thought hits me too late, like a sucker punch to the gut.

Couple goals dissolved.

~

"How's it going?" Knox calls out as he storms across the grass toward me, where I'm waving the metal detector I own back and forth over the lawn.

"Where's Genie?" Sebastian asks next as he accompanies Knox.

"She left." I don't bother glancing up at them, but I sense Sebastian stumbling to a stop.

Knox whistles low. "What happened?"

"Greetings Ambassador moved up their meeting to tomorrow."

"Why didn't you go with her?" Knox asks and I finally glance up.

"Because she . . . *we* lost the ring." I can't fault her. In my heart, I know she didn't do it intentionally. But I still cannot reconcile that it's gone. The last talisman of my mom. Vanished.

"You idiot." Sebastian seethes and my blood begins to boil. The twitching of a beast rumbles inside me. I hate being called names.

"Your most valuable thing . . . *no, person* . . . just left." He points toward the house. "And you let her go."

I could argue that I was going to lose Genie anyway, but it no longer felt true. She said she loved me. She'll come back to me.

Slowly, panic mingles with the loss boiling in my veins. *She'll come back, right?*

Sebastian is suddenly glaring at his phone and then it rings in his hand. He glances up at me while answering it and listens to someone speaking to him.

"Yeah, Vale," Sebastian states, still staring at me. "I just told him he was stupid."

The grief rumbling through me becomes anger. I drop the metal detector and rush my youngest brother. Knox catches me within inches of taking him down.

"I said not to call me that."

To his credit, my brother Knox is strong. Bricklaying does that to a man, and he holds me back as best he can but I'm still trying to reach around him and get at Sebastian.

"Fuck you, man," Sebastian yells at me.

"No, fuck you," I scream but it's not really my brother I feel like hollering at.

"What the fuck?" Ford's voice carries over the yard and Clay is suddenly standing next to Sebastian.

"He started it," Sebastian states pointing at me.

"Are we twelve again?" Ford turns on Sebastian.

"Everyone just calm the fuck down," Clay warns while Knox is still holding me back and anticipating every move I make as I try to break right and then left to dodge him.

I'm better than this. In the ring, I'm more alert, more perceptive of my opponent's intended moves. But these men are not my opposition. My brothers are not my enemy.

Eventually, I sag and then I'm folding down to the ground.

I fucking lost the ring. And now I'm losing Genie.

"What's really the issue here?" Clay squats before me.

"I lost the ring," I state again.

Clay shakes his head. "It's not the ring. The ring is a thing, Judd."

"It was Mom's."

"Yes, it was, and you've been wearing it as a way to keep her close." Clay sighs, glancing up at my brothers behind me, before staring back at me. "But Mom is in here." He taps his temple. "And here." He pats his chest.

He lowers his voice. "And Genie, someone you can actually hold on to, just left without you."

"I know." I cover my face as I sit on the grass. My heart conflicted.

"You don't need the ring, Judd. You have Genie instead."

My mouth falls open ready to argue but Clay holds up his hand. "I know you have it in your head that Mom's ring was meant for you. And maybe it was. Maybe it was her way of watching over you. But you don't need it anymore. You're where you belong. With someone who is right for you."

Genie. It's always been for Genie.

"But you all trusted me to hold onto it," I whisper, glancing at my brother like the eight-year-old kid who'd just lost his mother.

"And now, we're trusting you to love Genie."

"Fuck," I grumble. I scramble from the grass. As I stand and face the house, Stone is crossing the lawn next.

"What'd I miss?"

"He tried to rush me," Sebastian states, still sounding petulant. Stone's brows lift in surprise as he glances at me.

"This about the ring?"

I don't need to repeat that it's lost.

Clay is already shaking his head. "We already covered everything."

How it's a symbol of Dad's love for our mother but it was also a reminder of his demise. A reminder that he lost his shit when I took it and nearly beat me to death.

Stone would never say I deserved the beating I got. *Never.* But he's staring at me like I should understand. When you lose something precious belonging to someone you love, it can make you go a little crazy. I certainly feel out of my head with this loss.

I feel like . . . my dad. Like I'm coming unhinged. The ring is gone. *So is Genie.*

I need to get her back, because I can win her back.

"You are not him." Stone steps closer to me, like I'm a caged animal about to pounce. He cups the back of my neck and squeezes like he does when he wants your attention and repeats himself. He brings his forehead forward, close enough to touch, but we don't meet. "You are not him."

Knowing I lunged for Sebastian, I might be more like my father than I thought, and that frightens me more than anything else.

No, losing Genie scares me the most.

"I messed up."

"Nothing you can't fix," Stone says.

"I lost the ring."

"I'm talking about the girl," Stone chuckles.

There's always a girl, Genie once said. And I don't want to lose mine.

44

———

[Genie]

My meeting with Greetings Ambassador was amazing. I was taken on a tour of their current in-house creative rooms. They continued to praise Quirky Girl Calendar and loved my preliminary ideas for a future calendar line. I hadn't been at my best during my presentation, and I was grateful for under eye patches and make-up as I'd cried most of last night. I talked a bit numbly through the interview, but they still made me an offer before I left the building.

It was everything I'd dreamed of happening with them.

And I couldn't wait to get out of New York.

The city was too loud and crowded. The streets shadowed by tall buildings. A constant chill in the air despite the heat of late May. I only saw a sliver of the sky.

Twenty-four hours has passed with no contact. I'd sent Judd a long text, explaining that I loved him and apologizing again for losing the ring, allowing him the time and space to concentrate on finding the lost item.

He didn't answer.

And it hurt. Like throat clogging, sternum aching, gut punching hurt.

Losing the ring had been an accident, but Judd made a promise to me, and he reneged on it. And all my insecurities rushed back in. All my reasons not to commit to someone, not to believe in someone, nearly chokes me.

Despite the silence from Judd, I worry about him. I miss him.

Eventually, Vale sent me a text to check on me. She'd already listened to me apologize profusely for losing a family heirloom that was incredibly sentimental and invaluable.

Vale swore that Judd was overreacting and just being an idiot as boys can be, especially when I said I didn't want us to end.

"Why would you end?" She'd asked. *"You're engaged."*

How did Vale not know the truth?

"People don't call off weddings for losing silly rings."

I disagreed. My mother had shut down marriages for lesser offenses. But I was not my mother.

And I needed to get back to West Virginia.

As the hired car drops me off in front of the hotel, I stall, surprised by a man holding a bouquet of sunflowers and pacing in front of the building.

"Judd?"

He stops moving and steps closer to me, pausing short of hugging me. "I'm sorry I'm late." He holds up the flowers, then lowers them like he's disappointed he doesn't have something grander to emphasize his apology. "I missed the flight. Got caught in the delay of a later one. Spent the night in an airport in Ohio."

"Ohio?"

"*That* plane was grounded for technical problems." He sighs. "All the airport shops were closed. I didn't have a charger for my phone, which died. Only this morning was I able to catch a flight and find a charger to borrow."

He stares at me with those hopeful eyes. "So, I'm late." He exhales out a breath. "But I made it."

He didn't stand me up.

I close the final distance between us, wrapping my arms around his neck and holding tight to him. "Oh, baby. I'm so sorry again. Did you find the ring?"

As I pull back, Judd lowers his head and shakes it. "We didn't. But it's okay." His gaze latches on me. "You're the most precious thing in my life, Genie. You. And I'm sorry I lost my head for a minute." He brushes my hair over my ear and cups the side of my neck.

"I love you," he reminds me. "More than anything. You're what I'm fighting for."

"You've already won me. And I'm so glad you're here. I love you." He made it to me. He came for me. Then I chuckle. "It sounds like you've had quite a night."

"I was doing everything I could to get to you this time."

I press up on my toes and kiss him. With a bouquet in his hands and people walking by, we kiss on the New York street until Judd is lifting me by my thighs.

"Take me to your room?"

"Absolutely."

When he sets me back down, he takes my hand, and I lead him to the elevators. Once inside the lift, he says, "How did the meeting go?"

"It went really well. They have the latest graphic technology and so many ideas for the line."

Judd nods, lowering his eyes as we stand close in the enclosed space. "I'm so excited for you. When does the transfer happen?"

When do I hand over my company?

"Actually . . ." I pause until Judd is looking at me. "I've had a change of heart."

"Really?" Judd watches me.

"A certain someone ran my financials and a certain someone else then gave me some ideas on how to make this work on my own. Or rather with some help."

Judd's mouth slowly curls. "Oh, yeah? Anyone I know?"

I swat at his chest and lean toward him. "I think I might be more of a hometown girl than a major conglomerate cog. With a little help from Sylver Seed & Soil's merchandising manager, you're looking at the new Quirky Girl Paper Company, and the designer of a future line exclusive to Sylver Seed & Soil."

Judd's thick brows crease. "Are you certain about this decision?"

Sheepishly, I glance up at him. "You said you'd help me, right?" I didn't want to rely on Judd, but he is knowledgeable about financial matters, and Clay had been pretty adamant he could help me as well when I had a more official meeting with him earlier this week. I wanted comparative information before I met with Greetings Ambassador, and I'd been fortunate to have more details about doing this on my own before this moved-forward meeting.

An open-mind helped as well.

"Anything you need, firefly. Anything." Then Judd kisses me against the elevator wall until we reach my floor.

We stumble out of the lift and down the hall, awkwardly kissing as we walk. When we reach my room, we practically tumble inside. Judd drops the flowers on the dresser, and I leap up into his arms, circling his waist with my legs.

He drops me to the bed and then it's a whirlwind of clothing being removed and kisses in between until we're naked and breathless.

Judd flips me to my knees, crawling up behind me and

wrapping his arm around me. He flicks at my clit while nipping at my neck.

"I never want to lose you, firefly."

"I'm not going anywhere."

"Come home with me?"

"Live with you?"

"Couple goals," he murmurs to my neck, sipping at my skin but when he pinches my clit and slips inside me, all conversation is lost.

Couple goals. Living together.

45

[Judd]

Genie and I spend the rest of the weekend in New York City, just to say we've been there once. Then we fly to Knoxville, where we pack up her place and move her things to my house. For now, Genie wants to rent out her old place. Students are always looking for a good value and couples want rentals for a weekend away.

As we missed Sylver Sunday, as Genie likes to call the weekly meal, Stone asks us to come to dinner during the week. To my surprise, the entire family is present.

Genie and I arrive hand in hand, plus her other hand wrapped around my bicep. I love that extra touch of security. We're weathering together, sunny days and any storms.

"Congratulations," Enya calls out as we round into the backyard. "We heard the good news."

Genie tips her head, glancing at me. "Family group chat?" I've become only slightly more active in the stream.

"We should probably add you in," Vale says, setting a bowl of something on one of the two picnic tables pressed together.

I groan. "There's already too many of us in there." Not that I don't want Genie added. It's just the thread is a mess with seven siblings plus partners.

Genie chuckles. "Don't mind the grump." She nudges me with her arm. "But I probably shouldn't be added unless I'm officially family."

Everyone now knows Genie wasn't actually my fiancée, but she *is* my family. Married or not, Genie is my world.

"Well, congratulations anyway," Enya adds, offering a warm smile. "When is Quirky Girl Calendars officially part of Greetings Ambassador?"

Genie glances up at me again. "You didn't tell them."

"Figured it was your story to tell."

She clears her throat and addresses the group. "Actually, Quirky Girl Calendars is going to be renamed Quirky Girl Paper Company. And then . . ." She flicks a glance at me. "I have a new investor."

Clay slowly smiles. Mavis doesn't look surprised, but the rest of the group is a bit stunned.

Genie looks at me once more. "At first, I'll be exclusively distributed through Sylver Seed & Soil. Y'all every hear of that company?"

A rush of questions occurs. "What?" and "When did this happen?" and "How did this happen?"

Genie smiles. "I had a call with Clay before I went to New York, and he gave me some things to think about. Mainly, he offered me a different route, allowing me to maintain my vision and creative design, with more support."

I had gone through Genie's financials as she asked, and I showed her where she could spend some money to grow her business. I also suggested an investor, meaning me. I'd done it for Sebastian and his bakery. Ford and the baseball camp. Like I'd told Genie, I was good at investing.

She wasn't going to make the same money Greetings Ambassador promised to pay her upfront, but in the long run, she might make double with the expansion of her line. Clay was willing to help with the production details, as in finding suppliers until Genie had her own connections. Sylver Seed & Soil would be her first distributor, plus direct sales from her new, improved website.

"This is amazing," someone says.

"So happy for you," someone else adds.

"Does this mean you're staying in Sterling Falls?"

"That's the last thing to solidify in this merger of interests," Genie says, giving me a sly smile.

"What?" I turn toward her.

We've already moved her things. I don't want her to have any doubts. My home is her home.

Genie is adamant she needs to inform her mother of her new address. Whereas I'm of the mindset to simply leave Janet Hurley to languish in her own misery and bitterness, far away from my girl and her happiness. But Genie is a bigger person than I am, and she's stronger than me in so many ways. Her relationship with her mother may never be healthy, but Genie has checks and balances in place to navigate the situation. And she has me at her back, holding her hand through every storm her mother stirs.

Just like Genie has my back with my personal albatross. Although according to small town gossip, courtesy of Vale, Heather's little scheme with Tate backfired and she's run into some financial troubles. Heather's true nature revealed itself and set me free from any lingering guilt I felt at hurting her feelings. I don't wish her ill will in any way; I just don't think about her because all my thoughts are wrapped up in my firefly.

Genie turns toward me as well, taking both my hands in hers. Her fingers tremble and I squeeze them tighter, finding my palms suddenly sweaty. Her voice sounds serious, practiced even when she says, "Judd Sylver, a few weeks ago, you saved me from the corner of a room, a stuffy garden party, and a hideous yellow dress."

She chuckles and the tension loosens from my shoulders.

"Through a misinterpretation, it was assumed we were engaged." She quirks her brow. "But then we agreed to date for ten days."

"Checking yes," I mutter, keeping my eyes on hers, wondering where she's going with this recap of our short time together.

"There's one more thing I'd like you to check yes to, if you will." Genie reaches into the pocket of her summer dress and pulls out a folded piece of paper.

With hesitant hands, I take the note from her and read it to myself. There on light blue lines with a unicorn in the background, Genie has written:

Would you like to marry me? Check yes or no.

My head pops up. A grin so wide I can hardly contain it spreads across my face. My shoulders completely lose any remaining tension. In fact, I feel lighter than I've ever felt before. "You know I would."

Genie smiles, her eyes bright. "Then would it be weird if I asked you to marry me?"

"Not as weird as how fast I'd check yes." I turn toward my family, my voice raspy when I ask, "Anyone have a pen?"

Stunned, awed, and pleased faces stare back at us.

I turn toward Genie again. Pinched between her fingers is the newly minted, polished copper penny I'd given her.

"You're my wish, Judd. What do you think?" She laughs, reminding us both the question is the same one I'd said to her, when a certain someone misunderstood what was happening on the side of Genie's mom's house.

"I'd say, Genie Webster, will you be my wife?"

"Checking all the yeses." Her smile is so wide it is almost blinding, but I swoop her into my arms, spinning us in a circle before setting her on her feet and kissing her in front of my entire family.

"Does this mean he loves her?" Dutton's voice breaks through our kiss and when I pull back, Genie swipes at a tear in the corner of her eye.

"This means I love her," I admit to Dutton.

"Did you get her a new ring?" His innocent voice asks, knowing I'd given Genie the other ring. The one now lost.

"Not yet." I glance back at Genie. "But we can pick one out together. One that's special just for us." Because I didn't need my mother's ring to make a grand gesture for Genie to be mine.

I've learned that I'm enough for her, and she's all I've ever wanted.

Reaching into my shirt, I pull forward the silver chain with the platinum ring that once belonged to my dad. "And maybe it's time to give this one away."

I'm not certain anyone in the family wants the ring. The one tarnished by bad memories.

Stone steps forward, though, and holds out his palm. "I'll take it, for safe keeping."

Beside me Genie blows out a breath, knowing what the second ring meant to me. But I suddenly feel lighter. The weight of the ring was more of an anchor than a buoy and the memories were holding me down.

"I'm so relieved," Genie whispers.

"Why?" I whisper.

"Because I got you this." She reaches into her pocket again. "I thought we could make new memories, with you wearing this instead."

Genie holds up a silver ring with a strip of amethyst purple in the middle. "It's called meteorite. It felt fitting as we reunited on National *Star Wars* Day. But also, meteors are strong, vibrant and bright, like a shooting star. And people make wishes on shooting stars, so . . ." She smiles at me. "I wish on you."

I blink a few times, overwhelmed by what she's said. "It's beautiful, firefly." I'll wear it with pride, as this woman who didn't want to get married is going to be my wife. Apparently, the Force was stronger than she might have thought on that day.

I lean forward and kiss her, wanting to do more but knowing I'll have to save it for later. When I take my fiancée back to our house.

"Hey, Genie, do you know what today is?" I ask, pulling back but keeping my arms around her.

She tilts her head. "Really? That's what you want to ask me now." She chuckles. "I think it's National—"

"It's Get Engaged Day," I tell her, leaning in for another kiss and Genie giggles against my lips.

The sound as bright as she is in my life. As vivid as she's always been.

EPILOGUE
TWO MONTHS LATER

[Judd]

I'd been thinking about getting a new tattoo. One that matches my mother's ring before it becomes another lost memory when the strangest thing happened.

In the 1990 film *Ghost*, the main character has lost her beloved and he haunts her. Not a creepy as it sounds, and Genie and I have recently watched the movie. In the film, Sam proves he's present but sliding a penny against a door and then miraculously handing it to Molly as she watches it float through the air to her.

"Tell her it's for luck," he says.

The movie led to a discussion between Genie and I about ghosts, and believing in spirits. Not necessarily the bad kind but the healthy, watchful kind like a guardian angel.

I've heard stories of people who have an item that reminds them of a lost family member and how it mysteriously appears or moves about a house.

Quarters seem to be the story I've heard most often. A son who lost his life had a private joke with his family involving quarters, and the family would find quarters in odd places, like the middle of a bookshelf or on a bathroom sink, as if their forever-gone-child was sending a message, reassuring the parents he was okay.

Backing up, my attachment to my mother's ring started with a nearly forgotten memory of my father toying with the ring on his smallest finger. Just twirling it around the tip of his finger because his digits were too thick to wear something so delicate.

"Don't ever fall in love, runt. In an instant, your heart can shatter." The moment might be the only endearing one I remember about my father and his love for my mother. His backward advice evidence of how broken he was.

I remember him then fisting the ring in his hand and tucking it back in the nightstand drawer. Being a creature of habit, he didn't move the ring around which made it easy for me to find, and admire, and eventually steal from him when he threatened to throw it in the trash.

So, the ring became this talisman of my mother and when it was lost, while I finally accepted maybe I wasn't meant to keep it, the loss was still difficult.

Then . . . the ring was suddenly sitting on the island counter.

"Genie?" My throat catches and her name is more of a low croak than an actual call. As I stare down at the ring, my heart hammering in my chest, I can't move. Like my limbs are frozen in place. For a moment, I wonder if I'm having a heart attack.

"Genie," I squeak again, my voice rough.

"What's the matter, baby?" She eventually finds me stone-still staring at the island. She'd set up her new office in our dining room, loving the natural light and the large table as a desk for now.

"Did you . . ." I can't find the words. My throat is dry. My eyes are stuck on the thin gold band with an amethyst stone and two small diamonds. "Did . . ."

I swallow thickly still unable to form sentences.

Genie must follow my line of sight because she eventually gasps. "Oh my God. Is that—" She rushes to the edge of the counter, hovering her hand over the ring but then pulling back like it might not be appropriate to touch something so precious.

"Judd," she chokes out. "Where did you find it?"

Slowly, her head turns, glancing at me over her shoulder but I still can't move. Still can't force myself to step closer. To touch it.

"I . . . I didn't." I blink, lick my lips and then pull my gaze from the ring to lock onto Genie's eyes. "I was in the library. And then I was crossing the room to the dining room." I glance to my left as if I can see myself leaving the library and walking toward the dining room before doing a double take when something shiny caught my eye.

"I—" I'm still at a loss for words. How? Where? Why?

Since losing my mother's ring, and Genie giving me a new ring of my own, I've had one designed for her as well. With a silver band to match mine, Genie's ring has a square cut amethyst in a slightly darker shade then my mother's ring, plus a ring of diamonds around it.

"Do you think—" I swallow again. "Do you think it's a sign? From my mom?" I close my eyes suddenly feeling childish for the thought, and like a child, hopeful and innocent in asking.

"What do you think?" Genie asks. Her voice low, concerned but full of patience and love. "What do you want it to mean?"

I open my eyes and look directly at Genie. "I want it to mean she's happy with me." My choice in Genie. What I'd done to get the ring and how long I've kept it, waiting until I could give it to the girl I thought deserved it.

Losing it wasn't a curse or an omen. Losing it was a sign to finally let go of my past and race toward the future. Chase Genie, like Trudy once said I should have done.

"But why would it reappear now?" I can't even ask the questions of where has it been, or how did it get on the counter, in broad daylight on a random Tuesday morning.

"Maybe your mother is sending you a sign. That she is happy. She's resting in peace."

It never occurred to me that my mother might be restless in her afterlife. Watching what her husband did to her children, if she could. Sensing our loss in both her and him, and then ourselves along the way.

We each had our vice or our shield or our wall preventing us from giving love a chance.

Maybe that's my sign. My chance is now. My battle is no longer against myself but with my person.

Weathering the storm with Genie at my side. She's my good luck charm.

"I think." I pause. "I think, maybe it's time to just save the ring in a safe place." Not beneath my clothing on a chain or on Genie's finger in the open but some place special.

Maybe with that lucky penny I'd given Genie, and she made her wish on.

Genie looks a bit nervous as she watches me a moment, gauging with those dark eyes with flecks of light how stable I am with the idea of storing such a precious ring.

"I like the idea of saving it. For the future." Her hand covers her lower belly, flattening against it. "Maybe one day, we can give it to someone else who is special to us."

I stare at her a moment, not comprehending her meaning.

"We could give it to our little girl. Or our boy. Whatever." Genie shrugs and drops her gaze, chewing at her lower lip.

"Our . . . what . . . or . . . what?" I'm a stammering fool suddenly.

Genie's face turns light pink. "We've been going at it like

fireflies." She giggles anxiously at her own joke. Genie decided to stop taking the pill weeks after moving in with me, and she isn't wrong. We have sex a lot, although I am not complaining.

"Are you saying . . . Genie, are you pregnant?"

Genie nods, still biting her lower lip with concern.

This is a welcome surprise and one I'm still trying to wrap my head around, but I step toward Genie, tug her to my chest and hold tight.

"Genie. Oh my God, firefly. I love you so much. I love this so much." Panic rushes in and then washes back out.

Maybe this is the sign. I can love both my wife *and* my future child. I can do this. I am strong.

"Genie." I press her away from me by the shoulders. "We're having a baby?" I ask again like she didn't just confirm it.

She chuckles as tears fill her eyes. "I had the whole birth announcement planned. The unicorn paper and checking yes to being a dad, but now feels like the time to tell you . . . Judd, we're going to have a baby. We're going to be a family."

Her voice chokes on the final word. Judd, Genie, and baby makes three. Our family. One Genie and I will protect at all cost, fighting every day to show our child love.

While all of this is still a shock, I hug my fiancée again, then scoop her up in my arms. I want to celebrate us, and her, and our future.

"Wait? Is this okay?" I don't want to do anything to jeopardize our little one.

Genie laughs, scooping her hand around my jaw. "Cadence says being pregnant made her extra horny."

I scoff, knowing I can't get much hornier around my beautiful firefly.

But I'll give her all the love and sexing she wants, or needs.

Any wish of hers will be my desire and I know she'll be granting my wishes right back at me.

+ + +

Thank you for taking the time to read *Sterling Fight*.

Please consider writing a review on major sales channels where ebooks and paperbacks are sold and discussed.

Want a little more of Judd and Genie?
Click here.

Up next in Sterling Falls: *Sterling Touch*.
She's been off-limits ever since his friendship with her eldest brother ended. However, Vale Sylver is no longer a little girl. Despite the twelve-year age gap, he doesn't think he can stay away any longer.

CREDIT ON DATES

https://www.daysoftheyear.com/
https://www.naughty-events.com/naughty-news/2021/1/13/
naughty-holidays-to-remember

National Day Calendar –
https://www.nationaldaycalendar.com/what-day-is-it

Did you know you can buy a date and make it a special day? I didn't.

Here's to the special days, both on and off the calendar.

PETITE PLAYLIST

"Check Yes or No" – George Strait
"You Belong with Me" – Taylor Swift
"You Look Like You Love Me" – Ella Langley, Riley Greene
"If You Were Here" – Thompson Twins
"If You Leave" – from Pretty in Pink, Orchestral Manoeuvres in the Dark
"More Than Words" – Extreme
"Just Like Heaven" – The Cure

MORE BY L.B. DUNBAR

Sterling Falls
Seven small-town siblings muddle their way through love
over 40.
Sterling Heat
Sterling Brick
Sterling Streak
Sterling Clay
Sterling Fight
Sterling Touch
Sterling Stone

<u>Chicago Anchors</u>
When your eyes are on the silver fox coach more than the ball.
Elevator Pitch
Catch the Kiss

Parentmoon
When the mother of the groom goes head-to-head with the
single father of the bride.

Holiday Hotties (Christmas novellas)
Holiday novellas certain to heat the season.
Scrooge-ish
Naughty-ish
Grouch-ish

Road Trips & Romance
Three sisters. Three destinations. All second chances at love
over 40.
Hauling Ashe
Merging Wright
Rhode Trip

Lakeside Cottage
Four friends. Four summers. Shenanigans and love happen at
the lake.
Living at 40
Loving at 40
Learning at 40
Letting Go at 40

The Silver Foxes of Blue Ridge
Small mountain town, silver fox brothers seeking love over 40.
Silver Brewer
Silver Player
Silver Mayor
Silver Biker

<u>Sexy Silver Foxes</u>
When sexy silver foxes meet the feisty vixens of their dreams.
After Care
Midlife Crisis
Restored Dreams
Second Chance

Wine&Dine

Collision novellas
A spin-off from *After Care* – the younger set/rock stars
Collide
Caught

The Sex Education of M.E.
The original sexy silver fox.
When a widowed professor decides she'd like to date again,
and a local fireman volunteers to give her lessons.

The Heart Collection
Small town, big hearts - stories of family and love.
Speak from the Heart
Read with your Heart
Look with your Heart
Fight from the Heart
View with your Heart

A Heart Collection Spin-off
The Heart Remembers

BOOKS IN OTHER AUTHOR WORLDS

<u>Smartypants Romance (an imprint of Penny Reid)</u>
Tales of the Winters sisters set in Green Valley.
Love in Due Time
Love in Deed
Love in a Pickle

The World of True North (an imprint of Sarina Bowen)
Welcome to Vermont! And the Busy Bean Café.
Cowboy

Studfinder

THE EARLY YEARS

<u>Legendary Rock Stars Series</u>
A classic tale with a modern twist of rockstar romance and suspense.

Paradise Stories
MMA romance. Two brothers. One fight.

The Island Duet
Intrigue and suspense. The island knows what you've done.

Modern Descendants – writing as elda lore
Magical realism. Modern myths of Greek gods.

ABOUT THE AUTHOR

www.lbdunbar.com

L.B. Dunbar loves sexy silver foxes, second chances, and small towns. If you enjoy older characters in your romance reads, including a hero with a little silver in his scruff and a heroine rediscovering her worth, then welcome to romance for those over 40. L.B. Dunbar's signature works include women and men in their prime taking another turn at love and happily ever after. She's a *USA TODAY* Bestseller as well as #1 Bestseller on Amazon in Later in Life Romance with her Sterling Falls, Lakeside Cottage, and Road Trips & Romance series. L.B. lives in Chicago with her own sexy silver fox.

To get all the scoop about the self-proclaimed queen of silver fox romance, join her on Facebook at Loving L.B. (Dunbar) or receive her monthly newsletter, Love Notes.

+ + +

CONNECT WITH L.B. DUNBAR

9 781956 337495